Matching All the Way

A HESTON LAKE NOVEL

USA TODAY BESTSELLING AUTHOR
VERONICA EDEN

MATCHING ALL THE WAY

Copyright © 2023 Veronica Eden

Cover Design: Ink and Laurel

HESTON
HOCKEY

TEAM ROSTER

ALEX KELLER, #22, LEFT WING
THEO BOUCHER, #14, RIGHT WING
CORY PUTNAM, CAPTAIN, #17, CENTER
EASTON BLAKE, #24, CENTER
CAMERON REEVES, #33, GOALIE
SHAWN HIGGINS, #64, DEFENSEMAN
JAKE BRODY, #47, DEFENSEMAN
DANIEL HUTCHINSON, #16, LEFT WING
CALEB ADLER, #68, FORWARD

COACHES

HEAD COACH: DAVID LOMBARD
ASSISTANT COACH: COLE KINCAID
ASSISTANT COACH: STEVEN WAGNER
FORMER HEAD COACH: NEIL CANNON, RETIRED NHL PLAYER

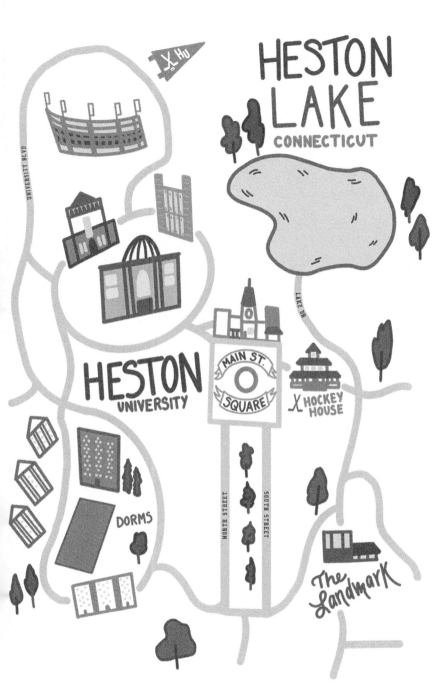

PLAYLIST

Sweater Weather — The Neighbourhood
Those Eyes — New West
Snowman — Sia
Wrapped in Red — Kelly Clarkson
Cardigan — Taylor Swift
Teenage Dream — Stephen Dawes
Habits — Genevieve Stokes
IYKYK — New West
Falling — Harry Styles
this is what falling in love feels like (Holiday Remix) — JVKE
People Watching — Conan Gray
Late Night Talking — Harry Styles
i don't want to watch the world end with someone else — Clinton Kane
Winter Dreams — Kelly Clarkson
Christmas Tree Farm — Taylor Swift
Call Me When You Heart This Song — New West
Everything Has Changed (Taylor's Version, ft Ed Sheeran) — Taylor Swift
Atlantis — Seafarer
ceilings — Lizzy McAlpine
Car's Outside — James Arthur
Adore You — Harry Styles
Paper Rings — Taylor Swift
Christmas Valentine — Ingrid Michaelson, Jason Mraz
Snow on the Beach (ft Lana Del Rey) — Taylor Swift
Feels Like — Gracie Abrams
Midnight Rain — Taylor Swift
All Too Well (Taylor's Version) — Taylor Swift
Yours — Conan Gray
What A Time (ft Niall Horan) — Julia Michaels
deja vu — Olivia Rodrigo
Seven (ft Latto) — Jung Kook
Tear in My Heart — Twenty One Pilots
Glow — Kelly Clarkson, Chris Stapleton
Until I Found You — Stephen Sanchez
Next to You — New West
Home — New West

CONTENTS

ABOUT THE BOOK

Nothing's more romantic than matching with the same guy every time you reluctantly download a dating app. Hotter than ever—check. Off limits—double check. Why does the universe hate me?

Cole Kincaid is unfairly irresistible and the one guy I'll never have. My brother's best friend is all grown up, but he's not here to witness my messy girl era. He's Dad's new assistant coach for Heston U's hockey team.

Match me once, we'll laugh it off and never talk about it again.
Match me twice, well this is awkward.
Match me three-four-*five* times? My resolve is only so strong.

Constantly enduring Cole's charm in this small town is tempting enough thanks to the pesky crush I never got over. We're **matching all the way** whether I like it or not. After a bad breakup, I'm only interested in avoiding loneliness through winter.

And at rematch number...I've lost count, it turns out he wants to help me with that.

ABOUT THE BOOK

What begins as an enticing game of sneaking around in secret turns into something neither of us can walk away from once the snow melts. The question is...how long can we hide this?

To all of us with ADHD who live in what I like to call organized chaos that only makes sense to us, between two times: not right now and RIGHT NOW, hyperfixation, and jump from hobby to hobby...

And to finding the right person who sees you, supports you, and takes excellent care of your praise kink.

Fall
NEW HOBBY FIXATION

ONE
EVE

November

WHAT IS it about the end of the year that seems to make everything fall apart?

The rest of the time I feel like I have everything under control, then as soon as September hits an impending sense of anxiety builds a cozy little cabin in my chest. By the time it's November I realize *no*, in fact, I don't have it together and I'm out of time to change that.

There's next year, sure. Except we all know it'll be the same cycle over and over.

Or maybe it feels that way because today is one of those days where everything has gone wrong. First, I managed to leave for work without the emotional support water bottle I take everywhere. Then I spilled coffee all over myself, and when I was in the bathroom cleaning it I noticed the inseam of my favorite jeans beginning to wear thin at the thighs.

And, once again, I've body checked an inanimate object at the end of my bartending shift at The Landmark.

Mondays? Hard enough to deal with on their own. Mondays when the holiday rush is in full swing and every calendar reminder keeps screaming at you that time is running out before a new year is upon us? The worst.

Mom's cheerful voice echoes through my mind with the admonishment she's given me my entire life: *slow down.*

I rub my throbbing hip and glare at the offending counter I clipped. I remembered to clear the door frame from the back room, swerving at the last second to avoid banging my shoulder into it, only to miscalculate the distance between my curvy hips and the spot I've dubbed the Corner of Hip Death.

"Did someone move that?" I ask.

A few of our older daytime regulars seated on barstools are doing a terrible job of containing their amusement. Even my dad's retired coaching friend Neil Cannon snorts, shaking his head.

It's been a slow lunch after what I like to call Hockey Weekends —the Thursday through Sunday crowd of locals, students, and the entire Heston University hockey team packing the place wall to wall. Those shifts bring in the best tips because the place is hopping. During the season, everyone ends up here to celebrate or commiserate after a game.

"It only seems to jump around for you." Mr. Boucher, the owner, chuckles while sliding a basket of wings and a beer to a customer at the other end of the bar. "Have a good night, Eve. Tell your mom and dad hi."

His sympathetic smile helps ease the ache in my hip. It'll bruise, though I'm used to how often I give myself minor injuries like this. At least this one won't be like the mystery ones I find that leave me wondering what I clumsily stumbled into and when. Terrible depth perception is just one of the super powers granted to me by my ADHD.

Hammy ambles over with his whole back end wagging and snuffles at my hand until I pet him. Mr. Boucher's lovable tan and white bar dog has an irresistible permanent smile you can't help but fall in love with.

"Sure," I say. "See you later."

I march myself out the door with renewed purpose and head for my boyfriend's place. I finished early enough for us to grab dinner together. His apartment isn't far from The Landmark. Nothing in Heston Lake is more than a short walk away.

The only way to turn around a bad day is finding something positive to focus on. Positives like my fun, colorful punch needle creations, my latest craft hobby obsession. I picture how cute a set of mug rugs and embroidery hoop wall decor with sassy sayings would be selling at the holiday market hosted in the square at the center of town every year.

I quickly discard the idea. Instead, I settle on my favorite activity: making my own earrings. The pink heart-shaped lollipop ones I have on are the latest pair I've made.

I love designing and making things. Sometimes I wonder if they're good enough to start my own business to turn my hobbies into a hustle. I've dreamed up a logo and imagined how I'd fit in at the craft fairs I love attending. It would be so fun to create things to make everyone's day brighter with a smile because of something I made.

Then I get overwhelmed by all the things that I'd need to do. I'm not business savvy the way Benson is. My brother followed his dreams and did all the right things to open his brewery with his partner by his side.

On my way to Shawn's, I pause at the corner where an old camper is out for sale. It's been here a few weeks without any bites. Each time I pass, I'm tempted to put an offer in. It's beat up, but if I could fix it, paint it with my logo—

No. It would be too impulsive. I'm working on that because my last three impulse buys that I was *sure* were going to be my new thing are gathering dust in my apartment. The camera I needed to start a photography career, the yoga mat I bought as a promise to get into a whole mind-body routine, and the cute planners I get when I see them then forget to use after a short time are all examples of why I need to hold back.

I love the rush of a new idea, but struggle with follow through. I spare the camper one more wistful glance before I'm on my way again.

If I'm making earrings, I want to see if the audiobook I requested is available to reserve. Otherwise I'll be blasting music, needing some sort of background noise while I work.

When I unlock my phone to check, two calendar alerts pop up to let me know Thanksgiving is in two weeks, kicking off what my family considers the start of the holidays. The second alert is to remind me to shop for presents, otherwise I'll be stuck stressing about getting or making everything last minute. Without my digital calendar keeping me on track, I'd be even more of a disaster human.

It's not that I'm a holiday-season-hater or anything dramatic. I love Heston Lake in the winter with its seasonal lights and charming historic atmosphere. New England winters are the prettiest with crisp mornings and the delicate frost. There's something magical about snow dusting the pine trees and sipping hot chocolate by the frozen lake. I enjoy watching Mom decorate every square inch of her house during her favorite time of year.

It was fun as a kid because my birthday is during the holidays. It always felt like the whole town was celebrating with me. As I got older, being lumped in with the festivities of Christmas and New Year's lost its sparkle.

There's nothing like December 31st sneaking up on me time and again to make me face that another year has crept by—quite literally, since it's my birthdate. No one tells you in college that once you graduate your life moves at lightning speed. Then you're looking up two years later, realizing you're about to turn twenty-five and you haven't done anything you planned yet.

It already took me an extra year to finish my graphic arts and marketing degree. I thought by now I'd figure my life out and know what I want to do with it.

Not even close. I live at home. Well, in the renovated apartment over my parents' garage. I still have the bartending job I got in college, though I do pick up a few freelance things here and there from online listings or small businesses around town that take pity on me.

The only major decision I've made lately is changing up my hairstyle. I give the ends of my ponytail a tug, running my fingers through the natural brown that fades in an ombré to blonde ends. At least my parents understand and aren't pressuring me.

Before I open the library app to browse the new releases in romance for my next audiobook, I'm distracted by hunger. It hits me like a flipped switch. I run back through my shift and nod to myself wryly. I had a handful of fries at the beginning of work, but I guess I forgot to eat a full meal again.

I should see what Shawn wants tonight. My pace slows so I don't trip as I walk and type simultaneously.

> **Eve**
> Done work!

> **Eve**
> I'm about to be at your place. What do you feel like having for dinner?

> **Eve**
> Maybe me? Or I can be your dessert [wink emoji]

Not even a minute later, he responds. Weird. Usually he takes a while to answer. He's the world's slowest texter. I can send him three to four rapid-fire thoughts as they occur to me before he answers once.

The message is a huge paragraph. Also odd. Brows furrowed, I scroll back up to find the beginning while waiting for the elevator in the lobby.

> **Shawn**
> I've been thinking for a while. We keep going through the same cycle. We can't keep doing this. It's time we both grow up and let what we had go. We're not in college anymore. I want to be able to put Heston Lake behind me and you're what's holding me back from getting out of this tiny ass town. I need to end this. It's what's best for both of us. We're over. This time it's for good. You don't have to say anything. Leave your key in my mailbox. Good luck.

By the time I reach the end, my ears buzz with rushing blood. The elevator dings. My legs feel like they're detached from my body as I shuffle inside in a daze. I read it again, most irritated by the blasé *good luck.*

He responded too quickly to have time to type it all out. There wasn't any indication he typed at all. It has to be prewritten. Copied and pasted to blindside me the moment I messaged him.

All those times I've caught him squinting at his phone lately, tapping away, I thought he was working on his resume. I imagine him drafting this breakup note while we ate meals, watched TV, before we went to bed.

A weak laugh of disbelief slips out of me. Not only does he want to break up two weeks before the holiday season begins, but he's doing it by a crappy one-sided text. I grit my teeth at his sheer douchebaggery.

By the time the elevator opens on the third floor, my blood is simmering, close to a boiling point. I inhale, trying to keep my rising anger at bay. Balling my fists at my sides, I steel myself for this conversation.

He can text me all he wants, but he's not dumping me so easily. Not without my own chance to say something.

There's a box of my stuff left in the hall outside his apartment. I recognize my glue gun and the knitting needles I decorated myself poking out from the top. That bastard.

Before I have time to pound on his door, one of his neighbors who lives alone across the hall comes out. I never got her name, but I've always waved hello to the elderly woman. She makes a beeline right for my box.

"Hey, wait!" Darting forward, I slap a hand over the box to keep her from taking it. "Sorry, this stuff is all mine. Shawn put this out without asking me."

The woman frowns, not backing off. She eyes my glue gun and her hand inches closer. I can't believe her audacity when she snatches it from the box.

"It's been out here all day for anyone to take. Says free right here."

She points to the other side where I recognize Shawn's handwriting. A sharp twinge throbs in my chest.

He really had this planned out, from what he wanted to say to me to end it to tossing out every trace of me.

Unbelievable.

TWO
EVE

SAVING my craft supplies from a wily older neighbor less than five minutes after my boyfriend broke up with me isn't how I pictured today going, but here I am.

"See?" She taps the writing on the box again when I'm too stunned to speak. "Free."

"And I'm telling you it's not." I huff. "These are my things."

I rescue the box by edging it behind me, then hold out my hand expectantly. The stubborn woman clutches the glue gun closer. For a moment, I debate how far I'll go to fend her off.

Thankfully, she plops it in my palm with a grumble, saving me from becoming hot Heston Lake gossip for tackling the elderly like a completely unhinged lunatic.

"Should've taken it earlier," she mutters. "Lucky you came when you did."

"Um, right."

With one last dour glance between me and the box I'm guarding, she toddles back to her apartment. Well, happy freaking holidays to her, too. I blink away my astonishment and throw a glare at Shawn's door.

I wanted to talk to him. He's definitely home. His car is parked outside.

Forget it. I just want to get out of here.

The situation is still hitting me as I put the glue gun back in the box, then skim the message he had locked and loaded to send me one more time. I don't bother answering it.

Instead, I dig out my key and chuck it at his door, gratified by the *thunk*. There are muted noises inside, as if he came to investigate. The door doesn't open. I narrow my eyes at his peephole.

Coward. Ugh, I shouldn't be shocked after he broke up with me through a text.

This is officially a new low for me. I can't believe him. What a fucking jerk.

We've been dating on and off since we met in college, but somehow we keep finding excuses to get back together. The last time we broke up after a fight, I at least had the decency to tell him to his face that I was done.

After this stunt, I'll never cave to his middle of the night sweet talk about missing me again. No dick is ever worth the inevitable heartache, and Shawn has brought me way more of that than he has orgasms.

I purse my lips, working to keep my breathing even. It becomes difficult as all his little criticisms hit me at once. Being with him used to be fun, but since we got back together all he does is rag on me for countless little things like how forgetful I can be, or when I struggle to manage my time, or how I'm incapable of sticking to a regular routine.

Those shortcomings are because my brain doesn't work the same way as most people's. I didn't understand why until I was diagnosed with ADHD. Rather than listening to me, he's been impatient whenever I hold us up.

My eyes sting as my vision blurs.

Shit. I won't cry over him outside his damn apartment. I refuse. Especially if he's still lurking to watch through the peephole. No way in hell will I give him the show he must be waiting for.

Screw this and *screw* him.

With a shaky breath, I swallow to ease the lump constricting my throat, give his peephole the finger, and take the stairs to leave with my box.

I'm so focused on getting away once I'm outside, I can't appreciate the satisfying crunch of brittle orange and yellow leaves dotting the brick walkway when I step on them. I keep my head down until I slam into something solid.

A wall of muscle stops me in my tracks. Cheeks heating, I gasp, trying to keep my balance without dropping my best craft supplies.

Despite my determination to plow my way right through town to the safety of my own space before shedding a single tear over Shawn...turns out I can't, in fact, go through physical objects.

The guy grunts at our collision, steadying me with large hands and a strong grip. Wow, he smells good. It's my first thought as the crisp breeze winds the spicy, warmth-infused scent around me. It's a welcome distraction for a second until I get my bearings.

"Whoa, hang on," he says in an amused tone that makes my stomach twist in a nice way. "I've got you. Where's the fire?"

"Sorry about that," I stammer. "I was, um. In a rush."

God, the last thing I need right now is for anyone in town to see me like this. My head threatens to spin right off my shoulders from the overwhelming last fifteen minutes of my life. Without fail, the end of the year is a sure sign everything I've managed to hold together up to this point is about to fall apart.

"I think I got that from your attempted hit and run. Maybe we should exchange insurance information."

He chuckles. I freeze, struck by the familiar sense of nostalgia that almost knocks me on my ass right there on the autumn leaf-speckled grass.

I know that laugh. Lifting my gaze, I confirm I'm in Cole Kincaid's arms.

Did I trip, hit my head, and slip into one of the fantasies of my seventeen year old self?

"Eve." His brows lift in recognition. "Hey. Good to see you."

His gaze passes over me, pausing at my earrings. The translucent sparkly pink resin heart lollipops are tamer than some of my quirkier ones I've made, like the dinosaur chicken nuggets, miniature potted houseplants, and rainbows with cute little faces.

My heart skips a beat under the full weight of his attention. His dark brown hair is as thick and tousled as always, slightly longer on top than he used to wear it. The corners of his warm green eyes crinkle with his handsome smile.

Too many responses crowd my thoughts at once. He drops his hands from my waist and steps back. I can't believe I didn't recognize my brother's best friend immediately, though I'm not exactly thinking straight.

"I didn't know you were visiting," I say. "It's been a while."

The last time I saw him, he was the best man in Benson's destination wedding three years ago. He only visited one or two other times before that. When he went to college, his family moved out west to be near him. The only thing left for him in Heston Lake is his friendship with my brother.

"Not just visiting. I'm back." His relaxed, uneven grin widens at my confused expression. He inclines his head. "For now at least. I don't usually stick in one spot for long."

"Back," I echo. "Didn't your family sell the house when they moved to be closer to you?"

"Yeah. It's kind of weird to be here but not living there." He pushes a hand through his hair, casting his gaze down the street before nodding to a nearby house at the end of the block. "I'm renting. Remember Mrs. Carter's place? With the cat we all liked to pet on the way to school? Now it's a duplex. I was lucky they offered me a month-to-month lease."

It was renovated into apartments like many of the other historic homes in town to save them from demolition and preserve our sleepy college town's charm. Most of them are filled with Heston University students that don't want to live on campus. A few older properties have become vacation rentals for the autumn and summer tourists.

"Yes, I went to the estate sale. Scored a whole basket of good yarn."

The edge of his mouth lifts. He studies me for a beat, smile falling as his brows crease with concern.

"Are you okay? You look like you might—Want me to carry that for you?"

I clutch the box, not in the mood to explain what I'm carrying or why. Hopefully it's not written all over my face that I was as easy for my boyfriend to throw out as this box he chucked out the door.

Crying in front of him would be way worse than Shawn seeing me upset. The last time he saw me shed tears over a boy who toyed with my heart, he found Benny and the pair of them beat the guy up. It wasn't until after they both graduated two years ahead of me that any guys dared asking me out again.

"I'm good. I'd better go, actually." I speak quickly, moving past him.

"You sure?"

"Super sure." I pause to turn. "Welcome back, Cole."

He gives me another one of his signature heart-stopping smiles. "Thanks. See you later, Evie."

My breath catches. I haven't heard that nickname in years.

Cole is the only one that's ever called me that. I might be turning twenty-five soon, but being around him always makes me feel like a teenager again.

My brain short-circuits, attempting to respond with two different things at once. "Glad to touch you later. I mean, thanks, you too."

Immediately, I cringe. Shit. I was trying to say I'd touch base with him later while also trying to say I was glad he was back.

Okay, it's fine. Just—breathe. That happened, and I have to accept it. He probably didn't notice even though I did.

More than ready to be out of there for the wicked breakdown I'm on the verge of, I duck my head and hurry down the street so I can do it in private.

This is just fantastic. Dumped and bumping, literally, into the guy I crushed on in high school in the same day. Mondays really suck.

* * *

It should've occurred to me Cole was serious about seeing me later when I drag myself down to the main house for dinner a few hours later and find him leaning against the kitchen counter. The sight of him sends me back about nine years, before he left for college and was a regular fixture at our place.

It's hard to believe. Long stretches of time often feel like nothing at all to me.

I blink, just in case this is some overstimulation-induced hallu-cination.

Nope, still there. Accepting a beer from Dad.

I feel a little more grounded after a tiny mental breakdown and a shower, but I'm not prepared to face him so soon after our run-in. My fingers curl in the cozy oversized sweater I bundled myself in, needing every form of comfort. It says *happy fall y'all* and has leaves embroidered on the cuffs.

"Hey, sweetie. Help me out and bring the potatoes to the table." Mom wipes her hands on a bright red dish towel covered in a snowflake pattern.

It's just the beginning. Soon every inch of this house will be covered in seasonal decor. This year I've actually convinced her to hold off until after Thanksgiving to give fall—and me—a minute to breathe.

I scoop up the serving dish and take it to the dining room. The table is set with the nice plates. She even pulled out the fancy cloth napkins and folded them with her brass leaf napkin rings. When it's just us, we eat at the kitchen table. That included Cole in the past, but I guess Mom's itching to host before the holidays are fully underway.

The front door opens, letting in a chill. Benson comes in alone, jerking his chin in a nod while unwinding the colorful scarf I knit for him last winter. He's got Mom's blue eyes and thick brown Lombard hair, like me.

"'Sup?"

Tossing a glance over my shoulder to make sure our parents are distracted, I skirt around the table and give his arm a soft jab.

"Dude. Way to not give me any warnings."

Some things never change. We might be older, but we're still siblings. We love each other in our own way and growing into adult-hood hasn't changed that. One minute we'll be squabbling like we're in Lord of the Flies, the next we're united and raising hell together.

He rubs his arm, unbothered. "Warning about what?"

I roll my eyes as he steals roasted carrots out of the bowl. "Why didn't you tell me Cole was coming back?"

"It all went down pretty quick. I just found out a few days ago when he texted to see if I'd be around to pick him up from the airport and help him move in. And he only brought two big duffle bags, so we were done in about five minutes." He shrugs. "Left us time to drink and catch up."

A sigh escapes me. I suppose I haven't always known what they were up to.

"No Jess tonight?" I flick his hand when he goes to snack on more of the spread.

"She had to fly out to meet with one of our new distributors. She comes back this weekend." He pretends to search the room. "No Shawn? Good."

What I had with my on-again-off-again boyfriend has never been like what my brother has with his wife. That kind of love is special. They're supportive of each other and they worked together to create their dream by opening a microbrewery.

I bite my lip. "Yeah, we're not—uh. Together anymore. As of today."

It feels good to tell someone rather than bottle it up. Sometimes I keep things to myself so I'm not unloading on everyone around me, but my brother's seen me through more than one breakup, including whenever things with Shawn have ended.

Benson's amused smirk drops. "Shit. Sorry. Are you okay?"

"I will be. Thanks, Benny."

"I stand by it, I've always thought that guy sucked. You deserve so much better than him." He holds up a case of bottles with the brewery's logo and drapes an arm over my shoulders to squeeze me. "I brought something that'll cheer you up. Your favorite fall cider."

My lips twist into a smile. "That does make my day a little less shitty."

He leads me into the kitchen, breaking away once he hands me a cider to put the rest in the fridge. When he's done, he moves to chill by Cole's side. I drift to stand next to Dad. He takes the bottle from me to pop the cap.

"I can open my own bottles." My cheeks heat when I accept the drink.

He shrugs. "Sorry. Helping your kid is a habit that's hard to turn off. I still remember teaching you to ride a bike and tying your first pair of skates when you demanded to come to work with me."

"Dad," I complain. "Seriously. Do we always have to rehash the life stories when I point out I'm not a kid anymore?"

Cole releases a husky laugh that makes everything worse because of the pleasant tingle it stirs in the pit of my stomach mixed with embarrassment.

"What?" Dad gestures to him. "Cole knows. He's like family. That's why we had to welcome him back with a meal."

"Thanks, Mr. Lombard. I appreciate the invite."

"Son, I told you. Call me David."

Cole nods ruefully. "Right. Tricky to get used to after only calling you Mr. L growing up."

This day needs to end. I hang my head back and take a sip, enjoying the hard cider's tart burst on my tongue.

"Cole, it's so nice to have you back with us," Mom gushes. "It felt like I lost one of my own when you went so far away for school."

"What about your actual kids?" Benson jokes wryly. "We're still here."

"Seems you might never leave." The sarcasm only lasts a moment before she bustles around the room with a crushing hug for all three of us. "And I hope none of you ever do. Stay close, right where I like you."

Benson claps Cole on the shoulder. "Send your parents my apologies because Mom's ready to sign the adoption papers and make this official."

Cole's deep laugh fills the room, piercing through me at the same moment I catch his eye. The corner of his mouth quirks higher in a smile that feels like it's just for me.

Oh no, he's still hot.

Correction, he's so much hotter now. He's broader in the shoulders and chest than the last time I saw him. The rolled up sleeves of his flannel hug those corded forearms like their lives depend on it. If I was the threads of those cuffs, I would be hanging on for dear life, too. With the defined jawline that gives him an edge of ruggedness and his comforting green eyes, he's a six foot two walking temptation.

I gulp as my old crush roars back to life. He's all grown up and my fluttering heart might not survive this family dinner. Memories flicker, unspooling in my head with all the reminders of how much I liked him in secret.

Playing street hockey in the summer with him and Benson. The time he told me I looked pretty in my Homecoming dress and I hoped he couldn't tell I was blushing. Going to their hockey games in high school and watching him the entire time. The first time he called me Evie when we were joking around and it made my stomach fill with butterflies.

Did these feelings for him ever truly go away?

No. But I've always hated admitting it to myself.

Because one thing's always been true when it comes to my brother's best friend: Cole Kincaid will never be mine.

I've hidden my stubborn crush because it won't amount to anything. It didn't when he grew up in Heston Lake, and it won't now.

Resigned to that fact, I follow everyone to the dinner table when Mom ushers us there. She leans close before we sit down.

"Are you okay? You're so quiet tonight."

"Yeah, just tired. I'll be fine."

Mom studies me with a small frown. Blurting out my breakup news at the dinner table is a big no from me. Especially while Cole's here.

It's not too surprising she noticed I'm off tonight. Typically I'm bright and bubbly.

This evening has been a lot at once and I'm close to hitting my threshold. It's easier to retreat inside my head to deal with it all.

Benson saves me. "Jeez, Ma. Did you save any food to make for Thanksgiving?"

"Like you won't eat it." She clicks her tongue. "You might not be a teenager anymore, Benson, but you still have enough appetite to eat your father and I out of house and home."

When Mom isn't looking at me, I nod to him in thanks. The edge of his mouth lifts.

I muster a reassuring smile. "Everything looks great, Mom."

She lets it go for now. I'll talk to her when I'm ready. Benson and

Dad take their usual seats, leaving me sitting across from Cole when I find mine.

As much as I want to endure this family dinner by turning invisible, he won't let me. He glances at me and makes attempts to include me in conversations the entire time.

Why does the universe hate me today?

THREE
COLE

It's strange to be back in Heston Lake after all the years I've been away. Some aspects of this small town are stuck in time, as if they've been waiting for me to pick things up right where I left them at eighteen. There's also a sense of what I've missed out on now that I've returned at twenty-seven.

The familiarity of having dinner at the Lombard house feels exactly the same yet not.

"Do you have plans for Thanksgiving?" Mrs. Lombard asks from her seat at the kitchen table while I take care of loading the dishwasher for her after dinner.

She insisted that I didn't have to, but she cooked dinner so I'm cleaning up after with Benson like old times. His dad refreshes her glass of wine and rubs her shoulders.

Eve disappeared as soon as she brought the stack of plates to the sink. Through dinner she was quieter than I'm used to. I wonder if it's because of that look on her face when I ran into her earlier today. The thought of anything dimming the lively spark I've always admired in her makes something tighten in my chest.

"No. Getting called in for the assistant coaching position happened so out of the blue that I didn't really think about it," I say.

Mr. Lombard hired me to fill the open job for Heston University's men's ice hockey team on a trial basis after the previous defensive coach retired. Honestly, I'm still shocked I got the call.

For now, I'm here. If it doesn't work out, I'll float around again until I find something else to do. It's how I've operated since I graduated five years ago.

Mrs. Lombard pats her husband's hand affectionately. "Well, now you do. I'll have plenty of food, so you should join us."

I shoot her a grateful smile. "I'd never turn down one of your meals. Thank you, that sounds great."

My relatives might be spread out across the country, but it's nice to still have my best friend's family feel like my own. They've always welcomed me.

"What about Christmas? Are you flying to visit your parents?"

"No. They booked a cruise, just the two of them. They like to get away a lot now."

"Good for them. And that settles it. You know you're welcome here."

I finish loading the dishwasher and start it. A sense of nostalgia hits me for all the time I spent over at the Lombards' growing up.

"If you're sure you can squeeze me in," I say.

"Of course."

"She still cooks like she's feeding an army," Benson chimes in.

"I might as well have been serving a hungry army anytime you brought your teammates over for dinner. You and Cole could pass as one with how much you both put away," she says.

Benson pats his stomach with a grin. "Hockey boys like to eat." He turns his attention to me. "You should. Jess wants to catch up with you, too."

"Yeah, okay," I say.

He points at me. "Also, you're joining the Brawling Bandits. No arguments."

"What's that?"

"Beer league team," Mr. Lombard answers. "Bunch of local guys. Steve plays for them when we're not away on a roadie. He's our other assistant coach. You'll meet him when you start on Wednesday."

"Okay, hockey talk is my cue." Mrs. Lombard snags her wine and kisses her husband on the cheek. "I'm going in the other room to watch a movie."

"I'm the current team captain," Benson says. "Your old number's

18

available. Not gonna lie, I've been hanging on to it for you in case you ever made a heroic return."

"Aww, bro." I lay a hand over my heart. "Is that your way of saying you missed me?"

Benson waves me off. "Shut up. It's about time we got some young blood. We need someone decent who can actually defend and skate at the same time."

His dad snorts. "My guys on D could wipe the ice with yours and half of them are barely old enough to order a drink."

"Not anymore, old man." Benson grins at me. "It's a new dawn for the Bandits. The Wall is back in play."

"Yeah, to work for me," Mr. Lombard counters smugly. "To help me shape my players into the best defensive line in our division. We're taking them all the way."

Pride swells in my chest at the chance to coach alongside him before I've even met the team. His belief in me makes me want to give this opportunity my all.

Not gonna lie, I've thought about coming back ever since I left Heston Lake. I was eager to get away when I chose to play hockey out west and have enjoyed all the traveling I've experienced. When my best friend's dad called me up with a job offer I wasn't expecting, it felt too important to pass up.

Back when I played with Benson in high school, I was known around this town for being too lax and unserious. That reputation followed me to college until I recently started looking for a change. It's what I'm working on, aiming to become more dependable. Still a work in progress.

"Have you been by The Landmark yet?" Benson asks.

I shake my head. "Why? Is it different? It's weird seeing new traffic lights and all the other little stuff that's changed around town."

"Nah, same as ever. Well, except that Eve bartends there." He puffs up proudly. "I have a distribution partnership with them now."

"No shit? Congrats. That's great."

"That's what really put us on the map. Now our stuff is popping up all over New England."

I clink my bottle against his. The mention of his sister brings her back to the forefront of my mind.

Which is exactly where she shouldn't be.

Eve Lombard has always been beautiful with her bright smiles and those amber eyes that glimmer with life, especially when she's talking about something that excites her. I always thought she was cute, except Benny would've put me through the wall if I ever even entertained the thought of touching my best friend's sister when we were teammates.

But now...

She's all grown up. The forbidden little spark I used to feel around her whenever she laughed or smiled at me hasn't fully gone away.

It's going to be much harder to resist wanting her. She stole my breath when I ran into her near my new place.

Her hair's different. It caught me off guard at first since she never used to dye it, but I like the dark brown fading into blonde at the ends. It was the sheer scarf she had knotted around her ponytail that I recognized first. Vibrant pops of color are a staple for her, followed by the earrings she makes. I've always been partial to seeing her wear the less understated ones, like clay popsicles and pastel dinosaurs.

Then she lifted those captivating eyes to meet mine, glossy pink lips parted. The universe shifted and spun off its axis because for a minute, something crazy happened. For a minute, I had her. She felt good in my arms, soft curves pressed up against me.

I can't help picturing what it would be like to explore her curves. Discover what makes her breath hitch and her body tremble. Hear my name fall from her perfect plush lips.

I meet her dad's eye and choke on the last sip of my drink, sputtering and hacking until Benson thumps me on the back.

"Dude, don't die," Benson says.

Fuck, does he know? Do either of them? Thinking about how hot Eve is while standing between her dad and her brother is risky. I hope my train of thought wasn't plain on my face.

What the hell is wrong with me?

I shouldn't be thinking about her at all. Not while I'm with them. Not while I'm alone, either. Especially then.

"Here, have another." Mr. Lombard—David, that's still weird to get used to—offers me a fresh beer.

"Thanks."

I take a long pull to get my mind off Eve.

Yeah, I definitely can't go there. She's off-limits. I need this job, and he went out on a limb to get it for me. If I want to stop being a screw up, I have to stop doing screw up type shit.

Lusting after the head coach's daughter is top of the list of Things Not To Do.

* * *

I can't believe I'm nervous. Makes me want to laugh at myself, yet I can't shake it on my first day on the job.

David was pleased when I showed up early this morning. He took the time to guide me around the college's huge state of the art ice sports facility.

Those nerves rear their head again when he ends the tour at the practice rink where the team is warming up with stretches and skating loose loops around the ice.

David rests his elbows on the boards and blows his whistle twice to get their attention. I'm impressed by how quickly they circle up in a group. It's clear they respect him.

"We all miss Kowalski since he retired suddenly, and we've made do up to this point in the season. I want to introduce a new addition to the coaching staff. This is Cole Kincaid."

The transition from player to mentor was trippy at first. I haven't felt these jitters since the first year I spent as an instructor at a youth camp. I'm used to showing little kids who are just getting down the basics of puck control how to improve their coordination.

I nod to the team and smooth a hand down my brand new Heston U Hockey track jacket, bumping the whistle dangling from a cord around my neck. David gave me both this morning. Beneath the logo it declares me as part of the program's staff, and the back reads *Assistant Coach Kincaid.*

This is the real deal. Legit coaching.

After my days of playing in college ended, this is a path I thought about following often. It just took me five years and a lucky break to get to this point.

"Glad to be here," I say when David gestures to me. "I'm looking forward to seeing what you guys can do."

"We kick ass, that's what we do," someone pipes up.

"No funny business. I'm talking about you, Blake."

He points at the young guy with messy brown hair and a huge grin that spoke. He's wearing number twenty-four and balances a puck on the end of his stick. Players snicker and nudge him.

"Let's get to work." David blows his whistle again. "First up, shooting. Then we're working on zone coverage rotation. Divvy up and, for fuck's sake, pay attention to the drill explanation. Don't waste everyone's time by daydreaming. Hear me?"

A chorus of agreements sounds. Half the team breaks off to form a line at the other end and the rest stick with me on my side. I don't even know their names yet.

The urge to glance at the roster David handed me is strong. I hold off for now, preferring to learn what I can about them without knowing where they stand on the team. Muscle memory kicks in when I put on a pair of skates and join them on the ice for a better view.

After they've run through the line, I break down the main thing David wants them practicing today.

"I'm sure you guys aren't strangers to this one," I say. "This exercise is beneficial for offense and defense. We're focusing on building foundations of communication during gameplay for the forwards passing the puck from different zones in the corners and behind the net. For the guys on D guarding those zones, I want you analyzing plays as they occur to develop better reaction time."

Their blank stares give me the urge to straighten my spine, which I decide I can't do because then I'd be losing whatever weird unspoken pissing contest I feel I'm being challenged with as they size me up.

These players are much closer in age to me. It's not like training kids. The specialty programs I bounced around in after college dealt with youth boys and girls divisions. Those seasonal summer and winter camps felt like a cakewalk compared to standing in front of twenty plus guys that have the skills to go pro if they have the drive to make it happen.

22

It was work, yet it never really felt like a true job since the programs only lasted for a short period. Then I'd move on and find another, enjoying traveling. David told me this was on a trial basis, but it already seems like a much more serious job than my previous experiences.

This is coaching high-level players. Something that could be a career, if I'm good enough at it.

Christ, will they even listen to me? Or will they buck my authority as a coach like the cocky little shit I remember being at their age? They probably think they know everything, and with Heston's overall stats and win record, I'm betting they think they're on top of the world.

"Any questions?" I prompt.

"You look young as hell, my guy," forty-seven observes. "Like you could be out here with us."

My lips twitch. He's got mouthy d-man written all over him.

"That's not really a question."

He shrugs. "All I've got."

"I'm not that young."

"Kowalski, our other defensive coach, was basically ancient. Dude was probably around when they were still attaching blades to the bottoms of their boots instead of actual skates," he says. "Neil Cannon even coached here after his NHL glory days."

Numbers twenty-two and fourteen stand side by side with their hands folded over their sticks. Fourteen looks familiar, but I can't place him right away. I glance at the roster to find their names, sophomores Alex Keller and Theo Boucher. Left and right wing, both starters on the first line.

Boucher—Mr. B's kid, right. It clicks when I survey him again, recognizing him as one of the twins that are always around The Landmark. Last I saw him, he was playing with the U13s. Kid's all grown up now.

"You're definitely not that old, bro," Alex says. "I'd say even Stevie has you beat by a solid decade at least."

I huff in amusement because I still feel like I have no idea how to be an adult. "I'm twenty-seven. And I bring fresh perspective because it wasn't that long ago I was where you all are."

Easton, the rookie wearing number twenty-four, perks up with interest. "You played? Sweet."

"Since I was old enough to join a team, all the way through college."

"So you're more qualified to coach than you look," one of the other guys says.

I hold out a hand with a silent question to the nearest player. Forty-seven—Jake Brody, another sophomore—offers me his stick. I nab a puck from the pile by the net and show off a little, skating quick and fluid. Rather than take a shot, I whip it back to them.

Coming to a stop with a scrape of my blades, I spread my arms. "Well? I'm not out here to practice my edge work. Are any of you going to try me, or what?"

Keller and Boucher exchange a look, grinning to each other before they're coming at me.

I can't pull off the full drill for defensive zone coverage without another defender to rotate with, but I incorporate some of the intended maneuvers while Keller and Boucher seek their opening. The guys watching sound intrigued by my ability to cut off the wingers from every move they try to make. A few of them pop off with chirps.

"Get him, Bouch. Show him how hard your slap shot goes."

"Come on, Keller. My grandma skates better than this guy. Get around him."

They *ohhh* in unison when I swipe the puck with a little extra flourish of stick handling, followed by a quick wrister to rip it into the net. Defense has always been my preferred position, but it's fun to show off a variety of skills in the arsenal I've spent years building.

I give the forwards a salute, then skate back to the side of the rink.

"Wicked," someone murmurs.

I tamp down on a laugh, feeling like I have their attention now as I return Brody's stick.

"So that's the general idea in this drill. Are you the kind of guys who need me to demonstrate it again, or do you have it?"

Easton eyes me up and down with a puzzled expression. "No prospect picks?"

I shake my head. "Not for me. But for some of you?"

When I leave the question hanging, there's a gleam in their eyes. A hunger that I understand well. If advancing to the next level is their goal, I want to help them achieve it.

I nod slowly, gaze flicking from player to player. "I live and breathe this game. I played hard, and now I get to have your backs."

They get fired up, a few of them releasing hoots and enthusiastic cheers. That's more like it.

"Now, who's ready for the drill?"

This time, they hustle. Satisfaction settles over me as I lean against the boards to oversee them while they work on their skills and coordinate with their teammates. It's only my first day but a sense of rightness flickers to life, settling in my gut to ground me. I just have to hold on to it while I'm here.

Until David Lombard finds someone more qualified to bring in permanently.

FOUR

EVE

As I MAKE it through the week, I feel more like myself again. By Wednesday, I'm proudly focusing on myself, as I should be. I'm fully invested in romanticizing my life.

This morning I spent time picking out my outfit and doing my hair so I feel cute and confident on my day off. I'm in my staple red platform booties, a cozy sweater dress, fun tights covered in hearts, and a pink scarf tied in my hair.

The initial shock from Shawn has passed and the breakup is beginning to sink in. This time it's final—I'll never get back together with him.

I smirk, the melody of one of Taylor Swift's breakup anthems with that sentiment playing in my head. I've blasted a playlist full of empowering songs the last two days.

Art inspiration struck me last night. I wanted a reminder to keep my head up when things are looking down. The adorable end result of daisies and the uplifting reminder of no bad days makes me smile.

No bad days. That's my new outlook.

I ordered stickers so I can plaster them everywhere when I need a positivity boost.

Ideas for products I could do other than stickers come to me as I stroll across Heston U's campus to meet Dad. Whenever I have time, I like to have lunch with him.

On my way inside the practice rink, a text distracts me. The

27

message from the group chat with my friends makes me smile. We bonded for life in college, and although we don't see each other every day like we did on campus, we get together as often as we can.

Caroline
Craft night soon? Please, I'm desperate for a girls' night.

Eve
You know it! How's next weekend? I have off Friday and Heston's playing away so I don't have plans.

Julia
Yes!!!!!!

Caroline
That's perfect for me. We'll bring the wine!

Lauren
I'm in, see you then queens!

I wonder if now's the right time to tell them about Shawn, or if I should wait for our crafty session. Pursing my lips to the side, I draft a few ways to word the news in my head.

"Keep it up. That's it. Get ahead of the play."

I stop in my tracks, head snapping up. I forget all about texting. Though I'm used to being at the rink to visit Dad, the familiar voice following the sharp blare of a whistle has me whipping around.

Cole is here. On the ice.

Not just on it, but skating with the hockey players geared up for practice. He borrows one of their sticks and demonstrates a defensive move I remember from watching him play hockey in high school.

He glides in my direction after giving the order for the players to run through it again. My mouth goes dry when he leans against the half wall separating us. He's tall enough on his own, but his height when he wears skates has always made me warm all over.

"What are you doing here?" I blurt.

Cole blows his whistle again, then turns to face me, resting his arms on the boards.

"Hey, Evie." His smile is crooked with the whistle caught between his teeth.

A pulse of heat hits my core.

Oh god. Why is that hot? My gaze sweeps him again, taking in the athletic jacket with a Heston U Hockey logo on one side of his chest. It says STAFF beneath it.

"I'm the new assistant coach," he says. "You didn't hear about it?"

I shake my head, unable to form words. I'm still stuck on seeing him on the ice in skates again. It takes me right back to my secret infatuation from when we were younger. He still looks just as good in a pair of skates—better, honestly.

There's always been this sense that he's at home when he's on the ice and it's no different now.

Once I manage to get a hold of myself, I wonder how I missed this. Between my dad and my job tending bar at The Landmark, hockey gossip is pretty much all I hear about.

"No, I had no idea. This is why you came back to Heston Lake?"

"Yeah. Crazy, right? I never thought I'd be coaching at this level." His green eyes glint. "I've done some youth programs and training camps, but never anything like this."

"It looks good on you."

His charming smile stretches with amusement. "Does it?"

I jolt at his inviting tone, realizing how that came off. "I mean, it suits you. Coaching. You look like you're happy doing it."

His eyes crinkle and he scans the rink. "Yeah, I think I might be. Today's only my first day."

Flustered, I look for my escape. "Is my dad around?"

"He's with Steve doing offensive drills." Cole motions to the other end of the rink.

"Thanks."

"See you later."

I suppose I will if he's here working with Dad every day. In my head, I add another reason why I'll never have him—besides the fact he never figured out how hard I used to crush on him. I almost laugh at myself because *used to* is such a lie. Those feelings are still around, and they only seem worse with him back, all grown up and irresistibly sexy.

Not only is Cole my brother's best friend, now Dad's his boss.

There's no way he'd be interested in his friend's younger sister and he definitely wouldn't risk pissing off the head coach by going for his only daughter.

Which will never happen, because I doubt Cole's ever looked at me the way I look at him when he's not paying attention.

Shaking my head to clear it, I walk around the rink. A few of the upperclassmen wave and I return their greetings.

"Hey." I hold up the takeout bag from The Landmark. "Brought our lunch."

Dad's a gruff man most days with a reputation for being a tough yet dedicated coach for this town's beloved D1 men's ice hockey team. That flies out the window when he's presented with Mr. Boucher's famous wings.

Mom's getting on all of us about eating better and moving more, so these are secret wings and burgers. They're our little thing. At least when we need some comfort food, which I totally do.

I don't really want to restrict myself with a diet like Mom always has. Not that she's too hard on herself, because she loves a good treat, but it's something ingrained in her from her mother. We don't talk to Grandma after Dad made it clear at one Christmas dinner that he wouldn't let her talk to Mom like that anymore before he made us all walk out.

Mom's been working on unlearning all the nasty things her mother put in her head since, making a point to always tell me positive affirmations to uplift me instead of nitpick my physical appearance.

I'm content with how my body is, with curves from my boobs to my ass and thighs. I don't mind that my stomach has a little pooch or the silvery stretch marks from growth spurts once I hit puberty. I'm a real-sized woman and it makes me feel beautiful because she instilled the importance of self-confidence in my body image.

I shake the bag. "I hope you're hungry. I needed emotional support fries this week."

"Is that right?" Dad's lips twitch. He checks his smartwatch with a quick nod. "Steve? Finish up practice after this. And send Cole over to me when you're done here."

"Got it." Steve doesn't take his attention off the action on the ice.

We take the food to his office. He clears a space on the desk and points at me with a fry.

"What's up with you? You've been in lurk mode."

I pull a face. "What the hell is lurk mode?"

"When you or your brother get mopey with teen angst, that's what your mother calls it. You lurk around the house."

My new positive outlook is a work in progress. "Okay, well I'm not a teenager now."

He gives me his stern coach face when his players mouth off to him, thick brows pinched and laugh lines deepening when his lips thin. I sigh in resignation.

"It's not a big deal. Things ended with Shawn. And before you go all *Dad mode*," I taunt. "It's permanent."

He frowns, then nudges the fries closer to me. He doesn't have to say anything else and I appreciate him for it, accepting his brand of comfort in the form of quiet solidarity. I love Mom to pieces, but Dad is who I gravitate to more often when I'm pissed off or upset because he helps me cool my head down and sort out my thoughts on my own.

"What do you want for Christmas this year?" I raise a hand. "And please don't say 'whatever'."

He closes his mouth, scratching his trimmed graying hair. "How about...anything?"

I melt in my chair. "Dad. That's the same thing."

A knock at the doorway interrupts. Cole leans in.

"Come sit." Dad waves him in, gesturing to the open chair beside me.

Cole takes it, shooting me a wink and a lopsided smile. Rather than sprawl in his chair like he might when he's at my family's house, he sits up straight in front of Dad.

"We're all wrapped up. Steve and I let them hit the showers. He said you wanted to see me?"

"Here, have some of this. We never finish the whole basket."

Dad slides the large order of fries closer to the edge of the desk. Cole stretches across me to reach for some. Awareness of his proximity lights up my senses. I cross my legs when his heady forest scent fills my lungs. My lashes flutter and I duck my face to hide a blush.

"I volunteered you for ice skating lessons at the lake again this year," Dad says.

My head pops up. "Again?"

Things at the bar slow down through the end of December into January while the college is on winter break. I planned to use the time to see if I could start a business at an online marketplace like Etsy. I've been toying with the idea after watching some studio videos from other small businesses that sell their stickers and stationary designs. It would give me the chance to start out small and test the waters.

"You said you liked doing it last year." His brows furrow. "Sorry, should I not have told Vic you would? I can call him back."

"I did like it, but..."

I trail off, wondering if it'll be a good way to keep myself busy. Then I don't have to think about Shawn. Or—I hold still so I don't look at Cole. There will still be plenty of time for everything else I want to do. I don't have to rush anything.

"Never mind. It's fine. I promised Victor last year I'd do it. Don't make him stress over who else would teach on short notice."

Dad's worried expression clears. "That's good. And Cole will be with you."

"What?" I blurt.

"I will?" he says at the same time in a strange tone.

"That's why I called you in," Dad explains. "The college partners with the owner of the public rink for a community program. It's been in place for the last five years. You're a good candidate to volunteer as an instructor with your background."

"Oh. Won't it cut into practice time?" Cole's leg bounces for a moment before he stops it. "You won't need me here for that?"

"Lessons are usually scheduled with that in mind," I find myself saying. "You won't miss anything. That's how it's always worked."

The hint of tension loosens from his limbs and he smiles at me. It's tinged with relief and something I can't name. My stomach dips. I'm not used to seeing him like this. Some part of me recognizes the need for acceptance, I think.

Dad interrupts the moment with an encouraging hum. "Right. Vic's an old friend and when he came to me with the idea of bringing our professional coaches and players out to revive interest in lessons,

I agreed it was a good idea for our guys. It only lasts a handful of weeks through the winter, then you'll be back to your usual duties here. Take any player with you, too."

"Yes, sir."

"When do we start?"

I pull up my phone calendar, focusing on what I can control rather than thinking about the fact I'll have to go through weeks of being around Cole.

Dad checks a sticky note. "After Thanksgiving. Vic will contact you with the details."

Cole stands. "I'll let you finish your lunch. Do you need me to do anything else right now? Set up for tomorrow's practice or help with player eval?"

"Steve will take care of that. Good work," Dad says.

From the corner of my eye, I notice Cole's chin dip a fraction before he leaves the room.

"I'm full. The rest is yours." I get up, collecting my purse. "Are you staying longer?"

"I've got some paperwork to take care of. Thanks for lunch, honey. See you at home."

"Okay, bye." I circle his desk to give him a kiss on the cheek.

Cole's lingering outside Dad's office when I come out, shoulder braced against the wall. He pops out of his lean with the fluid nimbleness of someone who has trained for so long their athleticism is ingrained in their body. I tamp down on my attraction to it.

I glance behind me before facing him. "Were you waiting for me?"

He slips his hands in the pockets of his coaching jacket and shrugs. "Figured I'd walk you out since I'm done for the day."

"Oh. Thanks."

We fall into step together.

"So, skating instructors," he muses. "I didn't expect that."

"It's not bad. They give us free hot cocoa."

"I've never taught anyone how to skate. Like, in an official class."

"It's just the basics, so it's easy. We're essentially signed on as babysitters."

A small laugh escapes me and I beam at him. His steps falter and he reaches out to catch himself on the open door to an equipment room to regain his balance.

"Are you okay?"

"Yeah, I'm fine." He clears his throat and swipes a hand across his mouth when he glances down at me. "Tripped on air, I guess."

I nod sympathetically. "Been there. Actually, I'll admit I pretty much live there."

Cole chuckles. "I remember your personal vendetta against gravity."

"That sounds way cooler than saying I'm naturally clumsy." Or that my equilibrium sucks sometimes. I squeeze my hands into fists and fake a jab with a gratified tilt to my lips. "I'm using that from now on."

I pretend to fight the air and he follows behind me.

"All yours." Humor and fondness are evident in his tone. He pauses outside when I start to walk in the opposite direction. "Wait, you're not heading for the lot?"

"I still don't have a car. I usually walk around town, or get a ride from—"

I cut off. Shawn let me borrow his when I needed it. That's out of the question now. It sucks because I've gotten used to having it as an option without having to rely on asking my parents or Benson.

"People," I finish haltingly.

"You were walking the other day. From that apartment building by my place. You carried that big box of stuff all the way home?"

I nod, eyeing him as he closes the small distance between us with a few long strides.

His attention drops to my favorite red boots. I suppress a shiver as his gaze sweeps up, traveling over my patterned tights dotted with hearts and my sweater dress to the bow tying my braided crown back before settling on my mouth for a beat.

A strong gust of wind kicks up a swirl of leaves around us. He moves into it without hesitation, blocking me from the brisk air with his tall frame. Even without his skates on, he towers over me in these chunky heeled boots by a head. He regards me with his dark brows raised.

When he looks at me, it's impossible not to feel caught up in that magnetic pull. Being around him is this inescapable force sucking me in.

"It's too cold out today. You don't have a coat on. It's supposed to snow, you know. Come on, I'll give you a ride." He holds out a hand toward the lot behind the training facility. "I'll give you one whenever you need it."

"Oh, no it's fine. You don't have to go out of your way to—"

He cocks his head with a slight smirk. "We can stand here and argue about it if you want, but this still ends the same way. Not accepting no for an answer, Evie. Let me take you."

A buzzing rush of warmth moves through me at the firm yet considerate tone he uses while teasing me.

"If you're sure you're not busy."

"I'm never too busy for you."

I tuck a piece of hair behind my ear as we head for the lot. He only means that I'm his best friend's sister. He's being as kind as he is to everyone. I shouldn't read any further into those words.

This side of campus is quiet other than the trickle of athletes coming and going. I bump into Cole's side a couple of times, then murmur an apology and put some distance between us until we drift closer again.

I stop when we reach his car, mouth curling at the corners. "You still drive a Bronco? Is this the same one you had in high school? This takes me back."

Countless memories from tagging along with Benny and Cole flit through my mind from endless summer days chasing sunsets to winters cramming as many people in as we could to hit the closest ski slopes. There were a few times when it was just us, too. When he'd give me a ride to my friends' houses when Benny didn't feel like it, and I would shyly peek across the center console to admire his profile while he sang along to whatever played on the radio with the wind in his hair.

He pats the blue frame of the SUV and opens the door for me. "Close to the same year. I sold mine when I moved away. Couldn't pass it up when I saw it for sale."

Climbing in, I'm sent right back to those memories. They blend with the present, this version of him just as out of reach as he was as the heartbreaker with a carefree grin that inspired so many idealistic fantasies when I was younger.

I'll blame it on my nostalgia, but I sneak glances at him the entire ride, admiring his shadowed jawline and the defined arm he drapes over the wheel.

FIVE

COLE

SOMEHOW THE BRONCO still smells like Eve's sweet perfume. Hints of vanilla and strawberry have driven me crazy for days. I finally left the windows down to air it out. I hope the snowstorm they're calling for doesn't start until later.

Tantalizing thoughts of her tights haunted my dreams again last night. I shouldn't have snuck glances at her legs when I gave her a ride home last week. But I also wasn't about to leave her to walk all the way home by herself.

I need to figure out how to shut off my reaction to her if we're going to be spending even more time together. How the hell did I keep myself in line in high school?

Whatever. Now's not the time to be thinking about ripping tights off the coach's daughter.

I dart my attention to the opposite side of the ice. David's bracing his hands on the boards. Licking my lips, I make a conscious effort to clear my head.

The jitters of my first day as a college-level coach dwindled after the initial practice. They're still there, but I'm getting a handle on them after a week.

Faking it with a smile until I skate by is how I've always operated since my wild teenage days doing dumb shit for laughs like tying rope from the back of an ATV to a trash lid to sled the trails.

Except this time I'm taking this seriously. Far more than I did

37

with my past jobs. I want to make it work instead of goofing my way through. Even if this is only temporary.

I love this game. I love the strategy and skill involved. The payoff when those hours of practice become an insane goal or the game-saving defense against all odds is the best damn thing in the world.

"Good, Reeves," I call from the boards when he kills the beautiful shot Alex Keller takes on the net during their scrimmage. "Watch out for your footwork, Brody. Get on the inside of that approach and you'll have the leverage to push him out of it before Keller shoots. Protect your zone. Keep that in mind for tomorrow's game."

Brody nods with a determined expression that ignites satisfaction within me.

Going pro was never my path in hockey. Not even when I had the chance to become a free agent.

This is. It's fulfilling to train talented young players like these guys to help them sharpen their game. I want to leave a lasting impression on them for however long I hold the assistant coaching position.

We've only played one Friday-Saturday series since I joined the program as a coach. They won back to back against UConn. Watching their successful chemistry as a team made me feel like I'm winning with them.

Each player on Heston U's roster has talent in spades individually. As a team, they're incredible. There's no question they're good enough to make it back to the Frozen Four again this year.

It's still sinking in that I get to be a part of that. They're out there practicing hard on the ice and I'm buzzing with inspiration now that I've seen what I'm working with. I arrived early again after a late night putting more effort into researching new ideas to bring to the table than I ever have.

From my college to high school teammates, even some as far back as junior league, I've always had the sense that they knew what they wanted compared to me. Even the Heston U guys give me the impression they know the direction their lives are taking, and they aren't afraid to chase what they want until they get it. With this job, I think I finally have an inkling of what that's like.

The other side gets a breakaway. I watch closely, assessing the play as it unfolds.

Theo Boucher passes to Keller when they cross into our end of the ice. Then Boucher needs to evade his opponents, so he sends the puck to the hotshot rookie center, Easton Blake. He receives it back when he's deep in the zone as he approaches the net. Boucher's cut off by Jake Brody racing in to stop him.

"Nice! That's how it's done!"

Boucher has no openings. He tries to push Brody on his own, testing ways to get around him. It doesn't work.

Brody hits the puck away and another one of our guys picks it up to turn the tide. He doesn't get far before Blake steals it back and goes for a goal with a wicked fast slap shot. His control is impressive as fuck. Reeves gets a piece of it, but it's clean.

Damn, I think that kid will go far.

Pride explodes, filling me with exhilaration at Brody's successful defense during the play. It grows when he turns to me with the look of someone that just figured out they're capable of great things. His teammates bump fists with him and pat him on the back in the shuffle to reset for a face-off.

"Keep it up just like that, got it? You know how to be fast, you just need to go for it instead of hesitating," I instruct.

"Yes, coach."

My stomach clenches for a beat. It's the first time I've heard one of them call me that. It feels damn good.

The scrimmage continues. David makes his way over for the rest of it. He surveys the game, occasionally tracking an individual player with a thoughtful hum before making notes on a legal pad tucked in the binder he carries. There's no doubt about his reputation as a dedicated coach.

"Settling in?" he asks when time for the game is almost up.

"I am, thanks."

He's my boss, not my coach. I'm not a player anymore. Yet I can't help but feel like I've got to prove myself and make a useful contribution the few times he's done this since I started.

"Glad to hear it. You're a good addition to our team." His laugh lines deepen when his mouth curves. "The players have taken right to you."

Sparks of happiness go off in my chest like tiny firecrackers. "That's good." A wry laugh shakes my shoulders. "A few of them have seen me around town outside of practice and follow me. Also, I've been meaning to tell you. Thanks again for trusting me with this job."

David studies me from the corner of his eye. "You weren't the first one I thought of to fill the position."

A weight drops in my stomach. "Oh. Right, of course."

Temporary, I remind myself.

"But I'm glad I called you in. So far, it's a better fit than I could've hoped for bringing on a change mid-season." He pats my shoulder. "Keep it up, son."

* * *

After practice, I go to Benson's microbrewery. The old brick industrial warehouse he turned into a thriving business with Jess in only four years still impresses the hell out of me.

"Yo," I call.

He pops out of the office area with a clipboard in hand. "Hey. Have a seat over there. I'll be out in a sec. Let me just finish bottle inventory."

I wave. "Take your time."

"Help yourself, there's a new pale ale we're taste testing."

The rough hewn island by the wall has stools around it. I snag one of the bottles in the mini fridge and sit.

I take a sip, groaning in appreciation for the perfect taste. Benson and Jess know what they're doing.

While I wait for him, I pull up an article I saved last night. I want to show it to David to see what he thinks about incorporating it into the team's development, but I haven't found the right opportunity yet. I need to work up the courage to bring it up to him.

Benson startles me when he hefts a crate of empty bottles on the counter. "Swipe right. If you're staring that long at her pictures, you want to bang her."

"No." I'm distracted by reading the article, then throw him a puzzled glance. "Huh? I'm not—no. I'm reading about mobility exercises for flexibility and balance training."

His brows shoot up when I flash him my screen. "Oh, seriously? That's a weird look on you. Are you about to turn into a workaholic? *You?*"

I hesitate to respond. His shock isn't a surprise. I've always had a reputation of being too easygoing everywhere but on the ice.

"Maybe. I don't know," I admit. "I like this job, though. I don't have the same expertise as a great coach like your dad, so I'm catching up in my own way."

Benson's joking expression falters. "Sorry. Ignore me. I never cured that inherent jackass gene."

I snicker. "It's all good. Kind of new for me, too."

"That's cool. You like it?" He circles the island and braces his forearms on it.

"I do. I—really do." I lick my lips. "I think this might be my thing. What I want to do with my life."

He nods supportively. "Staying here? Or anywhere?"

My fingers clench around the bottle. I don't know how long I'll get to remain with Heston U, but if I can I think I would. After only a short time, I like it.

I've always been passionate about hockey. I love practices most. Helping teammates work on whatever they were improving, or honing my own skills. Strategizing and analyzing plays. Coaching allows me to focus on all of those elements.

"Wherever I can," I say. "For now I'm here, though. I'm gaining experience by shadowing your dad. And these players, some of them are insane. I think we'll see some called up to the big leagues."

Benson smirks. "What I'm hearing is you need to get laid or you'll get all hyper fixated like Eve does. Let's see, Melissa is single. Savannah is, too. Actually, you should make a dating profile."

I pull a face. "I don't need that. And I sure as shit don't need to take a walk down a memory lane of past hookups."

He plants his hands on the island, leaning across with a grin. "Welcome back to small town life."

I snort and cover his face, shoving him. "Fuck off."

"It doesn't have to be anything serious," he points out. "We both know that's not you. Do it as a way to find out who's still around to reconnect with, or meet someone new. That's all I'm saying."

Maybe he's right. As simple as it is to go to places like The Landmark or Clocktower Brew House to flirt my way into someone's bed, it's not like my schedule will allow for relationships of any kind. The players have to put the hours in for practice and games, and as their coaches, we're right there with them through it all. This cuts to the chase.

Plus, I have no idea if my time here will last.

"Just casual," I muse.

"Yeah, man. That's the spirit. Sow your wild oats and shit."

I lift a brow. "What the hell is that supposed to mean?"

"Live it up. And let me live vicariously through you because as soon as I met Jess freshman year, she was the only one I wanted."

"Then why do you need a thrill?"

He shrugs. "I don't. But I want you to be happy like that."

I press my lips into a line. He's got it all—the drive to build his business and the woman he loves at his side growing it with him. It could be nice to find a connection like that.

Except I don't tend to stay in one place long enough to allow a relationship to get to a serious stage like theirs.

Eve flashes through my mind. It fills with her gorgeous smile, the way her cute laugh has always made me feel, those fucking sinful curves that have only become more tempting, and her colorful everything. Warmth expands, starting in my chest and spreading through me.

I shut down the forbidden train of thought before it runs away from me. Can't be thinking about her like this. It's a major no-go.

"Give me your phone. I'll help you take your profile picture," Benson says.

"What, can't I just use one I already have?"

He takes my phone and holds it up. "Work it. Give the ladies that famous Kincaid-brand smile that breaks all those hearts after you break their beds."

Laughter busts out of me. He takes photos from different angles with ridiculous encouragement. I swipe a hand over my mouth and goof off by striking a few poses.

"There, you should have some winners in there, you beautiful bastard." Benson tosses my phone to me. "You're welcome."

"Thanks."

I don't put too much thought into making a profile on the first app that pops up when I search for online dating. I keep it basic, listing my interests for hockey, being outdoors, and kicking back with friends. The rest can come if the vibe is right when I find someone to talk to.

It's not like I'm looking for the love of my life.

SIX
EVE

CRAFT NIGHT with my girls is hosted on Friday at my renovated apartment above my parents' garage. I have off from work. Usually if I'm not bartending on Fridays or Saturdays I attend the home ice hockey games with Mom, like most townies. We love to support our team.

So much so that Mr. Boucher saw the Heston U and hockey-themed stickers I made for my water bottle when their season started and asked if I'd make some more to put out at the bar. They go like hotcakes whenever I bring a new batch in. It makes my heart happy when people tag me in the photos of the stickers in use on social media.

Tonight's free since the Knights are out of town for an away game. The school's live feed is one of the many tabs open on my phone to keep track of the score.

Humming the song playing in the background on my speaker set shaped like a rainbow, I get everything ready for my friends' arrival.

Once I've cleared away some of the chaotic assortment of clutter —which always seems to pile up around my space no matter how often I attempt to keep it presentable and organized—I get out my things for crafting.

The closet is a mess. I cram all of my supplies in here when I have a random urge to clean everything for a mental fresh slate. Meaning, all my doom piles and things I've left out so I'll remember

45

them end up shoved out of sight more often than not. Right now it's a mix of hobby graveyard and stuff I've been holding on to.

Whispering a promise to not get sidetracked and bracing myself, I dive in.

First, I move my clay and resin supplies out of the way. Usually I keep them handy since they're my go-to craft activity, but I put them away so we have the room we need for wine and snacks on the table where my earring crafting station regularly lives.

The abandoned polygel kit is next—the one an ad on social media convinced me I had to have because it made me suddenly *need* to try doing my own nails. It was a fun process to learn, despite the five hours it took to do them. The fact I wasn't good at it right away made it hard to want to practice, even though some part of my brain acknowledges that's logically how skills work. Generally it's overpowered by the side of my mind that fumes when I don't immediately uncover a hidden skill for the brand new hobby I picked up on impulse.

I squint at the contents of the closet when I don't see my box of embroidery thread. It should be here. I think about it for a beat, then smack the door frame with a frustrated sigh. I know what happened. I'm sure I remember seeing it at Shawn's last, hit with a photographic memory of taking it there to work on some handmade gifts for the holidays. I'll have to endure seeing his face to get it back.

Shaking my head, I keep moving things around.

"There you are," I crow in success.

The landscape painting I picked out at Mrs. Carter's estate sale is perfect for tonight's craft session with my friends. We started with thrifted paintings and added in our own ghosts for Halloween, then decided we should keep doing seasonal ones. This painting will become my own cute holiday ghostie version of A Christmas Carol.

A knock sounds at my door.

"It's open," I call.

"We're here," Julia announces.

Grinning, I set it down and greet them with tight hugs.

"Oh my god, I'm so excited to make shit and talk shit," Lauren says.

"Same," I agree with a laugh. "It's so good to see you. We went way too long without a girls' night this time."

"I know." Caroline pouts. "Stupid work. Who let us be adults? With bills and responsibility? This sucks."

"And existential dread? No thanks," Julia adds.

"Hate it," Lauren says.

"Absolute bullshit," I confirm.

We all giggle. I invite them in and we catch up while preparing snacks and pouring wine. One of them puts on Pride & Prejudice— the 2005 version with the epic hand flex, obviously, although we're fans of every adaptation.

Twenty minutes pass before we touch our crafting activity.

Crafting is the best. It's the thing that makes me happiest. Sharing it with my friends is my favorite thing to do. We have the best time adding our own touches to the paintings, breathing new life into them.

"Okay, I really needed tonight," I say. "This cheered me up a lot after what Shawn did."

Lauren puts down her paintbrush and lays her hand over mine. "Are you two fighting again? You can tell us anything."

The memory of getting sidetracked from telling them last week by Cole in skates surfaces from the depths of my mind. Shoot, I knew I was forgetting something. Since I'd started the text, my brain accepted it as a completed task.

"I know. Shawn dumped me." I pause to wince, still pissed off. "By text this time. While I was showing up at his place after work and asking what he wanted to do for dinner. It was fucking awful."

The three of them scoff in anger.

"Are you serious?" Julia's eyes narrow at my nod.

Lauren is a ball of rage. She looks ready to hit something. "He's the world's biggest idiot."

"Want me to call my cousin? He knows a guy who knows a guy." Caroline blinks at us innocently. "What? I have an active approach to problems."

I laugh. "No. But you're right, he's a loser. By text—who does that?"

"Cowards," Julia replies flatly.

I swirl my paintbrush through the water, biting my lip. A note of vulnerability creeps into my voice.

"It's just going to suck to be single during a time it's couple-central. And even if I think he sucks, it's not like it's easy to go from falling asleep snuggled up with someone to nothing."

"Of course, he hurt you," Caroline says gently.

I nod, throat tight. "We weren't even fighting this time, which is usually how I know we're close to calling it quits. I mean, maybe things have gotten a little less steamy than when we were in school. It's been a while since we last had sex, but I just figured we were both busy."

We're all quiet for a few moments. I feel lighter talking it out with them. Their support helps the melancholy ease.

"The only cure for a broken heart is a new dick to make you forget the old one," Lauren says.

"I think I'm good on toys. As much as I love to read about hot fae men, I told you I'm not brave enough to buy one of those fantasy dildos you showed us." I stifle a laugh. "Be serious."

"I am," Lauren counters. "And I don't mean toys, although there's always room for an addition to our collections and I highly recommend the 4D reading experience. You should get over that idiot Shawn by getting back in the saddle. Find someone new."

I put on a regency-era accent to go with the movie playing in the background. "Because I meet so many eligible bachelors tending bar."

"Forget that. Obviously Mr. Darcy and every other fictional man are the standard, but they don't exist," Caroline says.

We all echo her with our woes that the fictional men we love aren't real.

"Algorithms are the way to go, babe." Caroline smiles wickedly around a grape. "Without them helping us wade through the no's and absolutely not's of the world, we might never connect with potential choices. Plus, I check off so many of my top fantasies. Like last month, while I was on a business trip in Chicago, I hooked up with this super hot businessman who railed me against his office window in a high rise. Like, he absolutely wrecked my shit."

She fans herself. We all fall apart with laughter and delighted squeals for our girl.

"I'm so done with guys like Shawn. I don't know if I want to rebound right away into a relationship. But I also am kind of dreading how many couple-y things are going to be in my face through the holidays." I pause, eyes widening. "No, my birthday party. Not only do I not have anyone to kiss at midnight, but now I don't have anyone to wear that sexy outfit I picked out for and they won't be peeling that little number off me at the end of the night."

I don't always like to celebrate my birthday on the real day, but this year I decided a New Year's Eve birthday bash would be perfect to ring in twenty-five. Now I'll be one of the few single people on the guest list.

"You're still wearing it," Julia insists.

"For yourself," Caroline agrees. "But also, you could totally still enjoy the night with someone if you find the right match to invite. You're closing yourself off to so many possibilities, and half the time you never see them ever again."

I swing a skeptical look between the three of them. "So I just hop on Tinder like a meat market?"

"Or Hinge, or any of the services," Julia says. "Despite what they advertise as the user experience, they're all pretty much the same."

I love my friends, and I know they support me. Sometimes I can't help but feel as if they have it together and I don't. Caroline scored a job for a marketing firm with global reach that sends her traveling around the world. Julia is working in PR for the NHL in Boston. And Lauren teaches lectures at the college while working on her PhD.

They're totally winning at the transition into adulthood post-graduation while I'm left lagging behind with a fake-it-til-I-panic approach.

I mull their suggestion over. Dating is challenging enough.

It's partially why I was content to stay with Shawn. He was... easy. Familiar. He might not have understood my interests or my neurodivergent quirks all the time, but the idea of finding someone else that will accept every facet of me, including my ADHD, is daunting.

Obviously I want to share my life with a partner that accepts me for who I am and doesn't believe I'm too much or too hard to love. Everyone wants that.

Maybe they're right. This doesn't have to be serious, it can just be for fun. I could find someone who doesn't want to be lonely for the next few months, either.

Someone who's down with a no strings attached arrangement.

Pulling out my phone, I browse through app options. Love Struck catches my eye with its retro-inspired pink branding. It's new. I overheard some Heston U students raving about it while I was bartending.

"This one seems cool," I say.

"Do it, do it," Lauren chants enthusiastically.

"We'll help you with what to put in your profile." Julia shuffles to sit on my other side.

"Fine, you win," I say.

I feel silly creating a dating profile, but we all giggle as I download the app. They're with me every step of the way to fill it in.

By the time the second bottle of wine is nearly finished off, I'm all set up on the app. The movie's over and our paintings are done.

Lauren squeezes my hands when we're all saying goodnight. "Just remember to have fun."

"It's what I deserve," I say.

"Hell yeah, you do." Caroline smiles and hugs me. "You deserve everything, so go out there and get it. That's the *fuck you* Shawn's earned."

"Love you guys. Thanks for everything."

After they leave, I run a bubble bath and pour myself the last of the wine. I add a scoop of bath salts and hum when I sink into the warm water.

I start a short, spicy audiobook on my library app, enjoying the narrator for the guy. His seductive rasp is perfect for all the dirty things he tells the heroine. I forget how his appearance was described, picturing thick dark hair, green eyes, and a chiseled jawline like I do for most romance book heroes.

My thighs slide together. The thrum of arousal burns through me, tingling across my skin. I pause the audiobook to take a sip of wine, then end up distracting myself when I see a notification from the Love Struck app at the top of my screen.

Settling back against the tub, I browse through profiles it pulls up in my area when I open it. A few promising ones make me pause, but most have cleared the pleasant haze I was enjoying while listening to the romance book.

Fictional men will always be superior to reality.

The hazardous thing about online dating apps when you've lived in the same town your whole life is that you know every one of the guys in the pool.

You know Peter who picked his nose and smeared it on you on the playground in elementary school.

Swipe.

You know Zach who asked you to Homecoming only to disappear five minutes after arriving so he could make out with his ex-girlfriend.

Swipe.

You know—

I freeze at the profile picture.

No way.

No fucking way.

You know your brother's best friend from high school. The same hot hockey player who definitely was oblivious to how much he owned my heart before he moved away. The same guy who just moved back to Heston Lake to work as assistant coach...under your dad.

Cole's photo stares back at me with a handsome smile, green eyes crinkled at the corners. At least he's not holding up a freshly caught fish like most guys on dating apps.

Unlike them, he's laughing genuinely at something. It easily makes him even more attractive, drawing me in with his natural magnetism.

Swipe, I tell myself. Swipe now.

The more I want to swipe away, the more opening it is the only thing I'm thinking about. Licking my lips, I drum my nails against the edges of my phone to ride out the temptation.

Looking wouldn't hurt, right? He doesn't have to know I saw him on here. We're both just two people avoiding singlehood.

Impulsive curiosity wins out over logic. I tap into Cole's profile.

His bio is briefer than mine, but I smile at the photos of his travels. He looks happy surrounded by kids in hockey gear. Coaching looks good on him.

Then again, everything about him looks good.

The match notification jumpscares me.

"What?" Water sloshes when I jolt upright.

The Love Struck app has our photos framed in pink hearts, declaring that he's only 1.4 miles away from me in Heston Lake, Connecticut. It gives me options at the bottom of the screen to start a conversation, send a heart, set up a date, or unmatch.

My face heats when I realize we're both wearing Heston U Hockey fan gear in the pictures we picked. Mine's a striped long sleeve shirt in Knights' colors that I made myself with a heat press to add the logo. His is a heather gray t-shirt that stretches across his broad chest beneath a shearling-lined utility coat that looks damn good on him. It gives him a rugged vibe to go with his athletic build.

I bite my lip, rubbing my thighs together beneath the sudsy bathwater. A shiver runs down my spine from the silky feeling of the salts I added.

Maybe he didn't get a notification. I hope this app doesn't work that way. I'll just unmatch him.

New message from Cole K.

There goes my hope that the dating app wouldn't notify him that it thinks we're a good fit. How do I tell this app he's off-limits—no, double off-limits?

I open the message. At the bottom, the app asks *Has love struck? Take this match to the next level.* It also offers activity ideas, letting me know the planner found upcoming events happening in our area, suggesting the hockey game for a date.

Oh good. Of course there are read receipts. I can't stalk the chat without responding. He already knows I've seen his message. Love that for me.

MightyPuck: What the fuck? No way.
CraftyCutie: Awkwaaaard [laughing emoji]

MightyPuck: I can't believe it haha. How did we match? What are you even doing on here?

I relax. It seems he's more amused by this than weirded out.

CraftyCutie: Me? Why are you on here, hmm?
MightyPuck: Don't worry about it.
CraftyCutie: Who says I'm worried?
MightyPuck: Bet your brother will get a kick out of this [laughing emoji]
CraftyCutie: Hell no! Don't you dare tell him. OR my dad!
MightyPuck: Okay. I've always got your back, Evie. They don't have to know anything. It'll be our secret.

The smile I didn't realize I had while we were having fun challenging each other drops off my face. My thumbs hover over the keyboard while my heart beats hard and fast.

Maybe it's the nickname only he uses. Maybe it's the way I'm able to picture his sincere expression perfectly.

Hell, maybe it's the wine going to my head.

I start to type out a confession I've kept to myself for years.

I've always through about y—

Before I finish, I delete it quickly. My cheeks heat. I can't believe I almost told him I've thought about him. Thought about being with him. Fantasized about it.

Shaking my head, I huff out a laugh and reach for my wine glass, downing the last of it.

"That was close," I murmur.

CraftyCutie: Soooo, we're going to pretend this didn't happen and never talk about it again, right?
MightyPuck: If that's what you want, my lips are sealed.

A flutter tickles my stomach. I swipe my tongue across my lower lip while trying not to think about licking *his*—or any other part of him. Why does he have to be so unbelievably hot *and* sweet, considerate, kind, freaking sexy as hell—

Okay, okay. I need to stop.

It would never work between us. He fits perfectly with my family and they've always loved him. What if it ended badly and it was on me for making things weird for everyone?

Besides, there's no way he sees me that way.

It's just a silly old crush. Who doesn't crush on their older brother's best friend? It's a rite of passage. Growing pains that you laugh about.

Except I'm not laughing and the flutter dancing between my chest and my stomach isn't going away on its own.

I'm sure I'd do something to drive him away like my other exes. It would gut me for Cole to get frustrated by the things I do that drove Shawn crazy because I couldn't just *function like normal people.*

I gulp past the lump that sticks in my throat at the memory from one of our past fights, the words still embedded deep on my heart. He would get so annoyed every time I bought a new planner, muttering that we both knew I wouldn't stick with it, or when I would get overstimulated and need to change outfits ten times before going out, then he'd be a dick about my time management.

I rest my cheek against the edge of the bathtub, reminding myself that Shawn is an insensitive, selfish asshole. I can manage my neurodivergent brain with therapy and medication, but there's nothing to fix being a fucking douchebag.

Surprise hits me when Cole texts me. I didn't think he'd still have my number. Not that I ever deleted his from my contacts. I hold my breath as I read it.

> **Cole**
> I unmatched. Don't worry, I won't tell anyone. Good luck.

> **Eve**
> Thanks. You too. Did Heston win? I didn't check the final score.

> **Cole**
> Yeah. They're awesome. The team bus is on its way back now. I'm riding with them.

> **Eve**
> They didn't see anything, did they? The...you know. The thing that we're not talking about.

> **Cole**
> No we're in the clear.

> **Eve**
> Good. They're cool, but there's no way I'd trust them with that information.

> **Cole**
> See you on Thanksgiving if you don't stop by the rink to have lunch with your dad. Night.

> **Eve**
> Night.

Sighing, I sink lower until the water comes up to my nose. If only he wasn't Benson's best friend or Dad's assistant coach. If we could be two random people who matched on this app. Maybe then we could flirt, and flirting would lead to a date.

And that date would lead to knowing how Cole Kincaid kisses. Whether he's soft and teasing, or commanding and dizzying. Either way, I'd want it.

I'm left wondering *what if* until the bubbles dwindle and the bath cools.

SEVEN
EVE

On Thanksgiving, people all over Heston Lake are coming together to spend time with their families. Their fireplaces add a cozy note of smokiness to the autumn air.

And I'm standing in the cold outside Shawn's apartment building with my arms folded tightly across my chest, tapping my foot in annoyance.

I need to go in there and get the embroidery box he forgot to pack up with all my other stuff when he dumped me.

"Just do it," I mutter.

I've been encouraging myself with a promise that this will be an in-and-out thing, going over how I imagine the conversation will go. Rubbing my forehead, I ready myself to get through this situation.

Since he ended things between us two weeks ago, I've moved from hurt to anger toward him. It's not that I'm mad over the breakup, though the way he did it sucked. The deeper pain is caused by this feeding into the niggling anxiety that I'm too much and I'm easily thrown away.

My therapeutic response has been sending him middle finger emojis whenever I think about the breakup. Not my most mature reaction, but I stand by it. The messages stopped delivering, so I assume he blocked my number.

Which is why I'm here in person instead of asking him to give the last of my stuff back over text.

Centering myself with a few deep breaths, I mumble, "No bad days, girl. Rip him off like a bandage. Or a self-wax strip."

I shudder at the phantom pain I'll never forget from the first time the girls decided it would be a great idea to try it.

Rolling my shoulders back and lifting my head high, I march inside. His neighbor that tried to steal my glue gun is in the elevator on her way out. I plaster on my sweetest smile and wish her a happy holiday.

I practice what I'll say on the ride to Shawn's floor. The hallway is unchanged, yet feels so weird when I walk down it. I no longer belong here.

There's no answer when I knock. I give it a minute, then try again. At last, the door opens.

It's not Shawn. I blink at the woman. She's gorgeous and put together. Her hair is a fashionable chin-length dark bob and her chic dress clings to her lithe frame.

"Can I help you?"

"Uh..." I resist the urge to check if I got the apartment wrong somehow. "Is Shawn here?"

Recognition crosses her face, along with a hint of regret that I hope I'm imagining. "Oh, you're—He's not here. He went out to buy our pie. Do you need something?"

I open and close my mouth. "I'm just here to get something of mine that I left. A box of embroidery thread."

She ponders for a moment, then holds the door open for me. I hesitate.

She waves me inside. "I haven't seen it, but I have an idea of where it could be. Come in while I look."

A strange, tense sensation settles in my chest when I step through the door. The place smells different. Like perfume—one I'd never wear. There's a candle lit on the side table in the entrance that's not mine, along with other feminine touches that stand out as I catalog the differences from the bachelor pad I knew his place as.

The table is set for an intimate holiday meal for two and something mouthwatering roasts in the oven. I don't want to believe what my instincts are picking up. It's hard to ignore the signs piling up one after the other the further I venture into the apartment.

"Wait out here. I'll only be a minute," she says.

While she's gone, I peek in the hallway closet. A few pairs of her shoes sit next to his, along with her coats. There's a calendar he didn't own before tacked to the wall in the kitchen with handwriting much neater than his.

This woman lives with Shawn. It's only been two weeks. There's no way he fell so head over heels for someone else that he'd ask her to move in that quickly.

Which means he was cheating on me. I purse my lips, willing my swirling emotions to vanish. Blood rushes in my ears.

Is it hot in here? It feels way too stuffy.

How long was he stringing me along while he cheated with someone else? Is that why he broke things off with me? Does any of it even matter? Did I?

My eyes slam shut. It only helps a little. I try to stop feeling everything all at once, attempting to rationalize that things were never serious between us. It was a college fling that lasted too long because it was familiar.

Still. That asshole didn't have to cheat on me if he met someone else. I thought he was a coward for texting me to dump me. A bitter laugh escapes me.

I cover my mouth as things click into place. Flimsy excuses lately about not being able to have me over. Things moved around that I wrote off as nothing.

My gaze snaps to the hall leading to the bedroom. She recognized me. She must know I dated Shawn. But was she aware of what he was doing behind my back? Did he do it to both of us?

The flash of guilt on her face is telling. Talk about not being a girl's girl. I could never do this to someone else.

This is too much. I rub my temples while my heart beats hard enough to burst from my chest at any moment. I'm not interested in confronting this girl or waiting around for Shawn. I don't want to hear either of their explanations or apologies. I need to get out of here. *Now.*

"Sorry, I have to go. Emergency turkey situation." I call out the lie without waiting for her to answer before I'm out the door.

In the elevator, I realize that I got so worked up, I ended up forgetting my damn embroidery box. Irritation tugs at me, skittering along my skin until I feel like I'm vibrating with it. I force out a breath to release some of the overwhelm from my emotions drowning me.

I'm not going back for it again. I'll have to rebuy it.

The ride goes by in a blur. I leave the building as fast as my legs will carry me without breaking into a run.

I love my red boots. They make me feel like a confident boss bitch. Running in them? Bad idea. With my luck, I'll catch the chunky heels on something and break my ankle. I'm not spending Thanksgiving in the emergency room or explaining to anyone how I hurt myself.

The further I walk through town, the easier it is to breathe again. I stomp on an especially crisp looking leaf, pretending it's my ex's face. It's marginally satisfying and gives me an outlet.

"Fuck him," I mumble.

Shawn doesn't deserve another second of my time or an inch of space in my mind. I'm so fucking done with him. And I sure as hell won't let him ruin my day.

I shove this bullshit with him to a corner of my mind and turn down the tree and lamp-lined road that heads through the center of town. The historic lamps are spruced up with seasonal banners and snowflake light decorations that illuminate at night.

I stop in my tracks when I come to the corner where the beat up old camper is for sale. It's seen better days. The siding is mismatched and missing in some spots from rusting away. Once again I picture how great it would be with a makeover for my business.

It would be impulsive to buy this thing. I don't even know if this whole idea will go anywhere because perfectionism tends to slow me down.

My impulsivity feels like a blessing and a curse because my brain operates on two timelines: *right now* and *not right now*.

When I have strong urges to do something, it has to be then and there to satisfy myself. On the other hand, when I lose interest or am feeling overwhelmed, it goes firmly in the back of my mind to wait until later, if it comes at all.

My mind screams at me *right now, right now, right fucking now*.

Screw it. I have a decent amount saved up from tips, and I've heard it from my friends, my family, and people all over town countless times that the creations I craft are good enough to sell. Then they all turn around and warn me off when I feel like charging into something because I'm gripped by an idea.

This could be my chance to take the next step in my life. I've been floundering since I graduated from Heston U. Am I going to remain a bartender forever, or am I going to have the guts to chase my dreams?

I don't want anything to hold me back.

Without giving myself time to chicken out, I text the number on the sale sign. The owner answers eagerly, more glad than anything to have someone take it off his hands. He agrees to come by the bar next week to make the sale and lets me know I can pick it up whenever I want.

A giddy squeal bursts free. I do a little happy dance, laughing when a passing car honks. I wave, recognizing Mr. Boucher and his son Theo that plays on the hockey team. His daughter Lainey is probably in the back with her nose in a book.

"Hi! Happy Thanksgiving!" I shout.

They give the horn a few more taps and drive on. I feel much better on my way home.

There's nothing I can do about Shawn cheating on me. We're over. I just want to move on and not think about him anymore. Fuck him very much. I hope he has an exceptionally mediocre life that brings him no fulfillment whatsoever.

And me? I'm going to strive for no bad days.

* * *

It's almost noon when I get home. I was only gone for a little over an hour, tops, but Mom's transformed the house.

A fir garland winds around the banister on the staircase dotted with frost-tipped fake leaves and a string of lights. The pinecone animals that decorated the mantel in the living room have been replaced with tapered candles and her bottlebrush tree collection.

This is nothing compared to how it will be by this weekend. Only some of her numerous boxes that house her holiday decor have been pulled out. She loves the winter season and Christmas most of all. Usually her decorations go up on November 1st, adorning every room in the house with a seasonal touch that doesn't come down until well into January.

Mom loves the holidays so much that she ended up with me, her Christmas baby. Well, I was meant to be born on Christmas Eve, but I didn't arrive until December 31st. Either way, it's why they named me Eve. Dad teases both of us for my stubbornness about Mom's plans from the start.

Cheerful instrumental carols play softly throughout the house, getting louder as I approach the kitchen.

"You've been busy."

She pops up from checking on the turkey. "There you are!"

"What can I help with?" I shrug out of Dad's utility coat and drape it on the hook where he keeps it through winter.

"The food's all cooking. Thanks for making the mashed potatoes this morning." She gestures for me to follow her into the front room. "Look what I got for your door."

After rummaging through the boxes, she presents me with a wreath. It's smaller than the huge one she puts out every year with a sheer gold ribbon woven around it and tied with a big bow at the bottom.

She fluffs the pine branches, grinning joyfully. "Isn't it so cute? It reminded me of you since you're always tying ribbons in your hair. They came in a three pack and I had to have them. I'm sending your brother and Jess home with one, too."

At my poorly contained amusement, she jumps in before I make a comment. "Don't start. You're my snow angel baby. You know how I get."

"I do, and I love you for it."

"Good. Take this for your bathroom, too. I put a set in all of ours."

She hands me a couple of decorative hand towels and a battery operated tea light in a silver votive with tree shaped cut outs.

"Mom," I say in fond exasperation. "It's only me over there."

"It adds atmosphere!"

"Okay, you win."

She kisses my cheek. "Is Shawn stopping by for dessert? I'll have Dad grab the extra folding chairs from the basement since we have Cole for dinner."

I scoff. "Nope. I'm done with him. More dessert for the rest of us."

There. Now the last person in my family knows and I can move past him.

Her brows fly up, though she recovers quickly. "My beautiful baby girl deserves the world and someone who cherishes that big generous heart of yours."

I hug her. She squeezes me tightly.

"Love you."

"Love you more, snow angel. You're still my best gift of the season."

A content smile curves my mouth. "I'll be back in a minute. I'm going to hang up the wreath."

It's blustery when I leave through the side door to the driveway. The wind sends a fresh trickle of leaves to the ground. They're nearly gone from most trees with winter approaching.

I wrap my long cardigan around me and hurry up the steps to my apartment above the garage. Once I run in to drop off the bundle in my arms, I use the hook Mom gave me to add the wreath to my front door. It looks great against the pink color I painted it last summer for a pop of personality.

Cole's there when I come back inside. He has a wreath that matches the one I just put up.

I bite my lip around a smile. "She got you, too?"

He lifts it with a chuckle. "Yeah. She handed me this and said if I wanted to borrow anything else to 'doll up'—" He does a scary good impression of her. "—my place, I was welcome to it. I'm surprised she waited this long into November."

"That's my doing. I convinced her to wait until this weekend so we could all be together to decorate as a family like we used to as kids."

His smile is crooked. "Remember when we were trick or treating, and when we got back she had half of your Halloween decorations down and was putting out the wicker reindeer that light up?"

I laugh. "Oh my god, yes."

Warmth flares in his gaze and an attractive dimple appears in his cheek. "You were dressed as a mushroom fairy."

"I—yeah," I stammer in astonishment. "I made the costume myself. You remember that?"

"I'll always remember that."

Butterflies dance through me. His gaze roams from my half-braided hair tied back with a tan suede ribbon to my signature boots.

"You look nice, by the way."

I smooth a hand over the russet v-neck I paired with jeans beneath the cardigan. "Thank you. So do you."

His unruly hair is styled. He has on dark jeans and a sweater with the collar of his blue plaid dress shirt sticking out at the neckline.

"Eve," Dad interrupts gruffly while I'm trying and failing not to ogle the assistant coach like he's a main course on our menu tonight. "We're eating soon. Mom needs everyone's help setting the table."

I avert my eyes and bolt for the kitchen before he finishes. "Yup. Got it."

"I'll help." Cole follows me.

I swear I hear one of Dad's cryptic hums before we leave the room. I hope my crush on Cole wasn't written all over my face.

"Pick a dish and take it out," Mom directs while she oversees the gravy.

We reach for the same thing. Cole clears his throat and nods with his chin for me to go first.

"Do you need help carving the bird?" he offers.

Dad claps him on the shoulder with a hearty laugh. "That's my job. Are you gunning for that one next?"

"No, sir," he answers too quickly.

"Relax. I'm not that old, but I'm not that young, either. Eventually I'll retire."

I take a bowl of potatoes to the dining table. Cole trails after me with roasted vegetables.

"Where should I put this?"

"Anywhere you find room," I answer.

The table is fully decked out with place settings and an autumnal centerpiece. I spot an open area. We move for it simultaneously.

Our hands brush when we set our dishes down side by side. The brief touch sends a thrilling jolt through me. I startle with a small gasp, putting space between us.

I move so quickly I hip-check one of the chairs. Biting back a grunt at the minor pain, I rub the dull ache. It's not bad. In a moment it will be gone.

"Are you okay?" His hands hang in the air as if he's reaching for me before he drops them.

"What? Yeah, I'm good. Excited to eat."

He inclines his head, studying me from the corner of his eye. "If you're worried, I'm not going to say anything."

My breath catches again. I push him away from the table. He goes without complaint, watching me while I herd him backwards until he's against the wall. His abdomen is firm beneath my palms. I enjoy it for a fraction of a second before I yank my hands off him.

I glance at the door to the kitchen, then back to Cole. All those what ifs I thought about come rushing back.

"I thought we promised not to talk about that?" I whisper. "You know, the thing that shall not be named that definitely didn't happen."

His green eyes flicker between mine, making my heart beat harder. "Right. Sorry."

We stare each other down. He smells incredible. The spiced, woodsy aftershave makes my head spin in a good way. I rub my fingers together to keep myself from putting my hands back on him while he studies me, quiet and unwavering as if we're the only two people in the world.

The moment between us breaks when Benson arrives with Jess. I realize how close we're standing. We both tear our gazes from each other. He goes to greet my brother and his wife.

After a moment of saying hello, Jess sidles over to me while the guys talk. I give her a wry smile and she walks into my open arms, returning my hug. I love her laid-back nature. She's been the perfect balance to my chaos since she became part of the family when she met Benson in college.

"Hey girl," I say. "Missed my battle partner."

She sweeps her sleek dark hair over her shoulder. "I know, I'm sorry. This new distributor insisted one of us fly out to sign the paperwork."

"That's so great. Soon enough you guys will be everywhere."

She crosses her fingers with a smirk. I hook my arm with hers and we stroll together to get glasses of wine from the bar cart in the corner.

"Speaking of kicking ass at business, I feel like I have to tell you first."

Her expression shifts with interest. "What is it? Wait—are you going to do it?"

I bite my lip, nodding. "I think so."

I've had a few false starts since graduating from Heston. She was one of the first people I told about my idea for a lifestyle brand to sell the things I create and she's helped me with suggestions for getting started.

"I want to get it up and running with what I've designed so far," I say. "And... I bought a camper. I know that's sort of cart before the horse, but I'm telling you it's a great opportunity to do pop ups. It needs work first, though, so that's down the line."

"Oh my god, girl, that's amazing." She clinks her wine glass with mine. "I'm so proud of you."

I relax from my instinctive defensive stiffness, glad that she gets it. "Thank you. I'm nervous, but really excited."

"Are you still using the same name and branding you told me about?"

I touch my earrings, a trio of translucent resin maple leaves that dangle. "Yeah, Sweet Luxe, for living luxe with things that make women smile."

"Love that," Jess says. "You've got this. If you need any help, hit me up."

"Okay. Thanks."

A rush of motivation hits me. Usually at the end of the year I feel like my life is falling apart, but maybe I'm turning that around with the drive to start my boutique online business.

"Okay, let's eat," Dad calls all of us while carrying the turkey platter.

"Did someone get the rolls?" Mom asks on her way to the table.
"I'll grab them."

I go to the kitchen and find the basket of fresh baked rolls on the counter. My steps falter on the way back.

Mom and Dad sit at each head of the table. Jess and Benson are seated together on one side.

And Cole is on the other, next to my open chair. He shoots me a furtive glance meant only for me as I take it. Is the same thing on his mind?

Awareness buzzes along my side. I'm acutely conscious of exactly how much distance is between us at any given moment throughout dinner with my family.

He's shared a meal with us hundreds of times before. I've sat next to him. Yet this is torture.

Pretending I'm not secretly matching with Cole in front of my family might test me more than this old crush reawakening.

Winter

QUARTER-LIFE CRISIS

Q DOES IT COUNT AS A MIDLIFE CRISIS IF YOU'RE ONLY 25?

EIGHT
COLE

December

WHEN I ARRIVE at the Heston Lake public rink for the first lesson the following week, I'm pleased to find Cameron Reeves is early, too. He's hanging out by the log benches outside the entrance messing around on his phone.

On David's advice, I brought this opportunity up at Monday's practice. Reeves was the most interested in joining me to get some volunteer hours under his belt. They're not required, but advised to do community service and outreach to give them valuable experience.

It hasn't been long since I met the players, but I really like this kid. He has a chill vibe, is level-headed tending the net when we trial him as a goalie in practices, and his loyalty to his teammates is admirable.

"Hey, coach." He adjusts his backwards baseball cap and offers a fist with a lighthearted grin.

I bump it with a smirk, feeling more like an older brother than his coach. "Just you, huh?"

He ticks off on his fingers. "E's hitting the weight room because Bouch told him his conditioning routine to improve his speed. Keller, Hutch, Adler all have classes. Captain is getting a jump-start

71

studying for exams." He hesitates, gauging my reaction. Either I pass or his honesty wins out. "And I think Brody's sleeping off a hangover."

I nod along, chuckling at the last one. "Sounds about right. Don't worry, I won't tell Lombard. I'm no stranger to what college is like."

I was a fan of testing my limits and showed up to more than one practice feeling the consequences.

"Cool."

I lay a hand on Cameron's shoulder. "Come on, let's head in."

The outdoor rink is built onto the lake. It looks festive with garland and lights everywhere around the cabins and the picnic tables. A few early parents sit near the space heaters with their kids. There's a cabin that sells food and hot cocoa that opens to this area and the rink. Skate rentals are in the cabin on the other side of the courtyard.

He puts on his skates while I go into the office between the snack and rental buildings. A girl who must be a student at the college shows me where to find the list of student names along with their parents' numbers.

It's almost time to start when I'm finished. More kids arrive and get checked in at the rental cabin while I don my skates.

"Eve's not here yet." I check my phone to see if she texted, finding nothing.

"Should we wait?" Cameron asks.

"Let's get started. It should be fine between the two of us on the first day. When she gets here, she'll jump in."

I've never exactly taught beginner lessons, but with the youth camps we sometimes had to brush up on basic skills. I draw on that experience to decide we'll work on balance first, then falling down and standing up.

We introduce ourselves to the kids. The group isn't too large to manage. Around fifteen of them, the youngest about four and the oldest about ten, sit on the long bench outside the rink.

"Show of hands, who's ready to learn to skate?" I prompt.

Their little gloved hands shoot up and a few of them bounce in place.

"First things first, rink rules."

I run through a brief list of safety rules for them to follow about their skates and no rough-housing. Then I quickly explain what we'll be doing to learn how the ice feels under their skates.

"Now do we get to go on the ice?" The question comes from a small girl at the end of the bench.

"Yes. Who here likes trains? We're going to make one."

I motion to Cameron. We get them lined up one by one, taking them out to the ice. We have them crouch down while holding on to the PVC training bars, towing them until they're in a row facing the boards for leverage.

"Show them how it's done, Cameron."

"Okay, watch me. Then it'll be your turn."

He borrows a PVC bar and slides each foot back and forth, then carefully lifts his knees one at a time to demonstrate his balance.

Once the kids test it out themselves, I let Cameron glide up and down the row on his own. He stops to give a thumbs up and helps a few that struggle, showing them to put their weight on the bar like they're pushing on a table. It's easy to see he'll be good at this with his attentiveness and his friendly smile when he high fives the ones who gain confidence.

I watch the kids do the exercise as they get a feel for balancing on ice. My mind drifts off in a direction it frequently does lately.

In the short few weeks since I've been back in town, I've done my best to keep Eve in the off-limits column where she's always been. Where she needs to stay.

Was she always this much of a temptation? Her laughter and smiles made my chest feel funny, but now whenever she's around it's like she's the sun in the room. And I'm a planet that doesn't know how to fight the pull of her orbit. She's all I'm able to look at.

Especially when she keeps wearing those hot little sweater dresses. Fuck, she looks good in them.

Growing up, I knew to keep my hands off her because she's my best friend's sister. She was never a possibility then. With her dad as my boss, I still shouldn't risk anything. Not if I want to try to keep this job.

And I do, I really fucking do. Coaching Heston U's guys has quickly become something that feels right for me.

I've been constantly moving around, unable to stay in one place. All because I believed I wasn't cut out to coach officially, not wanting to face that I didn't know what the fuck to do after my time as a hockey player ended. Working with the team on their development and having a part in guiding them to the top of their game is an honor. It's unreal to think I could help skilled guys like Keller and Blake reach the pros.

This job means everything to me right now. Not as a stepping stone to find a coaching position elsewhere, but staying here, with this team, this college. This is an amazing opportunity and I'd be an idiot to screw it up.

So of course my dumb ass had to find out if Eve was still on the dating app over the weekend.

The first time we matched before Thanksgiving was more of a funny surprise, then it evolved to intrigue the more I thought about it. It was on my mind throughout dinner with her family. She was within arm's reach sitting next to me, tickling my senses with her sweet scent.

I haven't been on Love Struck much otherwise. Curiosity made me look for Eve's profile while I took a break from researching more skills and drills training to bring to the table. We matched again somehow. I dutifully resigned myself to hitting the unmatch option. Maybe I'm better off deleting the app.

A distressed shout pulls me from my thoughts. Eve jogs along the path that follows the frozen lake from the parking lot. Her hair is in two thick braids and her workout pants look painted onto her curvy legs.

Don't look at her tits, don't look at her tits, don't fucking look at her tits bouncing, man.

Too late.

I clear my throat, wrenching my attention back to the group. "Hey, Cam? Keep them going for a minute."

"Sure." He gives me an easygoing smile and a little salute.

I linger for a moment, watching him guide the kids. It's evident he's enjoying this. I see a lot of myself in him. I'm glad I brought him.

Skating off, I meet Eve outside the rink. She's pushing herself so hard to get here, she doesn't have time to slow down. I catch her against me, then she scrambles back, nearly losing her balance.

"I'm sorry, I'm sorry!" She pauses to catch her breath before launching back into an explanation I don't need. "I mixed up the dates when I put the reminder in my phone. I went all the way to work thinking I had a bartending shift when I was supposed to be here."

I take her shoulders. She cuts off, looking up at me with a shining gaze.

"Don't worry about it. You didn't miss much. I had it all under control with Cameron. Here, sit down."

It doesn't take much encouragement to nudge her to the bench.

"I wasn't really dressed right, so I had to run home to change," she continues rambling. "Then Dad called to remind me, but I—Oh! Shit, I forgot my skates. I know exactly where they are. I put them by my door so I wouldn't forget them."

"What size are you?" At her flustered glance, I tip my head toward the rental cabin. "We'll rent you a pair today."

"Oh. You're right. I'm an eight."

I go take care of her skates, kneeling at her feet once I return. She doesn't stop me from helping her put them on, more focused on sending worried glances around. I wrap my fingers around her ankle as I guide her foot into the boot.

"Hey, it's okay. You made it here. It's not a big deal."

She nods distractedly. I soothe her by running my palm along the side of her leg. She begins to calm down and the knot of discomfort at seeing her frazzled loosens in my chest.

"I didn't mean to mess up," she murmurs.

My touch lingers on her calf and I peer up at her. "You don't have to be perfect. I'm not. No one is."

She's stunned by the encouragement. I offer her a supportive smile that comes all too easily for her. I'm relieved to help her feel better because I'm not used to being there for anyone else.

"Um," Cameron says from the rink. "Sorry, these little gremlins are bored of the basics already."

Two kids dangle from each of his arms while he skates around.

Eve laughs, her eyes sparkling. She captures my attention once more. It's difficult to take my eyes off her.

"Come on. I don't want Vic telling Dad we were slacking off." She grabs my hand and tugs me to the ice.

"I want a turn!" Two kids latch on to me.

"How about we save this for the end? Everyone say hi to Eve first. She's your other teacher."

She waves with a bubbly smile that lights up her beautiful features. "Hi everybody! You're all doing so well. Are you having a good time so far?"

The group erupts with cheers. More than half of them have a good handle on balance, some even abandoning the bar to venture with shuffling slides.

"Next up, we're going to make sure we know how to get back up when we fall," I say.

Cameron demonstrates by pretending to fall, sliding around on his knees. "Oh no, how do I get up?"

The kids giggle. Eve kneels next to him and shows them what to do, climbing back to her feet with Cameron.

"Let's take turns," Eve says.

I find myself observing her during the rest of the lesson more than the kids. She's a natural on the ice.

It takes me back to my hockey practices in high school when she'd finish running through her figure skating routines before we took over the rink. She only did it for a while when I was still there, but I liked watching her lose herself in it.

As promised, when we're done teaching the kids how to get back on their feet if they fall, we end the lesson by the three of us carting a few kids each while we skate around in loops.

When the time's up, we herd the students off the ice to wait for their parents to pick them up and help them change back into their shoes.

"I'm heading back to campus," Cameron says after we've got them all wrangled.

"Good hustle, Reeves. Thanks for coming out," I say.

"I'd be down to do another class."

"We'll get you set up for volunteering again."

Eve rustles his messy brown hair when he takes off his hat. "I'll be cheering for you guys this weekend against Elmwood. Wings on me at The Landmark Saturday night if you win the home game with a shutout."

His brows shoot up. "Yeah? Bet."

"You motivate them better than I do," I murmur once he's gone.

"It's easy. Everyone loves food."

We wave goodbye to more kids as they leave. I get both of us hot cocoa while we wait around for them to trickle out. She holds the paper cup between her hands, inhaling the steam with a serene expression.

It's mid-afternoon, the winter sun dipping low behind the pine trees on the other side of the lake to wash everything in soft light. It casts her in a distracting backlit glow and I'm having trouble not staring at her.

"Nothing like hot cocoa, right?" Eve freezes mid-sip, setting her cup down. "Ohh, that gives me an idea. Cozy nights and..."

She trails off, head bent over her phone. Sensing my curious gaze, she holds it against her chest.

"Oh, don't mind me. I'm thinking out loud."

I smirk, sipping my drink. "You say that like I'm a stranger who doesn't know you."

She rolls her lips between her teeth. "I was making a note for a design I want to make."

"A design?"

"A sticker. Maybe an enamel pin, we'll see. I haven't made any of those yet." She purses her mouth to the side in thought. "Maybe a keychain would be easier to tackle."

"What's all this for?"

She blinks as she realizes I'm genuinely interested. I give her my undivided attention.

"You know how I make stuff, like my own stickers and my earrings? I'm making a business out of it to sell them online. I have a lot I've made over the years, but since I decided to do this the ideas are flowing like crazy."

When I don't stop her, she shares more with me. She gains confidence, getting excited and gesturing wildly with her hands as she explains. I'm captivated by her lit up and passionate about what she wants to do.

"And—Don't laugh."

I swipe my tongue across my lip. "Wouldn't dream of it."

She taps her finger against my chest. "Seriously."

The corners of my mouth twitch. "I'm being serious. Go ahead. What were you going to say?"

She ducks her head, playing with the end of one of her braids. "I know this will sound wild, but I'm buying this camper. It's used—like, really used. I don't even know how to repair the rusted siding. I guess I'll have to figure that out."

Hesitation stalls her from continuing. She pinches her hair, seeming self-conscious after being animated a moment ago.

"What's wrong?"

Her gaze flickers when she lifts it. "I'm waiting for you to tell me I shouldn't do it."

I pull a face. "Why would I do that? I think it sounds cool."

Her eyes widen, full of wonder. When she looks at me like that, my heart drums hard.

"You do?"

"Yeah. I'll help you fix it up." I put an arm around her in a reassuring side hug. "What do you plan to do with it?"

Her giddiness returns as she launches into an explanation about pop-ups and vendor markets, then going into her plans to build a book cart inside the camper with a small library of romance books to borrow. She cuts off sheepishly after she's been talking nonstop for a few minutes.

"Sorry, I'm always getting carried away. I don't know when to stop once I get on a roll."

A chuckle slips out and I feel like some of her enthusiastic energy has overflowed to me. I tell myself I'm imagining the hitch in her breath when I shift closer.

"You can do it." I touch the earrings she has on—realistic chicken nuggets shaped like dinosaurs. The kids got the biggest kick out of them. "You can do anything."

The pink flush in her cheeks darkens and her pretty amber eyes grow large. "You think so?"

"Yes. In all the years I've known you as we grew up, I've seen what you're capable of when you put your mind to something."

"Thank you," she murmurs. "That means a lot to me."

"I'm in your corner," I promise. "I wouldn't be your friend if I wasn't."

I ignore the warmth spreading through me when she beams.

Not long after, we're waiting on the last kid's parents. Eve curses under her breath. He's oblivious, absorbed in playing a game on my phone to keep him occupied without any of the other kids here to entertain him.

"Everything okay?"

"It's nothing." She frowns, typing out a message on her phone.

"Doesn't sound like it. Tell me. If I can help, you know I will."

Her shoulders slump at the response that pings on her phone. "It's—I'm picking up the camper after this. Benny was supposed to go with me, but he had to bail. I just asked Dad if I could borrow his truck, but he can't because he went out to view a potential player he might want to scout."

"No problem. I don't have anything going on. I'll go with you to get it."

"Really?" Her relief is palpable.

"Of course."

"God, you're a lifesaver."

It feels good to be the one to put the cute smile back on her face. I bump my arm against her shoulder.

Once the last kid is collected, I walk her to my car and follow her directions to the middle of town. On the ride, she fiddles with my radio and blasts the heat on us, asking me twice if I need my vents adjusted while she holds her fingers over hers with bliss written all over her face. *Cute*, I think before tearing my gaze away. I need to stop thinking about how much I like having her in my car.

The guy selling the camper waits outside when I pull up. He's a middle-aged man with a protruding beer belly that strains against his winter coat. Eve told me he's a regular at the bar and gave her a good deal below his asking price.

She hops out of the Bronco. "Hey, Big Al!"

"Hey, Miss Eve. Thanks again for taking this old thing off my hands." He pats the small camper as I come up to her side. Glancing between us, he winks at her. "Let's get this hitched up to your boyfriend's car."

"Oh, he's not—we're not—" She flails, darting an unreadable look my way.

I wrap an arm around her shoulders and murmur in her ear teasingly. "Come on, *sweetheart.*"

"Cole," she hisses.

I chuckle, moving away when she swats at me, then turn back to blow her a kiss. Her mouth pops open and she gives me a look that says she's going to get me back for rolling with this.

I swipe a hand over my jaw to contain my amusement. "Need me to swing around?"

"Yeah, back up to here," Big Al says.

It doesn't take much time to get the camper attached. I switch places with Eve and have her drive the Bronco slowly while I help Big Al ease the camper off the curb. She hugs him when it's done.

I hang back to shake his hand while she gets in the car. "Thanks."

"Treat her good," he says.

My face goes slack. "What?"

He thumps his fist against the camper. "This old girl. She was good to me and my wife before she passed. We liked to go out to the Catskills."

"We will," I say.

It's not until I'm walking away that I realize I said *we.* I rub my forehead, mouth twisting wryly.

Eve has her elbow resting against the window, chin propped in her hand when I climb in the driver's seat. There's a faraway look on her face. My gaze softens when she turns to me.

"Thank you for coming with me and towing the camper," she says.

I stretch out to rest a hand on the back of her seat, pulling out on the main road to take her home.

"It was no trouble at all."

NINE
EVE

Clocktower Brew House is packed when I go in for a caffeine fix. Students are in a mad rush to leave town before it snows, otherwise they'll be trapped here for a few extra days into their winter break.

I get in line, noticing the outgoing waitress that started working at The Landmark recently. Typically when we hire freshmen they have a quick turnover, but I get the feeling she'll outlast the others and be at the bar with me for a while.

"Reagan, hey." I wave when she turns.

Her strawberry blonde hair is hastily braided with some pieces falling loose. She's wearing a teal crewneck with Heston University across her ample chest in block letters. Even dressed down, she radiates confidence in herself.

"Eve! Hi." She joins me in line. "I swear, if they run out of coffee before we get up there, I'll riot. I'm in desperate need if I'm going to handle my drive."

"It's the crazy rush. I remember it after finals. Are you heading home for break?"

"Yup. I'm coming back right after New Year's, though. Mr. B said he'd give me a couple shifts if I promised to take the stage." Her nose crinkles with her laugh. "I'm excited for the chance to sing for an audience, even if it's only The Landmark crowd."

"You'll rock it. You're an amazing singer." I bump my shoulder with hers and smile. "And I bet we score better tips."

We shuffle forward when the line moves. The bell on the door jingles when it opens, letting in a gust of chilly air.

"Hey," a deep voice says behind me.

I smile slowly, scraping my teeth across my lower lip. It's pointless because there's no stopping the warmth that spreads in my chest around him.

"Cole," I answer without turning around.

"How's the camper, sweetheart?"

That gets me to spin. He winks, only teasing. I wish he weren't.

"Okay, enough of that. Big Al isn't around," I say. "The camper is fine. I've gotten as far as dusting it and scaring myself half to death when I thought I needed to fend off a huge spider. Turned out it was already dead."

"Yikes," Reagan says with a grimace.

"Tell me about it. I wanted to get one of Dad's old hockey sticks from the garage, but I was terrified if I moved, I'd lose it. So it was just me and the carcass in a fifteen minute showdown before I worked up the courage to throw a shoe at it."

"Solid move." She shivers.

"You should've called me," Cole says. "Dead or not, I would've rescued you."

I roll my lips between my teeth and play with the beaded bracelet loop attached to my phone case. He needs to stop being so sweet and caring or I'll never get past this inconvenient crush. It's already worse from how kind he was the other day listening to me gush about my aspirations to start my business, genuinely interested in my goals.

"I'll keep that in mind next time I'm engaged in battle," I sass.

The corners of his mouth curl, bringing out the dimple in his cheek. He rests a hand over his heart with a slight bow.

"I await your call to arms, my liege."

Reagan shifts her gaze between us, then raises a brow at me. I give her a subtle shake of my head. We're up next to order.

"This is on me for both of you." Cole interrupts when I turn to him to protest. "What do you want, a mocha latte?"

My jaw snaps shut. He still remembers my coffee order after all these years? We used to stop by here every morning before he drove me and Benson to school, then we'd play Rock Paper Scissors at the ice rink before their hockey practices to see who would go out for coffee.

I nod. "Thank you."

"Same for me. Thanks, dude," Reagan says.

"You're welcome. Do either of you want anything to eat?"

"I'm okay. What?" I press at his doubtful expression.

"You're not hungry?" He lifts a brow when I shake my head.

"There are two things I never say no to: free coffee and baked goods." Reagan leans close to whisper to me. "Babe, he's all green flags. Keep him."

I hush her. His eyes glint with humor. I'm sure he heard her, but he's pretending he didn't.

He cocks his head in that confident, attractive way that leaves me breathless. "Are you sure you don't want anything else, Evie?"

You.

Not on the menu, unfortunately.

I wasn't that hungry. Not until he points at the fresh pastry twists as they're put in the display case. My mouth waters. I tap the glass and he smirks knowingly.

"Thought so. You've got it."

He puts in his order and pays while I contemplate how I got to a point in my life where my brother's best friend knows when I'm hungry before I do. Not that I'm always conscious of it, the sense often muted when I'm preoccupied until the moment I realize I've skipped a meal by accident and, oops, I'm starving.

When we shuffle over to the pick up counter, we bump into each other. He steadies me with his hands on my shoulders, walking behind me.

While we're waiting, Reagan spots some of the guys from the hockey team. They've claimed the armchairs and sofa around the low table in front of the crackling fireplace. They come in often enough to hang out at the bar that she's befriended them since she started working there.

She waves. "Hey guys."

They're happy to see her. Higgins, one of the seniors that plays defense, offers her his seat. He's a big softie despite his intimidating vibe.

"'Sup, Reagan?" Theo bumps fists with her when she takes the open spot on the couch.

Cole hands me my drink and cruller, then we follow her over to them. The guys get rowdier when we join the group.

"Eve, when are you gonna marry me?" Daniel Hutchinson gives me a slow grin.

I hum, pretending to consider as if he hasn't greeted me like this for the last three years since he was a freshman. "I don't know. Make me a good offer."

"You'll be in the shit if Coach Lombard finds out how much you flirt with his daughter, Hutch," Alex Keller jokes.

They share a laugh. Cole stiffens at my side. Daniel's laughter chokes off and he sits up after Cole shoots him a warning look.

"You could always flirt with my brother, but his wife might come after you instead of my dad. Maybe they'd team up." I hide my giggle at their spluttering by sipping my coffee.

"Yo, Kincaid." Jake Brody nods with his chin. "What are you doing today? The boys were just saying we wanted to get a pizza. You in?"

"I'm not here to see any of your faces outside of working hours. I, too, drink coffee," he deadpans while giving Reagan her cup. "Shocker, I know."

Easton snorts. "Have a seat, man. Shoot the shit with us."

"Why?"

"Because you secretly love us." Cameron grins unapologetically from his slouch in the other arm chair.

Cole exchanges a look with me. When I shrug, he offers the armchair to me instead of taking it. I perch on the arm, smirking at him when he narrows his eyes playfully, then sits down. I hum in contentment at the bite of my pastry, then break off a piece to offer to him.

"You moved on fast," a snide voice cuts through the cozy atmosphere of the coffee shop. "Guess you weren't that torn up. Does this guy put up with all your neurotic crap? Are you going to drag him down, too?"

Everyone in the group goes quiet. A leaden weight crashes to the pit of my stomach, crushing my good mood. I turn slowly, finding my ex-boyfriend. Heston Lake is a small town. Of course I'd run into him eventually.

Cole stills, then gets up in one quick, fluid motion. "What did you say to her?"

The demand is brittle with an edge of danger. My shoulders hunch.

"Nothing. Ignore him."

His big hand brushes the small of my back. "Sorry, Evie. I can't do that."

I try to convince him that he doesn't have to, but my heart is in my throat. He glares at my ex, standing at his full height.

Shawn is Cole's opposite in every way. His light brown hair is buzzed. He's shorter by a solid five inches and is much leaner than Cole's rugged build. His mouth is turned down in a natural, off-putting frown. Everything about his presence is cold compared to Cole's warm and inviting personality.

Seeing the two of them side by side, I question what I ever saw in Shawn.

"Apologize to her," Cole grits out.

"I'm good," Shawn says.

I swallow past the burn in my throat, rising to my feet. He doesn't get to be the asshole who gives me shit for moving on when *he* dumped *me*—and was secretly cheating. It doesn't matter that I'm not with Cole or anyone else. I won't allow my ex to cut me down with belittling comments because it makes him feel bigger than me.

"No," I snap.

Shawn swings his attention to me. "No?"

"No. I'm not dragging anyone down. If you felt like that when we were together, that was all your own doing, you absolutely pathetic piece of work. You don't have a leg to stand on. I know what you did."

He scoffs. I hate his smug bravado.

"I cut the fat from my life." He eyes me up and down with a sneer.

My jaw works as several responses fly up my throat at once. I bite them all back, taking a breath to remain calm and cool for once instead of feeling my emotions so acutely. I don't want to make more of a scene than he already has in the middle of the coffee shop.

"You broke up with me so you could move your other girlfriend in." A hollow laugh leaves me at his caught out expression. I narrow my eyes. "Yeah, I know you were cheating on me. Is that why you wrote out that wall of text explaining why you were breaking up with me out of the blue? Was I in the way? Did it take you all day to draft so you had it ready to send me at a moment's notice?"

Cole stands by my side, allowing me to say what I need to. His jaw locks and his fists balls tight enough his knuckles turn white.

"It doesn't matter because I'm not sitting up pining after you. Have a long, boring, terrible fucking life, Shawn. I'm glad I don't have to be in it anymore because you're a miserable person and a really shitty partner. A soul-suck. A gloomy poison that infects everyone around you until you eat away at their light and creativity and energy because all you know how to do is take."

I'm proud of myself when my firm tone only shakes slightly.

"Damn," Reagan murmurs somewhere behind me. "Tell him, girl."

Shawn's chest rises and falls for a few beats, then his face contorts with anger. "You bratty fucking *bitch!*"

He manages to take one step toward me before Cole and the hockey guys move to protect me. Cole grabs him while Easton tugs me back until he's blocking me. Cameron puts a hand on my shoulder and Theo hovers at my side, pausing his glare to throw me a wink.

My heart swells. I love these guys. Their bond as a group runs deep, and they treat me as if I'm part of their little family, too.

Cole wrenches Shawn by the unforgiving grip on his baggy hoodie, walking him back into the corner near the fireplace. He doesn't raise his voice enough for us to hear. The line of his chiseled jaw is rigid as he scowls and speaks in Shawn's ear. Shawn goes pale.

This fierce protectiveness charged with the barely contained threat of violence shouldn't be a turn on, yet it is. It reminds me of how hot I found it when he'd check his opponents playing defense. I will my body to stop being such a thirsty disaster.

Shawn nods at what Cole is saying. He stumbles when he's released, blurts an apology without looking me in the eye, and scrambles for the exit.

Cole watches until he leaves, then turns to me. He grasps my arms and dips his chin.

"Are you alright?" he mutters.

"Fine. Really," I insist when he doesn't buy it. "I swear, I'm good."

"So," Theo drawls. "Who's still up for pizza?"

"Yeah, I'm gonna go," I stammer. "Thanks for having my back guys. Cole."

I meet his concerned gaze and a fresh wave of fire spreads in my cheeks. Before he says anything else, I grab my latte and half-eaten pastry from the coffee table and dash out of the cafe with a hasty goodbye.

* * *

The coffee shop by campus was crowded, but The Landmark is mostly dead during my shift later in the afternoon. It started snowing on my way in, dusting everything in Heston Lake.

I'd love to be hiding away in my apartment after the scene at Clocktower Brew House earlier, but unfortunately I need to make money to live. Who decided that? Rude.

I'm more humiliated than angry about running into Shawn. He showed his true colors in all their douchebag glory. Having Cole and half the hockey team jump to my defense is as heartwarming as it is embarrassing.

Mom and Dad are going to hear all about the incident. No doubt. Who knows how the story will be twisted by then.

I text Benson and ask him to help me out with damage control before the town's gossip mill gets crazy. He responds with a string of emojis I'm not bothering to decipher. I take the peace sign, heart hands, beer glass cheers, and laughing emojis to mean that he's on it.

I'm braced to hear some version of it, but our usual regulars only talk hockey, hockey, and more hockey. I tune to the game on the flatscreens for them and they leave me be unless they want a refill.

It's slow, but I have an eighty pound tan and white shadow with a wagging tail and humid dog breath ghosting at the back of my legs to keep me company while I pass the time. Hammy follows me when I'm on the move and leans against me when I'm not busy.

In the middle of my shift, Cole comes in. He takes a seat at the bar a few stools down from Neil Cannon, the town's local retired NHL legend. People ask for his picture or autograph when they recognize him. To those of us that grew up here, he's just Mr. Cannon. He's a sweet guy, if somewhat grouchy.

Cole shakes his hand and buys him a round when he orders a beer with a burger.

"Coming right up." I salute before pouring his drink.

He scrutinizes me. "You all good?"

"Yup," I say brightly as I set his beer on a coaster in front of him.

He grasps my wrist gently to stop me from pulling away. "But for real?"

I duck my face. "Yeah. Thank you."

His piercing gaze is unwavering. "Tell me if that guy ever bothers you again. I'll make sure he's not a problem for you. No one treats you like that."

My knees grow weak. I nod, gripping the sink behind the bar for balance when he releases me.

"Not eating dinner with my parents tonight?" I ask when I have myself under control.

The side of his mouth quirks. "I wanted to keep you company."

I twist my fingers in the bar rag. Hammy interrupts my fluttering heart with a *boof*.

Smiling, I give him a scratch behind his ears. "You're the best company."

"I am, aren't I?" Cole jokes.

I huff out a laugh. He leans on the bar and props his chin in his hand.

"The dog," I correct.

"Woof." His grin stretches slowly at my amused eye roll.

I drift around to check on everyone. Once I handle refills, Cole's food is ready. I pop into the kitchen to get the order, then return to find Hammy has Cole off his stool to pet him. My brother's also arrived.

"Hey. Are you here for a drink?"

"I just stopped by to talk to Matt about brewery stuff," Benson says.

"Mr. B's in the office." I jerk my thumb to the hall that leads back there.

"You too good to drink with me?" Cole pauses from showering the dog with attention to elbow Benson.

"Fine, fine. Pour me whatever's on tap."

I get it for him, keeping half my attention on Cole and the dog while they chat about an upcoming practice for their beer league team. I bite my lip around a smile. He's beyond enamored with Hammy. I don't blame him, Hambone is one of the sweetest dogs ever.

Folding my arms and leaning on the bar, I watch them playing together. "You should get a dog. Didn't you talk about it all the time?"

Cole hums, massaging Hammy's ears. He leans into Cole's legs, tongue lolling in bliss.

"I would in a heartbeat. I just worry about having enough time with all the travel. If I got a dog, I'd want to give it all the time I could, or it wouldn't be fair," he says.

"The team doesn't travel that much. Except when they make it to playoffs and the championship. You could get someone to watch him. Like me, I'd do it."

"I would, too," Benson says. "You could take it to the rink."

Cole's shoulders shake with an amused huff. "Yeah, that would be awesome."

His expression shutters. A pang echoes in my chest at the flash of uncertainty, wishing I had some way to take it away for him as easily as he's done for me recently.

Hammy butts Cole's hand to ask for more petting. I get the jar of treats we keep behind the bar for customers to give to him when he begs and offer it to Cole with a shake. He shoots me a soft smile.

"We'll see," he says. "Until then, there's this guy."

Hammy's body wriggles under his attention. He gobbles down

the treats he's presented and plants himself by his new best friend when Cole sits.

Benson finishes his drink and heads to the back office.

"Your food's getting cold." I steal one of his fries. "Eat this."

"But look at his face." He gestures to what I like to call Hammy's seal eyes—big, round, adorable.

"I know, he's hard to resist. Just looking at him gives me a boost. It's free serotonin."

Lainey Boucher comes through the entrance with an armful of books. Snowflakes melt in the loose strands of dark blonde hair that fall from her ponytail to frame her face. She nudges her slightly fogged glasses up the bridge of her nose. She looks just like her twin brother, though Theo carries himself more confidently.

"Hey, Lainey."

"Hi," she mumbles quickly.

She's super shy when there are too many people, but we bond over romance books when it's quiet.

"There's plenty of open booths to chill in today," I point out.

"Great."

She goes to the far corner. The dog follows her, laying at her feet under the booth while she takes out her laptop and bends over a notebook. Whatever she's working on has her completely absorbed.

"Now you can eat your food without guilt," I tell Cole.

He smirks, spinning the basket so the fries are closer to me as he picks up his burger. I resist for a moment, then snag another fry.

During another lull not long after, I check my phone. I don't mean to, but I open the Love Struck app. The match screen with Cole is becoming way too familiar when it pops up.

I freeze, checking to see if it notified him. His phone lights up on the bar. He lifts a brow, tapping the notification.

A beat later, his gaze finds mine.

Damn it.

How many times has this been now? Three? Four? I'm losing count.

It wouldn't keep happening if I could stop myself from downloading it to my phone rather than leave it deleted. Every time I do, it takes my profile off of hiatus and treats it like a clean slate.

My thumb hovers over the options. He remains silent. I feel the weight of his observation.

Neither of us say anything while I quickly select unmatch and set my phone face down on the bar. I don't touch it for the rest of my shift.

TEN
COLE

On Christmas, I don't have anyone else to celebrate with. Rather than sit around my apartment alone, I spend it with the Lombards.

Yesterday, before joining them for the annual Christmas Eve pizza and beer night that they've hosted for as long as I can remember, I FaceTimed my parents to catch up while their cruise was at port. They're thoroughly enjoying the traveling they've been doing more and more since I graduated and moved out.

I get my love of travel from them, and I'm glad to see them doing all the things they dreamed of that they put off for my sake.

I turn up at the Lombards' place in the afternoon with a bottle of wine and a bag of gifts I scraped together two weeks ago. A bit last minute, but at least I got something. I wanted to avoid coming empty handed, and to show how grateful I am that they always treat me like I'm part of their family.

The sight of Eve's new camper parked in the driveway brings a smile to my face before I head in through the side door. David and Mrs. Lombard are in the kitchen. I shake his hand and she gives me a big hug.

"Here, I brought you this." I hand her the wine. "Thanks again for having me over."

"Of course." She pulls down the reading glasses perched on her head to read the label. "Thank you. You're such a sweet boy."

"Can I help with anything?"

"You can help by getting out of my kitchen until I need your muscles to cart all this food to the table." Mrs. Lombard shoos me with a wave of the holiday-themed dish towel in her hand. "Go on, the kids are in the living room."

I head there to find Eve, Benson, and Jess hanging out.

"Merry Christmas," I say warmly.

"Didn't we do this about twelve, thirteen hours ago?" Benson lumbers off the couch.

"Shut up." There's no heat in it.

"I told you last night, you should've crashed here."

My gaze darts to Eve—drawn to her first whenever I walk in a room these days—before I force it back to him. "My duplex is only a five minute drive from here."

He gives me a bear hug. "Merry Christmas, man. Glad you can be here with us."

Jess is right behind him. I hug her next, then freeze when I face Eve.

Before I left yesterday, I was able to hug her, no problem. But she wasn't wearing one of these sweater dresses that fill my head with ideas I shouldn't be entertaining, like fisting the soft material and peeling it off to unwrap her like my own filthy little present. The deep green dress has a wide neck that shows her shoulders, and her hair is half down with big curls, the top swept back from her face in two braids tied off with a dainty burgundy bow.

"Merry Christmas, Cole," she says.

My eyes close when she slips her arms around me. Her hair smells nice. I resist the urge to squeeze her closer just to find out how her curves feel pressed against me.

"Happy birthday. Almost," I add.

She sticks out her tongue, then brandishes a mug. "Mulled wine —which is amazing, but super potent this year—or hot cocoa?"

"Hot cocoa," I decide because she's having it and it smells as sweet as she does.

Her teeth sink into her tempting bright red lower lip and her beautiful eyes gleam. "I was hoping you would say that. Come see what I put together."

She all but drags me over to a hot cocoa station. It's got mugs on a wooden tree, a variety of mix choices, and all sorts of toppings. She also included labels for everything and a menu with suggested combinations.

"Nice," I say.

"It's a masterpiece," she gushes. "I had fun designing the signs."

"I'm torn. Do I want marshmallows and a peppermint stick, or whipped cream and cinnamon powder?"

"It's the holidays. Go big or go bigger."

I snap my fingers and point at her. "True. Do you need a refill?"

"Please."

She hands me her mug. We work together to create two of the most ridiculous looking cups of cocoa I've ever seen. They'd fit right in with those milkshakes with full pieces of cake on them from a popular restaurant down in the city.

I watch her enjoy her first sip and rub at the pull in my chest. If she wasn't my boss' daughter and my best friend's sister, I would've taken my shot with her ten times over by now. She's fun to be around with her energetic personality. She's kind and has the biggest heart of anyone I've ever known. She's beautiful, inside and out.

I don't make time for relationships, but if I did... Eve's the type of girl I'd want to share a deeper connection with.

Except we can't. Friendship is all we get to have together.

Suppressing a sigh, I clink my mug with hers.

"To good times and the sugar high these will give us."

She covers her grin. "Too late. I'm three cups deep and have been feeling the oncoming hyper jitters for the last half hour. Catch up."

I snort. "You've already got the zoomies?"

Her amber eyes gleam and she releases a laugh that isn't unlike a little gremlin. I secretly get a kick out of it when she gets like this. I'm glad she's still comfortable enough around me to show me her goofy side.

I pretend to mess with her hair. A wild laugh escapes me when she gets me back by poking my side until she finds a ticklish spot.

How could that asshole she used to date not see her and think she's the most awesome girl he's ever met? How could he tarnish this vibrant light she shines with?

It doesn't matter. I'm here to protect her from guys like that, just like high school. Her brother and I took care of the few that hurt her.

If I had five minutes with him on the ice, the gloves would fly off and I'd end him. I rein myself in, rolling my shoulders to dispel the instinct to find her ex and give him hell. It's a holiday and I'd rather be here with her and her family.

A commotion at the front door draws our attention. We head to join everyone welcoming Mr. Boucher, Theo, and Lainey. Neil Cannon is right behind them.

"Stopped by to wish you all a happy holiday," Mr. Boucher says.

Theo spots me and high fives me. I ruffle his hair before he switches places with his shy sister to greet Eve.

"Mr. Cannon." I shake hands with one of my hockey idols growing up.

While he was still coaching for Heston U with David, he'd come by our junior league games in high school from time to time to give us pointers.

"Good to see you," he says gruffly.

They stay long enough to have a couple of drinks. David and Neil start reminiscing about their days of coaching together while Mr. Boucher talks with Benny and Jess.

Theo gives me shit for not getting him a present when I pass out gifts. Eve promises to make him something, darting out the door and returning with two balls of yarn in Heston colors and a crochet hook.

Lainey watches with interest while she works, talking quietly with her about books while the four of us sit together in the living room. Twenty minutes later, she holds up a finished hockey stick that Theo rubs in my face for getting the best gift. I smirk, not telling him about the scarf she made me with my name in block letters and hockey sticks lining the edges.

Once we're seated for dinner after they leave, Benson lifts his glass. "I'm glad we can all be together as a family this holiday. Before we eat, there's something we want to share."

Jess lays a hand on her stomach. "We were keeping it a secret until we were sure after finding out recently. We're having a baby."

"Holy shit."

I'm the first one to break the beat of silence before Mrs. Lombard gasps and everyone else bursts with elation. We all get up to hug and congratulate them.

David's face is red and he swipes at the few tears he sheds. Eve hugs him when she's done fussing over Jess with her mom.

"Dude," Benson says through a laugh when he turns to me.

"You're gonna be a dad." I hug him again. "I'm so happy for you."

"It's crazy. I don't feel ready, you know?"

"Does anyone?"

"True."

"You're gonna be a fantastic dad."

His eyes shine. "Thanks, man."

As I take my seat, I get a sense of what I'm missing. After I finished my time as a hockey player and graduated, I only needed myself. Maybe I'm ready for something more.

I don't feel like I'm here displaced from my family. I'm right where I feel at home. I fit in here. It's not hard to picture staying in Heston Lake. I could build a life that makes me happy, one where I don't feel like I need to stay on the move to keep ahead of my own doubts.

This town knew me as a guy that was a little too lax and got into trouble too often. I have the chance to overwrite that if I continue to change into a dependable guy, rather than move before anyone realizes I don't know what I'm doing and haven't made an effort to figure anything out after college.

Eve snags my focus when she tries one of her mom's dishes and mumbles that I have to try it. I should take a page from her book. She's starting her business and it gives me the courage to pursue my passion with the same conviction.

Before now, I thought I was playing it safe. I think I was afraid I'd fail and go back to my old ways. Maybe it's the same with the impression I've always gotten from my old teammates, and the guys I coach now. It's not that they have things more together than I do because they're not secretly struggling. They're the ones who have the guts to believe in themselves, win or lose.

I take hold of that drive, not only motivated for myself but to show the people in my life who matter to me what I'm truly capable of when I start to believe I'm good enough.

Later, after another round of presents and dessert, David dozes in an armchair by the fireplace with the football game muted on the TV. Mrs. Lombard isn't far off from napping herself, lounging on the sofa with the new book Eve gifted to her. Benson leads me and the girls down to the finished basement.

It's been our hangout spot for years. Some of our old posters still plaster the walls by the air hockey table, though it looks like the furniture we trash picked in middle school has been replaced and there's a sweet mounted flatscreen.

"Why am I—?" Eve stares at the bundle of ribbons she collected from the wrappings that she carried with her. "I didn't mean to bring this down here."

"Are you sure you're turning twenty-five and not ninety-five with that spotty memory of yours?" Benson teases.

"Shut up," she says with a sigh. "I picked it up because I didn't want to forget it, but got sidetracked. I meant to put it by the door so I'd take it for my craft supplies when I went to bed. Don't let me leave this down here because once it's out of sight, poof—gone."

She shakes the ribbons to underline her point. I cover her hand with mine, ignoring the thrill contorting my stomach.

"I'll remind you."

"Thanks." She looks past me at her brother. "See, that's called being helpful and supportive. Cole's a team player."

He waves her off while searching for something to put on in the background. The girls pull blankets from the basket in the corner and sit on the couch.

"What else is going on this week? Feel like hitting the slopes with me?" I ask.

"I have to get back to work tomorrow. You know how it is. Eve's party is coming up this weekend, though. You should come." Benson gets her attention. "Cole's invited, right? To your birthday party."

Her giggling with Jess trails off and her gaze flicks to me in surprise. "Sure." She lifts a brow playfully. "It's not one of my birthday parties until you crash it."

The corner of my mouth tugs up. When we were kids, I'd always be Benny's guest to her parties at the skating rink or when her parents allowed each of them to bring a friend on a ski trip her family

98

took to Vermont to celebrate her birthday. It was a given that if he was going to be there, so would I.

"Duh, free junk food and your friends in high school were sorta cute," Benson says.

Eve rolls her eyes while Jess snorts and pinches his arm. He grins, murmuring an apology with his hand resting over her stomach.

"Don't be mad, baby cakes. It was all in the past before I knew you existed. You're the only one for me."

She groans. "I hate it when you call me that."

"No you don't," he teases. "Not when I—"

She covers his mouth before he can finish his sentence. His brows bounce suggestively.

"God, you two are gross." Eve mimes gagging. "We get it, you're married."

My gaze lingers on her. "I'll be there."

Her face flushes and she tears her attention from me, fussing with the ribbons.

Once again the thought enters my mind that this is what it would be like if I stay in Heston Lake. If I make this place my home again. The more the possibility takes shape in my head, the more I want it.

ELEVEN

EVE

New Year's Eve comes before I'm ready. I'm officially twenty-five.

Single. Unsure if the direction I want to take my life in is the right choice. Living at home with my parents. Well, sort of. I think it still counts since I'm in the garage apartment. No one's going to change those things or tell me what I should do except myself. I'm not big on resolutions since I can't stick to them to save my life.

But there is one thing I'm certain about. I'm excited to create a business with all the things I make. It's what I've dreamed about without taking the leap. Getting the camper was my sign it's my time.

Tonight I vow not to worry about any of that. I want to let loose and have fun on my birthday.

The girls came over to get ready with me, then we all crammed into the back of Cole's Bronco. Jess was supposed to be with us, too, but the first trimester has her exhausted.

The club we're partying at is in the next town over. I thought about hosting a big celebration and inviting more friends from college, but I wanted to keep this intimate. Only me and my closest people.

"There are two rules tonight," Caroline says as we arrive. "Make some damn good memories because this is how you're sending this year off."

"What's the second rule?" Cole asks.

He's standing right behind me, close enough that the heat from his body radiates against the open back of my little black dress. I gulp, angling my head back for a glimpse. He meets my gaze, eyes hooded. I whip around when I realize I'm being super obvious and take a small step to put space between us.

I swear he closes the distance.

Caroline smirks at him. "The second rule, and this is really the most important one, is that the birthday girl doesn't buy her own drinks. Got me?"

Everyone whoops.

"Car," I protest. "You guys don't have to do that."

"Yes, we do! We're here to celebrate you." She takes my hand. "Come on! First round of champs is on me, then we're hitting the dance floor to shake our asses."

An excited squeal escapes me as she leads us through the crowd. I reach behind me blindly, expecting Lauren or Julia to latch on so we don't lose each other.

The hand that takes mine is big and warm. I peek, finding Cole giving me one of his lethal smiles. He squeezes my hand and sticks close until we reach the bar. He doesn't release it right away.

I allow myself the tiny pleasure of shifting nearer. My eyes fall shut as his woodsy scent envelopes me. I sway to the pounding beat of the music, brushing against him. He laces our fingers together and my breath catches.

Caroline breaks me out of my private fever dream. "Here you go. Cheers."

Cole drops my hand, leaving it tingling from the loss. I accept the glass of champagne, clinking it with hers. Benson passes out more drinks until we all have one.

"To Evie," Cole toasts.

The others echo him and I'm caught up in a group hug. I take a hearty sip, downing half of it.

"Let's dance!" I announce.

The girls go with me and the guys stay behind. We join the dance floor on a good song we all like. A happy buzz begins to build within me by the third song.

I feel amazing and confident tonight. The dress I picked out is bold. It hugs my body with a shimmery black material. I know I look hot because I draw more than one eye. Though none of the guys who show interest in dancing with me are who I really want to spend my night with.

Does Cole like how I look in this dress?

I bite my lip and lose myself in the next song, imagining him behind me, hands resting on my hips possessively, pulling me back against his firm chest.

One of my girls hands me a fresh glass of champagne without missing a beat. I keep spinning and laughing as the song ends until I move too far away and bump into someone.

My mind conjures up Cole, but this guy isn't built like him. He's not muscular or tall enough, and doesn't smell the same.

I blink open my eyes. My smile falls. Shawn.

"What are you doing here?" I demand.

The once over he gives me used to excite me. All I feel now is acid upsetting my stomach.

"Actually," I cut him off when he opens his mouth. "I don't really want to hear it. You should go."

He scoffs. "Why? It's New Year's Eve." He spreads his arms. "I didn't know you'd be here. Doesn't look like you rented out the club, babe. This place is open to the public."

It takes serious effort not to roll my eyes. Of course he'd feel entitled. How did it take me so long to recognize how selfish he is?

My handmade tiered disco ball earrings jostle when I shake my head. "Whatever. Just stay away from me, then."

"Happy fucking New Year to you, too," he shouts over the music when I walk away.

I hold my hand above the crowd to flip him off as I navigate to find my girls. They pull me into their circle with cheerful yells.

Lauren notices my irritated expression first. "What's wrong?"

"Nothing. Just Shawn. He's here."

Caroline stops dancing. "Oh absolutely the fuck not. Come with us, we need to forget he even exists."

I point at her. "Yes. That. Let's do that."

"Shots! Shots!" Julia chants, grabbing my shoulders from behind as she enthusiastically nudges me closer to the bar.

Cole's there with Benson. He's leaning on his forearm with his sleeves rolled up. One foot is propped on the low railing that runs the length of the bar. He nods to us when we arrive.

"Ready for another round, birthday girl?"

My stomach dips. When he calls me that with a playful, sexy tone, it stirs heat in my core.

"Yes, please."

He pushes out of his slouch fluidly, eyes hooding as he peers down at me. I swallow thickly. My thighs slide together at the alluring languid air he has going on. He touches my disco ball earrings with a smirk, then gets a bartender's attention. Hot and cold tingles race across my skin.

People crowd around the bar. We get separated from Benson and the girls while they move further down to get their shots.

Cole takes my elbow and brings me closer to the counter, bracketing me with his arms from behind to shield me from getting bumped. A shiver zips down my exposed spine from his chest brushing my back.

His mouth dips to my ear. "Do you want whiskey? Vodka? Tequila?"

"Whiskey."

A rumble of approval vibrates in his chest. I feel it against my skin and stifle the noise that threatens to escape me.

"Good girl."

Heat spills through me at the praise. It ignites a heady fire in my veins that leaves me dizzy. My thighs press together to stave off the building ache.

The bartender slides two glasses in front of us and pours. Cole takes one and gives me the other. I twist part way to see him.

He holds his shot glass to his lips. "Bottoms up."

I toss mine back, forcing out an exhale at the smooth burn. Emboldened by my dress, I spin within the circle of his arms to face him fully. He stares me down, then slides his hands together on the bar. His thumb knuckles graze my skin above the low cut of my outfit, giving the barest stroke.

"Are you having a good time?" he asks.

Words catch in my throat. If I say anything, he'll be able to tell how much he affects me. I nod, gaze drifting to his mouth. Is it my imagination, or does he inch closer?

"There you are!" Lauren's shout reaches us before they appear.

Cole inhales sharply and backs away. No one noticed the position we were in, or how red my face is in the dim light of the club. I sigh in relief that Benson's bringing up the rear, distracted by the dance floor.

"Thank god you're tall, Cole," Julia says.

Caroline hooks her arm with mine. "Come on, dancing queen. We've still got time before the ball drop."

"Hell yes! Let's go!" I blurt with too much enthusiasm to cover.

My heart beats hard for a long while, though it's not from the exhilaration of the party atmosphere or from moving my body with the music. It's all Cole's doing.

It's close to midnight when I run into Shawn again on my way back from a bathroom break. He blocks my path at the edge of the dance floor, herding me back into the shadows.

"What do you want?" I fold my arms across my chest.

His eyelids are heavy and his attention falls to my cleavage. Pursing my lips, I try to sidestep him. He winds an arm around my waist.

"What are you doing? Get off." I break away from him.

"Come on. Don't be like that."

Shawn tries to pull me in again with a grip on my wrist. I search the club, hoping to spot my friends or my brother. His words slur and the alcohol on his breath makes me turn my head away.

"Stop it."

"I messed up." He ignores my efforts to push him off, repeating himself until his mouth grazes my cheek. "Taryn was a mistake. She's gone, babe. Come on, we're so good together."

Is he serious? I muster all my strength to get out of his arms again. He's wrenched away from me before I make a move.

Cole holds Shawn by two fistfuls of his shirt, nearly lifting him off the ground. His shoulders are set in a rigid line, anger rolling off him in waves. My heart stutters in surprise and relief. He always protects me when I need him.

"Here's how this is gonna go. I'm going to pretend I didn't see you trying to touch Eve when she clearly doesn't want that."

Cole speaks through his teeth, giving Shawn a forceful shake. His veins stand out on his flexed forearm and the back of his hand.

"Listen up, because this next part is simple. You're going to walk away," Cole continues, slow and brutal. "Call a ride and get the fuck out of here. Leave Eve alone, jackass. Permanently."

"Or wha'?" Shawn sneers.

Attempts to, anyway. He just comes across as a sleazy drunk.

A muscle jumps in Cole's jaw. "Didn't I already tell you at the coffee shop? You don't want to find out what I'll do to you if you try me."

I suppress a shiver at his stormy tone. The ache he stirred in me earlier returns with the wave of heat crashing over me.

"Be for real, man." Shawn shoves at Cole, but it doesn't break the hold he has on him. "Eve, tell this guy to back off."

A low growl rumbles in Cole's chest and he pins Shawn against the wall. "Eve isn't yours anymore, so get her name out of your goddamn mouth."

I lay a hand on Cole's arm, stepping into his side. As hot as it is to have him defending me against my ex, I want to have my own say in this. He seems to understand that, making my stomach tighten with a pleasant warmth.

I steel myself, meeting Shawn's eye. "There's nothing in this world you could do to make me want to be with you again. We're beyond done. You made sure of that when you cheated on me behind my back. You don't exist to me anymore, Shawn. Goodbye."

Cole's burning gaze locks on me, eyes glinting in the low light with pride and admiration. It's incredibly attractive that he's fiercely protective and more than willing to fuck Shawn up if he messes with me, yet also supportive of my need to stand up for myself. He's a man that would stand by me on equal ground, in front of me to guard what's his, and behind me knowing I can handle myself while he holds my purse.

I swallow thickly, wishing for the impossible to happen between us.

"Want me to hold him for you?" He flashes a disgusted glance at

Shawn. "Make sure he gets the point before we send him on his way."

I huff, lips twitching. "No. I don't want to hit him."

Cole smirks, inclining his head. "Are you sure? It might make you feel better. I bet you'd be cute as hell if you got a little violent."

Pleasure tugs in my core. I duck my head to hide my expression.

"I'll be right back. Stay here." He waits until I meet his piercing leer again. "Wait for me. Okay?"

I'd wait a lifetime for him. Not that he's aware of it. I try to speak, but words lodge in my throat. All I manage is a jerky nod.

The corner of his mouth lifts before he hauls Shawn away. He leans down, but he's speaking too quietly for me to hear whatever he's telling my ex. Shawn flinches away from him, but Cole holds tight. The crowd swallows them up.

It's not long before Cole returns alone. He offers his hand and I take it, marveling at how good it feels to be engulfed by his touch. He stares me down, attention flickering between my eyes, then dipping to my lips, fixated when my tongue wets them.

"I made sure he left. You don't have to worry about him anymore. He understands what will happen if he comes near you again."

"Thank you."

His big hand is warm around mine. Tingling awareness spreads up my arm when he sweeps his thumb in a light caress. Instead of taking us back toward everyone else, he leads me the opposite way.

My heart beats in double time. The countdown to midnight begins.

I follow Cole into the shadowy hallway. I'm not sure what's about to happen, but every inch of me quivers in anticipation. My fingers squeeze around his palm.

And he grips my hand tighter.

TWELVE
COLE

It feels like a live wire is tangled around my heart. There's so much going on in the club for the countdown, but all I'm aware of is Eve's hand fitting perfectly in mine.

She follows me down the hallway without letting go. I caress her silky smooth skin with my thumb again. Has it always felt this nice? The need to explore every inch of her to discover the answer beats in time with the thump of my pulse.

"*Nine...eight...*"

I'm not thinking straight. Hell, I'm not thinking at all. Not about everything I should be.

Tonight started with me being on edge. All because Eve looks like she walked right out of my fantasies with her hot as fuck shimmery dress that hugs her curves and has a low back exposing her skin.

Until Benson dragged me away, I was prepared to stand behind her all night to keep any other guy's eyes off her. It's been hell posted up at the bar, watching them all undress her with their hungry gazes.

I almost kissed her earlier after we downed our shots. If we hadn't been interrupted, I would've claimed her mouth with a searing kiss.

"*Seven...six...*"

Seeing her ex-boyfriend in her face, trying to put his hands on her was my breaking point. I was moving through the dance floor looking to join her. I found her at the edge of it, struggling against that piece of shit, then I saw red.

"Four...three..."

I pull up short. She nearly bumps into me with a gasp that could be my undoing.

Drawing in a deep breath that does absolutely fuck all to stop me, I gently turn to her. Nudge her against the wall. Brace my hand by her head while my attention falls to her mouth.

She's my best friend's sister. The head coach's daughter. Everything off-limits to me, and it should give me pause. But it doesn't. Not for a second.

I don't care. I can't. Because right now every fiber of my being is fixated on this moment.

"Two...one..."

Ten seconds. That was all it took for me to decide I'm kissing Eve tonight.

Less—far fucking less—if I'm counting every moment I've ever thought about kissing her.

"Happy New Year!"

Distantly, I'm aware of the people shouting and cheering. Lights flashing down the dark hall I've hidden us away in, and the music turning back up.

Eve stares up at me. She's stunning, her expression open, so damn open. The depth of her beautiful eyes swallows me whole.

I take her chin between my thumb and finger, lifting it slightly. Her lips part and her tongue darts out. Fuck, I want to chase it.

"Happy birthday," I rasp.

Then I brush my mouth against hers. She smothers a tiny sound. It makes my fist clench against the wall so I don't grab her. So I don't bury my fingers in her perfectly braided hair and muss it up while I devour her mouth.

This isn't how I want to kiss her. It's light. Too soft and barely there.

I want it as hard and desperate as the burning tightness in my chest from being near her. I want her melting for me, and to hear how she sounds when she moans. For her to be gasping little pleas between kisses while she tugs at me because she can't get enough.

I want to hear her say my name. As an urgent whisper. As a cry of pleasure. Screaming it.

She presses into me, hands splayed on my chest. A groan catches in my throat, swallowed back before I let it out.

Christ, it's killing me not to touch her more than this. Not to slip my hand beneath this sexy dress and sink my fingers into her or fall to my knees and taste her.

We kiss longer than could be considered a polite New Year's kiss between friends. I want more, so much more, but she already panicked when we matched on Love Struck the first time. Every time since then, I've almost told her how much I've thought about asking her out, to hell with the consequences and the unwritten rules I shouldn't break.

It takes all my willpower to stop kissing her. I pull back slowly, savoring every moment, committing it to memory.

Neither of us say anything. She blinks once, twice. Touches her plush lips.

Those gorgeous eyes flit to mine. Her chest rises and falls with her rapid breaths. The tightness in mine is back, constricting my heart. Shit. She kissed me back. Does she regret it?

I'm about to ask if she's alright when she surprises me with one of her radiant smiles that steals my breath faster than the hardest hit I've ever taken in a game. She slips her hand in mine.

"If we don't get back out there, everyone will wonder where we went," she says brightly. "The birthday girl can't go missing from her own party."

I shift back a step, because if I don't I might do another stupid thing, like keep her caged against the wall for another kiss. A real one.

When she turns, my gaze rakes over her exposed back to her ass. I'm still drunk on her sweet scent of strawberries blended with vanilla and the taste of her lips.

"Happy New Year, by the way," she throws over her shoulder. "Thanks for making sure I got a midnight kiss."

"Right," I respond woodenly.

I let her lead me back out to the main area of the club. We find the others not far into the dance floor. The girls are hyping Benson up while he dances with zero rhythm.

The moment Eve's hand leaves mine, I curl my fingers into my palm.

"There you are!" Julia exclaims.

"That bathroom line was insane. Thankfully the men's was empty. Cole stood guard for me." Eve pats my chest.

"You missed the ball drop," Caroline says.

Eve waves her off, cheeks flushed. "It's fine. Let's get a few more songs in before last call."

Benson sidles up to me while I stand there watching her. I tense, then force myself to relax. Hopefully he can't read me as well as he could when we were teammates because I don't want to end the night with his fist in my face for kissing his sister.

"Thanks for always watching out for her," he says.

My mind blanks. I grunt out some form of agreement. It's all I manage, otherwise I might give myself away.

I forget all about him when Eve swings around, laughing with her friends while they dance. Her gaze finds mine, the corners of her eyes crinkled.

Christ, the way she looks at me does me in. How can one glance from her make me so crazy? I don't care if she's Benson's sister, or any other reason we shouldn't cross the line. I've fought my need for her all night until I couldn't any longer. And now that I've had a taste?

It's official. I'm fucked.

THIRTEEN
EVE

THE KISS WON'T LEAVE my head. It's still on my mind from the moment I pulled Cole out of the hallway, on the ride home when we stopped for post-drinking chicken nuggets at the drive-thru, as I peeled my dress off and found an old oversized t-shirt from my days at Heston U.

Downing a glass of water—thinking of the kiss. Helping myself to a slice of bread—reliving every moment of his lips on mine.

I try to direct my thoughts in any other direction. Easier said than done, especially when it comes to Cole Kincaid.

And kissing.

Cole kissed me.

Even though it could hardly be classed as one. More of an obligatory, friendly peck because it's midnight and it's what's done on New Year's Eve. Right?

It probably didn't mean anything to him.

Still, every millisecond plays on repeat. The way he put one hand against the wall by my head and grasped my chin. The way he smelled—the memory alone of his heady aftershave ignites a fresh wave of desire in my core.

Maybe I'm still a little drunk.

And turned on.

I wish he'd kissed me for real so I'd know for sure if it's anything like I've imagined.

Raw passion. Pent up wildness breaking free. One that I could drown from. That could ruin me for anyone else. A kiss dreams are made of.

Oh, screw it. I need some self-care.

I go to the bottom drawer of my nightstand to pull out one of my trusty favorites from my collection of toys. It's an insanely good vibrator with pulses of air that send me right over the edge to a knee-shaking orgasm when I use it on my clit.

Especially at times when my release feels like it could wander off on me in the middle of pleasuring myself, this thing is a total godsend.

I needed it with Shawn, or I'd never get off. He hated that I liked to use a vibrator when we had sex. Complained he could give me everything I needed, yet never was willing to put in the extra work it sometimes takes for me to finish. He sure as hell never understood that toys aren't his enemy or replacement.

I could be moments from coming and a single stray thought could distract me enough that—*poof*—the orgasm is gone, back to the starting line. It wasn't until I spoke with a therapist about my troubles during intimate moments both with partners and by myself that I learned there was nothing wrong with me at all.

Stripping off my underwear, I stretch across my bed with the vibrator and my phone. I'm debating between playing some of the spicy scenes I've bookmarked from my favorite romance audiobooks, or going for one of those erotic audios when a notification flashes at the top of my screen.

Love Struck: It's a match! Open to find out if love has struck.

Too curious to leave the notification unread, I tap on it. Then freeze.

It's another match with Cole. How the—?

This is fate. It has to be.

Actually, I don't care what we call it. All I know is that my resolve is only so strong. Resisting him is impossible.

He messages me first.

MightyPuck: Funny seeing you here. I thought you were deleting the app?

MATCHING ALL THE WAY

CraftyCutie: No comment.

That was the plan. I was all for sticking to the plan, maybe picking another dating app to try.

Then Shawn unblocked my number a few days before Christmas to text me in the middle of the night trying to score a booty call. This time I blocked him, then re-downloaded the app to find someone to help me forget all about my ex.

I wasn't thinking about rematching with Cole at the time, although I ignored every other person the app connected me with. What does this make it, six? Seven times? I don't know, I've lost count over the last several weeks.

CraftyCutie: The real question is what are you doing online late at night looking at my profile?
MightyPuck: ...no comment.
CraftyCutie: This is all because I put 'hockey players are sexy' in my profile. That has to be why we keep matching.
MightyPuck: I'm a hockey player.

My heart stops. It doesn't simply skip a beat. I think the damn thing gives up then and there.

And honestly? I don't blame it, because all I'm picturing now is Cole in his hockey gear with all that fierce, savage energy that gets me hot.

With my inhibitions lowered, hockey-related fantasies about him run rampant through my mind.

I don't care if the locker room stinks in reality, if he wanted to fuck me there, I'd one hundred and ten percent be down for what would surely be one of the hottest experiences of my life. I'd let him have me any way he wanted. With his jersey on, without it, with me wearing it and him gripping a tight fistful for leverage to drive into me harder and—

I fan myself, squeezing my thighs together against the insistent pulse of desire throbbing in my core.

CraftyCutie: You *were* a hockey player. Now
you're a coach. Which...okay, there are some hot
coaches out there.
MightyPuck: Am I one of them?
CraftyCutie: [lips zipped emoji]

Cole goes quiet for a bit, then three dots appear and disappear while he types. The air in my lungs gusts out when it finally comes through. My head is still spinning just enough from the amount of champagne I drank.

MightyPuck: Are you mad I kissed you tonight?
CraftyCutie: No.
MightyPuck: Good.
CraftyCutie: Thanks for being my kiss at midnight.
MightyPuck: That's not why I did it.
CraftyCutie: It's not?
MightyPuck: I did it because I would've regretted
not kissing you.
CraftyCutie: What do you mean?
MightyPuck: I wanted to kiss you all damn night. I
still want to. I can't stop thinking about it.

My eyes widen. I can't believe it. He actually wanted to kiss me at the club? *Still* wants to?

I have to know for sure. All this time I've crushed on him believing my inconvenient feelings were one-sided. I never thought he looked twice at me as anything more than his best friend's sister.

CraftyCutie: Wait. Sorry, drunk brain. Are you
saying you're into me?
MightyPuck: Yes. Thought I was being clear about
that by kissing you.
CraftyCutie: Shut up! Omg this is blowing my mind.

We're treading into dangerous territory.

If we're confessing things to each other...

116

CraftyCutie: Can I tell you something?
MightyPuck: Anything.
CraftyCutie: I just…don't want to be lonely this winter. That's all. It's why I made my profile to find someone to keep me warm through the winter and forget Shawn
MightyPuck: I'm interested in helping you with that. If you let me.

I stare at his last response. It took a few moments after my admission for him to send it. Could we really do this? It feels like I'm in a dream.

An idea strikes me. It's absurd and toes the line, but as soon as the thought crosses my mind a whole new world of possibilities opens up.

CraftyCutie: I just thought of something.
MightyPuck: What?
CraftyCutie: Soooo, this might be crazy, but hear me out. What if we aren't us?
MightyPuck: Meaning?
CraftyCutie: We pretend we're someone else. You can be…Colin. You're a hotshot player in the AHL looking for some fun. And I'll be Evangeline, a rich, unbothered goddess of seduction who's driving you wild.

He sends a few laughing emojis at the intricate backstories I weave for our characters.

MightyPuck: How would that work?
CraftyCutie: It'll be like a game. Roleplaying and stuff. We'll keep it secret and only message each other here.

I roll over to bury my face in the pillows to smother a giddy scream. This is insane, isn't it? Sneaking around with him online might be even more torturous, like sitting at dinner while we message each other on the down low.

Or it could be exactly what I need.

My phone vibrates. I hold my breath to see what he says. He didn't send a text in our chat. Instead it's a voice recording. I scrape my teeth over my lip and press play. Cole's sultry voice washes over me.

"You want to pretend with me, Evie? Are you sure you can handle playing games?"

Not Cole, I attempt to remind myself. It doesn't work, not when he calls me Evie. I close my eyes, picturing him tonight, his thick brown hair falling across his forehead, the sleeves of his shirt rolled up over his sculpted forearms.

Just for tonight...

Then we'll be Evangeline and Colin instead of Eve and Cole. This will be our little secret. No one will find out, especially Dad and Benson.

I'm too nervous to respond with a voice clip. My fingers shake as I type out the rest of my proposition.

CraftyCutie: I can handle it. This is just physical. We can't have feelings involved. It would be too messy.
MightyPuck: If that's what you want.
CraftyCutie: So we keep it casual. Just for the winter, then we can stop.
MightyPuck: Deal.
CraftyCutie: You'd be okay with that?
MightyPuck: However you want to do this, let me be the guy when you need someone to make you feel good. Okay? Promise it's me you'll call.
CraftyCutie: Okay. I promise.

This is so crazy. My heart drums with hard, exhilarated beats. I'm about to ask him what he wants to do when he sends another voice clip.

"This club is dark but I've had my eye on you for hours. Thinking

about all the things I want to do with your mouth at midnight while you tease me with that hot as fuck dress that barely covers you. When the countdown starts, I lead you down the hallway."

Is he—? My pussy throbs with need as I realize what he plans.

He's recreating tonight. If we were strangers and there was nothing to complicate this pull between us.

I play along, adding to the idea with my own flair. I text him how I would've spotted him early in the night, wanting to tempt him until he was powerless to resist my allure. Excitement would race through me when he takes me into the shadows away from the crowd. Anyone could find us, yet that makes this even more thrilling.

He chuckles in a new recording. *"I wasn't able to resist you from the moment I saw you, baby. I push your back to the wall to kiss you the way I've wanted to all night."*

I imagine the devastating kiss sweeping me away. How I'd wind my arms around his shoulders while his hands drag all over my body, squeezing my breasts, skating down my sides to grab my ass while he claims my mouth. I trail my fingers over myself, giving my hardened nipples some attention.

"I'm sucking your neck when I move my hand beneath your dress. Naughty girl, you're not wearing any panties. Nothing to stop me from sliding my fingers right into your pussy."

A hazy moan slips out. We've hardly started and I'm already drowning in lust. My touch becomes his in my mind and I follow what he's doing. I tell him how good it feels when he fucks me with his fingers, then fumble with the phone to play his next recording. In the background, I can hear a rustle of fabric, then the faint sound of what I think is him stroking his cock.

"Fuck, you're so sexy. I need to get my mouth on that pussy right now. I drop to my knees and push your dress up to your waist. Mm, you look so good like this. I might kill anyone for seeing you right now, but I'm not stopping until you come all over my face. I hook your leg over my shoulder and swipe my tongue over you."

"Oh god," I breathe.

I clamp my thighs together with my hand trapped between them, grinding against the heel of my palm while struggling to type out that I love how his mouth feels on my pussy.

"Suck your fingers. Get them nice and wet for me, sweetheart."

Another breath shudders out of me. I take a photo of my lips wrapped around two fingers.

"That's it. Now pet your clit nice and slow. Picture it's my tongue. I could spend all fucking night on my knees tasting you like this."

The end of the recording trails off with a rough groan. Oh my *god*, this is so hot. My imagination overflows with a vivid fantasy of Cole kneeling in the hallway, head buried between my legs while he devours me with his mouth.

My thighs tremble at the first touch. I replay his last message while rubbing my clit, the deep, rasped words and that filthy groan washing over me again until the next one comes.

"Your fingers aren't enough, are they?"

No. I need so much more to satisfy the ache in my core. My pussy clenches, begging to feel full and stretched to the brink. My fingers shake as I type out a plea for more.

"Do you have any toys? Something thick and long for your needy pussy? A vibrator to tease your clit with?"

A strangled whimper escapes me, a rush of tingles racing across my body. I fumble around to find the one I abandoned in the covers and answer him.

"Show me."

With a shaky breath, I send a photo of it teasing along my bare thigh. A thrum echoes in my clit. I want to put the pulsing vibration over it and come so badly.

"That's my good girl."

I ask if he's going to fuck me.

"Is this what you need, sweetheart? To get fucked in the dark of the club where anyone could catch you taking my cock like my good little slut?"

Jesus, his mouth is amazing.

I tell him how wet he's making me and beg him to make me come. I'm too impatient to wait any longer, turning my vibrator on. I bite back a gasp when I tease it between my legs.

"Turn around and hold on. I'm going to fill you up and fuck you until your tight, hot pussy is dripping all over me," he rasps in the recording, cutting off to exhale a curse.

My hips rock as pleasure coils tighter from the toy. The fantasy has both of us unraveling quickly. My breaths thicken as I picture him thrusting into me, pinning me to the wall with his body as he drives inside me hard and fast.

I'm close. Tremors wrack my body and small urgent cries escape me.

When I fall over the edge, I find the courage to record it for him, gasping from the intensity still erupting through me as I hit send. He replies with a short clip.

"*Fuck, baby. So good for me, moaning for my cock like that. Oh, shit—nngh—I'm going to come so fucking hard.*"

The clip ends with him panting as he jerks himself. Then a choked off noise as he finishes.

Oh my god. The sound of Cole coming is permanently imprinted on my brain. I can't believe this experience, or that his hedonistic undoing is because of *me*.

He stops responding for a few minutes. I don't keep track, too lost in the divine sensations of the vibrator pulsing against my clit for one more orgasm.

I float on the waves of ecstasy for a moment, shivering with the aftershocks. My body sings with bliss.

MightyPuck: Look at what you did to me.

My eyes go round at the photo. *Holy shit.*

His cock is in his fist. It's bigger than I imagined. Thick and long, come splattering his knuckles.

The first thought to cross my mind is how much I want to ride it. I cover my face, muffling my giggle.

Out of everything we just did, the photo he sent feels deliciously obscene.

MightyPuck: You okay?
CraftyCutie: Very okay [wet emoji]
MightyPuck: Just wanted to make sure.
CraftyCutie: That was quite honestly one of the hottest experiences of my life

MightyPuck: Mine too.
CraftyCutie: What do we do now?
MightyPuck: Bed. I came so hard I feel like I'm still lightheaded from it. You wore me out.
CraftyCutie: True. It's almost 4, oops.
MightyPuck: I'll be waiting until the next time you need me. Goodnight.

Possibilities fill my head as I drift off to sleep. This is my chance to explore what I've always wanted with Cole. And no one has to know.

FOURTEEN
COLE

January

I'VE LOST my fucking mind.

Or rather, Eve is driving me even more insane than she did before my resolve not to go there with her snapped and crumbled to dust on her birthday last weekend.

Evangeline, I should say. We're supposed to be the fake identities she made up for us. Except it wasn't a pretend version I thought about while I jerked off and told her everything I wish I could've done to her that night. It was all Eve—filling my head with her beautiful eyes, those perfect lush lips, her gorgeous curves.

This arrangement is a way for us to cut this new tension growing between us. Get each other out of our systems while still keeping a line in the sand. There hasn't been a single moment since her birthday that I haven't wanted to say fuck it and erase the line. Fucking obliterate it for the chance to kiss her again.

Yesterday, she sent a photo to our DM. Her face was cropped out, but she had on this red satin bra that cupped her plump tits and hid her nipples with a ribbon tied in a bow I wanted to rip open. I had to dodge her brother's invite to go out, more interested in telling her to touch herself.

She rewarded me with a video of her slowly tugging the bow free until she revealed what I wanted to see, leaving the ends of the ribbon dangling at the sides of the bra, tits spilling free. Then she traced her fingertips across her cleavage while arching to tease me. Her mouth was visible, curling into a seductive smirk as she played with her breasts.

Christ, it kills me that I can't drive over to her place and fuck her so hard her bed breaks. This is the only way I get to have her. In person we have to act like nothing's changed.

I shake my head to get myself on track. Refocusing on practice, I scan the ice. The team is in good shape today. We have them split into offense and defense, then we're moving into some new skills routines that were my suggestion.

When Eve shows up during practice a few minutes later, I can't help but watch her from the corner of my eye. She waves to her dad and Steve at the other end of the ice, then to a few players that call out to her as she finds a seat in the front row of the stands closer to the end I'm at with the d-men.

It's normal for her to visit practice. So ask me why I'm thinking of every anti-boner thought in my arsenal to keep my cool?

"Brody, Higgins, you're up," I say from where I'm posted up at the boards.

I keep one eye on the defensive pair skating through their passing drill while drifting closer to Eve. Today's earrings are a pair of dangling bows, more understated than her usual flair but still her style. The corner of my mouth lifts. The tan plaid pencil skirt and knee-high boots look good on her. She's giving off a hot librarian vibe and I'm into it.

She's right here in front of me, yet I can't touch her. In the last week we've been insatiable, and I have to pretend I don't know what her body looks like or how she sounds when she comes.

"Hey."

She glances up from drawing on her iPad and smiles at me. "Hey, you. How's practice today?"

"Good. We've got some new drills to try." I duck my face, smile stretching. "When I showed some videos of them to your dad he liked the fresh approach."

"Look at you, Mr. Hotshot Coach."

Something pleasant bolts through me, nearly knocking me off balance from the force. "Yeah, well. I can't slack off, right?"

I use sarcasm to cover the hint of truth creeping beneath—that this matters a lot to me. I think she sees right through me because there's something a little too close to understanding in her gaze.

"You look nice today," I say.

"Thanks. I had to go down to City Hall to finish registering my business, so I wanted to look presentable." She smooths a hand over her skirt, then plays with her necklace. "I didn't want them to think I have no clue what I'm doing. Which I don't. But the point is, they don't know that."

It's my turn to soften with understanding. After college, somehow we're supposed to know how life works. I haven't got a clue half the time.

I offer her my fist. "You've got this."

She bumps it, holding her knuckles against mine. "Thanks."

We both pause, our attention drawn to where we're touching. A spark moves through me while time stands still for a beat. Her skin is soft. Capturing her hand in mine would be easy. I graze the back of my fingers against hers with a light caress. Her lashes flutter, then she pulls away too quickly.

"I'm proud of you for taking the next step," I murmur.

"This totally makes it feel real," she admits. "Now I just have to launch my online store."

"You've got this. I'll be first in line." I point at her water thermos covered in stickers she's made. "I need to get some Knights rep."

"Oh, no, you don't have to do that. I can just give you a sticker pack if you want."

I pin her with a sardonic look. "Then how am I going to support you?"

"Cole," she mumbles.

"Eve," I tease.

"Okay, okay. You win. I appreciate your support."

I smirk, watching the players on the ice. She's quiet for a moment. My phone notification goes off with a new message. I don't answer right away. Not until she catches my eye and tilts her face with a deliberate expression that says *well?*

I'm not expecting what I see when I open our Love Struck DM thread. I almost drop my damn phone reading it.

CraftyCutie: Bet I'd look nicer naked and spread out for you like a five course feast.

"Eve," I mutter.

"What?"

That innocent tone draws a smoky chuckle from me. She's not fooling me with that act. What I would give to throw her over my shoulder right now and drag her sexy ass out of here.

"I need to get back to work. With your dad, remember?"

She gestures to the opposite end of the rink. "He's all the way over there."

"Funny, it feels like he's breathing down my neck when you send me messages like that," I whisper. "I've gotta get back to practice."

She holds her hands up. "I'll be here, working on this illustration."

"Behave."

As I walk away, she texts me again. I swipe my tongue across my lower lip and tap out a quick response.

CraftyCutie: Make me.
MightyPuck: I deal with hockey players all day. Handling a brat to keep her in line isn't a problem.

Her breathy laughter follows me every step until I'm rinkside. She continues messaging me.

CraftyCutie: I like it when you get bossy.

By some miracle, I manage to read it with a straight face.

CraftyCutie: I think you should tie my wrists with that whistle and put me on my knees, Coach Bossy.

This time I risk glancing at her. She waves with a mischievous grin that makes me want her hair wrapped around my fist and those lush red lips around my cock.

I whip the green Heston U Hockey hat off my head and rake my fingers through my hair a few times before jamming it back on. She goes silent for a while. I start to relax and focus on practice while she's preoccupied with her design.

Then the vibration of my phone sends a shot of heat right to my dick before I even read the notification.

CraftyCutie: Last night I had a dream about you making me sit on your face. It was so hot that I woke up with my pussy throbbing. I fucked myself with one of my toys in the shower while I fantasized about riding your cock. Want to see a picture of it later?

I choke back a groan. Who knew the head coach's daughter could be so naughty?

One of the junior d-men gives me a funny look when he's done squirting water in his mouth. I clear my throat and nod to him.

Shit, I'm supposed to be working. Coaching this team rather than playing filthy texting tag with her.

If that's how she wants to play this while she sits in the stands to watch practice, I'm upping the ante.

MightyPuck: Be my good girl. Go take your panties off.

An electrifying thrill surges through my veins when she gets up a minute later. I track her, heartbeat drumming in time to her measured steps. It's not my imagination that she sways her hips because she glances over her shoulder, gaze colliding with mine. She smirks.

Blood rushes south. *Fuck.*

I want to follow her. Watch her while she takes them off. Kiss her again. Fuck her senseless somewhere in this training facility to show her how crazy she's making me.

I exhale forcefully. I need to get a grip before I do something stupid, like give us away.

Once the guys wrap up their drills, we call them to center ice. I put my skates on and pair up with Steve to go over the next maneuver we're working on. I borrow Easton's stick and drop a puck to the ice.

"Watch as I move through this. I'm coming in." I skate toward Steve with the puck. "Then I'm keeping control before he reacts."

I finish off by passing the puck under his stick and pick it up as I skate past him.

I'm in the middle of explaining the evasive entry skills we're aiming to improve when Eve returns to her seat. A moment later, she types something out on her phone. Mine buzzes in my back pocket while I go through the demonstration with Steve.

We shouldn't be playing this secret game while I'm at work, but there's something exhilarating about sneaking around with her.

I return Easton's stick. "Got it?"

He's got an intrigued gleam in his eye. The rookie loves techniques like this, and with his speed he'll level up his game once he gets it. Our lightning quick wingers, Alex and Theo, too.

I move off the ice to watch how they do. After I've seen a few of them run through it successfully, I check my phone.

CraftyCutie: Brrr [kitty emoji][snowflake emoji]
MightyPuck: Did you do it?
CraftyCutie: You'll see.
MightyPuck: I will?
CraftyCutie: Now I'll be cold, so I hope you'll warm me up.

I can hear her giggle behind me in the stands.

My grip tightens on my phone. I put it down on the boards and cross my arms tight enough my shoulders strain to keep myself from seeking her out.

I give a short blow with my whistle, waving Alex and Jake over to me. They hustle over from the line.

"What's up, coach?" Alex asks when he scrapes to a stop.

"I want you to run it again together this time. Brody, look for ways to control the puck so you recognize how to counter it during a game. Keller, keep it up. See if you can do it faster and cleaner."

They agree and high five. My phone lights up on the boards at my elbow. Alex reaches for it. I grab it before one of them reads the message on the screen. I level them each with a pointed look.

"Stay dialed in during practice."

They linger for a quick drink break. While they're distracted, I check what Eve sent to our DM.

I inhale sharply, fist pressed to my mouth at the photo. A sheer red mesh thong with a heart pattern dangles from her hooked finger. She's sitting with her legs crossed on a surface I recognize—the fucking desk in my office.

CraftyCutie: Hid these somewhere for you to find. Have fun on your treasure hunt.

Anyone could've caught her in there. Where did she hide her panties? Did she touch herself while perched on my desk?

Fuck, fuck, *fuck*.

My mind goes wild with the idea of her spreading her legs, pencil skirt hiked up around her hips, making a goddamn mess all over it as she makes herself come with her fingers while I'm out here. Will I catch a hint of strawberries and vanilla when I go in after practice?

Alex raises his brow and smirks. I stiffen, realizing I must've made a tormented noise.

"You good, coach?"

Schooling my features, I point at the ice. "Get back to practice."

I overhear Jake suggesting too loudly that he thinks I got a booty call on their way to the back of the line for skills practice.

It takes all my self control not to look Eve's way.

FIFTEEN

EVE

Since I bought the camper, it's chilled in the driveway while I lost myself in a research blackhole to learn how to renovate it. Saved browser tabs are open across all my devices with links I've looked at between serving drinks at The Landmark, sitting up late working on my products, and going to Heston U's home games.

I have so much information. Tons more than I likely need, yet making myself begin this project has been difficult.

If Cole didn't offer to help me, who knows how long I would've put off getting started. We've been at it for three afternoons in a row so far. When he's done with work, he comes right over.

"Here." He takes off his glove and offers a hand to help me up.

I ignore the tingle racing through me as his fingers curl around mine. He holds on until I find my balance, watching me. I make a conscious effort not to use his firm chest to steady myself. His comforting forest scent envelops me and his body heat seeps through my clothes.

It's not exactly spacious inside the hull of the camper.

I slide my lips together. "Thanks."

He releases me after a beat. Rather than paying attention to the section of flooring he wants to show me, I'm staring at his forearms. The sleeves of his gray henley are pushed up, the flannel he stripped off tied around his waist. The shirt stretches across his broad chest when he swipes the back of his wrist across his forehead.

131

I tear my gaze away, hissing out an uneven breath.

"See how this is all warped under the linoleum we pulled back?"

I lean over where he crouched in the cramped corner at the back. He puts a flashlight in his mouth and yanks on a loose board. My mouth goes dry at the way his upper back and biceps flex.

"Shit," he mutters.

"Is it bad?"

He turns a grim expression on me. "There's definitely water damage. Not the end of the world, but unideal. It means we'll have to rip this all out to replace the floor."

My stomach sinks as he gestures to the discolored piece he pulled up. I tug on the ends of my hair.

"Wow. This is going to take longer than I thought to fix."

Sighing, I hop down to the driveway. He follows me.

"I don't know, maybe I took on more than I was ready for. The further we get into this reno project, the more we find wrong with this thing. The rusted out siding let the elements in, and now we have to fix water damage. There's a tire that needs to be patched. I'm pretty sure a family of field mice has moved into one of the storage compartments."

As I list off all the work we need to do, my breathing speeds up. My skin feels too tight. I peel my hoodie off when the neck feels like it's choking me. I get more agitated while I pace back and forth, as if moving will help me stay ahead of this problem. Rubbing my forehead, I fight the tightness in my lungs.

"Hang on."

Cole catches me by my shoulders and keeps me still before I spiral out of control. His touch feels good. It distracts me from the thoughts piling up in my head, making me focus on him.

"Let's take a breather for a second. Then we can tackle this one by one. Deal?"

I roll my lips between my teeth and force an exhale through my nose. "Okay. Yes, you're right. One thing at a time. It's impossible to fix it all at once. Thank you."

He squeezes. "I've got you."

A lump forms in my throat. Cole has a knack for recognizing when I'm overstimulated. It doesn't frustrate him or make him dismissive. Not only does he ask me what's wrong, he offers his support without making me feel bad about being overwhelmed.

The midnight kiss from my birthday has been on my mind the last few weeks. We might be fooling around online together because it's a much lower risk, but it means I still don't get to have my brother's best friend the way I've always wanted. Our conversations online are full of wickedly delicious fantasies and show me a side of him I'm growing addicted to. The new connection we have makes moments like this more special to me.

This is enough. His friendship. His support.

I promised myself not to involve our feelings in this arrangement. Because mine are so much bigger than his could possibly be. I have no doubt now that he's attracted to me. That's as far as this thing between us goes.

We'll have our secret, no strings attached fun, then we'll walk away once the snow melts.

"Are you okay?" he asks.

"Yes. Thanks for keeping my head on straight."

He captures my gaze, his green irises swimming with something that makes my pulse flutter. My attention falls to his mouth. Am I moving in or is he doing that?

The alarm on my phone goes off, making me gasp. My pulse speeds up as I silence it.

It's time.

I sit cross-legged on the pavement, pulling up the draft of my online store. Jittery butterflies fill me. Moment of truth.

"What's that for?" He drops to the ground beside me, drawing a knee up to drape his arm across.

"A reminder for my launch. Today's the day my shop goes live."

"Yeah? Cool."

His charismatic smile makes my heart skip a beat. He runs his fingers through his thick dark hair, then hands over my water thermos.

"Here, have some water. I've barely seen you drink any while we've been working."

After glugging half of it to make up for my lack of hydration, I play with the straw and admit, "I'm pretty nervous."

"Who wouldn't be? It's nerve-racking to put yourself out there." He nudges his shoulder against mine. "Don't worry. You've got this."

I trap my lip with my teeth, keeping my gaze on him while I press the button to publish my listings. My eyes widen and a little scream leaves me.

"That's it. I did it. My store's live."

His grin stretches slowly, eyes bouncing between mine. "Congratulations."

I open the public link and dance at seeing everything I've been working on out in the world. It's surreal.

When I look up, he's studying me with something soft and unreadable swirling in his eyes again. It gives me goosebumps.

I hold up my phone. "Hey, can you see if this works for you?"

"Sure. Anything you need."

"I'm texting you the link."

He pulls out his phone and shows me my store open in his browser. Excitement buzzes through me.

"That's so weird to see it launched. Still feels like I'm staying up too late in Photoshop to mock-up what I wanted it to look like."

He climbs to his feet and grazes his fingers over one of my braids. "I'm proud of you for going after what makes you happy, Evie."

My throat tightens with a swell of emotions. I blink back tears, feeling silly.

A notification on my phone distracts me from succumbing to my sappiness. I pop to my feet, grabbing his arm.

"Cole! Oh my god! I got my first sale already! I haven't even posted that the launch is live yet!" I'm barely able to hold my screen straight, bouncing with joy.

He hums a quiet laugh. "Congratulations."

I open the order and all the excitement halts. Oh. It's from him. He bought the Heston U Hockey and Heston Lake themed sticker packs.

"Why didn't you say anything while I was jumping around freaking out?" I cover my flaming face.

"Because you're cute when you're excited. I wanted to be your first order." He gives me a dimpled smile while slipping his phone in his back pocket. "I had to support you."

Warmth overflows within me. "Oh. Thank you."

I put up the posts I drafted to announce my official opening to the social media accounts I made for Sweet Luxe. I also share them to my personal pages. Sales come in from my friends and family, along with texts to wish me congratulations.

"Okay, done." I beam at Cole. "I'm all yours."

His gaze snaps to me, eyes burning with an intensity that makes my stomach dip. We drift closer, lured by a taut invisible thread.

The moment breaks when Mom pulls into the driveway. She waves.

"Need help bringing in the groceries?" he offers, already grabbing a heavy bag for her.

"Yes, thank you," she says. "I'm making chili tonight. Want to stay for dinner? I bet you kids are cold from being outside all day."

He glances at me when he answers. "Sounds great. Thanks Mrs. Lombard."

After we finish, we get back to work on the camper. While we're looking up the flooring we need to replace, my phone goes off again. Twice. Three times. My features go slack when I find more orders, this time from people I don't know.

I didn't expect to get any sales when I launched. Cole proved me wrong about that, but I wasn't sure if I'd get more from customers that don't know me at all.

"Someone just ordered a pair of my french fry earrings!" I gush.

He slings an arm around my shoulders to give me a side hug. "That's awesome."

"I can't believe it."

"I can."

My attention darts up from my phone. His eyes rove my face. I swear they land on my mouth for a beat before darting away. It's funny how easy it is to act as we normally do, as though nothing's changed. At the same time, the slightest touches are charged with an undercurrent of enticement.

"Never doubted you for a second. You're amazing."

His sincere stare pierces my heart. I'm at a loss for words. The best I manage is a wobbly smile. He steps away, stealing all my air. It takes a moment to recover from dizziness.

Light snow flurries begin to fall. I tip my head back, closing my eyes.

It's really happening. I don't know if I'd be here without the people in my life pushing me to start my own business.

There's a long way to go, but the possibility of growing it floods me with incandescent emotions. My dreams feel within reach, all I have to do is believe in myself to have the courage to make them come true.

SLUTTY MIDNIGHT MUSINGS

SLUTTY MIDNIGHT MUSINGS

COLE

12:48AM

MightyPuck: Have you ever been so tired that you're weirdly horny for no apparent reason? Like I'm about to crash on my pillows but I'm wishing they were a nice rack like yours. They would make the perfect pillows.

CraftyCutie: Wow, you're up late.

MightyPuck: Looks like you are too. Were you waiting up for me?

CraftyCutie: Can't sleep. Midnight creativity struck. I got this idea for more snack-themed earrings and I've been designing them on my iPad for the last two hours before I tackle it with clay.

CraftyCutie: Actually, erase that last message from your memory. Because *Evangeline* is a total goddess of sexual energy and she doesn't hunch over iPads, she lounges in seductive little lace numbers with wine. Way more sophisticated than ADHD girlies with gremlin energy late at night.

A DROWSY SMILE tugs at my lips. Seems we both suck at pretending we're someone else when we do this.

Practice ended almost an hour ago. After briefly going over things with the other coaches, I dragged myself home. I drop the phone to the mattress and strip down to my boxer briefs before stretching out diagonally across the bed.

MightyPuck: Show me when you finish. Sounds cool.
CraftyCutie: Show you what? [raised eyebrow emoji]
CraftyCutie: These?

She sends a photo through our chat. It shows a cropped view of her laying back with her colorful sweater pushed up enticingly to reveal her breasts. It's hotter than any racy lingerie and it sends a thrum of lust right to my cock.

The lighting is dim. Doesn't change how much my mouth waters when I picture licking and sucking them until she can't take it anymore.

MightyPuck: Are you trying to distract me with your tits?
CraftyCutie: That's kinda the point. Did it work?
MightyPuck: Yeah.
CraftyCutie: Good.
MightyPuck: My turn to distract you.

It's only fair after she showed me hers. I'm shirtless with a pair of gray sweatpants riding low on my hips. The outline of my hard cock is visible.

CraftyCutie: Fanning myself, here. There's nothing sluttier a man can do than wear gray sweatpants.
MightyPuck: Is that what does it for you?
CraftyCutie: Yes. That and nice suits. And the ultimate: rolling up your sleeves to show off your forearms. Panty-melter. Every time. [fire emoji]

MightyPuck: I'll keep that in mind. I like knowing what will drive you crazy for me.
CraftyCutie: Are you threatening me with a good time?
MightyPuck: Absolutely [smirk emoji]
CraftyCutie: To answer your question, yes. But usually I'll lay down with a vibrator and give myself orgasms until I drift off. Sleepy orgasms are the best.
MightyPuck: Mmm. That's hot. I'd rather be wrapped around you, grinding my dick against your sweet ass while you play with yourself.
CraftyCutie: That sounds even better.
MightyPuck: I'd take that vibrator and tease you with it until I had you squirming for me and making cute little noises to beg me for more.
CraftyCutie: Then I'd want you to slip my panties to the side and push your cock inside me.

I record a voice clip of my pleased groan, telling her what I wish I was doing right now. "Yeah, baby. Gonna rock into your pussy nice and slow all fucking night."

I shove my sweatpants down and palm my erection with a satisfied sigh. She has me on the edge within moments. I'm picturing waking her up from sleep with my dick buried inside her tight heat, fucking her until I fill her with come.

The next photo she messages to our chat a few minutes later makes my balls draw tight. It's a view of her on her side, gorgeous ass displayed for me with her panties drawn aside by her fingers. Her folds glisten around the toy penetrating her.

My fist squeezes my cock, holding off my release. I press the microphone icon to record another clip.

"Look at you, begging for my cock to stretch you out. You gonna come for me?"

She types her answer. It's garbled, but that makes me hotter thinking she's swept in the throes of pleasure. I stroke my throbbing cock, staring at the photo.

"Let me hear you," I rasp into my phone's mic.

I grin when she sends a voice clip of her whimpering through her orgasm. Her sounds are unreal. I'm addicted to listening to her come, knowing she's falling apart because of me.

"That's my good girl," I praise.

I keep the recording going as my release rushes over me so she'll hear everything she does to me.

My limbs go slack until the aftershocks fade. I check our chat and chuckle at the parade of blushing emojis she sent. I love it when she goes from bold and sexy to shy. She asks if I feel better now.

"I always feel better when I talk to you. Goodnight, sweetheart," I murmur on a new voice clip. "Sleep well."

SIXTEEN
COLE

THERE'S NOT much for me to do during our ice time today. David and Steve have the team working on conditioning and shooting drills until everyone hits a quota.

I don't want to be useless. While they shoot wristers, backhands, and slap shots repeatedly on the net, I study the goalies, calling out advice. Cameron's doing fantastic guarding the net. He's fluid and has a damn good instinct for which way the puck will go.

"Nice read," I say when he stops another with a smooth glove save.

Eve's in the stands watching practice. She arrived a while ago and has been drawing on her iPad.

A few players go over to talk to her during a water break. David hasn't noticed yet. I follow them over after a minute to direct them back to the ice.

The group is rowdy, laughing and nudging each other. They're like puppies vying for her attention. I'm pretty sure Easton has actual hearts in his eyes. Alex and Theo are rolling their eyes. Cameron covers his face with his hat while his shoulders shake with amusement.

Jake Brody's slouched beside her, arm stretched along the back of her seat. I know she's not interested in any of them, yet it makes me pull up short. Something grates sharply in my chest.

Eve bats her eyelashes and pretends to swoon, but her smile is tired. "Is that line working on the girls you pick up at parties? Weak, bro. You need to up your game."

Jake shrugs with a cocky expression. "Works for me every time. Come chill and I'll show you how well I bag the ladies."

She scoffs, giving him a playful shove. Alex mimics the sound of a plane crashing and burning.

"Come on, you're not curious how I use these to make pretty girls like you scream?" He lifts the bottom of his jersey to flash his abs.

The grating sensation comes again, stronger this time. My brows pinch. I don't get the chance to step in.

Easton pales, punching Jake's shoulder and muttering a curse under his breath. "Dude, shut up, it's—"

"Did I just hear that right, Brody?" David's behind the group.

"Hey, Dad. How's practice going?" Eve hides a smile behind her hand, amusement dancing in her eyes.

"Wouldn't know. My players are too busy flirting to skate." He passes a stern look around that has the guys paling further. "I shouldn't have to make it clear that my daughter is off-limits."

I hope my face doesn't give me away because now I'm shitting the bed right along with the guys. If this is how he reacts to them joking around, what will happen if he finds out about what's happening between us?

David crosses his arms. "You'll be skating suicides for the rest of practice."

"Coach, that's like fifteen, twenty minutes," Theo points out grimly.

It's a long time for a drill that's designed to push skaters to their limit racing in groups from the starting point to the next line, progressing further with each round. Typically it lasts around five minutes.

David's eyes narrow. Alex pulls the rookies with him and the others follow. The team goes to line up, muttering curses to themselves. Once they're in position split into groups at opposite corners of the rink, he blows his whistle.

"Jeez, Dad," Eve mumbles a few minutes in. "Is this necessary?"

He grunts, moving away from us to oversee the team's penalty. I rub the back of my neck and sigh.

"They'll live. If he didn't say something to them, I would've."

She blinks, cheeks pink. Then she shakes her head, fighting back a shiver.

"The guys are harmless. I can handle players like Brody if it gets to me."

I rub at my sternum to dispel the remnants of annoyance. "What are you working on?"

She holds up her iPad to show me. "This motivational sticker collection. I started designing them last night. I thought it would be cute if I got some colorful pens and maybe some notepads to send out with them. Like a positivity journaling set."

She shivers again with a grimace, burrowing into the hoodie she's wearing. I frown.

"Here. Put this on if you're cold."

I shrug out of my coaching jacket and drape it around her shoulders. She peers up at me while I zip it for her, hands lingering when it hits me she's wearing my name. If she turns around, I'll see *Assistant Coach Kincaid* across her back.

Possessiveness burns in my chest. I curl my fingers into my palms to stop myself from pulling her into me the way I want to right now. Because wearing my name makes her look like she's mine.

"Thanks. It helps." She lifts the collar and tucks her nose inside, closing her eyes. "It's warm."

This jacket isn't one of my old hockey sweaters, yet the effect it has on me is just as strong seeing her in it. I used to think my old teammates were joking about wanting to see their girlfriends wearing their jerseys.

Now I get the appeal. Not only wanting to broadcast who she's rooting for, but also knowing her eyes are on me all the time. My mind flashes with ideas of her wearing it. Her riding me in reverse. Sleepy in bed on a Saturday morning, curled up with me. Out at The Landmark.

Damn. I fear I'll never work her out of my system because the more I'm around her, the more she draws me in.

"Aren't you cold? It's freezing in here today." She tugs the sleeves over her hands.

"Not anymore than usual."

She sneezes. "Must be me."

My brow wrinkles as she goes back to working on her design. She doesn't seem like herself today. Her hair is done in a more simple style than usual and she's bundled in comfy clothes. She's not even wearing earrings.

Her face is too flushed. I feel her forehead. She jerks in surprise. Gut clenching, I touch the back of my hand to her feverish skin again.

"Hold still," I murmur. "You feel pretty warm."

"I'm okay. I was just up late." She worries her lip. "I'm supposed to get a ride to work from Dad."

"Hang on. I'll give you a ride instead."

I hurry to David with quick strides. He's putting on the strict coach act, barking at straggling players to pick up their pace.

"Hey, I'm taking Eve home. I think she's sick. She's got a fever," I say.

His stony expression falls. "She's always pushing herself too hard." He checks his watch. "I'm meeting Neil for lunch at the bar. I'll let Matt know she won't be in for work."

"Okay."

He blows his whistle. "That's it for today. Get out of here."

While guys waste no time hitting the showers, I return to Eve. She has her iPad packed away in her purse and hugs her sticker-covered water thermos. She looks tired and pitiful. It's adorable.

"Ready to go?" I hold out a hand.

Her hum sounds scratchy and congested. She gets up on her own and follows me out. An icy gust of wind makes her hide behind me. I turn around and draw her into my arms to warm her up. She presses closer, accepting my help. I finally have her back in my arms, though not the way I'd like.

"Your dad's going to let Mr. Boucher know. You don't have to worry about calling out sick."

"Thanks," she mumbles against my chest.

"I'm taking you home so you can rest."

As we get in, I text Benson. I was planning to spend some time with him and Jess at the brewery. I let him know something came up.

Eve is quiet on the ride to her place. She doesn't comment on the detour I take when I start to head for my apartment first. It's how I know she's more out of it than she let on.

I think she was planning to power through the day, and now that she doesn't have to, it's hit her all at once.

"You know it's okay to slow down when you don't feel good?" I give her a sidelong glance.

She hums, head resting against the seat. Her eyelids grow heavy. I don't know if it registered.

My mouth quirks. I pet her head, enjoying the contented sigh she makes. It's nice to provide her relief.

We pull in the driveway. She doesn't move right away.

"Tired?"

She nods. "I was up until..." She scrunches her face. "Four? I don't remember. I was going to stop, but I wanted to finish. Hyperfixation is a real bitch sometimes. I'm basically delirious at this point."

I squeeze her knee. "Come on, Evie. Let's get you into bed."

She stares at me for a beat like she didn't hear me right. Her tongue darts out to swipe her lower lip. I want to follow it with my thumb.

"You want to take me to bed?" she whispers.

I do, but for a much different reason. A heavy exhale leaves me.

We get up to her apartment above the garage. My hand hovers at her lower back to keep her from losing her balance on the steps as she trudges up them with sad little groans. Once we're inside, I grab a fuzzy pink throw blanket from her couch and wrap it around her.

"Go get in bed. Do you have a space heater? It's cold as shit in here."

"Over there." She points to a small one in the corner.

I carry it, pausing on the threshold to her bedroom when I'm hit with familiarity from the sexy photos she's sent from here. Clearing my throat, I help tuck her in and sit on the edge of the mattress.

"Better?" I rub her arms through the covers.

She nods. "You didn't have to bring me home. Thank you."

"Can't have you getting sick." I feel her head again. "I'm going to get you some cold medicine. Do you need anything else?"

Her hand pokes out. "My hand is sore."

"Your hand?" I massage the ache for her. "Can't have that, either."

She melts with a sigh, lashes fluttering. "From drawing for so long without a break. Mm, feels nice."

My dick likes those tantalizing noises she makes as I work her palm. I swallow thickly, forcing my thoughts away from that path.

She gets me hard too easily. I feel like a damn teenager around her. It's never been like this with anyone else.

"Think you can eat anything? I can make you soup if you want. It'll warm you up."

She considers for a moment. I focus on stretching her fingers to keep from smoothing out the thoughtful wrinkle between her eyebrows. Her small pout makes it hard not to crumble to the desire to kiss her.

"I want...pancakes. It's what my mom would make whenever I was sick."

"My comfort food is mac n' cheese," I admit with a chuckle.

Her smile is sleepy. "Yum."

As she drifts off, I caress her cheek with my thumb. When I'm sure she's asleep, I bring her hand to my lips, brushing the lightest kiss over her knuckles before I gently tuck it beneath the blanket.

A flickering ember grows within me, filling my chest with a feeling I don't know how to name. Taking care of someone else is foreign. She awakens this impossible to ignore instinct, one that feels like a completely natural role to step into for her.

I sit for a few minutes watching her before plugging in her space heater and adjusting it until I'm satisfied she'll be comfortable.

I hover in the doorway, an unseen tether pulling taut with each step. I scrub my face with a short laugh for being weird. She's fine. I'll be back soon.

It doesn't take more than an hour to go to the store for medicine to fight her fever and pancake ingredients. It's early afternoon by the time I'm back at her place. I put her key on the labeled hooks by the door, then check on her.

Eve is still passed out. Snoring softly.

My mouth curves as I go to her kitchenette to look for a mixing bowl and pan. Her apartment feels like her, from the vibrant mug collection I find in one cabinet to her mismatched set of measuring cups from two different sets to the stash of coffee outnumbering everything else in her pantry. I like being in her space.

Not long after I start cooking, she wakes up.

"You're cooking?"

I turn from the frying pan to find her poking her head out from the hall. She looks more refreshed after her nap. I offer a crooked smile as she pads closer. She ditched the hoodie, but she kept my coaching jacket on.

"You wanted pancakes. I got you some tea too in case your throat is sore."

"You made me pancakes," she murmurs when she reaches my side. "Why are you the best?"

I switch the spatula into my other hand and rub her back. "Because it's what you needed."

A small noise catches in her throat. She ducks her head, covering her mouth. I pretend I didn't notice.

"Hungry?"

"Yeah, they smell amazing."

She steps back from the stove and sweeps her hair into a fresh ponytail. It draws my attention to her kissable nape until I smell something burning.

"Shit." I scramble to flip the pancake. "Sorry. I was on a roll without scorching any."

She releases a crackling laugh. "It's okay. I actually like them a little burnt."

"There's medicine on the table and I refilled your water bottle," I say while I finish off the last of the batter.

"I'm surprised." She tears into the packet and pops the dose.

"About what?"

"You. You're all domesticated now."

"Because I know how to make pancakes?" I ask dryly, bringing the plate to the table.

She smirks. "For starters. You've come a long way from the grunting hockey heathen that used to eat all of our Lucky Charms before I got a bowl."

It's my turn to smirk. "Gotta be fast."

"Oh my god, I used to get so mad when you'd say that and shake the empty box."

"I know better now," I say contritely. "Obviously I'd buy two boxes. You get your own."

She grins. "Bet you'd still eat both."

I pause from making her a plate to raise a hand. "I solemnly swear to share cereal fairly."

It makes her giggle until she breaks down in a cough. I get her water thermos from where she left it on the counter.

"This is annoying. I hate getting sick," she mutters.

"All the more reason to take it easy. You'll get better faster than if you pushed yourself."

"You're right."

I pull out her chair and set a plate in front of her. "Want a cup of tea? I wasn't sure what kind you liked, so I got chamomile and ginger since the box said it was good for colds."

She tucks a stray hair behind her ear. "Ginger tea sounds nice. Thank you."

I open the box, then pause, searching her kitchen. "Do you have a—?"

"Kettle? An electric one. It's in the same cabinet as the blender to the left of the sink."

After it begins brewing, I lean against the counter. She cuts into her stack with more energy than she had before she rested.

The first bite makes her hum. "These are great. Totally hits the spot."

My stomach tightens. I grip the edges of the counter to root myself in place.

"I'm glad you like them."

She studies me, sliding her lips together. "I appreciate the things you do for me. This—" She gestures to her plate and the medicine. "—helping with my camper. I know I keep saying it a lot, but thank you. It means a lot to me."

My heartbeat kicks up. I hold her gaze. It means a lot to me, too.

"Of course, Evie. I'm here for you whenever you need me. There's nothing else I'd rather do than be here right now making sure you feel better."

Every word is the truth. I could be hanging out with her brother or researching new techniques to present to her dad for training. None of that would make me as content as I am when I'm with her. Maybe it should scare me how well we fit together.

The kettle beeps, breaking the moment. I pour her tea and steal some pancakes for myself.

"Oh my god!"

I jolt, worried she burnt her tongue. She splays her hands on the table, pinning me with an excited look.

"Don't ask how, but this just reminded me of this show I got sucked into last night."

"What was it about?"

Her eyes sparkle at my honest interest. She plays with the cuffs of my jacket while telling me about what she watched while she was working on her design. Her feet bump mine beneath the table when she swings them. I stretch my leg out, anticipating the contact.

Listening to her start, then stop herself to fill in backstory for context, then get off on another tangent before she meanders back to the original explanation puts a stupidly happy smile on my face. I don't bother hiding it.

I like this. I like *her*.

Being with her, even when I can't do more than hold her hand. Taking care of her. Having her lean on me.

No one's ever relied on me before.

This might not be a big deal, but I've never had this. My last relationship wasn't serious. None of them have been. It worked for me when I was in high school and college because I was focused on playing hockey. Then when I traveled around without staying in one place for more than six months at a time there wasn't a point to look for something long-term.

If I'm remaining in Heston Lake, maybe it doesn't have to be like that anymore.

Eve's the one I see myself opening up to about the big unsettling stuff that falls on our shoulders as we figure life out the way she has with me. Being her sounding board and listening when she talks herself in circles to explain the unimaginable amount of thoughts running through her head stirs a warm and grounded feeling wrapped around my heart.

It's something I want to hold on to.

SEVENTEEN
EVE

February

AT THE END of today's skating lesson, we have some free time left. The best way for them to practice at this stage is to get out there and skate. Cole's racing some of the kids back and forth while I've slipped into some old flows from my figure skating days before I lost interest. It draws their attention, even though I'm rusty.

I flip around, gliding backwards with my arms out. When it feels good, I pop into a jump. I only manage one clean rotation, but the kids lose it.

Grinning, I keep going with an improvised routine of my favorite techniques. My muscle memory kicks in. I forgot how much fun this is. After I make a large loop, I finish off with a scratch spin, keeping my arms tucked against my body, twirling fast.

When I come out of it, I catch Cole watching me showing off.

The kids gape at me, several of them talking at once as they crowd around me.

"Whoa!"

"Where'd you learn that!"

"Well, my dad is a hockey coach. He taught me to skate when I was small like you." I crouch beside the smallest of our students.

VERONICA EDEN

"Then I learned figure skating because I wanted to be able to do the cool jumps."

Cole chuckles. "You should've seen her. She was amazing. We'd have competitions between her and the hockey team to see who could outskate the other."

"Who won?" a little girl asks.

"Me."

"Eve," he says simultaneously, meeting my eyes with a smirk. "Except forward speed. I had you beat there."

Something nostalgic tugs at my chest, sending me back to high school.

Cole leaned against the boards, geared up for practice. He tracked me as I ran through my routine. The other players were still trickling out from the locker room while I finished off my ice time, including my brother.

I pushed myself, going for a triple instead of a double toe loop when I leapt into the air. When I landed it, I gave up on the routine, whipping my gaze to him.

"Oh my god, did you see that?"

I raced across the ice, spraying him when I stopped. He caught me against him with a charismatic smile that made me dizzy. I wished he looked at me that way because he liked me back.

Breathless, I grabbed his jersey and gave him a shake. "I landed a triple toe loop!"

"I saw," he said. "It looked killer."

"You don't sound impressed. Do you know how hard it is? There's the speed, the balance, rhythm—all while rotating in the air."

He shrugged. "I bet I can do it."

"Oh yeah?" I pointed at the ice. "Try a spin."

He pushed off the boards with a cocky swagger. A few of his team-mates watched, hyping him up. He studied my demonstration, then attempted to repeat it without success. He frowned.

"That was a pitiful spin," I said through a cackle.

"Okay, how about this," he said. "Let's battle it out. Who's got it harder, figure skaters or hockey players."

"You're on."

We started with backwards skating. I won, then he crushed me in

154

forward speed, swinging around while I was at the halfway mark to chase me around the rink.

Challenge forgotten, I zipped around with unrestrained laughter until he caught me around the waist. My pulse sped up at the feel of him against my back.

"Got you," he muttered next to my ear.

"Yo, Cole!" Benson called.

My heart plummeted when he left to join my brother. I reminded myself he didn't see me the way I wished he would.

I'm pulled from my recollection when Cole announces, "Looks like that's time. Come on, some of your parents are already waiting for you."

"Show them how good you're getting," I encourage.

The group of students get excited, eagerly skating to the exit. We hang back, making sure they manage on their own without our assistance. It stirs a flicker of pride when each kid skates with confidence.

"Is it bad I'd rather hang out here teaching the kids than deal with their parents?" he mutters to me.

I smirk. "Getting tired of the single ones trying to hit on you after every class?"

I'd be lying if I said there wasn't part of me that gets irritated whenever I catch someone flirting with Cole. I want to shove our chat history in all their faces and stomp in a circle around him to warn them all to back off.

"Yes. They won't take a hint. It's getting awkward. I don't know how many ways I can say no, sorry, not interested."

He whips off his Heston U Hockey hat and sifts his fingers through his hair. I grab his hand once he puts it back on.

"I'll protect you."

"How?"

It's his turn to smirk, dimples appearing. He keeps me in place, drawing my chin up with his fingers. A flutter moves through me.

"Are you gonna kiss me, Evie?" His voice dips. "Here and now?"

I freeze, lips parted and eyes wide. "I, uh, I mean—we *could*, if that's what you think will stop them, but, well, people talk. What if word gets to Benson or my dad?"

His deep, rumbling laugh cuts off my stammering. "Relax, sweetheart. I'm not going to ravish you on the ice. Not unless you ask me nicely."

I'm burning from the tips of my ears to my toes. The corners of his gleaming eyes crinkle and he pats my head.

"You're so cute when you're flustered. Come on. If any of them try to put the moves on me, I'll tell them I'm taken."

I wait a full minute after he skates off, needing the breather to cool down. When I leave the ice, he's laughing with two of the dads he plays hockey with on the recreational team.

People filter out quickly. One of the moms flags me down before I sit to take my skates off.

"Oh, Eve! While you're here, I've got a question about these. Are they customizable? And do you take bulk orders?"

My store is open on her phone. It's still surreal a month after my launch, but my following is growing. I'm getting used to telling people I have a business when I receive compliments on my earrings or the stickers on my water thermos. Part of me worried no one would want to pay for what I make, but the loyalty from people around town touches my heart.

Sometimes the slow growth makes me impatient to be bigger and do more, but I'm so happy I started Sweet Luxe. I've never been more creatively fulfilled.

"Yes, I can do custom," I answer brightly. "What did you have in mind?"

"These ones." She shows me a set of my boho arch earrings. "I want to order ten for bridesmaid gifts for my sister's wedding this summer. They're too cute!"

I lace my hands together to keep from flailing with giddiness at my first big custom order, aiming to come off professional and collected. Inside, I'm totally screaming.

"Perfect. Send me a message and we can get that set up. Thanks so much for your order."

"I want Miss Eve's earrings," her daughter says. "Can I get some, mommy? We can match."

She laughs, hugging her. "You don't have your ears pierced."

"Oh, I think I have some clip-ons. It's an easy swap," I say. "They'll be special ones just for you."

"Hear that, Gabby?"

The little girl squeals in excitement. Her mom mouths *thank you* with a nod.

"See you at the next lesson." I wave to them on their way out of the courtyard.

They're the last to leave. I turn to find Cole watching with a soft smile. He still has his skates on and he steps back on the ice.

"There's an hour before the rink opens up for open skating hours. Want to keep going?"

"Okay."

The rink is empty and the lights come on just as dusk gives way to the inky winter night. It's beautiful to see the outlines of the pine trees around the frozen lake. No one's around to watch us skate laps.

Our hands keep bumping until he takes mine. I don't pull away. It feels right to hold his hand, the only sound the wind in the trees and our blades carving the rink.

This almost feels like it could be a date. It hits me hard how much I want it to be.

"It's nice being on the ice together again," he murmurs.

"Takes me right back to high school and sharing the rink with you hockey boys."

He squeezes my hand. "Yeah. I was thinking about that while you were showing off your moves."

"Me too."

The confession comes out soft, stolen away on the wind. He shoots me a crooked smile.

"You looked good out there. I always liked watching you." His voice dips. "Those training outfits and sexy little leotard costumes helped."

"Cole!"

I give him a light shove, fighting a blush. He keeps us balanced, releasing a laugh that echoes off the trees.

"I had fun, though," I say. "It was nice to do it again. I haven't figure skated in years."

"Why'd you stop?"

157

"Honestly? I just lost the spark for it. One second it was there, and then it just felt like a chore that was suffocating me. I only wanted to learn how to jump and spin fast, so it was less—shiny, I guess, once I learned how. I still love it, but my interest was pulled in another direction."

I lost my motivation to continue with it once it felt like I knew enough about the skill that drew me to it in the first place. It feels too big to admit the other half of the truth—that he wasn't at the rink anymore. Figure skating practice felt less fun without the time I got to share with him.

"There's nothing wrong with that. You have to do what makes you happy. Otherwise you'd start to resent the things you used to love."

"Exactly." My grip on him tightens. "I'm glad you get it. Sometimes it's hard to explain to people what it's like when something switches from fun to not in my brain. They think I'm a quitter. When I'm interested, it's all my ADHD wants to focus on—I live it and breathe it. Then as soon as I'm not, everything just feels like...forcing myself through sludge."

He chuckles. "I don't think you're a quitter. You've found other things to make you happy, right?"

"Yes. I'm happy now."

"That's good."

"What about you, are you happy?"

He glances at me with an indecipherable look before answering. "Yeah, I think I am."

"You like coaching for Heston U?"

"Love it." This time he responds without hesitation. "I feel like the guys didn't know what to make of me at first, but now we have a solid connection."

He sounds the way I do when someone asks me about my designs. I squeeze his hand with both of mine. A comfortable silence falls between us. It's nice just existing with him.

"Sounds like people are starting to arrive for open rink time," I say.

"I'll give you a ride," he offers.

I agree, following him to the exit. We wave goodbye to Vic and he helps me untie my skates without me asking.

He swings his keyring around his fingers on our way to his car, jogging ahead to open the passenger door for me. I tease him with a formal curtsey and he smirks, tugging on the pink and white polka dot scarf tied in my hair.

I love that he doesn't complain when I fiddle with the radio to pick out music. Unlike my ex, he shoots me a smile that stirs butter-flies in my stomach.

We're only on the road for a minute before drowsiness blankets me. I can't help relaxing around him, able to slow down because of the comforting effect his presence has on me. I blink slowly while Cole sings under his breath.

Warm and content, I give up the fight against my heavy eyelids and doze off.

EIGHTEEN
COLE

The offer to drive Eve home wasn't supposed to take hours. She fell asleep shortly after we pulled out of the parking lot and rather than finish the quick ride to her place, I'm still driving around. I'm not ready for tonight to end.

I keep circling town slowly, avoiding every speed bump and pothole out of fear of waking her. Music on the radio plays low. I turned it down after she drifted off.

My elbow is propped on the armrest of the center console. I hold it still, enjoying the slight pressure where we're touching.

A few texts from Benny light up my phone in the cup holder. I flip it around so it doesn't bother Eve. I'll talk to him later. Right now I'm with her and I don't want anything else to interrupt.

All I'm left with are my thoughts and the acute awareness of her —her shallow, steady breathing, the sweet scent of strawberries and vanilla, the point of contact between us where she's leaning toward me, arm pressed against the side of mine.

I round the bend to head in the direction of the lake for the third time since we left the rink. Being careful not to disturb her, I shift to trace my knuckles against her leg.

Watching her entertaining the kids with her old figure skating skills earlier made it so damn hard not to draw her into my arms to kiss her gorgeous smile. The need hasn't gone away, burning in my chest, tingeing every breath.

I sigh, clenching the fist draped over the wheel. It doesn't do anything to stop this inescapable feeling.

There isn't much time left in the regular season, or winter. Both of the things I want are supposed to be temporary. I don't want to walk away—not from her or this job.

"It's late."

Eve's muted observation cuts through my thoughts. I give her a sidelong glance, quelling the desire to brush hair from her face. I savor the warmth of her arm against the side of mine.

"Hey," I say, equally quiet.

With a drowsy sigh, she sits up, stretching. She blinks a few times, getting her bearings. I flex my hand, already missing the connection.

My lips slide together as I consider how she'd react if I rest it on her leg. Not because I want it to lead anywhere—I do, more and more, but not now. I just like touching her.

She studies me while I turn down another road that leads in the opposite direction than her apartment.

"Why are we still driving around?"

"I didn't want to wake you."

My throat bobs with the admission. Her soft laugh twines around my heart. I slow for the stoplight, turning my attention to her.

She smiles, resting her head against the seat. "That's sweet."

"Sorry. I'll get you home."

"No." She reaches for the radio and turns it up a bit. "Not yet."

"No?" I stare at her while the light changes, not putting my foot on the gas.

She holds my gaze. "Keep going if you want. I don't mind."

The corner of my mouth kicks up and my chest expands with a tender sensation. I turn left instead of right.

"Okay."

She gets comfortable, tucking one of her legs up. It bumps against my hand. She says nothing when I slide my palm over her knee.

"Hungry? You slept through dinner."

"Sure. Something with french fries, please."

After we stop for food, we drive without a destination in mind. She holds my drink up for me to sip from and feeds me fries. It doesn't matter that I could do it myself, I'm enjoying the small touches of her fingers against my lips.

My hand doesn't leave her leg.

I take us down streets at random while she talks energetically with her whole body, telling me stories and getting lost in her side tangents. My smile is permanent. I absently rub her knee with my thumb.

Riding with her while she slept was nice. This is even better.

It feels like we're the only two people in the world.

* * *

The arena is packed for tonight's home game. UMass is putting up a good fight, but we're not backing down. The guys dressed to play on tonight's roster are on fire from the moment they hit the ice for the first puck drop.

I keep an eye on our defensive pairs when they swap for their shifts through first period. They're providing great support for Cameron's first time officially tending the net in a game. My eyes narrow near the end of the period when Hutchinson takes a hit, the puck snatched away by their left wing that tears up his open lane. He evades Brody and Higgins. Cameron watches like a hawk to read him.

My fist presses to my mouth as he shoots. Cameron moves in a flash, sliding into the puck's path to stop it.

"Way to hustle, Reeves," I tell Cameron when he comes off the ice.

"Feels different than practice." His eyes gleam. "Better, just like you said."

The edge of my mouth lifts and I pat his helmet. "Good. Keep it up and remember what we've practiced."

"Right. Thanks, coach." He joins his teammates and they give him their own congratulations for a solid first period.

It's inspiring watching them doing well. I might've joined them in the middle of their season, but no one's prouder of these guys than me. I love working on their individual strategies to figure out how they can improve their coordination as a team.

Our overall ranking in the Hockey East conference is fantastic. This is one of our last regular season games and we already know we're heading for playoffs with our seed position from Heston U winning the national championship last year.

Early in the final period we're up by two from the goals Keller scores. I'm distracted from the action because Eve keeps sending flirty messages.

CraftyCutie: Making coaching look sexy in that suit. The view of your ass from here is [fire emoji]

MightyPuck: Are you watching me or the game?

CraftyCutie: Both. Pretending it's you out there, hot stuff. Two goals in a row. Will we get a hat trick tonight? I forgot to bring a hat. I guess I could throw my bra on the ice.

MightyPuck: Don't you dare. No one gets to see that but me.

CraftyCutie: Want me to go take a picture? The lighting in the bathrooms here suck, but maybe I can sneak into the coaching offices.

MightyPuck: You're being bad, baby. Are you going to shut up and take it like a good girl for me later?

CraftyCutie: If you make me. We both know how good you are at handling a big stick.

MightyPuck: I'm thinking you need that mouth stuffed while I fuck your pussy hard. Your toys better be charged because we're going all night.

CraftyCutie: Ohh, fuck, I want that. Keep talking and I might have to sneak away to get started without you. You're making me wet.

I slide my gaze to her section. She's seated with her mom and Jess a few rows behind our bench. Her Heston U Knights shirt isn't one I recognize from the regular merch sold to fans. She must've made it herself.

164

She looks damn good in those stands. I almost imagine she's here for me, as if I'm out on that ice with my girl watching. It gets me fired up.

The wink she flashes me sends a sizzling crackle of heat down my spine.

"Cole."

David's clipped tone makes me freeze. He's right at my shoulder. Shit—did he see my screen? I hope fucking not. I shove my phone in my pocket.

"Yes, sir?" It's a miracle my voice is even.

"Give me that." He motions to the iPad tucked under my arm.

Jesus. Nothing like looking your boss in the eye moments after talking dirty to his daughter to give a man a heart attack.

My pulse returns to normal and I unclench everything including my asshole. I hand it over. He was still using a whiteboard and print-outs until I put this together with everything we need for easy reference during games like stats, clips from game tape, and adapting our strategy on the fly.

While he's reviewing it, I glance at Eve. She waves without a trace of remorse.

We've safely avoided getting caught for now.

She doesn't send any messages for the rest of the game. At one point she disappears from her seat for a while. I keep checking my phone on the down low, expecting to get a sexy little surprise that will drive me crazy.

MightyPuck: Are you getting into trouble?
CraftyCutie: Long bathroom line. Making new BFFs though. They liked my shirt. I told them about my online shop and sold them on my motivational and mental health stickers.

My lips twitch. I'm not surprised she's easily making friends. Her warm, bubbly personality could draw anyone in within moments. She's the shining light in every room she enters.

The entire arena goes insane when Alex Keller's wrister sinks

165

into the net for a hat trick that secures our win with minutes to spare on the clock. Hats rain down on the ice.

I have no doubt his name will be on this year's NHL prospects list when it releases soon. It's not easy for college players to make it all the way to the pros, but he's got what it takes.

After the game, we have a meeting in the locker room to review it before we let the team loose for the night. Everyone's in high spirits.

"Did you see that assist?" Easton shakes Cameron. "Man, I was on fire tonight."

"We know, rookie. You won't shut up about it," Theo snarks playfully. "Good job, though."

"I'd say MVP for this game goes to Reeves for defending the crease excellently," I propose.

They erupt with cheers, ruffling Cameron's damp hair and patting him. David nods in approval. I grin, struck by a sense of belonging.

"Alright, that's all," I say.

"Be ready to get on the team bus early tomorrow," Steve announces.

David turns to me. "Come on."

"What's up?" I follow him from the locker room to his office where we get our coats.

"The girls are waiting. Aren't you coming with us to The Landmark to get a drink?"

"Sure."

We head outside and find them. Mrs. Lombard gives David a congratulatory kiss and Jess holds up her hand for a high five. I accept it.

Eve shifts as close as she dares with everyone right there. A chord ties around my heart, pulling me to her.

"Congratulations on another win. We're looking good for the championship," she says.

"That's all them. The team's working hard."

The back of my hand grazes hers. Her fingers are chilled. I make sure no one's paying attention and take her hand to warm it up. Her breath hitches and she peeks up at me through her lashes.

This is the hard part.

Playing our little game is addicting. Yet when we're near each other the best we get is a brush of our hands and fiery stolen looks when no one's watching, all while pretending we're nothing more than friends.

ALL TIED UP WITH
NOWHERE TO GO

ALL TIED UP WITH NOWHERE TO GO

COLE

MightyPuck: I think you'd look so fucking pretty tied up for me.

THE INSPIRATION for this has been on my mind for hours. I've been holding back all day. Almost started our game twice while I was at work.

It's all because she waltzed into the practice facility for lunch with her dad wearing a short leather skirt hugging her ass that could bring me straight to my knees. The bow tied in her hair was begging me to tug it free and use it on her.

She was the one that teased me before that I should use the cord of my whistle to bind her wrists.

CraftyCutie: Omg
MightyPuck: Does that idea make your pussy nice and wet for me?
CraftyCutie: ...yes [blushing emoji]
MightyPuck: Good, because I've thought about it all damn day. You on your knees, wrists bound with one of those ribbons you like to wear in your hair.

171

Desire rides me hard. I'm too swept up in it to pretend Eve is anyone else.

CraftyCutie: I'll do anything you want, Coach Bossy.

My mouth curves at the nickname. I bring the phone close to whisper into the mic.

"I want to hear you this time."

As soon as I see that she's read it, I hit the phone icon at the top of our DM window. The call connects us. A thrill shoots through me, anticipating all the sounds I want to draw out of her.

"Hey." My greeting comes out deep and raspy.

She's silent on the line for a moment, then answers breathlessly. "Hi."

"Good girl," I murmur.

She smothers a noise. I grin, enjoying the way she reacts to being praised.

"Are you still wearing the same thing as earlier?" I ask.

"Yes."

"Perfect."

I close my eyes when my dick throbs in anticipation. I press my palm against it through my sweatpants, then tear them off before taking a seat on the edge of the bed.

"Pull the ribbon from your hair and tie your wrists. I'm going to have your mouth tonight."

There's a rustle, then it sounds like she's muttering to herself. I swipe my tongue along my lip, gaze softening with affection as I imagine the sight of her at the moment.

"Are you using your teeth to tie yourself up for me?"

"Yeth." It's muffled by the fabric between her teeth. "Tricky."

I chuckle. "Show me?"

A moment later, I receive a photo that rips the air from my lungs.

"Oh, baby. You're beautiful like this."

Eve perches on her knees by the side of her bed with her mouth open, tongue out. She's stripped down to a red lace thong that sits high on the swell of her hips, plump tits squeezed between her arms as she holds up her wrists tied with the ribbon from her hair.

"I want to suck your cock," she says.

I draw a breath through my teeth at the tug of heat. "Open wide."

My eyes hood. I squeeze my shaft from tip to base as if I'm sinking into her mouth inch by inch. She makes sweet noises for me, making this better.

"You like being my pretty little slut? I've spent all day holding back from this, waiting to have those lips wrapped around me."

She answers with a moan that's garbled, closer to how she'd sound if she were sucking me for real. She's using something to simulate this fantasy, eager and fucking perfect for me.

"Are you taking my cock all the way in your greedy mouth?"

Her name almost slips out of me. I bite it back at the last second, slowing my strokes to hold off. I want this to last because I need more of her. How am I ever supposed to feel satisfied when she makes me lose my damn mind?

The phone dings with a new message. It's another photo in our DM within the app. I open it and drop my head back with a tortured groan. My fist tightens to stave off the heady rush of desire.

Eve's face is rosy, her lashes heavy and her amber eyes glazed with arousal. Her lips stretch around a dildo. The ribbon binding her wrists is driving me crazy. She probably has her phone propped up and set a timer to show me.

Mine.

A fierce rush of possessiveness crashes over me.

This is for me. No one else gets to see her like this.

"Fuck, sweetheart," I rumble. "Look at you with your mouth stuffed full of my cock. You take it so well."

She moans. It's made filthier by the sound of her sucking on the toy. I stare at the photo, jerking my length faster.

"That's it, baby, make it nice and sloppy."

My stomach concaves with the breath I force out at another one of her filthy, garbled cries. I close my eyes, envisioning her more vividly. Cheeks flushed, eyes watering but taking each of my thrusts deep, keeping her mouth open for me to use. I imagine taking hold of her bound wrists by the ends of the ribbon to tug her closer while I flood her mouth with come.

"Oh, f—I'm coming," I choke out.

She hums in pleasure as if she's swallowing every drop spilling on her tongue.

It takes a minute to recover, pleasurable electric sparks dancing along my nerve endings. I flop back on the mattress with a satisfied groan.

"How are you so perfect?"

"That was good?"

"Hell yes. So damn good."

I get up to clean up while I talk to her.

"I'm glad," she murmurs shyly.

"Do you want me to—?"

"I'm going to take a bath to take care of myself, but that means I can't bring you with me," she blurts. "At least not on the phone."

"How come?"

"I only have a shower in my apartment. The tub is in the house. I can be quiet in there, but someone could hear you on the phone with me."

I rake my teeth over my lip. "In that case, take your phone anyway. I'll have to tell you dirty things by text instead."

"I'd like that," she says.

I listen for a moment to the sound of her moving around her room.

"Good. And sweetheart?"

"Yes?"

"Don't forget to untie your wrists."

I laugh at her strangled yelp before ending the call.

NINETEEN
EVE

THE NARRATOR for my current listen is so good, I need to pause my crafting to fully experience his seductive voice in my ears. Lainey recommended the latest romance release from her favorite author and I'm loving it.

"Are you going to let me taste you? Lap at you until your sweet cries reach the rafters, pretty girl?"

The couple has taken shelter in a barn, caught in the rain after a trail ride. They're both soaked to the bone, their clothes translucent, clinging to their skin. He's skimming his fingertips up her arms and across her chest to catch the water droplets. Then he makes a show of stripping out of his shirt while she watches.

Just as the hero in the book is about to lower his mouth to go down on the heroine, the audio cuts out. I'm so absorbed in the story vividly playing out in my head, I don't realize why. There's a new Love Struck message from Cole.

"Getting ready to go to the game but I'm thinking of you right now, on your knees, lips stretched around my cock."

His voice is so close to the narrator's that my brain glitches from the sensual overload. There's water running in the background. He must be about to shower.

It takes a minute to answer. All I manage is a string of emojis to illustrate what he does to me.

175

MightyPuck: Did I interrupt something? We can have fun later. You're worth the wait.
CraftyCutie: I was listening to an audiobook on my phone when you messaged me. It was at a steamy chapter.
MightyPuck: Send me the name of the book and the part you're at.
CraftyCutie: You want to listen to it?
MightyPuck: Yeah. I need to know what else you like, sweetheart. Maybe I want some inspiration, maybe I just want to read it knowing it made you wish I was there to make your pussy stop aching.

My stomach dips. That's so hot. No guy I've dated has ever been interested in the romance books I read. They've reaped the benefits if a scene got me too hot and bothered, but they've never gone as far as reading any books themselves to find out what I find sexy.

MightyPuck: I can still help you feel good from far away.
CraftyCutie: Your talent is unmatched, sir.

He switches to a call. I answer it and set my earring project aside.

"Mm, want to help me out? I'm so fucking hard thinking about you in this shower with me."

I wet my lips, already short of breath. "We'd be all wet together. What would you do with me?"

"Fuck. Everything," he growls. "But first, get on your fucking knees for me."

A shiver zips down my spine and heat pools in my core. It's easy to moan across the line for him while I think of how he looks right now—corded forearm braced against the tile, fist stroking his rigid cock, water streaming over his body.

A ragged exhale tears from him. "Yeah. Suck it. Show me what's all mine."

The mental image of kneeling at his feet to blow him in the

shower, maybe with his hand gripping my hair to make me suck him all the way down ignites my desire.

I spot the mug of candy canes I left on my book cart. Grabbing one, I film a short video to give him a visual.

He groans when I send it. It sounds like his hand speeds up.

"Get me there," he rumbles. "Make me come, baby."

I could stretch across my bed with a vibrator, but I want to stay focused on him. Make him feel good.

"Want your come filling my mouth," I murmur. "I want to swallow every drop. Choke me with it."

"Jesus," he forces out roughly. "You like being my little cock slut, don't you? So good for me, taking me nice and deep while I fuck that mouth."

I moan again, making more obscene noises to make this lifelike for him. He bites back a curse that turns into the filthiest sound when he comes. A thrill races through me knowing I helped him get off.

"Thanks," he says with a warm, sleepy chuckle. "I used to have this pregame ritual where I'd always rub one out. It's more fun with you, obviously."

"I feel like I should be thanking you. Did your shower run cold?"

Talking to him while he's showering feels more intimate than him calling me while he jerks off. I lay my hand over my stomach. It doesn't help the flutter.

"Not yet. Water's still lukewarm."

I listen for another moment to the sound of him moving beneath the spray and rinsing his hair.

"I don't want to keep you or you'll be late."

"Wait, where did you get the candy cane?"

My gaze slides to the mug that's been living on my cart. "Don't laugh."

"I'd never." I can hear his smile.

"They've been sitting on my book cart."

"It's the end of February," he says after a beat.

As promised, he's not judgmental like others might be knowing how long stuff sits forgotten in my apartment.

"Yup."

"Lucky me. Now I'll be thinking about you as a naughty little elf." His hum is so sexy. "How do you feel about costumes? Think we can get some on discount now that the holidays are over?"

Laughter bubbles out of me. "Okay, I'm leaving now."

"Bye, sweetheart."

"Bye."

My smile doesn't fade. I settle back into making heart-shaped lollipop earrings. They've been one of my bestsellers since I launched. I can barely keep them in stock after my online store was featured on a Valentine's Day picks list.

I start the chapter over on my audiobook while I get to work.

As usual, Cole's the blueprint I think of for any romance book hero I read.

* * *

It's not until a few days later when I go to Cole and Benson's game for their beer league team that I see him. He nudges Benson during warmups and they wave to us before going back to passing the puck between each other.

Jess and I have great seats in the third row. I'm surprised their teams draw a sizable crowd for a recreational league, but apparently they're good enough the Brawling Bandits and their opponents both have fan followings in their communities.

I'm glad we got here early, even though I rushed out the door to meet Jess so quickly that I forgot my coat on my bed. It's chilly, but I have a thick sweater, jeans, and knee-high boots on. Some of Heston U's players show up before the game starts. They say hi to us before grabbing some open seats nearby.

Familiar exhilaration sparks seeing Cole on the ice. When the puck drops, we cheer for Benson winning the face-off. Cole watches his team's play unfold, on guard for any shift. Benson and the wingers take the puck down the ice, but the other team's defense shuts down their goal. Cole's ready for them, checking their center against the boards and firing the puck to his teammate.

I can't take my attention off him. He plays even better than he did in high school.

"Are you sure you don't want me to run back and get your coat?" Jess asks during the break after first period.

"Yes. Don't give me that look. This is fine." I make sure she has more of the blanket she brought for us to share. "I'll bounce my legs to keep warm."

"Want me to keep you warm, Eve?" Jake jerks his chin in a nod, opening his arms.

"I'm good. Got this cozy blanket to snuggle with my girl."

He scoffs. "But you could be snuggling with me. I'm great at snuggling."

"Pass," I say through a laugh.

Easton comes over and strips off his hoodie, tugging down his t-shirt underneath. "Here. You can borrow my hoodie if you need it."

"Thanks. I'm okay, though."

He opens his mouth to say more, then freezes when Cole clears his throat behind him. His team is in the locker room for their break, but he's out here with us.

Cole in his jersey and skates makes my brain melt and my stomach dip. He's wearing his old number from high school. His hair is slightly damp, curling across his forehead and his attention is solely focused on me.

"Hey, coach. Good game so far. What's up?" Easton rubs the back of his neck.

"Don't you guys bug Eve enough when she's watching you practice? Beat it," Cole says.

"Give 'em hell," Easton says before returning to his friends.

"Hey, Kincaid. Can I get your autograph? Will you sign a puck for me?" I joke.

Cole cocks his head, mouth twisting wryly. "Funny."

"Sign your stick for her." Jess snorts at the gaping look we both throw her. "What? I didn't say sign her boobs."

"Jess," I hiss.

"Kidding, jeez. You started it."

She pokes me and the blanket falls from my lap. I suppress a shiver.

"You know, the coach's daughter should know better than to show up to a hockey game without dressing warm enough," he says with a handsome smirk.

His teasing makes me blush. "I forgot my coat and didn't want to miss out on getting good seats. I'm taking one for the team."

Chuckling, he holds up the coat he brought over. "I figured. I saw you between my line's shifts sharing the blanket with Jess. We can't have you catching another cold, right? Here, wear mine."

He drapes his coaching jacket around my shoulders. His mesmerizing green eyes smolder as he zips it for me, stirring a flutter. This time I'm suppressing a shiver for an entirely different reason. My pulse speeds up, heart drumming wildly.

"Looks good on you," he murmurs.

Mentally, I'm kicking my feet and screaming. It means something to a hockey player when you wear his number. I can't help but wonder if this has the same meaning for him.

The Heston U players make a ruckus, cupping their hands around their mouths and elbowing each other.

"Ohh, coach got game!"

Cole flips them off without looking. "Can it."

"Thank you," I say.

"Better?" He rubs my arms to help me warm up.

"Much better."

"Enjoy the game, girls."

"Good luck out there."

His eyes bounce between mine. "Can't lose with you watching."

Jess bumps her shoulder against mine when the players take the ice for second period. "Um. How long has this been going on?"

"What?" I blink rapidly. "There's nothing going on."

"This is totally a thing."

I fold like a house of cards under the weight of her skeptical stare. "Don't tell Benson. We're not really—It's complicated, okay? He doesn't know I like Cole."

She mimes locking her lips. "Girl, that's your business and I support it. Benson won't know a thing."

"You're the best sister." I hook my arm with hers.

"I've always thought you'd be good together," she says after a short pause.

"For real?"

"Totally. I think you balance each other well."

I think of how much his support and kindness has helped me. "I didn't think he ever noticed me as more than his best friend's sister."

"He always looks at you whenever you're not paying attention."

She raises her brows when my eyes snap to her. There's no way that's true.

She must sense my disbelief because she adds, "I have video from the wedding to prove it if you don't believe me. In almost every candid clip, his eyes are on you whether he's aware of it or not, sweetie."

I find Cole on the ice. He's clashing with the offensive player he marked. He's a force to be reckoned with.

And when the play ends, he glances toward the stands. Is he looking for me?

I wave and he lifts his gloved hand with a crooked smile that makes my heart skip a beat.

My eyes don't leave him for the rest of the game.

Spring
PLAYOFFS

BE MY BOOK BOYFRIEND

BE MY BOOK BOYFRIEND
EVE

March
11:36 PM

It's harder to imagine Cole as the AHL player persona I made up for him on the fly with his voice in my ears. This isn't the first time we've been on the phone, but it makes everything more intense. He told me earlier he had something fun planned for tonight while he's on the road with the team for playoffs.

"How's the hotel room?" I'm unsure how to talk normally to him when we do this even though we're friends.

"Four walls. A bed. Nice view of an air conditioning unit," he deadpans. "Are you in bed?"

"Technically I'm on top of it. Not under the sheets."

"Is that right? What are you wearing?" I can hear his smirk.

I pluck at the hem of my old Heston U shirt. "Nothing at all, because I'm a seductress who lounges around naked like a queen."

"I'd better get on my knees then."

I wish I could experience his mouth devouring me for real. The way he describes it drives me wild every time.

"Remember the audiobook you were reading?"

My cheeks heat at the memory of what point I was at when he interrupted. "Yes."

VERONICA EDEN

"Play it."

"You want to listen to a romance book right now? I thought we were going to—"

"We're going to listen together," he corrects. "And act it out."

Words tangle on my tongue as I try to say too many responses at once. "Okay. That broke my brain."

He gives a soft, seductive chuckle that makes me press my thighs together. "In a good way?"

I bite my lip. "Yes. Super yes. Huge turn on. I've never recreated a spicy scene from one of my books with someone before."

Again, I wish he was here with me. My body aches for his touch and doing this with him has only made the desire more intense.

"Still there?"

"Yes," I say quickly. "Which scene did you have in mind?"

"Which one's your favorite?"

I consider how many good spicy scenes are in the book. "The dinner table."

"Not the barn?" He sounds surprised.

"The barn during the thunderstorm is hot, too. But there's something powerfully sensual about him capturing her gaze, telling her he's hungry, and slowly spreading her out on the table as his meal."

He rumbles in agreement. "I left you a present before going out of town. Did you find it?"

My face flushes. It's waiting on my bed.

I discovered the unexpected package when I checked if the new weather sealing we did on the interior of the camper held out against the snowstorm that blew through. Inside, I found a new vibrator with an app designed for couples to use long-distance. If he has the controls, it'll be more like he's with me.

"Yes. You're lucky my dad hasn't been in the camper this week."

"It was wrapped," he protests. "I'm dying to use it on you. Knowing I'm miles away but making you feel so good? Mm, I'm going to make you come so hard, sweetheart."

The flush spreads from my face, tingles dancing along my nerve endings. He releases a smoky laugh at the strained exhale that leaves me.

"Get your audiobook set up."

MATCHING ALL THE WAY

I open my laptop and find the scene, switching the call to speakerphone. "Okay. Ready."

"Strip for me," he murmurs. "Before we start, let me warm you up."

"What do you want me to take off first?"

"Start with your panties. How does it feel being bare for me?"

"Good," I answer quietly, enjoying the cool air of the room against my heated skin. "I'm getting achy already."

"Yeah? Now take your top off."

His quiet commentary makes chills breakout across my body. I bite my lip, peeling off my shirt. My nipples are already pert buds. I tweak them with a faint hum of pleasure, skimming my fingers lower, down the softness of my belly to pet my mound. My pulse thrums in my clit.

"Co—"

His fake name won't come out. I swallow thickly.

"Cole," I whisper.

"Yes, baby?"

"I want it."

His voice dips. "Use your words. Tell me what you need."

My lashes flutter. "I need to come. Make me come."

"Lay on your bed for me. Spread those thick, beautiful thighs. I want you rubbing your clit. Get yourself nice and wet."

"Already there," I breathe. "I'm so turned on."

A gravelly laugh sounds. "We're just getting started."

It feels like he's watching when I slide my fingers over my pussy, holding my legs open wide as if his gaze is setting me on fire. Just as I'm beginning to ride the current of heat uncoiling deep within me, his voice cuts through my focus.

"Now, get your new present. Push it inside slowly. Take it inch by inch."

Air flies from my lungs. "Okay."

I pat the bed, closing my fingers around the curved vibrator. It has a slight swell at one end that vibrates and makes a come hither motion when it's activated. The other end fits to the body, covering my clit with a rotating nub at the center that's similar to the stimulation of a tongue.

189

The velvety material feels nice when I circle my entrance. The tip slips in easily from how wet I am. I drop my head back, eyes hooding as I picture him stretching me with his cock.

"Does it feel nice?" he prompts.

"Yes."

"And now?"

The vibration inside activates. My lips part on a sigh, hips shifting to meet the sensual motion stroking me.

"Yes. Feels good."

He waits a few minutes, playing with me by increasing and decreasing the intensity of the toy. I'm warm all over, caressing my body.

"Start the chapter," he says.

My eyes blink open, dazed. I stretch to reach my desk, pressing play on my laptop. He goes quiet for the beginning of the scene, allowing the narrator to draw me into the story. My attention is split between listening to Wyatt and Lydia's conversation and the toy.

He's subtly adjusting the controls to bring me closer to the edge. The other end switches on, drawing a moan from me. The dual sensations inside and on my clit are overwhelming. It's so good, igniting a fresh burst of heat that grows hotter when he changes the intensity.

"I haven't eaten," Cole answers the question from the audiobook.

I'm too lost in the divine sensations of him using the vibrator to say Lydia's next response.

Wyatt captures my gaze and rumbles, "I'm hungry."

"Cole," I whimper.

"Shh." He continues playing out the scene. "Come here."

Every step is a blessing and a curse, the need for him rising until it's too overpowering to fight. He grabs my hips the second I'm within reach and sits me on the table before him. I swallow when he guides my thighs apart and finds I'm bare beneath my sundress.

The narrator gasps with me.

Cole hums, continuing to say Wyatt's parts. "Look at you, spread for me, glistening."

In the book, Wyatt glides his knuckle through Lydia's folds and licks his finger. Cole changes the speed pattern on the toy, making it writhe faster buried deep inside me and the nub on the outside tease my clit as if a tongue circles it. My fingers fly off my breasts and scrabble across the sheets for something to hold on to for leverage.

"Fucking gorgeous." He sounds more reverent than the narrator. "I'm going to enjoy every drop of this meal."

Before Wyatt's mouth descends between Lydia's legs, I'm shaking apart, my core erupting with ripples of ecstasy.

"Oh god!"

"You're not done yet, baby," Cole rasps. "I've barely had a taste of you. I want to spend all night fucking you with my tongue and fingers."

He recites Wyatt's dialogue, following along with the scene. He groans over the phone as if my pussy is the best thing he's ever devoured. My chest heaves with unstoppable cries while he uses the toy to take me apart.

I picture Cole in place of the book's hero, imagining him in the room with me. The toy's movements inside me are his fingers and the undulating vibrations on my clit are his mouth sucking me, licking, unraveling me at the seams.

"You taste like heaven," he narrates, improvising some of his own lines. "Christ, I want to have you like this always, Evie. Those luscious legs wrapped around my head and your sweet cries filling my ears. Every minute of the day I don't spend with my head buried in your pussy is a fucking waste."

A gasp sticks in my throat. My hips buck and another orgasm crashes over me.

"Fuck, oh fuck, oh f-fu—"

My thighs tremble from the strength. It goes on and on, making my eyes swim from how unbelievable it is.

"Those gorgeous sounds of yours are all I think about. You're always filling my head. You're sound so fucking sexy when you come, you know that?"

The praise washes over me with another change in rhythm from the vibrator. He's keeping my release going, the pleasure cresting once more. I cry out, arching my back with my fingers clawing the sheets.

"That's it. I've got you." There's a smile in his voice.

"I knew you'd make the best book boyfriend."

I murmur it more to myself while I'm floating in the afterglow, but he heard me. He pauses a moment, then steals my breath with his response.

"I'll be everything for you, sweetheart. Every fantasy. Every dream. Whatever you need, I want to be it."

SAFE SPACE

SAFE SPACE
COLE

9:37PM

THE FIRE EVE ignited tonight lingers in my veins as I catch my breath, come coating my knuckles after one of our online conversations. With a groan, I haul myself out of the hotel bed to clean up. She's making it bearable to be on the road.

I need to be at the rink early for a coaches meeting before tomorrow's playoff game, but I'm not ready to say goodnight to her yet. I bring my phone into the bathroom, typing a text with one finger.

MightyPuck: You made me make a huge mess, baby.
CraftyCutie: Hehehe [angel emoji]
MightyPuck: Not fooling anyone with that angel.
CraftyCutie: You love it.
MightyPuck: I do.

I sigh, staring at the message after I send it. Since we've been on the road for playoffs, I haven't seen her. As much as I'm enjoying the team's energy and drive to win, I miss her. I want to sit at the bar during her shift to keep her company and work on the camper with her. Ride around with no destination in mind.

Never thought I'd find the day I would rather be home than throwing myself into traveling the way I used to before I returned to

Heston Lake. I can't imagine leaving now. Not when a piece of my heart resides there with her.

The possibility looms over my head the closer the team gets to the end of their season. If I'm no longer needed and David finds someone to fill the position, I need to figure out what I'll do.

MightyPuck: What are you going to do the rest of the weekend?
CraftyCutie: I have a double shift at the bar but I also am thinking about some non-work crafting. It's been too long since I opened my shop that I've sat down and created something for me just because, you know?
MightyPuck: You should. Show me what you make.

I know I'm pushing it, coming right up against the boundary she set. I haven't put much effort in pretending to be someone I'm not when I talk to her online, blending reality into this game.

If she isn't going to say anything, then I won't stop. Breaking the rules with her is worth it.

CraftyCutie: The TVs at The Landmark will be tuned to the Knights' game tomorrow. We're all watching you guys. They're playing so amazing. You must be proud of what you've done with them.
MightyPuck: Yeah, I am. They're incredible guys. I think I'll always carry this season with me after it's over.
CraftyCutie: Next one will be even better I bet.
MightyPuck: I'm sure they'll do great, even if I don't get to be part of it.
CraftyCutie: What do you mean?

I massage my forehead, working out how to explain this without coming apart at the seams to unleash every stressful worry I've caged up. I haven't wanted to think about any of it, allowing myself to get swept up in the rush of post-season to put off my unknown future as a coach for Heston University's hockey program.

Leaving the bathroom, exhaustion washes over me. A thump followed by laughter and muffled music from the next room prevents me from face planting into the bed.

A wry smile twists my lips. I remember what it was like in the middle of playoffs with my own team in college. We felt on top of the world. I shoot off a quick text to the group chat they put me in and tell them to get their asses to bed so they're fresh for tomorrow's game.

CraftyCutie: Cole?

CraftyCutie: You still there?

CraftyCutie: You can talk to me about anything.

MightyPuck: Sorry, I didn't mean to worry you. I had to lay down the law for rowdy players that wouldn't go to sleep.

MightyPuck: So… I don't know if I get to keep my coaching job. I was brought on as a temporary measure to fill in on a trial basis.

CraftyCutie: Oh. But you love this job.

MightyPuck: I do. Can't picture myself doing anything that fulfills me like this. I can't go back to what I was doing before. The youth camps were fun, but I've realized I was just bouncing around to fill the time as a way to cope. It was a distraction because I didn't want to think about what I wanted to pursue after I graduated. Now that I'm aware I was using it to cover up what I didn't want to face, I can't go back to letting my life happen to me. I want to be in control.

CraftyCutie: Have you talked to my dad? If you want to stay, he'll want to keep you on.

MightyPuck: Not yet. He hasn't said anything yet.

CraftyCutie: I'm sure he wants you after everything you've put into this team. You work so hard to push them.

MightyPuck: I hope. I haven't been thinking about it because I don't want to plan what comes next if I'm let go. Since I've been back, I've worked on changing my old reputation. I want to be better.
CraftyCutie: What do you mean? You're amazing.
MightPuck: You know what I was like. The funny guy. The screwup…
CraftyCutie: I didn't think of you like that.
MightyPuck: Thanks. I want to change, though. I'm tired of being the guy who's too irresponsible. I'm trying to get it together and become someone dependable, but whenever I feel like okay, this is what I need to do, there's always something new to handle. I swear it seems like some of the guys I'm coaching have their life more in order than I do. Isn't that messed up?
CraftyCutie: Hey. You're talking to a professional disaster. It's okay to be in your feels and not know what the hell is going on. In the words a really cool person told me recently, no one's perfect.

My lips twitch and my gaze softens. I trace the edge of my phone with my thumb, wishing I had her in front of me. I need her.

She's the only one I'm not afraid to let in completely. I trust her to see me at my best and my worst. It's easy to open up to her, far more than I imagined. Not only because we've grown closer as friends, but because I've seen her struggle first hand.

I sink to the bed, struck by the fact it's my best friend's sister who sees me who I want to be seen as. My heart beats hard when I envision her brilliant smile.

She makes me want to be strong for her when she needs help to carry her burdens, but it's gratifying to know she understands and offers me the same in return when I need to lean on her. I don't feel as alone being able to share this with her.

Out of everyone in my life, she understands the uncertainty I'm feeling. I've tried to bring it up to Benson, but he's got a lot on his plate between his business and the family he's started. I love him like a brother, but it doesn't bring me the same relief to be open with him like this.

When I talk to Eve, there's no sense of judgment or comparison.

CraftyCutie: Everyone takes a different amount of time to figure it all out, too. There's no set way we all have to follow. Some people find their way early and some of us need longer.
MightyPuck: True. I really needed to hear that.
CraftyCutie: I'm glad it could help. I need that reminder every day. In fact, I'm totally making that an art print and I'm going to plaster it all over my apartment.
CraftyCutie: And it's working.
MightyPuck: What is?
CraftyCutie: Your self-improvement quest. You're the most dependable person I know. You've been my rock this year.

My heart squeezes.

If Eve believes in me that's all that matters. It makes me feel like every unknown will be okay. I'll be able to face whatever comes next because of her.

MightyPuck: Thank you. That means a lot to me. I appreciate you listening.
CraftyCutie: This is our safe space. No matter what, we'll figure it out. You've always got me in your corner.

A tender smile stretches across my face. I close my eyes, picturing her laying next to me. The future feels less daunting knowing I have her to confide in.

It's not just this connection we've formed that's become my lifeline. It's Eve. She's my safe space. My comfort.

SEARCH HISTORY

Q HOW NOT TO FALL FOR HOT HOCKEY COACHES

Q HOW NOT TO FALL FOR YOUR BROTHER'S BEST FRIEND

Q HOW TO AVOID CATCHING FEELINGS FOR BROTHER'S BFF

Q WILL YOUR BROTHER NOTICE IF YOU'RE IN LOVE WITH HIS BEST FRIEND

Q SECRET RELATIONSHIP TIPS

Q WILL ANYONE NOTICE IF YOU'RE HOOKING UP WITH THE ASSIST. COACH

Q TUTORIAL TO STOP BEING IN LOVE

SEARCH HISTORY: HOW NOT TO FALL FOR HOT HOCKEY COACHES/YOUR BROTHER'S BEST FRIEND

EVE

7:54PM

I CLEAR MY SEARCH HISTORY—TWICE, just to make sure—then slam my laptop shut. Not sure what I was hoping to find.

Some sort of community or forum for people pining for their sibling's friends? What to do when you think you're falling for your friends with benefits situationship that was only supposed to last for the winter? A guide to get rid of those feelings?

My lips purse as I lean back in my swivel chair, swaying back and forth. Maybe I just wanted an excuse to get these insistent thoughts out of my head for a minute.

This whole thing with Cole would be a hell of a lot easier if I was only physically attracted to him. Of course, that's always been the problem. My crush didn't begin just because he's hot. He is unbelievably hot, but that's beside the point.

How can he feel more like my boyfriend than any of my past relationships?

We're supposed to keep this arrangement feelings-free. Then he goes and does all these sweet things for me like helping me work on my camper and taking care of me when I'm sick. He never gets annoyed with me for my neurodivergent tendencies. In fact, he's so heartbreakingly supportive I don't know how to cope.

It's impossible not to fall for a guy who believes in you in every way. I feel so seen when I'm with him.

I should've known I couldn't keep this simple and uncomplicated.

The truth is I was a goner for him from the start, before we even began this situationship. The longer it's gone on and I've grown closer to him, the more I wonder if it's the same struggle for him.

It's not like anything has changed. Cole is still working under my dad and he's still my brother's best friend. Yet... I don't care as much as before. If there's a chance for us to be together, maybe we could work after all. If we do, I don't have to worry about any fallout tearing my family's relationship with him apart.

I'm afraid to bring it up in case it does cause a change, one that could end this before I'm ready to let go.

Naturally, I distract myself from one of my sources of over-thinking by focusing on the other—my business. I open my laptop again. I've had a browser tab open with an application to a maker's market at the end of the year for days. This would be a big step for me.

When I bought the camper, I imagined being able to do things like this if I was doing well with Sweet Luxe. It's not ready, though.

There's also the other worry—am I even good enough to apply? I've only been in business a few months. I thought it would be good to try, even if I didn't get in. I probably won't.

Trapping my lip between my teeth, I procrastinate on my phone. I end up opening my messages with Cole, then hesitate.

I listened when he needed me to. Of course I did—this is our safe space. It makes me feel braver than texting him for real. I always feel better when I talk to him.

CraftyCutie: Hey, are you busy?
MightyPuck: Never for you. What do you need?

It barely takes him any time to respond. A soothing warmth spreads around my heart.

CraftyCutie: Do you mind if I talk something out?

You don't even have to say anything. I just wanted somewhere to dump out my thoughts.
MightyPuck: Of course. I told you I'm always here to listen if you need me. Shoot.
CraftyCutie: You're the best. Have you ever been to a holiday market?
MightyPuck: Sure.
CraftyCutie: Cool, okay, so there's one happening near Boston at the end of the year. I'm thinking about trying to get in as a vendor.
MightyPuck: That sounds awesome.
CraftyCutie: It is! It would be, at least I think so. I've got the application, but I'm choking on filling it in. Whenever I start, I'm like, wait I'm a super small creator compared to the vendors that are accepted. Then I googled it and apparently this sucky feeling is imposter syndrome. I don't know, I think I'm just really in my head about it. But I still want to do it.
MightyPuck: Do you want my input, or would you prefer if I just listened?

I roll my lips between my teeth, fighting the tender affection that cuts through my stress. How does he know me so well?

I wish I could be wrapped in one of his fantastic hugs. They're the best. When I'm in his arms, it never fails to make me feel calm and balanced.

When did I get so reliant on him? It doesn't matter. All I know is I can't imagine not having him to lean on when I need him.

CraftyCutie: Solution-oriented suggestions are welcome.
MightyPuck: What's the worst that can happen if you submit and don't get in?
CraftyCutie: …nothing? I just continue on.
MightyPuck: But you tried, so that counts for something, right? You won't know if you don't try,

just like starting your shop. You can always apply
again.
CraftyCutie: Good point.
MightyPuck: And if you get in, that's amazing.
CraftyCutie: You're right. Will you stay with me
while I fill this in?
MightyPuck: Absolutely. Not going anywhere.

My heart swells. Knowing I'm not alone helps immensely. It's not as daunting to make my way through the application while he sends encouraging messages.

CraftyCutie: Okay… I'm gonna do it.
MightyPuck: Right here with you, sweetheart.

I rub my fingers together before hovering over the submission button. Just to be sure, I skim through the application again, adding a bit more to my bio section and reword a few other sentences. Blowing out a breath when I'm sure I'm ready, I send it off.

Popping out of my chair with a broad grin, I walk in a tight circle, shaking excess energy out with a flick of my hands. I bolt back to my phone as the adrenaline rush subsides to send him an update.

CraftyCutie: I submitted it!
MightyPuck: Good girl.
CraftyCutie: Thanks so much for doing this with
me. It was a huge help.
MightyPuck: I believe in you. Always will.

At a loss for the right words, I send a heart. He matches my response. I spend way too long staring at it, committing it to memory whether it means what I want it to or not.

TWENTY
COLE

April

THE ROAD to Frozen Four has been one of my proudest moments in life. More than my own days on the ice, because watching my guys dominate through the quarter and semifinals to this last game during the championship is thanks to all of the hard work we've put in together. I feel part of something profound as their coach.

If they win this, it's not just their win. It's everyone's who is part of Heston U's hockey program.

It's down to the third period. We're ahead by one. There's still far too much time left. Any wrong move and they could take this from us.

"Come on guys!" I clap for them, glancing at Steve. "How are you so calm?"

His shoulders shake with a laugh. "Years of practice. We're looking good. They need to keep this pace and not rush it."

I nod, turning my attention back to the rink. The printout of tonight's roster is rolled in my hand. It's falling apart from me taking out my stress on it.

We get two breakaways that don't result in anything. With minutes left, we're watching our boys fight the pressure while making sure the other team doesn't score.

"Don't rush! Keep it loose!" David yells.

One of the opponent's forwards has the puck deep in our zone and Brody's the one to stop their play.

He passes to his linemate, then Higgins sends the puck to Keller. He has impressive speed as he and Boucher tear up the ice ahead of our center. Even with their agility, Alex's pass to Theo is almost intercepted. Their defense gets a piece of it, but Theo controls it beautifully, getting around him with the evasive moves I taught him.

"That's how it's done!" I call.

Adrenaline courses through my veins as the puck flies across the ice to Keller. He charges toward the net and rips the puck into the crease. The goalie misses it.

Our entire bench is on their feet screaming. Theo collides with Alex, then two more Heston players in an emotional celly.

At the final horn moments later, our bench spills on the ice to surround their teammates. David and Steve are clapping. I feel like I'm underwater, then all the sound rushes in at once.

The arena is deafening and confetti falls from the rafters. A huddle of our guys hugging and celebrating shows on the jumbotron.

Holy shit, they did it. We won Frozen Four. Their season has ended with a huge success.

And my time with them has run out. The elation making me weightless fizzles, dragging me back to the harsh reality I've been avoiding.

Still stunned, I turn to shake David and Steve's hands. "Congratulations. They're unbelievable. I'm glad—honored, really—that I got to be part of it for a little while."

David laughs, exchanging a look with Steve. "Congratulate yourself. This is your win, too. You did good work, coach."

"Right. I learned a lot. Thanks for giving me a chance."

An uncomfortable laugh sticks in my throat. I wanted to talk to him about the possibility of staying, but it kept getting pushed off after playoffs to strategize for the championship tournament. I'll continue on as a coach, but it wouldn't be with this team, where I want to be. This was always supposed to be temporary from the beginning.

"Good. I expect the same next season," David says.

I don't follow. The confusion must be obvious because he chuckles and slaps my shoulder.

"Son, the trial period is over. The position is yours to keep if you're willing to stay on."

Static makes my mind blank while my brain struggles to process. I open and close my mouth, waiting for them to go *sike*.

"I told you it would've been better to tell him before we hit the road," Steve says. "You broke him."

David's amused expression falters. "You're going to stay with us, aren't you? That fresh perspective of yours is the edge we need in shaping our guys to be the country's top players."

"I—yes," I manage. "Yes. Sorry, I'm—I wasn't expecting this."

Steve shakes me by the shoulders. "Relax, kid."

Too many thoughts and emotions hit me at once to decipher. Happiness that I get to stay in Heston Lake. Eagerness to continue growing into someone this team can rely on.

Most of all, I want to tell Eve. I almost whip out my phone to tell her. The itch to race back to the hotel skitters throughout me.

"Thank you. This job is where I want to be."

"Good," David says.

Theo and Alex hoist the cooler of Gatorade, dumping it on the head coach. It drenches him and splashes on me and Steve. David barks in surprise. Their laughter is infectious. I swipe droplets from my face with a wide grin.

I reach for Cameron, dragging him into a hug. A laugh overflowing with relief slips out. Easton piles on by throwing himself at us. Then Theo, Alex, and Jake join. I've never felt closer to a team than this moment.

"Thanks, coach," Cameron says.

The others echo him until they're chanting *Kincaid! Kincaid! Kincaid!* I'm so proud of them, and fucking honored to be their coach.

After things wrap up, the post-game press conference goes by in a blur. David warns the players to behave when we finally release them. At last, I'm on my way to the hotel.

The minute I unlock my door, I call Eve on FaceTime. I'm so

swept up in tugging my tie free and riding the high of my good news that I don't think about it.

"Hey," she answers breathlessly when the video call connects. "Is everything okay?"

She blinks owlishly as if she just woke up, rubbing her face. I'm distracted for a moment, the buttons on my shirt left half undone because I'm wishing I could be there to wrap her in my arms.

"Yeah, it's all good." I'm out of breath and buzzing with energy. "I just got back to the hotel. We won and I wanted to tell you."

I can't wipe the grin off my face. Haven't been able to since David officially offered me the assistant coaching job.

"I saw. Well, I guessed it would be their game. I was watching the stream, but I fell asleep in the middle of third period when we were up in points."

My gaze softens. I sit on the bed, drinking her in.

"Sorry if I woke you."

"It's okay." She sighs with a sleepy smile. "It's nice to talk to you. See your face. Hear your voice."

"Yeah. I know what you mean." My throat bobs with a thick swallow. "After the game, I was talking to your dad. I wanted you to be the first person to hear it."

She's the only one who will get what this means to me. The only one who understands why I haven't put down roots.

She props herself up on her pillows. "What is it?"

"I'm staying in Heston Lake. He said the job is mine if I want it. Permanently."

She lights up. "Cole! That's amazing. Congratulations."

The same weightless feeling as earlier returns at her heartfelt response. I drag my fingers through my hair a few times.

"It's still sinking in that I get to keep being a coach for Heston U."

"You're awesome at it. I'm not surprised. Hey." She waits until I meet her gaze. "You've earned this."

Warmth expands in my chest until I'm full of her belief in me. I rub at it while I drift around my room.

"That really hits me. Thanks, Evie."

"I'm proud of you," she says softly. "You've worked your ass off to get here. And I'm really glad you're staying."

I stare at her. "Me too."

It's beyond gratifying to know I made this happen. I get to have everything I've been striving toward since I returned to town.

Well... Almost everything.

My gaze burns. Eve's mellow from sleep, hair mussed, and she's the most beautiful woman I've ever set eyes on.

There hasn't been a single second since we started this three months ago that I thought of her as anyone but herself.

Because there's no one in the universe that compares to Eve.

"Are you still tired?" It comes out smoky with desire.

She shakes her head, eyes hooding. I wet my lips slowly, gaze dragging up and down her as she stares at me. Her hand slides down the length of her body, out of frame.

We've been on the phone to fool around or sent photos and videos. It doesn't compare to being able to see her live, watching her reactions.

There's no fake names hidden behind a private conversation on a dating app. Our desires are plain as day.

This is all us.

She can't hide it if she wants me, and I'm done hiding it from her that she can have everything from me if she lets me give it to her.

"Hold on," she says.

Eve props the phone on a stand on her desk. She disappears from view, leaving me with her empty bed.

"What are you doing?"

"You'll see. By the way, that suit is really fucking hot on you. Thanks for the eye candy, but you should take it off."

My mouth quirks. I ditch the blazer and finish undoing the buttons. Her face appears at the edge of the frame to watch as I drag the shirt out of my pants, muscles rippling while I strip it off.

"Like what you see?"

She hums. "Yes."

"Why are you hiding from me?"

"I'm not."

She steps into view and immediately sends blood rushing to my cock. She's wearing my coaching jacket.

And nothing fucking else.

I forgot I lent it to her a few weeks ago. I'm not complaining because seeing her wear it makes me rock hard.

The zipper is open to her cleavage, the bottom skimming her bare thighs. She twirls for me, peeking over her shoulder when she displays my name across her back.

Her eyes gleam and she props her hands on her hips. "I thought this was fitting since you won tonight, coach."

"Fuck, Evie." It comes out gravelly.

"You like it, I see." Amusement laces her tone.

If I had her within reach, I'd grab a fistful of the jacket and drag her onto my lap. I'd need to open my fly and split her pussy apart on my cock until I filled her with so much come it leaks out of her.

"Fuck," I repeat. "I wish you were here."

"Me too," she admits.

"Is there anything under that?"

She shakes her head. My hand drops to squeeze my throbbing dick.

"Go to your bed. Spread those legs for me, sweetheart. I want to see that pussy taking your fingers while you're wearing my name."

Her lips part on a small gasp and her lashes flutter. She's quick to follow my directions. A rough groan tears from me when she leans against the wall and opens her legs for me. She's divine fucking perfection, on display, shyly peeking at me from the corner of her eyes.

"Evie," I rasp. "Look at you. You're so gorgeous, baby."

She shivers. "Can I see you?"

I look around, improvising a stand for my phone with the discarded shirt. Balling it up, I prop my phone against the lamp. Her focus is rapt as I unbuckle my belt and yank it off in one smooth move. She bites her lip at the *thwip* it makes.

The rest comes off until I'm standing naked before her. She takes her time admiring me. My cock makes her dart her tongue across her lip.

I wrap my fingers around the base, stroking it while we stare at each other. It's the most intimate, seductive experience. Neither of us are in a hurry.

"Touch yourself," I murmur. "Make yourself feel good."

I sit on the edge of the bed, bracing a hand behind me so she has a good view while I work my cock. She bites back a sigh of pleasure when she indulges herself with teasing caresses until she starts rubbing her clit. Her legs squeeze together.

"Keep them open. I want to watch your pussy get wetter and wetter until you make a mess all over your hand. It doesn't matter how far away I am, I'll still make you come. You're going to be my good girl and drench those fingers for me."

"Yes," she breathes.

Her thighs fall open again, wider. She pushes a finger inside herself. I grip my length harder, matching my pace to hers, picturing it's my cock sinking into her inch by inch. She adds a second, her hips rocking with the steady thrusts of her fingers.

Fuck, she looks so good like this. Face flushed, riding her fingers while wearing my jacket.

"You can take another," I croon. "Show me."

Her chest heaves with a strangled gasp. Her thighs tremble as she works a third finger in, breathing turning ragged.

She rips the zipper low enough that her tits spill free. Her teeth rake her lip while she plays with her nipple before it drops down to give her clit attention.

"So good for me, beautiful," I praise. "Love watching you fuck yourself."

"Cole."

My name on her lips sounds like heaven. It's a soft moan. I don't think she realizes she said it, too lost in her pleasure.

Possessiveness rips through me.

I want to be the only one that sees Eve like this. No one else gets my girl.

My name is the only one she'll ever whimper when she comes.

"Say it again," I grit out. "Say my name, baby."

Her hips falter and she cries out, "Cole."

My eyes are glued to her while I stroke my cock. "Are you going to come for me?"

She bites her lip, nodding. Those little noises she's making drive me closer to the edge.

"Look at me. Keep those eyes on me when you come."

Only look at me. I don't say it, but I mean it.

Her gaze collides with mine. It's hazy with desire. I know it a moment before her orgasm hits, watching it play out.

"Cole!" The plea breaks off in the sexiest cry of ecstasy.

"That's it, Evie. Does it feel good? I'm right there."

My cock swells thicker. I jerk it faster, all of my focus on her melting against her bedroom wall with my jacket slouching off her shoulder. I don't allow myself to take my eyes off her when my release hits. I bite back a groan as I shoot my load into my hand.

Once we've both caught our breath, we're grinning at each other. I can't stop staring at her as she sits up with a pretty blush.

"This is going to be on my mind every time I put that on," I say.

Her flush darkens. "If I give it back. I could keep it."

A rumble leaves me. "I like that idea, too."

We clean up and continue talking without any awkwardness. It's always easy with her.

I stretch across the bed. "How was your day?"

"Good. I spent most of it finishing a new design and packing orders."

"Did you remember to eat?"

She's silent for a beat. "Totally."

"You're about to make yourself a bowl of midnight cereal, aren't you?"

"Guilty," she mutters. "Thanks."

I chuckle. "Gotta make sure you're taking care of yourself when I'm not there to do it, sweetheart."

It takes three tries to say goodnight because we keep talking. I'm reluctant to end the call, but when we finally do I lay in bed with my arms folded behind my head.

This is wearing my resolve thin. Eve is the one who decided this should be no strings. I thought when we agreed to do it like this, we could both get what we needed but it isn't enough anymore.

Not by a long shot.

I want the real damn thing with her. Except sneaking around online has been a much lower risk than having an actual secret relationship.

It's agonizing that after all we have together hidden on our phones, I'm not able to wrap her in my arms and show the world how much I want her no matter the consequences.

After a few short months, I feel closer to her than anyone in my life. I can hardly imagine it without her at this point. She's the one I go to first when I want to talk about something. I've opened up to her about the things I haven't been able to admit to other people.

We've shared our dreams. Our fears. We've grown to be people we each lean on.

Eve doesn't realize it, but she shifted something between us by putting my coaching jacket on tonight. This isn't the game we started back in January. We're far past that. The rules have changed.

By wearing it, Eve told me she's all fucking mine. And once I have her, I'm not letting go.

Summer

NO BAD DAYS

TWENTY-ONE
COLE

May

Neither of us have said anything in the last few weeks about the night I called her on FaceTime. Almost a month has gone by and now the spring semester at the college is closing out. We talk online and see each other as much as we usually do.

I want to bring it up—so badly it's beginning to eat me up inside —but post-season has kept me busy.

Since David broke it to me that I officially have the job, I've thrown myself into preparations for training camp and researching new conditioning ideas I want to incorporate into our strategies to prove he made the right choice. Not only that, I want to give the guys every tool to hone their game.

Eve's also been elusive to pin down. I'd rather tell her how I feel in person than over text. Whenever I've tried to get her alone, her dad's nearby, or she has her friends over for craft night, or talks with Jess at family dinners to bounce product ideas off her. She's picked up more bartending shifts to help out with the nightly crowds now that the weather's nice and the semester's ending.

There's always someone else around, preventing the conversation I want to have about us.

The Landmark is packed tonight. It's wall-to-wall college

students celebrating freedom from their finals before summer break begins. Reagan zips around to take orders and deliver food.

She makes a stop by the far side of the bar with a service tray balanced on her shoulder. "Here you go, boys. And fries for the lady."

"Reagan!" Easton takes her tray for her to help out. "You're the best. Have we told you that lately? Because you rock."

"I do," she agrees. "I also accept cash tips and Venmo."

"We've got you," Cameron says.

I move my beer. She sets four baskets of wings in front of Theo, Alex, Easton, and Cameron, then gives the fries to Lainey Boucher, the quiet blonde tucked against Alex's side.

"Just because it's off-season doesn't mean you can blow off your nutrition plans completely," I warn. "Take it easy this summer before camp. If you show up with laziness, I'll put you through hell to get you back to peak performance."

"Coach," Theo complains. "Let us live a little."

"I'll be running extra miles for every cheat meal," Easton promises, two wings deep already. "It'll be nice when we get to move to the hockey house next semester. Running through town is nicer than doing it on campus or at the gym. Right, Reeves?"

Cameron's easy grin widens and they bump fists. "Upgrade. Our own kitchen. Choice bedrooms. It'll be nice as hell to live there instead of the athletic dorm."

"That's what you think." Theo snorts. "Good luck keeping anything stocked in the fridge, because Brody and Hutch eat everything in sight. If Keller wasn't there to remind them the carpet isn't edible, they'd go through that, too."

I down the rest of my drink, wondering how I ended up hanging out with my players. My gaze cuts across the room to the place I want to be: by Eve's side.

She's with her girlfriends. After she posted a photo online about being here, I decided to come instead of scrolling through her social media missing her.

Benson's out of town and it still feels weird to invite David out like an equal. When Alex and Theo spotted me, they dragged me into the corner they've taken over. I feel like an older brother chilling with them.

At least this spot gives me a good view of Eve.

The edge of my mouth quirks when she gestures with her hands, a bright smile curving her pretty mouth. She's telling her friends an animated story that has them in stitches.

When she joins them in laughter, a tender reverence stirs in my chest. I rub at it absently.

"You should go after what you want." Alex nudges my elbow, giving me a pointed look when his comment draws me out of my thoughts.

"What?" Shit, am I that obvious?

"Come on, coach." Alex glances from Eve to Lainey. "There's no point holding back. It just wastes time. Trust me."

Trust him. The twenty year old most discussed NHL draft prospect who is seven years younger than me. A short laugh shakes my shoulders.

Keller has a point, though. He's got the world ahead of him and he didn't hesitate when he started dating Theo's twin sister a few weeks before the regular season ended.

I don't want to waste anymore time when the girl I want is right across the crowded bar. My attention returns to her and her friends.

How do people handle feeling so much for someone else? I feel like I'm going insane.

Sort of sick to my stomach and exhilarated whenever we're in the same room. Fixated on little details like her choice of earrings, the rich brown to blonde strands of her hair catching the sunlight, and the way she smiles. Wondering what she's doing or how her day is when I'm in the middle of work. Wanting to spend even a few seconds with her because it's always better than when I don't get to be near her.

I never knew caring so deeply for someone could be so consuming. I guess I've only ever experienced superficial attachments because no one has ever made me feel the way I do about Eve.

There's no getting her out of my system. She's infiltrated every part of me. Changed me permanently because there's no going back to the guy I was before I grew closer to her.

Reagan takes the small stage in the corner not long after, transforming from the young bubbly sports bar waitress to a confident performer when she belts out a song. People cheer for her. The live music gets everyone on the dance floor, including Eve and her friends.

It's impossible not to follow her with my gaze. My focus is trained on her like a magnet. I tune out everything except her.

As she's dancing, she notices me. Her eyes light up, stealing my breath. She waves and I lift my beer in response.

Once she's aware of me watching her, she puts on a show for me. Every sway of her hips and arch of her back has me gripping the bottle tighter when she peeks at me from her periphery to see if she has my attention.

It's not even a question. If she's in the room, she's all that exists to me.

Every ounce of self-control keeps me leaning against the bar instead of closing the distance between us and showing everyone whose girl she is. I smirk when she drops low, rolling her body sensually to the song. If that's how she wants to play, I won't let her win the game that easily.

> **Cole**
> You shaking that ass for me, baby?

She checks her phone. Texting her instead of messaging her over DM doesn't seem to catch her off guard. Instead, the corners of her mouth curl and she flashes me another teasing look. Christ, I want to go over there and drag her against me.

> **Cole**
> You're so damn sexy. Keep it up and I won't be held responsible. You're making me want to come over there. Don't know what I want to do more, dance with you so you can feel what you're doing to me with my cock pressed against your ass or wrap your hair around my hand and put you on your knees for being so fucking tempting.

She reads it. I can't hear her laugh from here, but I recognize it's one of her low, seductive ones by her expression. She peeks at me through her lashes before sliding her hands over her curves with her head thrown back. Her movements drag the hem of her sundress up enough for a glimpse of her decadent thighs. She's touching herself everywhere I can't.

My jaw clenches when some guy dances up on her from behind, taking her display as an invitation. It wasn't meant for him.

Although she's startled, she doesn't deflect him right away. Instead, she slides me another tantalizing look while she dances with him. He's oblivious she's using him to make another man envious. I slam my beer down harder than I intend.

"You good, coach?" Cameron asks.

"Yeah," I answer without taking my eyes off Eve.

No. No I'm not fucking good.

Far from it because some other guy is putting his hands all over her and my jealousy is a raging inferno searing me from the inside.

Before I know it, I'm making my way over to cut in. I'm past temptation. She's mine and no other asshole should be dancing with her.

The guy takes her by the hips to yank her body against his, ignoring her when she pushes at his hands and throws an uncertain look at her friends as he moves further from the circle she was dancing in. My muscles seize at her clear increasing discomfort.

I lose the last shred of my patience at her exclamation when he tries to feel her up. With two strides, I'm at her side before her friends intervene, ripping his hand away from her body.

"Yo, what the fuck?" he barks.

"Get your hands off her if you plan on keeping them." He flexes against my strong grip, but I don't let up. "That wasn't a suggestion. You're done touching my girl."

Eve's wide eyes land on me, swimming with a mix of relief and shock. She has to know by now that if she's ever in trouble I'll always come for her.

She tries to move away while I have the guy distracted, but his free arm bands around her waist. White-hot fury sears through my veins.

"*Your girl* is busy. Fuck off, man," he says. "We're dancing."

My fingers dig in harder and I speak in a slow, dangerous tone. "I said let go of her. Now."

We're drawing a small audience from the people surrounding us. I dare him to fight me with my fierce glare. I'd love nothing more than to wrench his arm and break every bone in it for thinking he has any permission to touch her.

He stares me down for another beat, then loses his bravado, paling at the way I twist his wrist. He lets her go, stumbling back. It puts more pressure on the position I have his arm in. His eyes bulge.

"Okay, okay, chill, my guy!"

"Apologize to her," I growl.

"I'm sorry," he yelps.

I glance at her. Her breath hitches at my intense gaze. Realizing I'm waiting for her decision, she gives a small nod. My lips thin. I'd prefer if he made a better effort, but the sooner he's away from her the better.

"Go learn what consent looks like before you ever step foot in here again, asshole. I'll be watching."

When I release him, he pushes past the onlookers without a backwards glance. Once people realize the show's over, they resume dancing, jostling us. I shift to block her from being bumped.

Blowing out a breath, I take her hand and tug gently. "Come on, Evie."

She clutches it, her gaze searching. Whatever she reads on my face makes her stifle a faint, surprised noise. I barely make it out over the music.

This is like New Year's Eve at midnight all over again.

The need to kiss her scorches me from the inside out, far more intense than any of the countless moments I've wished to in the last four months.

It would be so fucking easy. An inch of distance to erase, then my mouth would claim hers for this whole damn bar, this whole damn *town* to know Eve Lombard is my girl.

She turns to her nearest friend that's watching us with interest. "I'm going to head out." She reaches for a hug without dropping my hand. "Love you guys."

"Call us this week," Caroline says with a pointed glance at me.

"Yup," Eve says brightly with a nervous laugh. "Definitely. Craft night soon? Okay, great, bye!"

She steps into me. I stare her down and lace our fingers. It makes her scrape her teeth over her lip.

"Let's go," she says.

I keep her close as I lead her to the exit. The group of hockey guys I was with are still in their corner, unaware of the source of the commotion and back to joking around with each other. Good. I don't need them noticing us right now.

Walking out of here holding her hand is enough to get residents talking in Heston Lake if they were able to spot us amidst the crush of college kids. Kissing her in The Landmark would've set the rumor mill on fire.

I only hope this isn't enough to get back to her dad or her brother, but I can't find the will to care about pissing them off more than I want her to know how I feel about her.

TWENTY-TWO
EVE

THE NIGHT AIR is balmy and thick with humidity. Cole doesn't let go of my hand and my heart drums harder with each step.

We reach his Bronco and he still doesn't break our connection. I'm hesitant to shatter this moment because it feels so good to have his hand wrapped around mine. He's the first to end the silence, squeezing my hand.

"Did he mean anything?"

He asks so quietly it breaks my heart. I swallow, trying to slow my racing heart.

"No," I promise. "Nothing at all."

The tense set of his shoulders eases. "Then tell me this..."

He corals me until I'm leaning against the car. The loss is palpable when he drops my hand. I swallow when he braces a palm beside me as if he's forcing himself to stay at arms length.

I hardly dare to breathe. "What is it?"

"Have you ever thought of me as Colin or as my actual self this whole time? You were dancing for me in there, weren't you? What about when I FaceTimed you and you put on my coaching jacket? Were you thinking about me as the fake AHL player then?"

His stare is piercing, as if he's able to see right through me. To see how much it affects me to be around him because it's impossible not to fall more in love with him.

I look away. He doesn't let me hide the truth from him, drawing my face back.

Cole's stare bounces between my eyes and his hand moves from cupping my jaw to loosely grasping my neck. My pulse thrums and heat rushes through me. I've wanted to feel his touch like this for so long. I can't believe this is real and not a vivid fantasy pulled from my dreams.

"I'm done fighting. Done standing around while other men think they can put their hands on you."

"Fighting what?"

My voice shakes when I force the question out, giving away how much I'm hoping I'm not imagining the taut band of tension between us stretched to its breaking point.

A muscle in his cheek twitches as he works his jaw.

"All of it, Evie. Every damn thing." His fiery gaze drops to my mouth. "Wanting you every fucking minute of the day. Telling myself I shouldn't cross this line more than I already have. Fucking needing you, baby."

My stomach bottoms out. Is this happening? I'd pinch myself, but I can't move.

"Cole." His name is a strangled plea.

He closes his eyes for a moment, drawing me closer by his hold on my throat. "Tell me you're tired of fighting it, too. I need to hear you admit it so I know I'm not the only one constantly going insane trying not to touch you and show you that you belong with me."

"Yes. For so long. Please."

The words are barely out before a groan of relief rumbles in his chest.

"Thank *fuck*."

Then his mouth is on mine. It's exactly what I wished his kiss was like at midnight on New Year's Eve. Hot and persistent. Dizzying.

I'm drowning in him. He devours my mouth with unwavering intensity. His hands are everywhere—in my hair, cupping my face, dragging down my sides to hold me tight while we make out.

Drunken laughter from somewhere far off in the parking lot filters through the haze of my desire enough to make me tear my mouth from his. Right. We shouldn't do this in the open.

We're at the back of the lot. It's darker, but that won't provide much cover if anyone comes close.

"Someone could see," I whisper.

He releases a rough exhale, scanning the area. "I can't wait." Rummaging in his pocket, he pulls out his keys and unlocks the Bronco. "Let's get in the back. It's roomier and the windows are tinted."

An electric thrill shoots down my spine. He gives my ass a smack when I climb in, then he follows me and drags me on his lap. With some maneuvering, I straddle him, shuddering at the hard ridge of his erection grinding against me through his jeans.

"Oh, fu—"

He grabs my nape and captures my mouth in another searing kiss before the curse leaves me. I rock my hips with his encouragement. He palms my ass, squeezing it with a groan when I suck on his tongue.

My clit throbs from the perfect friction and I toss my head back with a gasp, chasing my pleasure. A pleased rumble vibrates in his chest. He takes my hips and pulls me down harder on his lap while he kisses my bared throat down to my cleavage.

I seize when my core erupts with ripples of ecstasy.

"Look at you," he croons. "I can't wait to see you coming with my cock buried inside you, Evie. For-fucking-real this time."

I melt into him, seeking another kiss. The urgency between us hasn't ebbed. It builds back up within moments, both of us exploring what we couldn't have before. I glide my palms down his chest, then push beneath his shirt to feel his skin.

If I only get to have this tonight, I want to brand it into my mind so I never forget.

"Fuck me like this is the only chance you'll get," I say against his lips.

His grip on me flexes and he pulls back. "*No.*"

"No?" I breathe.

Cole pins me with a smoldering gaze. The way he's looking at me, as if I'm the most important thing in the world to him, lights me up.

"This isn't only for one night. That's not enough. Not even close."

My heart swells, rising into my throat. "It's not?"

"Hell no, Evie. As far as I'm concerned, we've been together this whole time without this part. Maybe we did it all backwards, but I'm done. I want you—all of you. I want you to be *mine*."

I've dreamed of hearing those words from him for so long, it feels surreal to have them growled against my mouth before he kisses me, fierce and all-consuming.

He pulls back too soon. I chase him for more, but he remains out of reach.

"Are you mine?"

I shiver at his hot breath ghosting across my lips. "Yes. God, yes. I've been yours for years."

His forehead presses to mine. "Good, because I'm not letting you go."

My eyes close at the force of my heart dancing with joy. His fingertips trail down my back and he buries his face in my throat.

"Kneel up for me."

I bite my lip when he reaches beneath my dress to drag my panties down. For a moment, he does nothing but pet my hips. I reach to touch myself. He stops me, gathering my wrists behind me with one hand.

He holds my gaze, bringing his free hand to his mouth to wet two fingers. Then he moves it between my thighs and finds my clit. My head falls back with a bitten-off cry when he pushes a finger inside my pussy.

"Look at me," he commands.

My attention snaps to him. He adds the second one, smirking when I move to meet his pumping fingers, silently asking for more. He keeps the same pace.

"I need to be inside you so bad it's killing me. I'm not holding back."

I stifle a moan. "Good. I don't want to, either."

"Later, I'm taking my time. Because I want to relearn you all over again, understand?"

I nod, past talking. "Please, Cole."

"I know. I've got you. I just want to make sure it's clear that this is only the beginning."

"Crystal," I choke.

His dimples pop out with his grin. Pulling his fingers free makes me cry out. He soothes me with a kiss before guiding me to turn around to face the front seat. I kick off my panties, stomach dipping at the sound of his zipper.

The insatiable frenzy that overcame us takes over once more. I'm panting with arousal when he positions his cock at my entrance. We both moan as I sink down his length.

"Fuck," he grits through his teeth. "Evie."

"I know."

We fit together better than I could've imagined. I move before he does, hissing at the feel of his cock filling me. His hands find my hips, lifting me before slamming me down.

"You feel like perfection," he utters reverently.

Neither of us can keep quiet despite our best efforts. I forget that we're fucking in the parking lot, too swept away in him.

There's no savoring this or going slow. It's not long before I'm bouncing, taking each of his sharp thrusts.

"Hold on to something," he rumbles.

My fingers scrabble for purchase on the headrests in front of us. He fists my dress and shifts his angle, hitting a spot that makes me go slack with pleasure.

"Oh god, don't stop," I whimper.

His arm slips around me, fingers seeking my clit and circling. It's too much. Heat spirals through me, cresting as he drives into me hard.

The orgasm steals my breath as the tight coil unravels in the most delicious way. He drags me against him as I ride it out. He keeps rubbing my clit and pushes his other beneath my sundress to knead my breast.

Euphoria-tinged wonder arrows through me because it's rare for me to come with a partner without extra stimulation to get there. He's so focused on me rather than himself, my body unravels easily for him.

"Who's fucking you?"

"You are," I manage breathlessly.

"Who?" he demands. "Who's cock are you making a pretty little mess on with your come?"

"Cole," I cry.

"Love the way my name sounds on your lips when I'm buried inside your pussy."

A strangled noise catches in my throat when he holds me against him and fucks me harder. My nails dig into his muscled arm when I clutch it.

"I'm close," he mutters against my ear.

My pussy clamps around him, unwilling to give this up yet. A harsh breath gusts from him.

"I didn't put a condom on. If we don't stop..."

"I know. I want it," I say. "Come inside me."

His grip flexes and his thrusts stutter to a stop. "Fuck. I've never —are you sure? There hasn't been anyone else, only you, but what about—?"

"We're okay." I twist to look him in the eye. "I'm done putting any barriers between us."

His forehead bumps my temple and his cock throbs deep inside me. I reach down to feel where our bodies connect.

"I want to feel you come," I murmur.

He groans, pace speeding up. My mouth falls open in a silent cry, eyes fluttering shut. His arms lock around me.

He goes rigid and I feel the pulse inside me when he fills my pussy with his release. It's a heady experience, setting off another burst of pleasure that races through me.

We're both fighting to catch our breath. His palms roam every inch of me.

"Are you okay? I didn't hurt you by being too rough, did I?"

"No. That was amazing."

We don't move right away. His fingers brush between my legs, stroking my sensitive skin stretched around him before he begins to soften.

He draws my hair to the side and kisses my neck. "Let's get out of here."

"Okay."

I grab my discarded underwear to clean myself with. He smirks, swiping them from me to stuff in his back pocket.

"Saving a souvenir?" I joke.

His tongue slides along his lower lip. "You started it when you hid that first pair in my office. I tore the whole thing apart after hours to find them."

Laughter bubbles out of me. "You're the one who told me to go take them off. I thought it was only fair to give them to you."

He grabs a handful of my hair loosely with a playful growl, drawing me into a kiss. Then he puts his shirt on and gets in the driver's seat, checking if the coast is clear before I dart from the back to the front.

Shooting me a crooked smile, he puts a hand on my leg before pulling out of the lot. I can't wipe the matching expression off my face.

We pass the street that leads to my apartment.

I swing my gaze from the window to his profile, marveling once again that this man I've dreamt of for so long is mine. I trace his knuckles. My stomach dips when his possessive hold tightens.

"You missed the turn back there."

"No I didn't." His thumb caresses my thigh before he tucks his hand deeper between my legs. "We're going back to my place. I'm tired of not having you next to me in bed."

TWENTY-THREE
COLE

HAVING Eve in my apartment knowing she'll be in my arms when we go to sleep settles something inside me. My chest expands with a soft, happy warmth watching her curiosity exploring my space.

There isn't much. The walls are sparse and I have a few boxes that are still unpacked from what little I brought with me. I didn't want to make it feel like home, worried I'd be leaving when the season was over. I haven't had the chance to make a dent in the last few weeks once I found out my job isn't temporary.

My hand hasn't left hers since we walked through the door. I let her lead me from room to room, fingers laced because neither of us is willing to stop touching.

The ride from the bar was like this, too. I held her leg and she wouldn't stop running her fingers over the back of my hand.

We're making up for lost time.

No more denying what we both want. No more pretending we're only friends.

Eve takes us back to the living room, almost pulling free from me. I draw her back, lifting her chin with a crooked finger to kiss her. It's unhurried and deep, learning the shape of her mouth, the glide of her tongue against mine. I commit all of it to memory.

I kiss her for the sake of kissing her, because I can. I don't take it further.

Of course I want her again. I don't think I'll ever have my fill of being inside her. We'll get there.

For now, this is everything I need. Just being near her. Being able to touch her as much as I've wanted for months.

We both end up smiling into the kiss. I'm not sure if I do it first or her. She giggles and I slide my arms around her waist.

"I can't stop kissing you," I murmur against her lips.

"I know. Me either."

She presses on her toes. I dip my head to make it easier for her to reach, resting my forehead against hers. I could stay like this for hours.

"You're mine," I marvel.

"I am. Which makes you mine, too." She sounds equally awed. Her voice drops to a whisper. "I've liked you for so long, Cole."

I hug her tighter. "You have? Since when?"

"Yes." She gives me a cute, self-conscious look. "I can't even remember when it started. God, I used to do anything to get you to smile at me. Past me would be flipping her shit right now to know I'm with you."

My mouth quirks and I study her tenderly. "Is that right?"

Eve hides her face against my chest. "Don't look at me like that, it's embarrassing."

"Like what? I'm just looking at my girl." I cradle her head. "You'd better get used to it because I plan to do this a lot."

"How is this going to work? We still have my dad and brother to worry about," she mumbles. "We can't just be like 'surprise we're together' at dinner. My dad would have a heart attack."

I walk backwards until I hit the couch, dropping down to bracket her with my knees. My fingertips graze the backs of her thighs, sliding up beneath her dress. She shivers at the contact.

Dating the head coach's daughter is still going to be a problem. Benson I think I could convince easier. I hope, anyway. My best friend might knock my lights out once I come clean about being with his sister.

If he's on my side, maybe I can win over David without losing my job for breaking his off-limits rule on Eve. As long as I continue proving I'm a good coach, I think this will work out.

"I'd say we've had damn good practice at sneaking around." I press my face to her soft stomach, peering up. "We can still keep us a secret for now until we figure out how to tell them. And I do want that."

"To tell them?" She cards her fingers through my hair.

"Of course. I won't hide how I feel about you forever, sweetheart. Don't you want to kiss me or hold hands whenever you want without worrying who sees? Dance with me at The Landmark instead of making eyes at me across the room? Sit next to me at dinner with your family without stealing glances?"

"Yes," she answers in a heartbeat.

I hold my hand up and she threads her fingers with mine. I bring them to my mouth, kissing her knuckles.

"Jess knows, sort of. She has our backs if we need someone to cover for us."

We'll worry about everything else later. I tug her to my lap. She comes easily, resting her head on my shoulder. I close my eyes. As long as I get to enjoy doing this with her now, I'm content.

"Are you hungry? I can make something, or we could watch a movie?"

She pulls back, covering her smile. "A movie? You're making me feel like I'm on my first date in college."

"I haven't actually dated a lot. Or had anyone I'd call a girlfriend. Things were usually more focused on getting a drink and getting naked." I squeeze my nape. "So I guess this is sort of in the first date territory for me. We're really doing all of this backwards, huh?"

She tilts her head with a fond expression. "A movie sounds great."

We pick something out. When I go into the kitchen to scrounge for popcorn, she follows me, hugging me from behind while I search the cabinets.

"You know you have a box in the corner that says plates," she points out.

"Yeah. I didn't bring much. That one's from my parents shipping extra stuff they thought I'd need. I only ended up unpacking the essentials."

She hums in understanding. "I want to get cozy. Can I borrow a shirt to wear?"

"Yeah."

I take her to the bedroom. She strips off her dress and unhooks her bra, standing bare before me. I rake my teeth over my lip. She doesn't hide. I saunter over, giving her curves a light caress. Her lashes lower in enjoyment.

Tearing my gaze from her, I pull a clean t-shirt and boxers from the drawer to give her. I also find a pair of loose shorts for myself. Pulling her panties from my back pocket, I set them on the dresser, shooting her a smirk.

I watch her in my periphery while she gets dressed, then change slowly for her benefit. She looks damn good in my clothes. My cock is half hard at the sight. If I make it through the movie knowing she's wearing my shirt and little else, it'll be a miracle.

"Comfy?"

She lifts the neckline to her nose. "Yes. I'm totally stealing this."

A rumble sounds in my chest as I bend and haul her over my shoulder. My arms secure her thighs and I grin at her squeal. She grips the back of my shirt, laughing.

"Are you ready to watch the movie? Because if not, I'm going to toss you on that bed and fuck you again."

"Mm, tempting," she sasses. "Let's watch the movie first."

Somehow it feels like we've been together forever and like everything is fresh all at once. I want to spend hours making her come, and also as long laying around with her head resting on my chest.

I just want to exist with Eve Lombard as the universe passes us by.

We settle on the couch with her nestled into my side, my arm draped around her shoulders. The film we pick out ends up being background noise.

I miss most of the beginning because I'm too focused on the talking we're doing with our hands. We're palm to palm, then entwining our fingers, exploring every bump and line.

She flips my hand to study my palm with gentle sweeping touches. I have no idea what's going on in the film because I'm captivated by her.

Halfway in, she gets up for water. Instead of returning to me, she pauses by one of the boxes I've been using as a side table. She plops down and moves the stuff on top to the floor before opening it.

"Want me to turn this off?"

She jolts, attention flying to me. "I'm sorry," she says automatically. "This is sort of bugging me."

I chuckle. "Don't be. I wasn't paying much attention to the movie, either. I was more interested in looking at you."

She blushes and climbs to her feet. I drag the box over to the coffee table so we can do it together.

"You're giving me a good excuse to finally unpack."

Her shoulders relax. "You don't mind?"

"No. Help me make this place feel more like a home?" I offer my hand.

She takes it with a relieved smile. "You always do that."

"What?"

"You get me. I never have to explain myself, you just roll with it. You don't get mad about my ADHD or think it's annoying when I'm distracted like this."

"Why would I? It's part of who you are. And if I haven't made it clear enough, I like everything about you, sweetheart."

She bumps her shoulder against mine. I take her chin and kiss her.

The movie continues while we make our way through the box. She finds spots for my hockey trophies and gives me shit for having some NHL merch for west coast teams when most of Heston Lake follows teams in the Eastern Conference in addition to their support for the Heston U Knights. I wrestle with her until I get her into one of the jerseys I collected while I was away at college and tell her how cute she looks.

It's late when we strip down to go to bed, but we don't sleep right away. We lay awake talking. It doesn't matter that we've had nights like this talking through the dating app or on the phone in the last few months.

This is better. She's exactly where she belongs.

I have her in front of me, my leg tucked between hers. The sweet scent of her shampoo fills my lungs and it will be all over my sheets.

In the middle of talking, we end up kissing. Then she pulls on my arm at the same time I give in to the urge to roll on top of her. She opens her thighs for me and I settle my cock against her, grinding against her until she has her legs wrapped around me.

"Need you," she begs.

When I slide inside her it's my own personal heaven.

This time we go slow. I take her hands and pin them above her head with our fingers threaded together. I swallow each gasp as I hit her nice and deep. The flutter of her pussy when she comes is too fucking good. I drop my forehead to hers, a groan scraping my throat as I finish.

Afterwards, I have Eve wrapped in my arms. She moves her ass back so it's against me and I drag her close enough to feel her heart beating in time with mine. I bury my face in the crook of her shoulder, more content than I've ever been in my life.

TWENTY-FOUR
EVE

WHEN I STOP by campus for my usual lunch with Dad two days later, the rink is empty. I find the team gathered in a room near the coaching staff offices. I squeeze through the guys standing at the back and decline with a smile when Theo offers me his seat.

They're wrapping up their final team meeting of the semester by reviewing game tape to break down their season performance. A projector screen shows a hockey arena. It looks like they're up to their Frozen Four win.

"See this rebound?" Cole points to the play when it pauses. "Here. This moment."

It doesn't matter if I've watched Dad coach my whole life. Cole's passion for this fills me with delight.

He notices me, lips twitching up at the corners for a split second. I give him a subtle wave. Dad thinks it's meant for him.

Cole clears his throat. "Higgins gets it to Adler, but it was luck. If this was controlled and fluid, more windows of opportunity open up."

"We scored a goal right after that," Brody says. "Nice one, rookie."

He bumps fists with Easton across the table.

"Don't let it go to your head. The minute you do, your game gets cocky," Dad warns. "The next win is never guaranteed. Wins mean nothing if you're not doing the work it takes to earn them."

241

"Keep yourselves loose over break," Cole says. "Your individual conditioning regimen recommendations are on the table. Make sure you grab it on your way out before you clean anything you need out of the locker room. We'll see you back here for training camp in August."

The team jumps up in high spirits with their summer upon them. In their hustle, Cole slips through the room and snags my wrist without making eye contact. I bite my lip around a smile and sneak out with him while Dad's busy talking with Steve.

We follow the flow of players, falling behind. Then he pulls us into the equipment room and locks the door.

"No one should need anything in here," he says. "Hi."

I step into him, resting my hands on his abdomen. "Hi."

He cups my elbows. "That's it. That's all I brought you in here to say. I had to steal you away for myself for a minute."

Husky laughter leaves me. "You're not gonna kiss me?"

"Risky." His brow lifts.

"That's an interesting way to say fun," I sass.

He grasps my waist, walking me back against a shelf. His head dips, lips meeting mine. It heats up from sweet to passionate, neither of us able to slow down.

"Eve," he says reluctantly against me.

I don't respond, kissing him until his composure fractures. His grip flexes on my waist.

"We shouldn't be doing this. Not here. We could get caught."

He's right. He's so right, and yet—

"Fuck it. I don't care."

If I don't touch him in the next minute, I'll combust. My palms slide up his chest, bumping the whistle hanging around his neck.

Cole groans, dragging me back in for another filthy kiss, fingers digging into my hip while I clutch his coaching jacket. His words come out ragged and hot against my lips.

"You drive me insane."

"The feeling is absolutely mutual."

A laugh that's more of a gasp escapes me as his mouth moves down my throat with rough, branding kisses that could easily leave his mark of what we're doing all over my sensitive skin. I tilt my head back to give him better access.

One of his hands slips under my top to fondle my breast, the other pushing down the back of my shorts to squeeze my ass. I'm as ravenous as he is, seeking any inch of skin within reach. Then his mouth claims mine again.

It's been like this any moment we've been near each other since the other night at The Landmark. I don't know how two people could be so consumed with an unending need to touch one another, but that's how we are.

We both jump when the door handle jostles and unlocks before we have a chance to react. It swings open right as Cole yanks his hands from beneath my shirt and inside my shorts, but there's no hiding what we were doing.

"Umm." Easton grins like an idiot, holding the key.

Cameron has the decency to avert his eyes, smacking his friend's shoulder. Cole recovers first and shifts in front of me.

"You didn't see anything," he warns.

"We saw nothing," Easton parrots immediately, lifting his hands in surrender. "We know nothing."

"I'm serious," Cole says. "Not a word to anyone."

"Got it, coach," Cameron replies.

"Got what? Do you see something other than equipment in here, Reeves? I'm just getting more tape for my stick to take home with me over summer break." Easton winks. After a beat, he adds, "I actually need the tape, though, if you could just—"

"Blake." Cole sighs in exasperation.

I find it on a shelf by my elbow and toss it to him. He salutes us, then lays a hand over his heart.

"For real. Your secret's going to the grave. We won't let you down. I'd say have a good summer, but, uh, looks like you've got that covered."

"Dude," Cameron hisses.

"Get out of here," Cole says.

"Going. Here." Easton tosses the key to Cole and backs away.

Cameron covers a snicker, dragging his teammate off by grabbing his t-shirt. The door shuts. Cole wastes no time locking it again, pocketing the key.

After he makes sure they're gone, he braces his hands on the shelves on either side of me and hangs his head with a groan.

"Feel my heartbeat."

I place a hand against his firm chest. His heart drums hard.

"What if that had been Steve? Or your dad?" he mutters.

"That's half the thrill," I tease.

He puts a hand at the small of my back to tug me against him, dipping his face to press a smirk to my throat.

"I'll show you a thrill."

"Please do," I encourage.

He mouths at my skin, turning my stifled giggle into a gasp.

I end up missing lunch with Dad, texting him an excuse about needing to leave.

* * *

Cole gave me the key to his place when we were sneaking around at the training facility earlier. Yesterday, I snuck home early after our first night, then ended up back in his bed last night. My calendar reminders are piling up with this week's tasks that I keep putting off to spend time with him.

It's still sinking in that Cole Kincaid is my boyfriend. I never thought matching with him on the dating app would lead us here.

I'm waiting for him with a pizza by the time he makes it home from work. He finds me in the small kitchen, pausing in the doorway. I'm so happy to see him, I'm unable to control my beaming expression. He eyes me like I'm the more enticing dinner.

"This is the best thing to come home to," he says.

"Hungry?"

His devastating grin turns wolfish. "Don't ask me that unless you like cold pizza."

"Who doesn't like cold pizza?" I trace the low neckline of the t-shirt dress I changed into before coming over. "Cold pizza is the best."

With two strides, he's on me. His mouth collides with mine and he boosts me onto the counter. My knees open to accommodate him. His fingers thread in my hair, tipping my head back as he kisses down my throat.

Heat pulses between my legs when he lowers himself to his knees. When his hot breath hits me through my panties, air gusts past my lips. He hums, slipping a finger beneath them, stretching the material as he slides it up and down.

His green eyes flicker to mine, darkening. He pulls my panties off. I spread my legs wider and he hooks my knee over his shoulder.

"I'm starving," he says before his mouth covers my pussy.

It's not quite like the scene we recreated from my book, but it's just as arousing.

My hand buries in his hair and my mouth falls open with a cry. It feels amazing. He caresses my thigh and hip as he devours me.

"Oh, oh yes. Like that, please," I beg between gasped moans.

"Wanted to taste you all day after you left," he croons against me.

My chest heaves and tremors of pleasure race through my limbs. My core clenches, then erupts with wave after wave of ecstasy.

"Oh god, oh my god, I'm coming," I whimper when he doesn't stop.

He takes me right into another orgasm before the first one fades, his mouth relentless on my clit.

"Cole," I wail. "You're—oh!"

He growls against me in satisfaction. My eyes roll back from the stimulation to my sensitive pussy.

At last, once he's melted my brain and my body, he sits back on his heels with a smirk. His chiseled jaw glistens with saliva and my wetness.

My stomach dips when he swipes the heel of his hand over his mouth. It's one of the hottest things I've ever seen.

"You taste fucking delicious when you're crying out my name and coming all over my face, baby."

It takes me a second to form words. "You broke me I think."

I give him a thumbs up. He chuckles, helping me down from the counter. My legs are still shaking and I sway against him. His arms cinch around me.

"Need some water?"

"Yes." My desire flares at the bulge in his jeans. "What about you?"

He kisses the top of my head. "Later. Don't want you to be sore or have you forgetting to eat again because we're too busy fucking. I'm taking care of you."

My stomach somersaults. "Okay."

"Good girl."

The praise makes me shiver. He grasps my chin, giving me an affectionate expression before kissing me.

I put my underwear back on while he gets my water thermos from the table and cleans off the counter. I crack open the pizza box.

"Still warm," I say.

He steps behind me, massaging my nape. "Didn't spend enough time with my tongue buried in your pussy, then."

I twist to swat at his chest. We take our pizza slices into the living room and put on a random show while we eat.

I end up getting sucked into it by the end of the first episode. I brought some new earrings for my summer collection that need their hardware. Cole pulls my legs across his lap while I craft, absently stroking my calf.

On a whim, I grab my phone to take a short behind the scenes recording. Once it's finished, I end up checking my email out of habit. My eyes bulge and my stomach drops off a cliff.

"Oh my god." My hand flies out blindly, latching on to him.

"What is it?"

Tears prick my eyes. "I got in. Look!"

He takes my phone, scanning the acceptance message for the maker's market he encouraged me to apply for. The corners of his mouth curl and he shakes my leg.

"Good job, Evie. This is amazing. Congratulations."

I squeal, falling back against the cushions, kicking my legs. He chuckles, then drags me by my ankle until I'm partially across his lap, lifting me with an arm beneath my shoulders.

"Look what you can do when you put yourself out there," he murmurs against my lips before kissing me.

I sway into him, fingers tangling in the hair at his nape. We stay snuggled like that when we part, my mind brimming with ideas as we watch TV.

An hour later, there's a knock at the door. He checks his phone and mutters a curse.

"It's your brother. He just texted me."

"Oh, shit. Give me a second. Make sure he doesn't see the two plates in the sink."

I sweep my craft supplies into my tote bag, not bothering with packing them up nicely. Hopefully the clay popsicles survive. I nearly collide with Cole when he's coming back from the kitchen.

He takes me by the shoulders. "Should I get him to leave?"

"No, it's okay." I press on my toes to give him a quick kiss. "He'll get suspicious if you keep dodging him when he wants to hang out."

"I could tell him I have a girl over," he suggests. "Which is true."

"Yes, but then it could backfire."

"How?"

"He might want to meet her. I'll hide, then you can sneak me out."

He sighs, tangling our fingers. "I don't want you to go."

"I don't either. But I actually have a bunch of store orders I need to pack up before tomorrow. They were on my to-do list and I pushed them off to go out with the girls for drinks, and then..." I trail off, leaning into him. "Someone has barely let me leave his bed for the past two days."

His lips twist ruefully. "Fair enough."

Benson knocks again, yelling through the door. "Dude, are you dead or just taking a shit?"

Cole rolls his eyes. "I love him but I also kinda want to kill him right now."

I'm frozen by indecision on where to hide for a moment until he nudges me in the direction of the bedroom. I hurry into his closet and text Jess an SOS.

It's difficult to hear clearly. Benson makes a commotion when he comes in. I only catch half of it, relieved when he mentions a beer run. Jess answers and agrees to be my getaway ride. The walk isn't far, but it's quicker and erases any risk of my brother spotting me walking through town while they're out.

Cole opens the closet, startling me. He gestures to the door with a nod of his head.

"We're leaving. Told him I needed my phone charger," he whispers.

"Perfect. Jess is going to give me a lift."

He grasps my throat in a loose hold, dragging me in to steal a kiss. I clutch him, reluctant to leave the happy bubble we've formed in his apartment to spend the night alone in my own bed.

His forehead rests against mine. "What about tomorrow night?"

"Family dinner," I remind him.

"Damn it. Right. At least I'll get to see you."

"I'll sneak over after."

"Okay." He kisses me again. "Good luck with your orders. You'll get them all done."

"Cole! You ready or what, man?" Benson shouts from the hall.

We both stiffen when his voice grows closer. Cole throws a frown at his door.

"Relax, I'm coming!"

"Bye," I breathe.

He gives me one last smoldering look before leaving with my brother. I wait until the apartment goes quiet, then text Jess that I'll meet her outside.

Before I go, I steal one of Cole's shirts. If I can't sleep in his arms, at least it will feel like he's close if I wear his clothes to bed.

TWENTY-FIVE
EVE

June

AFTER THREE WEEKS, the giddy excitement of being with Cole hasn't worn off. Technically, I suppose we've been together much longer than that. It all still feels new—nerve-wracking and amazing all at once. When we're alone together, he lights me up with every word, look, touch.

Being with him is better than I ever dreamed. He makes me so happy. I don't care if we have to sneak around. It's worth it. *He's* worth it.

Then my mom gets one of her ideas in her head. She's impossible to persuade otherwise once she's thought one up. Maybe I get it from her because I can be the same.

Except this isn't about when seasonal decorations should go up or why she's stubbornly a Rangers fan in a family of Bruins diehards.

She believes she's doing me a favor by springing a surprise blind date on me today. All the hints she's been dropping this week make sense. I thought it was weird she was asking me if I met anyone lately.

I couldn't exactly tell her, oh yeah, I'm totally getting my insides rearranged on the regular by Cole.

She also wasn't listening when I tried to say thanks but no thanks, insisting how much it would mean to her friend if I met her nephew.

Eventually, I gave up, deciding it would be easier to go and tell her it didn't work out.

Cole finds it funny. His exact words when I called him about it were, "You don't need my permission to go out. I know you're my girl, and you know it. You'll be in my bed tonight, not any other man's."

Then he made me stay on the phone with him while I showered and used the vibrator he bought me to make me come three times as I promised I was only his.

While I got ready, I had him on FaceTime listening while I worked out how I'm going to let down my blind date. He offered to be my escape plan.

When I walk into The Landmark, I steel myself. Stalling for time, I wander over to the side of the bar where Mr. Boucher has let me display some of my stickers for sale along with a collectible bar coaster I designed just for him. I also have my own small shelf at the bookstore for my earrings and handmade bookmarks, plus a spot at Clocktower Brew House, too. It's surreal and heartwarming to see my things supported by so many in Heston Lake.

Maybe Cole and I should work on the camper again. It's been on hold for a while when my orders boomed from social media and him getting busy in the spring with the championship tournament.

"Are you Eve?"

I spin. The unwanted blind date is at a table for two by the wooden columns in the middle of the bar. I have my escape plan at the ready as I go over.

"Hey. I'm Dylan," he says.

He's a nice-looking guy with short hair and an open smile.

I hover by the table, braving the awkwardness of the sentence I practiced on the way over. "Listen, I just want to let you know this isn't going anywhere. My mom set this up and wouldn't get off my back about it, but I'm not actually—" I wave my hands as I stumble over the words. "I have a boyfriend, she just doesn't know it."

Dylan blinks for a second, then gives me a friendly smile. "Thanks for letting me know. In that case, I have a confession, too. I'm also not looking for anything out of this."

I unwind the tense set of my shoulders. "Oh. That's great."

"I'm just making my aunt happy while I'm visiting her before I go back to Boston. It's her mission in life to set me up. She doesn't understand why I haven't settled down yet."

I droop against the table with a relieved laugh. "Oh my god, same. My mom's been dropping hints about me finding someone to 'cheer me up' after my last relationship ended. It was faster to come out to meet you and get it over with to appease her before she went into full-blown matchmaking mode than explain to her I'm seeing someone secretly."

"Listen, if you want to walk out the door right now, I'm cool with that. Here, you can even splash a beer on me." He frowns. "Can I have another sip first? This is really good."

I smile, recognizing the light hue as one of Benson and Jess' summer ales. "It's fine. I'll stay for a drink."

"As friends," he says.

Once I order, we end up chatting about the dating scene and general life struggles post-college. He shares that, like me, he took longer to graduate from college because he kept switching majors.

I plant my hands on the table and lift a brow, being dramatic. "So why aren't you settled down, Dylan? Don't you know by twenty-five you should be married, have a house, and you're losing the game if you haven't thought about kids by now?"

He snorts. "My aunt never lets me forget it whenever I'm in town. She's worse when it comes to my sister and can't accept she's choosing to live her life child-free."

"There's nothing wrong with that."

He shows me a picture of both of them on his phone. "We're more invested in our careers. Me especially since I felt like I needed to catch up."

"Yes! I totally know what you mean. If there's anything I've figured out, it's that none of us know what we're doing. It's pretty reassuring. Except the times I'm going through it feeling like I'm the only one who doesn't have my shit together."

We toast to not knowing what the hell is going on in our twenties.

Cole and Benson arrive shortly after, spotting me while I'm laughing at the story Dylan's telling. Cole's features harden for a moment, then he veers for our table with my brother in tow.

"Well, look who it is." Benson sidles to me and messes with my hair before I bat him off.

"Shocker, you guys found me at the most popular place to go out for a drink within town limits," I deadpan.

Cole edges closer, looming over Benson's shoulder. I can't help but feel like he's sizing Dylan up. While the others are distracted, I slide my hand beneath the table to brush against his hip out of sight. He inches toward me.

I swallow at the memory of his voice echoing off my shower tiles earlier while he controlled the toy I had inside me. With my brother here, I can't introduce Cole as my boyfriend.

Benson glances between me and Dylan. "What's up, I'm Eve's brother."

"Dylan. Word is, my aunt's friends with your mom." He shakes Benson's hand, then turns to Cole. "Are you Eve's brother, too?"

Cole and I both freeze. He shakes his head.

"No. I'm Cole. Friend of the family."

"You'd think it from how he acts." Benson snickers and slaps Cole on the back. "But nah, we just grew up tight. He's basically family at this point."

"Want to move to a bigger table?" Dylan suggests.

"We don't want to interrupt. Have fun." Benson smirks, winking at me. "Come on, Cole."

He thinks he's being helpful without realizing he's wrong. On their way to the bar, Cole takes his phone out.

Mine lights up at my elbow with his text. I duck my head to keep from looking his way.

"Sorry, that's my boyfriend."

Dylan waves a hand. "Go ahead."

Cole
Ready for your out?

Eve
He's not so bad. He's not interested in a blind date either and offered to let me toss a beer in his face.

Cole
Say when. I'll be waiting for you.

I send him a heart emoji, peeking in his direction. He's joking with Benson. No one would suspect we're talking to each other.

"If you need to go, it's cool."

I sip my half-finished drink. "I can hang. He's, er, out right now. We have plans later."

We go back to talking for a bit. When I bring up my online store, he's interested in how it works being my own boss. I get wrapped up in talking about it.

My train of thought disappears when I notice Cole has texted again.

> **Cole**
> Every minute since I walked in here I've wanted to come over there and kiss you until you're melting against me.

> **Cole**
> Thinking about the first night I fucked you in the truck. The way you sank down on my cock and rode me. No one knows what pretty sounds you make for me.

> **Cole**
> Be my good girl and meet me in the bathroom. I want to fuck your pussy and fill it with come.

A flush spreads over my cheeks. I find Cole watching for my reaction, leaning against the bar with a smug expression. I slide my thighs together to alleviate the ache of desire he's stirring.

"Sorry, what was I saying?"

"About starting your own business," Dylan supplies.

"Right. I'll get back to that in a second, let me just..." I split my focus to text Cole.

> **Eve**
> Are you getting jealous after all?

> **Cole**
> Just telling my girl what I want to do to her right now. Why, is it distracting you?

> **Eve**
> I'm not even dressed sexy right now. I literally put no effort into this outfit.

> **Cole**
> What you're wearing never matters to me. You're always sexy, and I always want you.

I bite my lip around a smile. If he wants to tease me, I'll tease him back. It's fun to rile him up knowing we get to go home together.

> **Eve**
> Hmm, I'm not feeling particularly distracted. I think you'll need to try harder.

> **Cole**
> Oh yeah? Does it get you hot when I send you dirty texts?

> **Eve**
> You know it does. Who will break first, you or me? Winner gets to do whatever they want tonight.

He doesn't respond, but I feel his attention on me when I get up to order a second drink while Dylan's using the restroom. My hips sway for his benefit when I pass. I catch his eye before licking the salt rim on my cocktail. Heat flares in his gaze.

He tracks me back to my seat. I make a show of sucking on an ice cube before Dylan returns.

The game goes back and forth with me putting my best effort into appearing unaffected by the texts he sends. I can pass off the spreading tingle of warmth on the alcohol, but I can't pretend the messages aren't getting to me. He knows exactly what to say to drive me wild.

> **Cole**
> Keep squirming, baby. It won't help if you cross your legs.

> **Cole**
> I'm what you need. Your whole body is begging for me.

> **Cole**
> Your pussy wants to take every inch of my cock, doesn't it? I can see how hot and achy you're getting from here.

> **Cole**
> Ready to break yet? I promise to make it better. I'll make you feel so good tonight.

Licking my lips, I risk a glance toward the bar. He stares at me over the rim of his glass, nodding at whatever Benson's saying.

"I'll be back. I'm going to run to the bathroom," I blurt.

"Want to order another drink?" Dylan asks.

"Um, you can. I—oh, shit." I nail my hip by clipping the column in my rush to hop down from the high chair. When he jumps up, I stop him. "Oh, don't worry. I'm good. Just bumped it."

Dylan sits. "Okay."

I hurry to the bathroom to splash cool water on my face.

> **Cole**
> Are you touching yourself in there? I want to come find you and feel how wet you are for myself.

I choke back a hazy gasp, glad there's no one else in the room. My thighs clamp together against the insistent pulse of heat in my core. Teasing him has been fun, but I'm tapping out. He wins. I'd rather be in his arms right now than sitting across the bar unable to be with him in the open.

> **Cole**
> Leave your date.

> **Eve**
> I thought we agreed this wasn't a date?

> **Cole**
> Go home. I'll make it worth your while because I'm going to spend all night reminding you that you're mine.

He's too good at the whole jealous boyfriend thing, and I'm a little too turned on by it when he gets like this.

When I head back into the bar, I meet Cole's eye on the way over to Dylan. His charming victorious smile steals my breath.

"Hey, I'm sorry, but I'm going to go. My boyfriend called," I say. "Thanks for a fun time."

Dylan shakes my hand. "It was cool meeting you."

"Likewise. Enjoy the rest of your visit with your aunt. And good luck putting your foot down about her setting you up on dates you don't want."

"You too."

I wave my phone. "Already on it."

On my way out, I tell Mom bummer, we aren't interested in each other, then warn her off setting me up again.

I feel the weight of Cole's gaze until I reach the door. I glance back, catching his eye with a smirk before texting him that I'll be waiting for him at home.

TWENTY-SIX
COLE

As MUCH AS I want to leave with Eve—hell, as much as I want to toss her over my shoulder so there's no doubt she's mine—I have to wait.

Because we're still a secret.

When she explained her mom set her up on a blind date, I didn't have a problem with it. I trust her.

I didn't expect to get so jealous seeing the other guy make her laugh. The rational side of me recognizes that she's not laughing the way she laughs with me, more like how she does with the guys on the hockey team or around her friends.

It's not that I'm worried she'd be interested in him or that he could steal her from me, my problem is that I don't get to do the same thing with her.

I count the minutes, debating with myself what an acceptable amount of time is before I leave her brother to follow her home.

Once Eve begins sending me sexy selfies of her waiting for me, missing a different article of clothing in each photo, I'm done. She doesn't get down to her bra before I let her know I'm on my way.

"I'm beat. I'll see you later, man."

"What? I thought we were hanging out," Benson protests. "You're always running off on me lately. What's the deal, are you seeing someone?"

My gut clenches. "No."

"Have one more drink."

"I see your mug at dinner with your family twice a week, minimum." I cover his face with a laugh and give him a light shove. "You'll live."

Once my tab is paid, he messes with me by trying to wrestle before I leave. I snort, winning by going for the spot he's ticklish. It always worked when we'd screw around in the locker room before practice and games. He howls, pushing off me.

"Still can't beat me," I joke.

"Cold, brother. Cold!"

He clutches his side, calling after me without any heat. I wave without looking back.

It only takes me five minutes to drive home instead of the usual ten. She's waiting for me when I come through the door, leaning enticingly in the hall a few feet out of reach in only a bra and panties.

"Finally," she sasses.

"I had to get away from your brother first," I mutter, more focused on drinking in the sight of her.

I toss my keys at the bowl she made for the table near the entrance, missing by a mile. They drop to the floor. We both ignore them.

"You win, so you get anything you want."

"Easy. You're what I want. Just you."

She tilts her head. "I thought you said you'd make it worth my while if I left?"

I'm a fucking goner whenever she does the cute little head tilt. There's too much I want at once.

Keeping myself planted in place, I reach behind my head to tug my shirt off. Her eyes brim with desire, admiring my physique. I drop it, gaze locked on her.

"I'm a man of my word, sweetheart. Come here."

She bolts at me with a giggle, jumping up. I catch her, mouth descending on hers as I press her back to the wall. My fingers dig into her thighs and a groan tears from me as she writhes.

"You're still wearing too many clothes," she says between kisses.

"Let's fix that."

I carry her through the apartment, kicking the bedroom door wider. When I toss her, she bounces on the mattress. She ditches her bra while I flick the button open on my jeans, shoving them down with my boxers in one go. My gaze rakes over her as I stroke my cock.

"You can do anything you want with me." Her fingertips run over her body enticingly. "You can kneel over me and fuck my mouth. Flip me over and fill my pussy. Use me."

Jesus. My grip tightens around the base of my dick to ride out the heat.

"Don't move. I know exactly what I want first."

The bed dips as I join her. Her lashes flutter when my touch skims up her leg, delving between her thighs to graze her pussy. Her panties are soaked. The corners of my mouth curl. I take them off and settle between her legs, kissing a path across her skin until I reach her slick folds.

"You're so wet," I praise. "Is this for me?"

"Yes," she breathes.

I lower my mouth to swipe my tongue through her folds. She shivers, already so responsive.

"Oh, you need to come badly, don't you?"

"Please."

I've teased her enough tonight. I'm ready to devour her.

She moans as I lick and suck the way she likes, working her slowly until she begins to buck beneath me. When she's ready for more, I give it to her, sinking two fingers inside. They slip in easily from how aroused she is. I pull them out shortly after and she cries at the loss.

"Look at this pretty cream all over my fingers." I hum, sucking them clean before fucking her with them again. "You taste so good."

She reaches for me, scraping her nails across my shoulders as she tries to tug me up. I catch her wrist and thread our fingers, placing a kiss to her clit.

"I want to touch you," she whimpers. "Make you feel good, too."

"This isn't about me right now, Evie. I'm erasing every man who looked at you tonight and thought they could have you."

As I speak, I crawl over her, bracing my arms on either side. The hitch in her breath makes her hardened nipples graze my chest.

"No one wanted—"

"They did. I'll spend all night reminding your body why it's mine, sweetheart."

"It knows," she says, half laughing, half gasping in pleasure when I shift to circle my tongue around her nipple. "Oh god, Cole, please. I'm only yours."

"That's right, baby. Say it again."

"Yours," she whispers like a prayer.

"Can't hear you."

I kiss a trail down her body. With each one, she repeats it louder until she screams it when my head buries between her legs again.

Her plush thighs clamp on my head when she's close to coming. My tongue swirls around her clit while I caress her hip with my free hand. I read every sound she makes and the way she clenches my fingers to devour her the way she needs.

"Oh! I'm—ah!"

Her body contorts, hips bucking against my jaw, greedy for her pleasure. I oblige my girl, giving her what she wants until she whimpers and pushes me off when it's too much. I lift my head to watch her. She's trembling, chest heaving as she gasps with tiny moans. I love taking her apart like this.

"You like when I make you come with my mouth, sweetheart?"

"Yes. So good," she mumbles.

She's the most stunning woman I've ever been with. I want to worship her luscious body every minute of the day. *Cherish* her. Eternity won't be enough for me.

I love having her bare, but an idea pops in my head. I drag myself from her momentarily to reach for one of her toys and the jacket draped over a chair in the corner.

"Put this on for me." I toss it to her.

Still breathless and languid from her orgasm, she sits up. Her mouth stretches in a pleased grin when she slips her arms through the sleeves.

"Your coaching jacket? Why?"

"Because I like seeing you wearing my name." I return to the bed, pinning her to it with a kiss. "Looking like you're mine."

"Possessive," she teases.

"Yes." I nip her bottom lip. "You like it."

"I do. I like everything about you."

I hum in satisfaction. "You like me, huh? Show me."

She twines her arms around my neck to draw me into a kiss. I knead her waist with one hand, enjoying the way she arches against me. Then I take a fistful of the jacket and bring my mouth to her ear.

"Good girl. Now let me eat your pussy while you're wearing my name."

I resume my position, pulling her legs over my shoulders and switching the vibrator on. I work around it, alternating from using it on her clit while my tongue dips inside her entrance. Her moans are music to my ears. I take my time, enjoying every second of pleasure I bring her. My hips rut against the sheets because her sounds are too damn good.

"Please, please," she urges after I've made her come over and over.

I tear my mouth from her pussy. "Please, what?"

"Please fuck me. I need you so bad."

"What do you need?"

I'm already moving, lining up at her glistening entrance. She tries to angle her hips to get me to penetrate her. I caress her side.

"Use your words, sweetheart. Tell me."

"You. Inside me. Please, Cole."

I drive into her with a sharp thrust that makes her back bow and her mouth open in a silent scream.

"Is that what you wanted? My cock?"

"Yes. God, yes."

I collapse over her, claiming her mouth in a scorching kiss and swallowing every noise she makes. She meets my thrusts, legs locked around me.

"Flip over," I rasp. "I want to watch you taking my cock with my name across your back."

She moans with a shudder, pussy tightening on my dick. Both of us stay in the same position for a moment longer before I let her turn onto her stomach. She lifts her hips and a ragged breath tears from me.

"Fuck, you look incredible like this, Evie."

My palm splays on the small of her back, skimming her spine to touch where the jacket reads *Assistant Coach Kincaid*.

I search the bed for the abandoned toy, giving it to her. "Make yourself come on my cock."

Taking her hips, I sink back into her with her name falling from my lips. She circles her hips, tossing her head back when I fuck her hard and fast. I grip the jacket for leverage to slam into her. She gasps and I feel it when she comes.

She's perfect. Fucking perfect.

I hold out as long as possible, but my orgasm crashes over me. My body seizes, fingers digging into her, ragged breaths scraping my throat. She sighs in pleasure when I pulse inside her, filling her pussy with come.

"Feels so good," she murmurs.

She slumps against the sheets and I'm right behind her, making sure I don't crush her.

"Oh my god," she mumbles once we catch our breath.

"Yeah." A weak chuckle leaves me. I run my fingers through her hair. "Are you okay? I didn't hurt you, did I?"

"No. That was amazing."

She twists to face me with a pretty, fucked out smile. Something loosens in my chest. I kiss her gently.

"You relax. I'm going to clean you up and do all the work."

I help her out of my coaching jacket, kissing each of her hands when I pull them free. Then I lift her into my arms. She hums and rests her head against my chest, tracing my jaw with her fingertips. I dip my head to brush my lips over hers.

In the bathroom, I put her down, keeping her steady against me while starting the shower. It warms up quickly and I help her step into the tub with me.

The water feels great raining over us. We stand beneath the spray holding each other. I rub her back and she places soft kisses on my chest.

Turning her around, I reach for a washcloth. One arm slides around her waist for support as I run it over her.

"Lean against me," I encourage.

She tips her head back as I swipe it lightly between her legs. Her sigh is tinged with an echo of pleasure. I play with her pussy a little, but neither of us are inclined to go further. This is more about touching for the sake of it than wanting to make her come again. She needs rest.

"Close your eyes for me. I'm going to wash your hair."

My chest expands with warmth when I use my shampoo on her. She's used it once before when she forgot hers.

I take my time lathering her hair, pulling the suds through the wet strands and massaging her head.

"Oh," she murmurs. "You're good at that."

"I'll wash your hair for you anytime you want, sweetheart. Keep your eyes closed, I'm going to rinse."

Once we're clean, I switch the showerhead off and fill the tub. I guide her between my legs when we get in, kissing her cheek, her throat, her shoulder. Anywhere within reach.

She twines our fingers together and lays back. "I could stay like this forever."

"Me too."

We talk quietly about our lives when she brings up her next goals, but there's no urge to fill the comfortable silences. It's enough for both of us to enjoy each other's company.

"I think it would be cool to have a storefront space for Sweet Luxe, you know? I put it down on my vision board. One that has a living space attached or above it would be great. What do you think?"

"Planning like that is still a new concept for me. But I think that would work." As long as it's with her.

"Imagine if a space opened up on Main Street Square? Somewhere we could fit all my crafts and your hockey gear. And where Knights players will fit when they inevitably drop by."

I chuckle, enchanted by the life she paints. "And a dog, too."

"Yeah! We definitely need to get you a dog."

Eventually she falls asleep against my chest. I sit there for a while longer, chasing water droplets across her silky skin. When the water goes cold, I carry her out, careful not to wake her. Once I dry her off, then myself, I get her into bed.

Everything feels right with Eve.

The thought crosses my mind as I lay there with her tucked

against me. This isn't simply sex, it's much deeper than superficial lust. My heart beats steadier when I'm around her. She makes me want to be the best version of myself to become everything she needs.

I kiss the top of her head and hold her closer. I never want to be apart from her.

TWENTY-SEVEN
COLE

SINCE WE BEGAN DATING in secret, most of our time together is spent at my place. Eve thinks it's too risky to sneak me into her apartment with her dad right next door. I'm happiest when I have her over, but we don't get to have everything typical couples do because we're hidden away.

Today I plan to change that.

"Ready to go?"

She tosses me a confused look. She's only been out of bed for a half an hour, perched on the arm of the couch next to me while sipping a mug of coffee. I'm absently stroking her bare leg.

"I'm only wearing one of your t-shirts," she points out.

"Just how I like you."

I drag her down to my lap and kiss her cheek. She stretches to set her empty mug on the coffee table.

"I want to take you out. Just you and me, the whole day."

"Like a date?"

"Exactly. We've only been doing them in secret and, as much as I love our movie nights and cooking for you here, I want to go somewhere with you. Last night that was all I could think. That it should be me you're out with."

Her tender smile is everything to me. I trace it with my thumb and slide my fingers into her hair.

"I want that, too," she murmurs. "Where will we go?"

The corner of my mouth lifts. "While you were sleeping in, I was planning. It's a surprise. Go get dressed. I'll give you one hint: you'll need more than the clothes you've left here. We'll stop by your place first so you can pack a bag."

She pulls a sly face. "Sneaky, sneaky. We're going somewhere overnight?"

Instead of giving away the plan for this impromptu trip, I capture her lips.

"Nice diversion, but I'll keep guessing," she says against my mouth. "Now stop being distracting, otherwise I'll never get off your lap."

I hold her waist with an interested hum, trailing kisses down her throat. "What if we take a shower together?"

"Later." She pushes against my chest with a giggle that becomes a gasp when I nip at her skin. "Cole!"

"Alright, fine."

She gets up, then pauses. "Wait, what about work? I was supposed to have a shift tomorrow."

"I took care of it. Texted Mr. Boucher from your phone earlier for you. He said Theo's got you covered. And your Dad doesn't need me in on the weekends during off-season."

Excitement sparks in her eyes. "We're going out on a date."

"We are. Somewhere we won't have to hide anything."

Happiness settles over me. I'm looking forward to being with her the way we both want out in the open.

It sucks that we have to sneak around at all, having dates behind closed doors or out of town just to be together. I'd love to take her to The Landmark and walk through the center of town hand in hand. I want her at the hockey games I play and the ones I coach as my girlfriend, not my friend.

For now, this is what we have to do. As long as I'm making her happy I'll do anything to be with her.

Once Eve finishes getting ready, we swing by her apartment. She tells her parents on our way there that she's going out of town to surprise her friend with a visit. Thankfully they don't read into me supposedly giving her a ride there.

Then we're on the road to our first destination. The windows are down and my hand rests on her leg. This is heaven.

She keeps guessing our agenda, searching on her phone. "There's a new exhibit at the science center in Hartford. Is that where we're headed?"

"Nope." I swipe her phone. "Don't you trust me?"

She giggles, snagging my wrist to bring me back to her leg. "Well, you did tell me once that you don't know how to date."

I shoot her a wry look. "And I've learned since, haven't I?"

"You're a fast learner."

"It's easy when it comes to you. We were already friends, so I know what you like. Just added feelings to the mix."

"Feelings, huh?"

She rests an elbow on the door and covers her broad smile. I squeeze her leg and she does the same to my wrist.

"Feelings," I emphasize.

She turns on the radio and sings along to almost every song that comes on. The pink sheer ribbon she tied in her hair flutters. I twine it around my finger.

We drive for an hour before I pull off the highway south of Hartford in central Connecticut. Eve perks up, scanning the signs with guesses about our destination. My smile grows wider as she gets more competitive about it for no apparent reason.

When I turn down the road to the fairgrounds with signs for the festival I found, she gasps, quivering with mounting excitement. We pass beneath a banner announcing the dates for the summer festival, advertising live music and over a hundred vendors. It's drawn a big crowd judging by the amount of cars already parked when I find a spot.

Her eyes sparkle with delight on our way in. "This is such a good surprise."

"Yeah?"

She turns to me with an energetic nod. Her joy wraps around my heart, making it thump insistently.

"Lead the way, sweetheart. Where do you want to start?"

She browses the pamphlet she grabbed at the entrance. "There are so many shops here. I don't know what to pick first."

"Start at one end and make our way through to the other?"

"Sounds good."

She slips her hand in mine and we head for the first vendor booth. Each one we visit catches her interest. I love watching her passion for the art and craftsmanship.

"Oh, I love these! How cute!" Eve shows me the squat clay animal figurines, picking out one with a blue bandana. "Here, it looks like it could be a Heston U mascot. Until you're ready to get the dog you want, you can have this one for your office."

Smirking, I draw her close, bringing my lips to her ear. "Maybe I don't need one. I already have a good girl, don't I?"

She turns an enticing shade of pink, elbowing me.Her head ducks to hide her smile. I rub her back affectionately while she buys it.

"I love your earrings," the girl says as she packs it up.

Eve touches them. "Thank you."

"Where did you get them?"

"I make them. This is me." She shows the girl her online shop on her phone.

"Oh! I've seen these. I found you through one of your cute order packing videos. I totally have some saved on my wishlist."

Eve blinks, smiling in wonder. "You do? Small world. I just started this year, but I'm hoping to do something like this soon. My first pop up is in December."

"Good luck."

"Thanks."

Eve clasps my wrist and pulls me away. Once we're out of earshot, she does a little dance with a muted squeal. She hugs me and I crush her to me, kissing the top of her head.

"Did you hear that? A total stranger knows about my stuff."

"I did. Proud of you, baby."

She runs her fingers through her hair a few times. It's how she likes to reset.

"Okay. Sorry, I just needed a minute to freak out."

"A well-deserved celly if there ever was a time for one."

She pulls a face. "Oh, come on, that was way more dignified than riding a hockey stick like it's a horse or pretending it's a sword."

I raise my hands as we continue down the row of booths. "The fist pump or skating a lap are more my style. They're simple, classic."

We bump our shoulders together as we laugh. She runs through a list of recognizable celebrations and rates them while we share food from one of the stalls.

This is nice. No one knows us here. We can just be ourselves, strolling hand in hand.

This is how it should be. When we're back, I intend to start easing Benson into the idea of us together.

We try on ridiculous hats at one stall, taking photos of each other and together. I take about a million of her smile. Once she realizes how many I'm snapping, she flirts with the camera, blowing kisses until she's close enough to trap in my embrace.

"Ready to go?" I ask when we reach the other end of the fair-grounds.

"I think so. We've hit all the booths. I've got so many good ideas for how I can set up mine for the maker's market in December," she gushes. "I can't wait to plan it out now that I have a better visual."

"I'm glad you liked it."

She slips her arm in mine on our way to the car while I carry most of the shopping bags. "I did. So far this is the best date ever."

"Not gonna try to find out what's next?"

"Nope. I'm along for the adventure now."

My shoulders shake with amusement. "Good."

After another stretch of driving, we check in at the hotel I booked in New Haven. She doesn't know the plan for tonight, but I made a dinner reservation for the rooftop restaurant.

While she's finishing her makeup in the bathroom, I sit on the end of the bed to put on shoes. When she comes out in a colorful floral dress with a neckline that falls off her shoulders, I still. Her hair is tied half up with a cream bow, the ends curled in bouncy waves.

"Wow," I breathe.

She does a twirl. "It looks okay? I wasn't sure since I bought it without trying it on."

"Yes." I smooth a hand down my shirt as I stand. "You're stunning."

"You look amazing, too. I really like you in suits."

Her gaze flares with appreciation as it roves over me. I take her waist and swallow the surprised noise that escapes her when I kiss her.

"We'd better go before I mess up your makeup and tear this dress off of you," I mutter against her lips, reluctant to part from her. "You're too tempting."

She sways when I pull away. "So are you."

I fall back a step, then another, holding her hands. "First, let me show off my girl. Then tonight you're all mine."

Her breath catches when we reach the rooftop. "This is super nice."

The sunset streaks across the sky, casting her in an ethereal glow. My touch rests on the small of her back when we're led to our seats.

"Are you having a good time?"

"I always have a great time when I'm with you."

"Me too."

I lay my hand on the table, palm up. She slides hers into it.

Our server interrupts us. "Are we celebrating anything tonight?"

My thumb caresses Eve's knuckles. "Yes."

When he leaves, she leans in. "What are we celebrating?"

"We're enjoying a weekend to ourselves."

She props her chin in her hand, nose scrunching with her cute smile. "Think they'll give us a free glass of wine? Or maybe cake. You should tell him it's our anniversary when he comes back."

"You've got it."

Her attention drifts to take in the sunset. Mine stays on her.

"No bad days," she murmurs.

"What's that?"

"My little positivity mantra. A reminder to pick myself up if I'm having a crappy day because it won't last." She meets my eye. "It feels like all I have are good days with you."

My heartbeat stutters and a glowing peace emanates within me.

"Yeah, I know what you mean. It's the same for me, Evie."

TWENTY-EIGHT
EVE

July

WE SETTLE into a routine for a couple of weeks after we return from our weekend away. I spend more nights in Cole's bed than not, only going home when I need to change out craft supplies or when we have dinner with my family.

No one suspects a thing between us.

This morning, neither of us plan on leaving bed. It's nearly eleven. We've been up for close to an hour, dozing tangled in each other and fooling around.

We're not in a hurry. I'm trailing languid kisses across his firm chest, enjoying when I move lower and earn one of his sexy, sleep-tinged rumbles.

"You going somewhere?"

His fingers sink in my hair, giving a slight tug that lights up my nerve endings and ignites heat in my core. I shiver, lashes fluttering.

"I could be."

"Fuck, when you lick your lips like that it makes me want to use your mouth, baby." He takes my chin, thumb pulling my lower lip.

I smirk. "Ask me to suck your cock nicely and I will."

A rough noise tears from him and he captures my nape with his big hand. "Bring that pussy up here while you put that pretty mouth to work."

We're so wrapped up in each other, it catches us off guard when there's a distant slam in the apartment.

"Hey, man, I called and texted, but you're not answering! We're going to be late."

We both go rigid at Benson's voice.

"Shit," Cole mutters. "He must've used the spare key I made for him when he helped me move in the new TV console."

He reaches for his phone. I lean in, seeing a string of missed texts from my brother.

"Cole, dude! Are you even awake? I know you don't sleep til noon these days."

I'm frozen with indecision. There's no time to race from the bed to hide. My only option is to dive beneath the sheets as my brother's voice grows closer.

"Oh—shit, sorry," Benson stammers when he reaches the bedroom. "I didn't think you'd have anyone over since you keep dodging my attempts to be your wingman."

"What are you doing here?" Cole's tone is flat.

"Did you forget? I've got the beer for the barbecue. You said you'd help me bring it to the lake before everything gets started."

"Damn it." Cole's voice muffles like he's scrubbing his face. "I did. Alright, could you give me a minute here?"

"Oh, right. Yeah, of course." He's silent for a beat too long and Cole stiffens, setting me on edge. "Isn't that Eve's laptop?"

Fuck! We left it on the nightstand after watching our show last night.

Cole covers quickly. "Uh, yeah. She lent it to me. Mine's a piece of shit. Keeps freezing on me."

Benson buys it. "I'll meet you at the brewery and we'll load up."

"Fine."

I listen to the entire exchange, cringing at the fact that there's only a sheet covering me while my brother is right there talking to his best friend.

There's another pause, then Benson jokes, "What's up, mystery girl?"

I press my face against the mattress, wishing I could disappear.

"Benny," Cole snaps.

"Just saying hi. You're going to land yourself back on top of the town's hot gossip list if you've got a secret girlfriend."

Cole groans. "Benny, fuck off."

"Going, going. Don't take too long. I promised to get everything over before one."

I remain hidden until Cole lifts the covers to peek at me.

"Sorry, I forgot all about him asking me last week."

"It's okay. I forgot today was Fourth of July." I emerge with a sigh, leaning against his shoulder. "I guess we have to get out of bed after all."

He blows out a breath, dropping his head back. It thunks on the headboard.

"I think my life flashed before my eyes."

"Yours? What about mine? He thinks you're hooking up with some random chick, but I have to live with the fact he caught us in bed together."

He swings a smirk at me. "I'll see you later?"

An exasperated sigh leaves me. "Yes. I'll be the cute one, so don't go mistaking anyone else for me."

He pretends to be offended, pinning me to the bed with a grin. "I'd never. You think anyone else has tits as nice as yours?"

I savor his kiss as the last one I'll get until late tonight, after the town-wide party's over.

* * *

Heston Lake's annual Fourth of July barbecue is open to all residents. The beach is dotted with picnic blankets and camping chairs. Younger kids race around, splashing at the edge of the water while older ones dive from the dock anchored deeper from shore. Music plays on the speaker system. The savory aroma of grilling meat wafts through the humid air. It's a fantastic atmosphere.

I'm chilling with Jess, Lauren, Julia, and Caroline on beach chairs my family brought. I tip my face into the sun and clink my fruity hard seltzer against Caroline's.

"So," Julia drawls. "How are *things*?"

I smirk at her emphasis, matching it. "Things are fantastic."

I wave to Mr. Boucher and his twins when they arrive with Alex Keller. He has his arm around Lainey, accepting congratulations from people about his NHL draft pick. If anyone hasn't already heard, Theo boasts about his teammate's achievement.

They make their way over to us.

"Hey, Eve." Theo bumps my fist when I hold it out for him.

"Where's your dad?" Mr. Boucher asks.

I push my sunglasses onto my head and scan the party. "Over there with Mr. Cannon and Steve, manning the grill."

Mr. Boucher heads over. Theo sprawls on the blanket while Alex and Lainey stroll down the beach. I nudge him with my foot.

"Enjoying your summer?"

"I'm eager to get back on the ice instead of waiting tables for dad," he says.

"What, am I not fun to work with?" I pretend to pout. "I thought we had the bond of friendship and teamwork."

Theo snorts. "Yeah, yeah."

Cole and Benson come back from the water's edge, playfully wrestling each other. Cole wins, trapping Benson in a headlock and ruffling his hair. Benson breaks free with a grunt, going to kiss his wife while Cole takes the empty seat next to me.

His foot inches closer until we're touching. While my brother's distracted, his eyes rake over me before meeting mine, darkening with desire. I stretch my arms overhead for his benefit, the lightweight plaid shirt knotted at my stomach opening more to show off my bikini top.

"Evie," he mutters low enough for my ears only.

"I'm starving," Benson says. "Did we run out of chips and dip already?"

"Five girls left alone with snacks? That would be yes," Lauren says.

I swirl my can, judging I have less than half left. "Anyone need another drink?"

"Yes, thanks," Caroline says.

"You're a peach," Julia chimes in.

"I'll come with you." Cole helps me to my feet.

I adjust my snug shorts so my thighs don't chafe and follow him. We don't make it far before some of the girls we went to high school with recognize us. One of them is a year younger than me and one was in the same class as him with Benson.

"Cole, I heard you were back in town," Marie says.

He offers them a polite smile, sticking close to my side without being obvious. "Yeah, for a while now. How are you?"

"Good. I can't complain. Teaching first graders keeps me busy. I'm always living my days by my to-do list."

"Same," I say.

"That's cool. Have you seen the ones Eve sells?" Cole turns to me. "You have to-do list notepads, right?"

"Right." I blush at him peddling my products for me.

"I'll check them out," Marie says. "I saw your earrings at Derby Bookshop. My students like the bookmarks."

"I'm glad."

Vanessa is the younger and bolder of the pair. She points out their spot while twirling her hair. "You should come hang out with us. We're over there. If you're feeling like getting up to some trouble."

Cole shuts her down. "I'm here with the Lombards, and trouble's not really my deal anymore."

"We've heard," Marie muses. "I suppose your wild days of infamy are over. No more getting busted snowboarding through the square hanging off the back of cars or hopping the wall at the ice rink to skate on the open lake."

"Nope." He grins reminiscently.

"Are you seeing anyone?" Vanessa asks.

I choke on my drink. It saves him from answering her, at least. As I splutter, he pats my back.

"Are you okay?" His hand lingers, thumb grazing my nape.

"Uh, sorry," I say hoarsely. "Went down my windpipe. Breathing and drinking at the same time, still haven't mastered it."

Jess comes to our rescue when she passes, drawing their attention away from Cole to her baby bump. As we slip away from the conversation, she winks at me. I give her a grateful smile.

My shoulder brushes his arm and he touches the backs of his

fingers to mine. I steal a glance at him, rolling my lips between my teeth when I find his attention on me.

"You look pretty," he murmurs. "I haven't had a minute alone to tell you yet."

I tilt my head, peering over the frames of my sunglasses. "You like it because my cleavage is out."

His dimples appear. "Okay, yes. You got me. I wish I could kiss you right now."

"Later," I whisper slyly.

His smoky chuckle makes my stomach dip.

We spend the rest of the afternoon into early evening stealing glances where we can. During dinner, we sit at the picnic tables near the grills with our knees touching out of sight. It's a miracle we keep it together without anyone looking too closely, though we've had months of practice at this point.

When the sun sets, I help Mom gather our trash. Dad lights up a cigar and the guys go with him.

"I'm going to go wipe my hands," I say when we're done clearing the picnic table.

"They're in my bag," Mom says.

I head back toward our spot on the beach, waving to my friends as they take selfies by the shore before the light fades. I kneel beside Mom's bag to look for her hand wipes.

Benson's voice drifts over from the card table we set up before we ate. "I'm glad we've got you around to help make sure all these idiots eyeing Eve up stay away."

Cole's silent for a beat, then he clears his throat. "What do you mean? She can handle herself."

"Still need to chase off the chums, you know? Like that limp dick Shawn and the loser we took care of after he toyed with her back in high school, remember? I'm glad Shawn knows not to show his face at events like this."

"Last I checked, he moved out of town," Cole says.

I blink. I didn't realize that. All this time I've been passing my ex's apartment building to get to Cole's duplex down the street, not thinking of him once.

"Oh yeah? Good."

MATCHING ALL THE WAY

"They're all boys," Dad mutters. "None of them deserve to go near her. They don't know how to treat her right. Her heart's too big for them to handle."

I freeze, disbelief rocking me to my core. I can't believe what I overheard. Indignation burns through my veins at the idea that they get to decide anything about my love life out of a misguided sense of protecting me. It's absolute bullshit.

What's next, a fucking dowry?

As surreptitiously as I can, I peek at the guys. They're unaware I'm listening.

Cole's jaw clenches. His broad shoulders are rigid. He sets his beer down on the table, shoving a hand in his pocket and swiping a hand over his mouth.

My heart pangs watching his composure threaten to break. I want to go to him, wrap my arms around him to take away his distress. It kills me to be a few feet away and act like nothing's wrong. He catches my eye, hard gaze losing some of its edge.

"Right," he says stiffly. "Not good enough for her."

"It's hard having a daughter," Dad replies, oblivious to the irrevocable doubt he's clearly put in my boyfriend's head. "No one ever feels worthy."

"Don't say that, Dad. If my kid's a girl—which will obviously be the best damn thing to happen to me—I already know I'll end up in jail for murder," Benson says.

Dad chuckles. "Good luck. I won't be able to bail you out. We'll be sharing a cell."

"I'm going to get another drink," Cole says before walking off.

There are too many people around for me to tell him to come with me. I send him a text instead.

Eve
Meet me behind the rentals shed.

Cole
Be right there.

Before I go, I consider storming over to Dad and Benson to give them a piece of my mind. I waver only a moment, deciding it's more important to check on Cole.

No one notices me slipping away from the party in the fading twilight blanketing the lake. I head down the beach to the water sports area where people rent canoes, kayaks, and paddle-boards to take out on the lake. I'm only waiting a few minutes before Cole finds me there.

He eats up the distance between us with powerful strides. "Hey. Everything okay?"

"I'm fine. You're the one I'm worried about. I heard what Dad and Benny were saying."

Even in the near dark, I'm able to tell when he's upset. His brows pinch and he squeezes the back of his neck.

"You heard it all?"

"Yes." I hold his sides. "Don't listen to them."

He curls his fingers around my upper arms as if he's afraid to break me. "How are we ever going to tell them if they're lumping me in with any other guy they think doesn't deserve you?"

I shake him. "I don't care what they think. You make me so happy. I lo—"

I break off, throat constricting. Not yet. I'm not ready to tell him he means so much to me. That being with him has shown me what being in love truly is. He's had my heart for months—years if I count all the moments in our life he's stolen pieces of it with his charming smiles and loyal friendship.

Cole makes me feel cherished in a way I'll never find with anyone but him.

"I love being with you," I finish.

His eyes swim with reverence as they bounce between mine. He cradles my face, swiping his thumbs over my cheeks.

"I love being with you, too," he rasps. "You're the one who decides if I'm worthy enough for you. Not your dad, not your brother —only you, Evie."

I nod, eyes closing. "That's right. If they're not ready to face that we're together, we'll just have to wait. I don't want to put your job or your friendship with Benny in jeopardy by blindsiding them."

"I won't give you up." He sighs, tension leaving his body. "There's nothing that will make me walk away from you."

"We'll figure it out," I promise. "Let's hold off for a while longer."

He releases a rough noise and kisses me. It sweeps me away, taking my ability to breathe with every glide of his tongue against mine.

Fireworks explode overhead, illuminating the sky in streaks of color. We end our kiss. He turns me around, then tugs me against his front, embracing my shoulders. I hold his strong forearms.

"It's pretty," I say.

"Not as beautiful as you. Nothing comes close," he murmurs against my ear.

A slow smile stretches across my face. "That was smooth. Are you trying to get some action behind the canoe rack, Cole Kincaid? I'll have you know, I never made out with anyone in this spot."

He chuckles. "Don't knock it. My first kiss was back here."

My mouth pops open. "I didn't know this. Who? When?"

"Hailey Rutherford right after I turned fourteen."

I gasp dramatically. "Should've seen that one coming. She made eyes at you that whole summer."

The fireworks wail when they shoot into the sky. They reflect off the calm water of the lake.

"By the way, it wasn't a line, sweetheart." His hand splays over my heart. "I meant what I said. It's because you're gorgeous in here that you shine brighter than those fireworks."

I spin in his arms, pressing on my toes. He meets me in a tender kiss that stokes a warm glow within me.

Nothing else matters as long as we're by each other's side.

TWENTY-NINE
EVE

August

"And here's how the interior is looking," I narrate as I film a clip for my social media showcasing the progress on the camper renovation. "Not super exciting yet since we just finished installing the new floor. Soon we'll get to the fun part—hopefully in time for my first in person event later this year. There's my brother and his best friend, Cole. Give a wave for your fans, guys."

Benson goofs off with a flex, brandishing a primer-coated paint brush at me. Cole snorts and paints a smiling face on the back of Benson's t-shirt.

He grunts, twisting in an attempt to see it. "I'll get you back for that."

"Try it. I dare you," Cole taunts.

"Nice," I say.

My following has doubled since I started documenting the project. The more open I am about honestly sharing my struggles along with the good, the more response I get. They're interested in a lot of the behind the scenes of my business growth. Well, and whenever I show Cole. My comment section is always flooded with questions about him.

I step outside and pan the camera to show the display shelves I'm creating with my friends. "And over here, we're crafting away. These pegboards were a great choice, thanks for your input. Oh! The sign's almost done, let me show you."

I finish off filming my logo made with a bright pink acrylic. It's going to look great hanging inside the camper.

Once I post the video, I sit on the driveway with the girls. We're painting the pegboards in varying shades of pink and peach to match my business cards.

When they're complete, they'll be able to display everything from my handmade earrings to my stationary sets. Cole was the one to suggest modifying the shelf template I found online to make them portable so I can use them at the market in December.

"Thanks again for helping out," I say.

"Of course, girl. You know we've got you," Caroline replies.

"This is fun," Lauren chimes in.

"I can't wait to see it all finished." Julia leans back on her hands, studying the camper.

"Me too. I probably shouldn't have slacked off on it for so long. We'd be done by now."

"It already looks so much better than when you first texted us photos," she assures me.

"It's getting there. Still a long way to go," I say.

"Progress is progress," Jess says from the cushioned chair Benson brought out for her in the shade of the garage. "It's all part of running your own business. We can't do it all at once, no matter how much we wish we could."

"True."

I paint for a while, getting through two more pegboards. Brushing my hands off, I check on the ones we've set aside to dry.

Mom brings Jess a fresh cold water. "Looking good, sweetie. I'm going to call your dad and see how long he'll be with lunch."

Cole pokes his head through the window. "Come help with this, Evie?"

I pop inside the camper. All morning I've bounced between working outside with the girls and helping him.

"Where do you want me?"

He shoots me a playful look while Benson's back is turned at the

282

opposite end of the interior. I purse my lips, but a smile breaks free anyway at the silent innuendo passing between us.

"Hold this while I drill." A hint of flirtation tinges his direction.

"That's what she said," Benson replies automatically. "Or would that be what he said?"

Cole waggles his brows at me, mouthing *later*. I cough to cover a laugh and steady the butcher's block counter while he installs it over the new cabinets he built for me.

My teeth scrape my lip as I admire the definition of his bicep and the way his forearm flexes when he drills. He notices when he repositions to get the next screw lined up, smirking. Heat blooms in my cheeks when he adjusts his grip to make his veins stand out prominently in the back of his hand and his corded arm.

He checks that Benson is absorbed in paining before moving behind me, bracing his hands on the counter.

"Is it aligned right?" His hips press against my ass.

I tip my head back, holding my breath. The risk of being caught by my brother makes my pulse race.

"Yes."

"Good girl." The mutter against my ear is barely a breath before his voice returns to normal. "Keep it like that."

I mourn the loss of him when he moves to install the other end of the counter. His smoldering gaze collides with mine before he ducks inside the cabinet.

Once the countertop is secured, I stretch my neck, rubbing stiffness from my muscles. He bats my hand aside and clasps my shoulders, massaging them. I close my eyes, enjoying the treatment. We'll both use any excuse to touch each other if we can get away with it.

"Good work," he says.

The corner of my mouth lifts and I twist to sass him. "Yes, I'm excellent at standing around looking pretty, aren't I?"

"Don't answer that," Benson cuts in without looking over his shoulder.

I flip off the back of his head. "Who asked you?"

He spins, pausing when he realizes how close we're standing. His attention zeroes in on Cole's hands on my shoulders. My stomach clenches when he flicks a suspicious look at his best friend.

Shit. Is this it?

"What? You want a massage next, buddy?" Cole offers nonchalantly.

Benson's suspicion clears and he snorts. "Yeah, and I'll take a beer after you work me over. It's my turn to stand around looking pretty. Here, Eve, you can take over painting."

Cole chuckles. "The counter's in, the floor's done, painting in progress. What's next?"

"I made some resin knobs to upgrade the cabinet hardware with. They're in my apartment."

I walk out to get them. Cole joins me. He snags my wrist once we're behind the camper, tugging me out of sight.

"What are you doing?" I whisper.

He answers by checking our surroundings before taking me by the waist to press me against the siding with a heart-stopping grin. Then he steals a kiss. It's slow, torturous, and over way too soon.

I chase him when he pulls back. His handsome green eyes crinkle.

"Had to kiss you or I'd go crazy," he murmurs. "Needed a dose of you to recharge me."

I bite my lip around a smile. "We already cut it close with Benson right there. You're going to get us caught."

"Nah."

When he looks at me like I'm the most important person in the world, it's difficult to catch my breath. We gaze at each other, the world falling away outside of our stolen moment.

"Anyone see where Cole went?" Benson calls from the other side of the camper.

Reality sets back in. My eyes widen. I push at Cole's chest. He doesn't budge.

"I think he went inside," Jess says.

Cole grins and claims another short kiss, kneading my waist. Then he's gone, circling the camper.

I slump against it, laying a hand over my racing heart until I calm down. This man. I swear he'll be the end of me.

Even though it's disappointing that we're still keeping our relationship hidden after what happened last month at the lake, we're happy. The looming possibility of my brother and dad finding out about us and the potential fallout from that isn't enough to make me walk away from this.

My heart is firmly tied to his.

I wait a few more moments before coming out of hiding to retrieve the knobs. When I return, Dad and Mr. Boucher have pulled up with provisions from the bar.

A few other cars arrive with Heston U's hockey players. Their summer training camp started this week. They lope up the driveway messing around with each other. Theo, Easton, and Cameron I recognize. The beach blond guy is a new face on the team this season.

"Hey guys," I say.

"Hey yourself," the freshman player replies with a wink.

"Easy, rookie. Coach's daughter is off-limits and about a million miles out of your league," Theo warns. "This is Noah."

I wave. "Hi. What are you doing here?"

"Coach Kincaid roped us into helping yesterday," Easton says.

"How?"

Theo smirks, ruffling Cameron's hair when he pulls his hat off to flip it around. "Lost a shootout against him. He bet us all he could get more in than us."

"And I did. Still got it," Cole says when he comes over to stand beside me. "Consider it specialized training as part of camp."

"Bet you wouldn't have lost against Keller if he was around," Theo says.

Cole shrugs. "That's why he's going pro."

Easton's eyes glitter. "Hell yeah. Miss having him around, though."

"Heard his game is killer," Noah says.

"It is," Theo agrees proudly. "I'm ready to get tickets when he plays on NHL ice for the first time."

Easton and Cameron whoop. Noah goes with the flow, doling out high fives to each of us. When he gets to me, he claps his palms against mine and holds on with a wink. Laughter bubbles out of me.

"Sorry, I'm immune to flirting from Heston's hockey boys," I say.

"But you haven't met me yet," Noah answers.

"Alright, get a move on," Cole says mildly.

They fall in line, their respect for him clear. It stirs a spark of delight.

Before we put them to work, they eye the food Dad and Mr. Boucher spread out on folding tables. When Dad invites everyone to help themselves, they descend on it.

"Hope you brought enough," I joke with Mr. Boucher. "Hungry hockey players are dangerous creatures."

"Don't I know it," he replies. "What'll I do when I lose you soon at the bar?"

"Eventually," I concede. "I'm not ready to go full-time yet, so don't go giving my job away."

"There will always be a spot open for you as long as you need it."

"Thanks."

I grab a plate to load up with wings, but my brother stops me.

"Hang on. We got you a surprise," Benson says.

"What? Who?"

"Me, Jess. Mom and Dad chipped in, too."

"Hey," Cole says.

Benson waves a hand. "Credit where credit's due, this was Cole's idea. It's an early birthday present."

He goes into the garage and moves some old hockey gear out of the way. Mom's giddy with her phone held up to record my reaction. I throw confused glances at my friends, the hockey guys, finally landing on Cole. Everyone seems to have an idea of what's going on.

Benson drags a long box out to the camper. It's not clear what it is until he lifts it against the new siding.

Oh, wow. It's a bigger sign than the one I ordered for inside. This one's neon. I spent a month in late winter looking at them before deciding I couldn't do it without getting a really expensive one.

"Cole looked up how to wire it with the camper's electric," Benson explains.

"We're so proud of you," Dad says. "Always will be. We want you to know that."

My eyes mist and my voice trembles with emotion. "You guys."

Cole's fingertips glide up my spine before he wraps me in a half-hug. "What do you think?"

I lean into him as much as I can get away with as his friend in front of everyone. He slants a handsome smile my way.

"I love it."

The camper still has a ways to go before it's done, but my heart is full. I'm so thankful I have an amazing support system in my family and friends. Most of all in Cole. His belief in me bolsters my confidence in myself.

Falling
WITH You

THIRTY
COLE

October

Before I know it, fall sets in again. The weeks fly by after training camp, then the start of the semester. I blinked and August has sped along to the end of October.

I get how it must be for Eve when she says she feels like time slips away from her too easily. Maybe it spills through my fingers so quickly because she makes me happy.

The regular hockey season is underway. Our first few games were good in my book, though David gave the team an earful in the locker room and on the bus home after Saturday night's away game. We definitely have room to work out the kinks and get the guys connecting fluidly.

It's getting late on a Tuesday. The athletic facility is shut down for the night. I'm still in my office reviewing game tape to search for anything else to address in this week's practices.

Narrowing my eyes, I scrub back to watch a breakaway. I tap a pen over the notepad I've filled with my observations. It's one of Eve's that she designed for her shop. The motivational messages she hand-lettered while we watched TV make my lips twitch affectionately.

As I watch, I pick up the dog figurine she bought for me at the festival. It always makes me think of her when I spot it on my desk.

I rewind the video to study the play again, frowning at the moment it falls apart. Easton's golden when he picks up the pass from Jake in our defensive zone, racing up the ice ahead of the Elmwood players. He's wicked fast and his control is beautiful. Then in a split second, it's over when a zippy forward poke checks the puck.

My mind whirs with the drills we can utilize to help Easton find a counterattack strategy. The kid's got so much raw talent, yet it surprises me he wasn't picked up by professional scouts in junior league. I know David personally recruited him to play here.

My phone lights up. I see Eve's name and just like that, I feel lighter.

> **Eve**
> Mission sneak in after hours successful.

There's a photo attached. She's standing by the practice rink, the image edited on her phone to make her look like a spy with a drawn beanie, sunglasses, and coloring her Heston U hoodie black.

I snort, glad I asked her to meet me here after hours. I needed the excuse to drag myself away from the overtime I've been putting in.

Pocketing my phone, I slip out of the office to find her. The practice rink has half the lights turned off, creating a more intimate vibe when I track her down. She's absorbed in typing something on her phone, probably a note to herself to get down whatever idea's popped into her head.

Prowling silently, I sneak up on her, clapping a hand over her mouth to stifle her surprised shriek when I wrap my arm around her.

"Gotcha."

She tugs my hand down and spins in my arms. "You'll pay for that."

"Oh yeah?" I grin, dipping my head to slide my nose along hers. "How?"

"No idea. But retribution will be sweet," she assures me.

My shoulders shake with humor. "I'll be waiting."

She points to her eyes with two fingers, then swings them to me. I take her waist, boosting her onto the boards. Her knees spread and I step between them, hands settling on her hips. She winds her arms around my neck.

"Hi," she chirps.

"Hi. Sorry I'm here so late. I got wrapped up analyzing the games we played over the weekend."

Her head tilts with a cheerful smile. "That's okay. What did you come up with?"

"We're shaping up. I think it's just early season jitters. When I have them on the ice this week, I want them working on their foundations for better chemistry."

"They'll find their groove," she agrees. "I have tickets for the home game on Friday. I'll be cheering real loud."

I hum, drawing her closer. "For me, right?"

"For my team," she sasses. "I scream for you all the time."

"Damn right you do. Because you're my good girl."

She shivers, biting her lip. I slide my hands up her back, loving her reactions whenever I praise her.

It amazes me that after we've been together for months, I'm still this starved for her, always turned on by her mere existence. She could be standing at the coffee maker with greasy hair from a three-day work binge and I want her with every fiber of my being.

"I totally used to dream about making out at the rink with you," she murmurs against the corner of my mouth. "You were so hot in your hockey jersey. I'd imagine practicing my routine and catching your attention. Making out in the penalty box."

"Yeah?"

I capture her mouth, deepening the kiss when she gasps in delight. Her legs lock around me and I shift closer. The memory of her figure skating overlaps with the girl who stole my heart. The girl who's all mine now.

I pull back to marvel at her. Her eyes remain shut, a serene smile gracing her beautiful features.

"I'll need to update my fantasy. Making out with a hockey coach is definitely sexier than making out with a player."

A rumble sounds in my chest and my fingers sink into her hair. "Come here."

We crash together in a rush of hot breaths and tongues. I swallow every sound she makes, hands pushing beneath her sweater.

A door bangs open at the other end of the rink. I tear away from her with a disgruntled sigh, helping her down.

"Campus security," I mutter. "Let's go back to my office so he doesn't catch us together."

We hurry from the practice rink without making a sound, carefully shutting the door. She muffles a giggle with the sleeve of her hoodie covering her hand as we jog the halls.

In my office, I lock the door. She perches on the desk, grinning when she spots the notepad I'm using. Taking her phone out, she snaps a photo of it in action and sets it aside.

I saunter over to her, grasping her throat lightly. "Where were we?"

She hums into it when I pull her to me for a kiss. Her hands slide beneath my shirt, nails scraping my skin when I nip her lip.

We separate only long enough for me to help her peel off the hoodie, then I'm on her again, dragging open-mouthed kisses along her jaw.

She plants her palms on my chest and pushes me. I collapse into the chair, watching intently as she lowers herself between my legs. She's only in her leggings and a bra. Thinking becomes difficult, blood rushing to my hardening cock.

Her hands splay on my thighs, inching inward until she reaches my erection. "Is that for me? I'll have to do something about it."

My fingers thread in her hair with a bitten off groan. "Evie. You're killing me."

"You've never thought about having my mouth on you in here, sitting between your legs under your desk?"

"Of course I have." My head hangs back. "Making out here is one thing, but I work here with your dad. All I'll be able to think about is my cock in your mouth if I let you give me head. I'll never be able to look him in the eye during a strategy meeting again."

She quirks a brow in challenge, giving my dick a squeeze through my jeans. "Are you sure?"

I fold like a house of fucking cards. I always do when it comes to her.

"We have to be quiet," I concede.

"Me, or you?" She leans into the hand I have in her hair. "You can be loud when I blow you."

"Both of us."

My stomach clenches in anticipation when she lowers my zipper. I help her shove my jeans down far enough for her to pull my thick length out. She hums, eyes flicking up to meet my hooded gaze.

She licks the tip, keeping her eyes on me the whole time as her lips stretch to sink down my shaft.

"Oh, fuck, baby," I rasp. "So good. Your mouth is perfect."

She gives it to me exactly how I like, taking me so deep I feel the back of her throat, then sucks hard. My breathing is uneven. I lick my lips, muttering praise that makes her cheeks pink.

She gets into it, finding a fast rhythm of bobbing her head. At one point she almost chokes herself, pulling back. I pet her head until she nods, working my cock like she's dying to swallow every drop of come I give her.

The pleasure is too much to handle. I inhale sharply at the bolt of it from her tongue curling around me.

Not yet.

I need to be inside her.

My fingers tighten in her hair. She makes a greedy noise that nearly finishes me off. Air punches from my lungs as I fight off my release. I hold her jaw, getting her attention.

"Up," I grit out.

I help her to her feet, then bend her over my desk. Her breath hitches when I tear her leggings down and glide the tip of my cock through her wet folds.

"You want this? You want me to fuck you on my desk?"

"Yes."

Her answer comes out hazy with arousal. I sink into her inch by inch, both of us gasping with pleasure. I savor the feeling when I'm buried deep, stroking her lower back.

"Come on," she goads. "I need you to move."

"In a minute, baby."

"Cole—ah!"

Her plea turns into a strangled cry when I slam into her. She presses back against me, body begging for more.

"Shh," I remind her.

"You shh." She moans under her breath.

"Feel good?"

"*Yes.*"

I fuck her hard and fast. The desk creaks and my pen holder tips over, spilling them off the side. She giggles, then stifles a hiss when I pull her hair.

"You're making a mess, sweetheart," I tease.

"You are," she snarks.

I snap my hips sharply. She gasps, fingers scrabbling across the surface, nearly knocking the empty coffee thermos over.

"Did you come? You're squeezing me like you did."

"Yes," she cries.

"Shh."

"Oh my god," she pushes out. "Don't stop."

We both freeze a moment later when her phone lights up on the desk with a call. It's her dad.

Her breath catches. She lets it ring for a few seconds until she glances back at me, then reaches for it.

"Evie—"

She answers, bright and breathless. "Hey, Dad. What's up?"

"Hey, honey, your—are you running or something?"

Everything goes haywire, my pulse a frantic thrum from adrenaline and arousal. What is she thinking? I start to ease out of her. Her hand flies back to grab my hip, holding me in place. Fuck, she kills me. I take her waist and try not to make a sound.

"Nope, I'm all good. I just had my phone at the bottom of my purse so I was about to miss your call. What do you need?"

She clamps on my cock. A ragged breath rips from my lungs, grip flexing. I hope to fucking god David can't hear it.

"Your mom's looking for the—What? You got it?" His voice grows distant before returning. "Sorry, she found it. I'll talk to you later."

"'Kay, bye."

"Jesus, Evie," I mutter as I snap my hips the second she hangs up. "Taking your dad's call while I'm inside you?"

She snickers. "Just keeping you on your toe—ah! Fuck!"

My hips snap at a punishing pace. "Take it."

"Yes," she whimpers.

I nudge my hand beneath her, finding her clit. She exhales unsteadily as I stroke it. I shift my angle to hit her deeper, smirking against her shoulder when she claps a hand over her mouth to hide her louder moan.

"Right there?"

She nods, arching to meet my cock as I drive into her. I kiss my way to her nape, intent on leaving my mark on her. She'll have to wear her hair down for days because I want to leave this memory on her body.

Eve trembles, choking back a cry, then I feel it. Her limbs go languid with pleasure.

I keep the same pace, focused on rubbing her clit. I want her to come again.

"Cole," she breathes. "Please."

"Come on. You can do another, can't you? Give me one more," I encourage.

My fingers circle her clit faster. She seizes, then arches her back with a sigh. Her pussy flutters with her orgasm.

"That's it," I croon.

I want to stretch this out longer, make her come more until she's wrung out, but I'm too close to the edge. My thrusts speed up, eyes slamming shut at her squeezing my cock like a goddamn vice.

Heat sears through me when I come. I cover her back, muffling a groan against the crook of her neck. She melts, hips circling as I empty inside her.

She's the first to speak after we've recovered. "What do you want for dinner? I'm starving. Forgot to eat since you were late."

I try to form words and fail, caressing her side. "Dunno. Brain isn't back online."

She giggles. "Did I break you this time?"

"Yes." I kiss between her shoulder blades and pull out carefully. "Goddamn, baby. Look how much you came on my dick."

"My own hat trick," she jokes. "With an assist."

I gape at her, lips twisted in a ridiculous smile. My chest expands with boundless adoration for her, the feeling growing so big my ribs might crack open.

Eve's just—perfect. The best damn thing that's ever happened to me.

She gives me a confused look when she finishes hiking her leggings back up and pulling on her hoodie. I shake my head, cradling her face to kiss her.

We leave my office with our pinkies linked. I can't wipe the grin off my face while she regales me with the plot of a new show she's obsessing over and has lined up for us to watch.

THIRTY-ONE
COLE

November

AT THE BEGINNING OF NOVEMBER, the hockey program partners with a local shelter to host a community event on the quad in front of the athletic facility.

The team mills around, some of them directing people to the booth to buy tickets for the game, some taking photos with fans and signing things. The rest are playing with dogs and taking people to the shelter's volunteer table to complete adoption paperwork.

Noah has a megaphone, helping draw people over from campus. "It's Pucks and Paws night, people. Yes, beautiful, I'm talking to you. Do you like puppies? Free pets all day—and you can pet the dogs, too. Come on down to get your tickets. All proceeds tonight will be donated to the shelter."

"Less flirting, Porter," I chide.

"But it's working, coach," he answers.

I wave him off and scrub my face, hiding my amusement.

"I love this event," Eve gushes as we stroll through. "When I was still here, I volunteered to design all the promo graphics. Still can't convince Dad to adopt a dog, though."

"Damn. What's that, twenty-five years and counting?"

"The man is so stubborn. He was mad he had to feed my goldfish

299

from the state fair one time—*one* time—and decided Benson and I weren't ready for a dog."

"Wait, I remember this. You made me win that fish for you because Benson wouldn't do it. I spent my whole allowance trying to win because you looked like you were going to cry."

Her lips roll between her teeth and her nose scrunches with delight. "You're the best."

We cross paths with her dad and Steve. Eve sidles up to David and nudges him.

"What do you think, Dad? Is this the year? Look at that sweet one over there, can't you picture her snuggled up with Mom on the couch while she reads? Feeding her snacks? Dressing her up for hockey games?"

David lifts his brows. "No. Don't bother with your usual tricks, they won't persuade me."

She gestures to him in exasperation. "See?"

"All hope is lost," I joke.

"Seriously," Eve agrees. "What about you, Steve-o? Are you adding a new buddy?"

He tips his head side-to-side. "We'll see. My wife wouldn't be too pleased, but she's a big softie. Whenever I bring a new rescue home, she's the one that ends up spoiling them."

"As she should. I totally need to come visit. Or..." Eve turns a pleading expression on me that I have trouble refusing. "Maybe I can convince other people to adopt so I can get a dog through friendship. It'll be fun, like a co-op."

"Eve." David sighs. "Leave my coaching staff alone. Don't let her talk you into anything, Cole."

She tugs me away by my elbow, calling over her shoulder. "Great talk. Bye, Dad."

I snicker, allowing her to tow me. When we're across the lawn, she slows down. I study her surreptitiously, trying not to be obvious about it while we're in public.

"I like those earrings on you."

She pokes the dangling arches. "Yeah?"

"You look cute in Heston U colors."

Her eyes glitter. "Yes! You're the first one that noticed. I made them for some Knights fan spirit."

"I notice everything about you."

My hand automatically lifts to find the small of her back, dropping away once I realize I can't. I settle for bumping my shoulder against hers.

Her gaze softens. "You really do."

I rub at my sternum, heart beating like it's trying to leap out of my body to get closer to her.

I'm glad I drove her ex out of town months ago so she can enjoy events like this without worrying if she'll run into him.

Shawn nearly pissed his pants the first time he found me waiting for him outside his building after the talks I'd had with him at the club and the coffee shop. I didn't do anything to him, only stared him down. Didn't have to lift a finger. It took three encounters before he packed up and moved.

It can't erase the ways he hurt her, but it satisfies me ensuring he's long gone from her life.

My hand flexes at my side, longing to hold hers. I prefer feeling physically connected with her.

"So, have any dogs caught your eye?"

I hang my head. "All of them."

She grins. "You keep saying you want a dog. This is a perfect opportunity."

"I know, but it's so tough to justify it when the hockey season keeps me—"

The puppy pen stops me in my tracks.

"Oh my god, they're so cute!" Eve crouches by the short fence, delighted when a mass of small black and brown lab puppies charge to greet her.

She steps inside and they follow her, circling around her feet. They're jumping on each other as they vie for her attention with excited yips. She sits in the grass, immediately ambushed by the litter. She falls to her back with a laugh, allowing the puppies to run over her.

"This is the best," she declares. "Instant serotonin boost."

Damn, that's adorable. I take photos for my ever-growing album of her on my camera roll.

"Get in here," she says. "They're so soft."

I kneel by the side, letting a puppy sniff my fingers. If I go in there, I won't want to leave. I rub my fingertips together. The kid inside me that's always wanted a dog takes over. I swing a leg over the pen to join her.

It's awesome when half the puppies veer toward me. I crouch with a grin, petting as many of them as I can. A small one that must be on the runt side of the litter sticks to me like glue when I move to sit beside Eve.

"Aww. That one really likes you."

"He's really damn cute," I say as the little black lab wriggles beneath my fingers.

"You could take him home," she suggests as we play with him.

"I don't know. This is only my second season here. Is it really a good idea?"

"I think so. Don't you?"

"Of course I'd love to take him home."

She tilts her head. "What's really holding you back?"

I sigh, scratching the dog behind his ears. "Habit. Doubt. Dogs need a lot of work and time."

I never got one before because I was always moving. I'm not living my life as if it's all temporary anymore.

"And since when have you shied away from hard work?" Her affectionate smile stretches slowly. "Don't sell yourself short. You're a reliable guy now, Cole. In fact, I think you always were. You never let me down. When I needed help, you stepped up."

My gaze meets hers. I lick my lips, considering the puppy. He's so tiny it plucks my heartstrings. Her encouragement reassures the old doubts that reared up.

"You don't have to do anything alone, either," she continues. "I'll help watch him when you're on the road for games."

"A co-op dog," I muse. "Adopt him together?"

"I like that idea. He can be ours."

As soon as she says *ours*, I'm swayed by the thought of doing this with her. "Okay."

She lights up. "Really?"

"Yeah. Let's take him home."

She squeals, crawling closer to hug me. I want to kiss her. Instead, I hold up the puppy between us.

"What'll we name him?"

"I might've made a list of dog names if I ever got one when I was a kid," I admit. "They're all hockey-themed."

"That's sweet. What's your top contender then?"

I pass the dog to her and squeeze my nape. "Bauer. If I ever got a dog, I really wanted to use that name."

"I like it! What do you think?" She lifts him and he releases a bark that makes us chuckle. "Oh my gosh, we can put him in a skate for photos, I can't."

Bauer squirms in her hands to get closer. I take a photo of them. He licks her face, her fingers, anywhere he's able to reach. She laughs.

I love that sound. Her joy is the most beautiful music in the world.

I love...her. I'm in love with her.

It hits me. Strikes me so hard in the chest it knocks the wind out of me.

I think I've known for a while, but recognizing it, giving this feeling a name seems big.

This is what I want. All of it's here in Heston Lake. I have part of the life I'm ready to build—coaching with a team I'm proud of—still afraid someone's going to turn around and tell me they changed their minds from the moment I found out I was staying.

I've never thought about my own future before this past year, let alone making one with someone else. Eve's who I picture having that future with. And if she's not part of it? I'm not interested in any future that doesn't include her.

It's time to put down my roots. But it's not the roots that matter, it's the person I want to ground me. The one I want to be with whether we're standing still or on the move, no matter where life takes us.

Eve. She's my roots.

The one who makes Heston Lake feel most like home—because she's here with me. I want to make our home with her by my side.

Because in small moments over the last year, I've fallen for her. Harder and more deeply than I have ever before in my life.

She's drawn me in with the way she shines brightly, her kind and gentle heart open to everyone around her, and an unwavering belief in me. We've grown to lean on each other. When something good happens, she's the first person I want to tell.

This didn't start after I finally made her mine. Our beginning was way before that, from the moment I kissed her on New Year's Eve. It was when we were teaching ice skating. When we were fixing up the camper. When she visited hockey practices and cheered us on to win the championship.

It was every moment I held her hand as her friend while my heart yearned to belong to her.

Maybe it started years ago, back when her smiles and laughter would stir the funny sensation in my chest I've come to recognize as my adoration for her. It grew the more I started doing things just because I know they'll make her happy—I'll do everything in my power to make sure she has a million good days.

At some point, she became a vital part of my life. Without her, I won't be able to breathe, to exist.

Eve is my person. Simple as that.

I don't want to hide my feelings for her or our relationship. She's mine and I want everyone to know it. Including her brother and her dad.

THIRTY-TWO
EVE

IT FEELS like my calendar reminder is mocking me every time it pops up at the top of my tablet. I swipe it away with an irritated flick, going back to the packaging design I'm illustrating for the market.

More like failing to illustrate because every line I draw feels wrong. I erase the crooked stroke and roll my neck. It eats at me when I can't connect to my creativity easily.

Once again, time has gotten away from me. It's the last week of November and I only have two weeks left before the maker's market. I'm dedicating as much time to prepping for it as I'm able to between my bartending shifts, helping Mom plan the potluck she's throwing next week, and squeezing time in with Cole.

We're at his apartment, lounging in bed. He's watching the livestream of the Flyers playing the Bruins at TD Garden on his laptop while I've been curating which of my products I want to bring. Even with all the research I've done and countless screenshots I've saved to give me ideas, it all feels like too much.

I switch positions for the millionth time from laying on my stomach to sitting up, lasting only fifteen minutes before my neck begins to ache from hunching over. I flop back on the pillows, propping my iPad against my leg. This is terrible drawing posture, but for a short time it works to get the idea down.

I hate it five minutes later, scrapping it to start over for attempt number three at this label sticker for my earrings.

"I know," Cole says at my sigh. "I can't believe that call, either. That goal was totally good."

I hum, feeling bad that I'm not really paying attention. It's not his fault that I'm having a bad day.

Closing the flap on my case to reset, I zone out. Thoughts collide with ideas crowding my head. I pinch my lip between my thumb and finger, brows furrowed as I sift through it all. There are way too many things on my mind. I know it's why I'm having art block.

I set my iPad aside, curling against Cole to watch the last ten minutes of the game with him. He grumbles when it freezes. I end up on my phone, looking through my inspiration board for my vendor table. Imposter syndrome prods at me, making me question who I think I am, taking part in this market.

He groans, shutting his laptop. "What a game."

At least I'm not the only person in the world having an off night. He puts his laptop away, then comes back to bed. A light in the corner of my eye distracts me.

"You have a text."

"Hand it to me?"

I unplug it from the charger and pass it over. He scoffs when he reads it.

"Who's that?"

He stretches across me and tosses the phone back on the nightstand. "Easton put me in this group chat with his teammates last season. They come to me first before they ask your dad for something they want."

"They're like you're little ducklings," I say with a laugh.

"Yeah, that blow my phone up at all hours of the day."

He lays his head on my chest. I play with his thick hair.

"It's nice to know they trust me enough to come to me when they need something. Makes me feel like I'm doing something right."

"At least one of us is," I mumble.

He lifts to his elbows to study me with concern. "What's wrong?"

"I don't know. I think I took on too much for a first event by doing such a big market. Maybe I should back out. There's so much more I need to prepare. The camper isn't ready."

"But you are. Come here."

He rolls to his back, taking me with him. His embrace feels so safe, as if he's the only one able to chase off the stressful doubts eating at me. I burrow closer, tucking my nose against the crook of his neck to inhale his warm, musky forest scent.

"Talk to me," he encourages.

"I'm overwhelmed," I admit. "When I applied, I didn't think I'd get in. Then I didn't think about how long it would realistically take me since I've never done this before. I should've looked for a smaller pop up event to try first so I know what to expect."

"Would you be happy with yourself if you back out?"

I purse my lips. "No. It would feel good because canceled plans weirdly feel freeing, but I'd be disappointed I missed out on this opportunity. I don't like giving up."

His fingers card through my hair. "Okay. So you're not going to cancel your table."

I sigh. "No. Doesn't make me feel better now, though. I'm checking things off my to-do list, then remember something else I need to get done. It's never-ending."

"Do you need help? You know you have me. I'm sure Benny and Jess would offer advice if you went to them."

I slide my lips together. He's right.

"I know, I just—I wanted to do it myself. I—"

When I break off with a frustrated sound, he soothes me with a calming touch, lulling me back from my snapping point once I'm too overstimulated.

"It's okay. Take your time telling me. I'm listening."

My throat twinges and I press my face into his skin. He always takes care of me. I swallow, gathering myself before continuing.

"This is hard to explain. I know it's better to ask for help when I need it."

"But?"

"I have trouble giving up control. I like doing all the parts myself. Except I know that means if I mess up by procrastinating or forgetting, I only have myself to blame."

"There's no blame. It's okay to not do everything perfectly, right? Waiting until you get it all perfect will only slow you down. You do what you can—and I believe in you, Evie. You're capable of so many

307

great things. You're putting yourself out there. That's something to be proud of."

His gentle, reassuring words wash over me. I cling to them, needing his comfort to anchor me from floating away into a spiral.

Perfect is impossible. No matter how much I fixate on my tendency for perfectionism. I have to embrace that owning my own business is messy. I can't control everything.

I trace patterns on his chest. "Why do you have to make so much sense?"

His embrace tightens. "I'd be a shitty coach if I couldn't strategize and give good pep talks. Take things one at a time, okay? And ask for help if you need it."

"Yeah."

"How about you take a break to give your mind a chance to reset. I'll make you a snack. Would that help?"

I mull it over. "I do like snacks."

"I know." He kisses the top of my head. "Let me take care of you, okay? Don't hide it from me when you're struggling. I can't be there for you if you don't rely on me."

I rise on my elbows to kiss him tenderly, pouring all my gratitude and love into it.

"Don't know where I'd be without you," I murmur.

"Hangry and skipping meals, I bet," he teases.

I scoff. He tickles my sides until I burst out laughing. When he lets up, I catch my breath, grinning at him. He cups my cheek, green eyes brimming with fondness.

"There's my girl."

THIRTY-THREE
COLE

December

IT SEEMS like half of Heston Lake's residents are at the Lombards' party when I arrive. Mrs. Lombard has outdone herself with festive decorations. Somehow they've doubled since Thanksgiving last week.

"Oh, Cole, honey!" Mrs. Lombard gathers me into a hug, almost crushing the plate of cookies I made with Eve yesterday. "You didn't have to bring anything."

"It's a potluck, isn't it? Couldn't come empty handed." I offer our contribution.

She fusses over me. "Thank you. I'll find a spot for these."

David and Theo greet me next. I shake David's hand and pat Theo's shoulder.

"They putting you to work?" I joke.

He lifts the tray of Mrs. Lombard's famous savory pastry turnovers. I don't know a soul in town who doesn't love them at parties or hound her for the recipe.

"Are you kidding? I volunteered to carry them when they were ready to go out." Theo grins at the platter. "First dibs are mine."

"Go easy on them. We don't want you slowed down next weekend," David says.

Theo groans. "I've been looking forward to them all day."

Covering a snort with a cough, I elbow him. Once David leaves, I stand guard while he shovels three into his mouth.

"Just make sure you hit the gym and keep yourself limber," I mutter.

"Got it, coach. Thanks for doing me a solid."

Smirking, I nab a brie and caramelized onion turnover for myself. He protests as I saunter away. I bypass the living room when I don't see Eve, wandering to find her. At last I hear the voice I want most behind me.

"Hey, you. Glad you made it."

Eve puts a drink in my hand, fingertips lingering. I hook her pinkie with mine and go in for a kiss to her cheek.

"You look great." *Hey, baby. You're so beautiful. Sneak away with me for a real kiss.*

She grants me a wink. My eyes rake over her quickly, not nearly long enough to satisfy me. Her sexy knit dress hugs her curves and half her hair is pulled back in a bow. My lips twitch fondly at her sparkly pink heart lollipop earrings.

"Cole! What's up, bro?" Benson claps a hand on my shoulder, steering me away from his sister.

I twist in time to see her wry expression while he shows me ten new photos of his daughter. A chuckle shakes my shoulders because they seem to be from the party. We end up in the back room with some of the guys on the Brawling Bandits, Theo, his dad, and some other guys from around town.

"I'm telling you, our rankings for this season? We've got this in the bag," Benson boasts. "Joe, you've gotta get out to one of our games so you can drink with us after."

"For sure. Heard you guys were robbed after getting far last year."

Benny nods vigorously. "We're out for revenge this year. Right, Cole?"

"Your D is solid." Theo cracks up at the round of groans from the innuendo. "But for real, coach. Top shelf skating."

"Thanks." I toast him.

"He's even sharper than he was on our high school team." Benson jostles me with a hearty laugh.

I shake my head, grinning into a sip of beer. After hanging around long enough to finish it, I wonder where Eve is. I ruffle Theo's hair on my way from the room.

"Where are you going?" Benson objects.

Tracking down your sister. "Snack run. I'm hungry. I want more of your mom's pastries before they're cleared out."

"Make me a plate, too."

I flash him a smirk. "Nah, you're on your own."

When I locate Eve again, I pause outside the dining room where the food is. She's laughing with Jess and holding her new niece, making faces at her to get the baby to smile. I watch for a moment, rubbing at my chest.

Eve spots me, lighting up. "Cole! Come here, Gracie always gets the biggest kick out of you."

I cross the room, reeled in by an invisible line anchoring my heart to her. The baby latches on to my finger when I offer it, gurgling happily. The girls laugh when I pretend it's a hockey stick and narrate Gracie scoring a goal.

"Soon enough you'll be ready for your first mini stick."

"Ohh, she's so enamored by your voice you struck her silent to process," Eve jokes.

"Nope, that would be poop face. That's my cue," Jess says.

"I've got her." Benson swoops in from behind, plucking their daughter from Eve's arms. He kisses Jess' temple. "Relax, babe. Enjoy yourself."

She smiles gratefully, following him. I envy their open affection.

"Alone at last," Eve teases in an undertone.

"Not as alone as we could be." I tip my head, indicating her parents' neighbors engrossed in conversation in the corner.

Her hip nudges mine and she bounces her brows. I return it with a secretive smile meant only for her. She glances at the neighbors before catching my eye. My abdomen clenches when she reaches for the cocktail wieners. Batting her eyes, she gives the tip a tantalizing lick, then closes her lips around it.

"Evie," I mutter.

"Mm, *delicious*." Her eyes gleam, aware of what she's doing to me. "Want to try it?"

I can't handle it anymore. My self-control snaps.

When no one's looking our way, I take her hand. She follows without hesitation. We slip away without drawing attention to ourselves, heading upstairs. I quickly bypass the bedrooms, pulling her into the bathroom at the end of the hall.

Her eyes sparkle when I press her to the door after locking it. "What's wrong?"

"This."

My mouth slams against hers. I swallow her gasp, kneading her waist. The kiss is deep, filthy, relentless. It's tinged with the force of my need for her.

"Is that all?" Her eyes cloud with a dreamy haze.

"No. I need to touch you." I fist her sweater dress, bunching it at her hip. "You drive me fucking crazy when you wear these."

Swinging her away from the door, I push the dress to her waist and lift her to the counter.

I groan at the sight of her stockings. "Garters."

They're integrated as part of her tights and they're sexy as fuck on her. My mouth finds hers in another smoldering kiss, swallowing her husky laugh at my reaction. I tug on the sheer material, wrapping the garters around my fingers.

"These protect my thighs from rubbing together," she murmurs. "They come in other colors, if you like them on me this much."

"Fuck yes. I'm buying you every single color."

Kissing my way to her neck, I blindly move her panties aside and run my fingers through her folds. I've barely done anything to her, yet she's ready for me.

"Have you been thinking about sneaking away with me? You're already wet."

"Cole," she chokes.

"I need to touch you."

Her protests die when I tease her clit, then glide a finger inside her. She parts her lips with a sigh.

"You like that?"

"Yes. More."

My mouth stretches in a smirk. I kiss her throat.

"My girl gets everything she asks for."

I add a second, curling them. She holds my arm, pulling on it to get me to fuck her with my fingers.

Christ, I want to drop to my knees and spend hours worshiping her. I want my tongue buried in her pussy until she comes on my face. I want to mark her everywhere, not just the places where no one will see.

Gripping a fistful of her bunched up dress, I use my fingers to make her fall apart. Pumping them in her pussy, pulling free to use her own wetness on her clit, sinking back into her. She's so responsive to my touch, planting her hands behind her to arch her body, mouth open with a silent cry.

As she gets closer, I whisper encouragement, nuzzling her jaw.

"That's it. You're right there, aren't you? Are you going to come all over my fingers?"

Her chest heaves with a strained gasp, then she bites back a moan. I smile against her cheek, slowing my fingers. When I step back, I'm burning with the satisfaction of making her feel good.

She's fucking gorgeous. Cheeks flushed, lips parted, hooded eyes locked on me.

I hold her gaze and lick my fingers clean, savoring her taste.

"All I'll be able to think about the rest of the night is your come all over my hand and those pretty sounds you tried to smother," I rasp.

Her lashes flutter and she spreads her legs wider. Heat pulses in my cock.

"Fuck me."

I inhale sharply. "Here?"

"Yes. Right now. I need you."

The plea makes me stagger, lightheaded from the rush of blood racing south.

"They're going to notice if we're gone too long."

She whimpers, fingers toying with her glistening pussy. "So be quick. Take me hard and make me feel you inside me all night."

"Fuck, Evie," I hiss, threading my fingers in her hair.

My hand covers hers and together we play with her clit until she shudders for me. I help her down from the counter.

"Turn around."

She leans over, flashing me her divine ass. I slip a finger beneath the garter built into her tights and snap it against her skin with a rumble. She arches with a strangled gasp.

I don't waste anymore time, getting my cock out, pulling her thong to the side, and lining up. Pushing into her wet heat is fucking heaven every time.

She has trouble controlling her volume when I pull back and begin driving into her again. I cover her mouth to muffle her cries and bring my lips to her ear.

"Scream if you need to. I'll keep you quiet while you take my cock like the good girl you are."

Her pussy flutters. I want to make her feel this all night long. To walk around freshly fucked, knowing she's all mine. For our eyes to meet across the room and remember what we did while everyone was downstairs.

Biting back a rough noise, I angle her hips the way she likes and give her what she begged me for.

"You're so fucking wet," I croon.

She whimpers against my palm and presses back to meet each thrust.

"Touch yourself."

Her hand moves so fast she almost knocks over a votive. I catch it before it topples over and right it without breaking my pace. I split my attention between watching my cock sinking into her and our reflection in the mirror.

She's watching us, too. Fingers working her clit.

"Look at you. So gorgeous, baby."

She stills with a strangled noise, her body squeezing me like a vice as she comes.

I'm so focused on her pleasure, my orgasm blindsides me. I grit my teeth, fucking her as long as I'm able to before my hips falter. Her pussy spasms as I flood it with come. With a ragged breath, I release her mouth and brace my hands on the counter, riding out the aftershocks.

Eve's still trembling when I pull out. I smooth a palm down her spine, a thread of worry tugging my heartstrings.

"Are you okay?"

She nods languidly. I help her stay on her feet, pulling her against me for support.

"Are you sore? Was I too rough?"

"No, that was amazing," she breathes. "So good."

I run the water in the sink and focus on cleaning her with care first, then making quick work of myself. She smiles softly at me in the reflection of the mirror. I kiss her head, then help her pull her dress down and fix her hair.

"Think anyone's noticed us missing?"

"I think they were all on their way to being drunk and merry, so they won't be too worried." She leans against the door. "I'll go first. Ready?"

"Wait."

I stare into her eyes, clasping her throat with my hand. I don't break our gaze as my mouth dips to hers in a sensual kiss. She melts against the door until I catch her with an arm around her waist.

"Okay," I rasp against her lips. "Now you can go back down to the party."

THIRTY-FOUR
EVE

IN THE END, I didn't finish the camper in time for the maker's market. I've come to terms with that thanks to Cole's reminders that I don't have to be perfect.

The impulsive side of me wanted to cancel my spot since it isn't ready. My nerves are a mess today. I haven't been able to eat anything yet.

Cole's tried a few times to coax me into having something other than coffee and water. Before we hit the road, he packed me a protein bar, a sandwich, and a bag of cereal to give me options.

"There's a rest stop up ahead at the next exit. Hungry?" He's checked if I want to stop at every sign for food we pass.

I shake my head, eying the thick gray clouds blanketing the sky from the passenger seat with a frown. "I hope the snow holds off."

"I have all-wheel drive. Take a breath for me, okay?" His thumb strokes my thigh comfortingly.

My head hits the seat and I close my eyes, drawing a deep inhale, holding it, then letting it out until my pulse stops skittering like a panicked rabbit.

"Good girl. Better?"

"A little. Sorry, I'm just so nervous. There are a million thoughts going through my head. Checklists, the order I want to set up in, the freebies I made." I gulp. "What if no one comes to my table?"

He shoots me an empathetic sidelong glance that stokes warmth in my heart, temporarily taking the edge of nerves away. When he untucks his hand from between my legs and offers it, I clutch it like my lifeline.

"They will, sweetheart. What will make you happy about today?"

"If just one person comes over," I push out in a rush. "Last night I dreamed no one could see me."

"I see you," he promises sincerely.

As usual in the face of my insecurities, he's patient. He remains calm and doesn't raise his voice. I've never felt like I'm frustrating to deal with.

I massage my forehead. "Sorry I'm like this. I know it's irrational. It's hard to switch off if I don't talk it out."

"No." He squeezes my hand. "You have nothing to apologize for. It doesn't matter if it's logical, what you're feeling is real. It's normal to be nervous and I want you to tell me so I can help. I'm listening. Do what you need to if it'll make you feel better."

If I didn't have him here, I think I would've turned around and driven home. He called out from the Knights' away game for me and arranged for Lainey to watch Bauer for the weekend. He told me I needed him as my coach more than the hockey team does right now.

"I'm so glad you're with me," I admit.

"I'll always be there for you when you need me."

My eyes water as a result of being overwhelmed. I blink away the tears, feeling silly.

"Want to listen to your audiobook? It might give your mind a minute to rest."

"Okay."

He gets my phone connected to the speaker system. The story sucks me in, creating a welcome escape from my imposter syndrome. He opens a protein bar, giving it to me when I glance at him, then gets another for himself.

I relax for a while. Until it begins to snow.

Needing an outlet—without bothering Cole with my indignation —I vent to my friends.

> **Eve**
> The weather better not fucking try me today.

Caroline
Major middle finger to the storm. My flight home is canceled. Chin up, babe. It won't stop you.

Julia
It's your day. Nothing can hold you down. We're cheering you on!

Eve
Thanks guys. I'm just dumping my feels here so I don't keep piling on Cole, ignore me.

Lauren
Never [heart emoji]

Julia
You know this chat is open to all therapeutic unloading because none of us have it together all the time.

Eve
Okkk, I needed that. [heart hands emoji]

We're less than an hour from the town north of Boston where the market is being held when the snow falls in fast, heavy clumps, decreasing visibility. It's nearly a whiteout.

"Damn," he mutters, pointing ahead. "They've got every lane blocked up there."

I lower the volume on the book. "What?"

The car slows to a stop as the one in front of us U-turns from the police cruiser and flashing caution signs. Cole lowers his window. The officer waves to the blockade.

"Sorry, folks. Road's closing down. We're asking everyone to turn around and get to safety from the storm. If you're coming from anywhere beyond fifteen miles, I recommend finding accommodations for the night until this lets up."

"We only have a bit further to go to our destination. There's no way around?" Cole asks.

"No. We're shutting all major roadways across the tri-state area. It's coming down faster than expected. It's not safe."

"I understand."

"Follow the detour. There are places to stay nearby in town."

"Thanks."

I listen to the entire exchange, but it doesn't sink in until Cole swings the Bronco around, taking the first exit. I twist to look at the highway disappearing behind snow-covered pine trees as we round the bend.

"I'm going to miss the market," I blurt, voice wavering.

All of my doubts rush back. This is out of my control, yet I feel like the world is telling me I'm not good enough to do this after all.

"There's still tomorrow," he says gently.

At the anguished sound that snags in my throat, Cole throws me a concerned glance and pulls into an empty parking lot.

He reaches for me. "Evie—"

"It's over. I can't go to the market," I choke out.

"Hey. Don't do that." He cradles my face, brushing away the tears leaking down my cheeks. "Don't run away. I know that's not what you want. You're not giving up."

My throat burns with frustration and the sting of failure. I shake my head.

"This is just a bump in the road. We'll figure it out together, okay?"

His gentle tone shatters my aching heart. I try to stop crying, crumbling more in the face of his tender treatment.

"I hate it when you cry, Evie," he murmurs.

I hiccup, sniffling. It hurts to swallow.

"I'm sorry."

"Come here." He draws me in, kissing my forehead. "You don't have to be sorry. I just want to take your tears away when you cry."

My eyes close as his scent surrounds me. He runs his palms over my shoulders and cups my nape, kneading until the tension ebbs from my limbs.

"You're okay."

"I don't deserve you," I whisper.

"Yes you do, sweetheart."

"You don't—" I break off with a strained gulp.

"What is it?"

Don't ask. Don't. There's no need to know.

"Do you ever think I'm too much?" My voice is small and cracked.

He releases a rough noise, practically crushing me in his embrace. "No. You're not too much."

A fresh wave of tears flow at his firm contradiction of my fear. He swipes them away, whispering reassurances until they dry.

My fingers tangle in his coat. "I should email the event organizers that I can't make it because of the storm."

"Let's get off the roads first. Do me a favor? Find us a hotel for the night. We'll keep an eye on the weather. In the morning, we'll get there. You still can make it tomorrow."

I nod feebly. Find a hotel. I can do that.

It doesn't occur to me until I've skimmed through nearby options and picked one that he offered me the task to give me a minute to catch my breath. I reset our GPS, accepting the situation.

While we're following the detour signs, Dad calls. I startle, nearly dropping my phone. Cole takes it from me and pulls over to the shoulder to answer it. Dad's brusque voice comes through the car's speakers.

"Hey, Eve."

"What's up?"

"I'm with the team on the bus to play Vermont, but we got snowed out. I wanted to check that you're not on the road, either. They're a mess in this storm."

"We're not," Cole says. "We're a little under an hour from Middleton and they just closed the highway."

"Sorry the storm stopped you, honey." Dad's voice muffles, pulling away from the phone. "What? No, you can't talk to them. Sit the hell down, Blake."

A huff leaves me. Cole smirks.

"We're going to try to get there tomorrow morning," I say.

"Alright." Dad's pauses. "Take care of her, Cole."

I exchange a look with him. He stares at me, hand resting on my knee. The corner of his mouth lifts.

"I will," he promises. "She's safe with me."

"Good, good. I knew I could count on you."

We smile at each other. I fight back a laugh, feeling lighter than I have all day. He squeezes my leg.

"Looks like you didn't have to call out after all," Dad continues. "Today's game will be rescheduled sometime later in the season. We're heading for a hotel. Get somewhere safe and hunker down. Call me when you do."

"We will," I say.

"Drive carefully."

"You too. Thanks, Dad."

He hangs up, shouting something at the players to keep them in line. We pull back onto the road and head for the hotel I booked.

"There was only one room left. It's a king," I say.

His head jerks with an amused huff. "Only one bed. Just like your current read."

I smile at the paused audiobook on my lock screen. "Look at you, learning the tropes."

"Gotta keep up with what my girl likes."

Once we arrive at the hotel, the world is blanketed in thick piles of snow. I check over my stock packed up in the back while he texts Dad and gets our bags.

"It'll be okay out here overnight," he says.

"You're right."

The room is nothing fancy. It'll do as shelter from the storm tonight. After setting our bags down, Cole's arms slip around my waist from behind.

"Should I put a pillow wall between us?" He kisses my cheek. "Or lay down some ultimatum about not touching each other?"

I play along. "Don't look into it if you wake up with me snuggled against you. It doesn't mean anything."

"We can't fight these feelings," he rasps, imitating the narrator for the hero. "I can't resist you anymore. I need you, even if it's only for tonight."

I spin in his embrace, winding my arms around his neck. "I'm glad I get you for more than one night."

"I'm not going anywhere. You get me forever."

I play with his hair and kiss his jaw. "Then that's how long I'm holding on."

"Good, because I mean it."

A chill wracks me. "I'm going to warm up in the shower."

"I'll join you."

We strip down in comfortable silence. Steam fills the bathroom by the time we step in. The hot spray feels good against my muscles. Cole helps by massaging me until I'm pliant.

"How are you feeling?"

"Okay. I wish this didn't happen, but I'm hoping we can make it tomorrow at least."

"I know it sucks right now, but this isn't a setback. It's like I say to the guys after a loss, you just keep going. That's how you turn it around. And you will, Evie."

I trace water droplets on his skin as he caresses my back. "You always know what to say to get my gremlin brain to stop being such a jerk to me."

"Because I love you," he says simply.

My heart skips a beat. Hearing him say it stokes an ember that echoes throughout me. I meet his warm gaze.

"I love you, too," I murmur.

He presses a smile to my wet hair. "I know."

"You do?"

"You're always showing me. The things you make for me, or when you bought me that dog figurine. How you melt against me when I have you in my arms. The way you smile at me is different. Like you're so happy you can't contain it."

I nuzzle into him. He's been telling me he loves me the same way, with his caring gestures like checking in to remind me to eat and always needing to touch me in some way.

His caress skims up my spine. I match him, shifting closer. His arms lock around me. It's more about intimacy and our connection than seeking anything out of it other than enjoying being pressed together with nothing between us.

"Thank you for being you," I say against his shoulder.

He responds by holding me tighter.

Even when I'm drowning from doubt, imposter syndrome, and fear, Cole doesn't leave me on my own. No matter what problem I'm facing, he's always here for me to help me through it. I have him to hold me up.

THIRTY-FIVE
EVE

It's day two of the market and set up starts in twenty minutes. We're still not there. The hotel we ended up at in the storm isn't far. I'm itching to get there, part of me still disappointed that I'm screwing up my first in person event.

In my head I know nature's at fault. I can't help feeling like it's my own shortcomings. If I was ready to go earlier, or if we'd arrived the night before the market began this wouldn't be a problem.

It was difficult to sleep last night. I'm sure I kept Cole awake as I tossed and turned. He didn't complain, simply pulled me back into his arms once I changed positions and rubbed my back to help me doze off.

He startles me when he comes back from checking us out at the front desk.

"We're all good. The roads were cleared out this morning."

My heart leaps into my throat and I tangle my fingers in my sweater. "They are?"

He takes one look at me and crosses the room to stop me from pacing by the window. The knot in my chest loosens when he pulls me into his arms.

"It's okay," he murmurs. "I know you're nervous."

I didn't voice any of my swirling thoughts. Didn't have to. He understands why I'm still worked up about this.

"Remember what I said yesterday. You've got me every step of the way. Once we get there, it'll be great."

I swallow past the lump clogging my throat, clinging to him. "Thank you. God, I would've spiraled without you here. You're my rock."

"You think I'd let you do this alone? Nah. Of course I'm here for you."

"Let's go."

We leave the hotel. I only spare a moment to admire the fresh snowfall sparkling in the morning light before getting in the car.

Time passes quickly in the car with the audiobook playing in the background. I don't take in any of the information, but I appreciate the sense of normalcy to anchor me. We'll listen to this part again on our way home tomorrow.

A slew of texts chime with a shower of support and love from the girls. Between the inside jokes that we've spent years collecting and their sweet messages, they make me smile.

Cole pulls up to the curb to help me unload. "Ready?"

I shake my hands out. "Yes. No."

He catches my wrist, bringing it to his mouth to kiss. "You've got this, okay?"

I nod, invigorated by his unwavering belief in me. We load the plastic bins onto a cart. After hours of YouTube research, more experienced artists agree this is the setup to go with.

I see what they mean when one of them tumbles to the snow. Cole gets it, giving me a thumbs up once he brushes it off.

"It's all secure. Doesn't look like anything moved."

My shoulders relax. We head inside the brick building, following another person who I assume is a vendor from their multicolored hair.

A kind yet frazzled looking girl with a clipboard pops up at my side when we pause to get our bearings in the main room.

"Hi, are you a vendor?"

"Yes. Eve Lombard, Sweet Luxe."

She runs a pen down the sheet and checks me off. "Great. The storm's totally got us turned around, so we're checking you guys off as you arrive. You'll be at table fifty-three."

A funny sense of relief blooms in my chest. "Other people have been delayed, too?"

"Over half. Yesterday we only opened for a few hours into the day before we had to shut down early for the road closures. We're so sorry about any inconveniences. Check your email later, we're offering a discounted rate for our next event in Mystic to make up for this mess."

I light up. "I love Mystic."

Her nose crinkles with her excitement. "Me too! It's my favorite event of the year."

"I'll definitely check that out."

"Have a great event! My name's Lena. Flag me down if you need anything, okay?"

"Okay! Thanks so much."

She waves, bustling off to meet another vendor. I grin at Cole. He returns it with a soft expression, hand resting on the small of my back.

"Here, let me push the cart. You lead the way to your table."

We weave through the room to find my row. It's surreal to see my business name labeling the table.

"Is it weird if I save this as a keepsake for my first event?" I ask as he wheels my supplies behind the table.

"Not at all."

The girl at the table next to me selling candles leans over. "I have a whole scrapbook page of my first time."

"Thanks. That makes me feel better."

I assess my space, battling the urge to do everything at once. I need to pick a place to start to tackle my setup in order.

"There's power," Cole confirms.

I clap. "Oh my god, there is? I can hang up the neon sign."

"I'll handle it. You go ahead and work on your displays."

"Right."

Setting up takes longer than I anticipated. I almost run out of time when someone announces the doors open in ten minutes. My neighbor and Cole help me get the last display shelf ready with moments to spare.

"Does this get easier?" I ask her.

"Honestly, I'm still wondering that myself and I've been at this for three years. But you just roll with it. Good luck today."

"Thanks, you too."

"Come stand out here a second," Cole says.

"But they're letting people in."

"I want to take your picture so you remember this moment, too."

My heart swells with affection. He takes a few, gaze flicking over the phone to me. Before he puts it away, I borrow my neighbor to have her take one of both of us.

"I don't need to be in it," he says.

I hug his waist. "Yes you do. I want to remember everything about today."

He plays with my hair while she takes our photo. A mom and daughter wander over, browsing my stuff. My eyes widen. I didn't expect to have anyone so soon. Cole thanks my neighbor while I jump behind the table.

"Sorry about that. How are you doing today?"

"Good. We wanted to come yesterday, but we're glad we could make it out today," the mom says. "This is where we do most of our holiday shopping."

"That's great! Thanks for supporting small business."

"Mom, look at these."

The daughter points out my eclectic earring collection. They light up at them. Glee fills me at their enjoyment right before my eyes.

"I have more options available online, and I take custom orders if there's a shape you have in mind."

"We'll take these ones." The mom nudges her daughter. "We like to match."

"That's so sweet. I'm also doing a special today for your choice of sticker if you buy two sets of earrings."

The daughter picks one out while her mom takes the free business card sticker I made that has a smaller version of my no bad days design. I ring them up on my phone, pulse thrumming with adrenaline.

"My first event sale," I murmur to Cole after they continue down the row.

He rubs my back. "See? I told you everything would be great."

I hum, lifting my chin to meet him in a kiss. His palm fits to my cheek, caressing it with his thumb.

"What the hell?"

We snap apart at Benson's surprised exclamation. What is he doing here?

My hand automatically finds Cole's out of habit. It draws my brother's attention, his brows flattening. He lifts his glare to Cole.

"Benny," Cole says warily. "Take it easy."

"How long have you been fucking around with my sister?"

Cole's jaw clenches. "Don't phrase it like that. We're not fucking around. She's my girlfriend."

"We wanted to tell you," I cut in. "We were going to."

"How long?" Benson ignores me, staring Cole down. "When did you go behind my back to start this?"

"Her birthday," he mutters.

Benson's eyes bulge. "Fucking New Year's?" He swipes a hand over his mouth until it dawns on him. "Christ, that time I came to pick you up in the summer. The secret girl I caught you with was my sister this whole time?"

I cringe. "Come on, Benny. Can we not?"

"No, I think we should," he says. "Because I came all the way out here to make sure you were good after the storm, and I find out you're both lying to me."

The commotion is driving people away from my space and the vendors near me. My chest constricts with worry that I'm hurting their businesses.

Cole glances around, then circles the table to snag Benson's arm. "Come on. I'm not doing this here."

Torn between staying at my table and making sure things don't get out of hand between them, I write a hasty be right back sign and dash after them.

Cole drags Benson down a deserted side hall off the main room. "Look—"

"Don't you 'look' me." Benson shrugs him off. "My sister, Cole? Really?"

"You got a problem with me and her?"

"I have a problem with you using her," he snaps.

329

"I'm not," Cole growls. "I'd never treat Eve like that. It's not like you ever said I shouldn't go for her. Do you think I'm not good enough for her?"

Benson narrows his eyes. "You said it, not me. I know how many girls you've run through." His voice raises when he notices me. "My sister won't be another one you're with for a minute before someone else catches your eye. Eve—"

"Hey," Cole cuts in harshly, shutting my brother up by grabbing his shirt and holding him against the wall. "That's enough. Say whatever you want about me, but I won't let you make a spectacle of Eve. Haven't you already made enough of a scene? We can discuss this later—hell, I'll let you punch me if you feel the need to take a swing—but you're not going to ruin her moment."

Benson's silent, gaping from his best friend to me, then back. He drags a hand through his hair, considering us for another minute.

"Shit," he mutters. "You actually care about her."

"Of course I do," Cole says. "Do you have a problem with that? Because if you're going to be an asshole about me dating Eve, I'm telling you right now I don't want you around her."

"Guys. Don't fight, please," I say. "You're best friends."

I tug on Cole's arm. He turns his back on Benson to hug me.

"It's okay, Evie. He's not controlling what we do. Either he comes around or he doesn't."

"*Shit*." Benson slumps down the wall with a short laugh, rubbing at the dark circles beneath his eyes. "Okay, I get it. You love her, man."

"I do. And I won't let anyone hurt her. That includes her family."

Benson nods. "You really have changed."

"No, I haven't." Cole sighs, offering to help him to his feet. "I just never met anyone I wanted to be serious with. Not until her. So all that bullshit you were spewing about my past isn't true."

He mulls it over and accepts a hand up. "I'm sorry I didn't notice."

"You've been busy," I say. "And Jess has been helping us keep it quiet."

His brows jump up. "I knew I wasn't going crazy."

"So we're cool?" Cole asks.

Benson hangs his head. "Yeah. I never imagined you'd go from helping me beat up the guys that made her cry to falling for her yourself."

"I'll still kick anyone's ass that makes my girl cry." Cole tugs me against him.

"Sorry." He scrubs his face. "Seriously, all my brainpower goes to keeping my baby alive. I keep wondering how the hospital let us leave with her because it's hard, terrifying work. Feels like I'm running on like five minutes of sleep a day. I didn't mean to be a dick to you guys, I just—you surprised me."

"It's okay as long as you're not going to do anything irrational about our relationship."

Benson waves me off. "Nah. Now that I'm thinking about it, you two actually make a lot of sense. Who else knows?"

"Just you, Jess, and my friends," I answer. "We haven't told Mom and Dad."

"Okay. They won't hear about it from me."

I sag against Cole, relieved that my brother is back on my side. "We want to tell them soon. I don't want to keep it secret."

Benson follows us when Cole leads me back to my table. "Now I'm glad I didn't bring Mom. She wanted to come with me, but she's fussing over Jess and the baby."

I smile, pointing at the opposite end of the room. "There are handmade ornaments sold down that way. I already ordered some for her, but you should bring her back more."

"Good call." He starts to walk off, then backtracks. "Hey."

"Yes?"

"I'm proud of you. I should've started with that."

"Thanks, Benny."

He crushes me in a hug. "I'll be back in a bit."

Once he leaves, we exchange a look. Cole shakes his head in exasperation, drawing me in to kiss the top of my head.

"Think we should've brought him into the fold sooner?" I wonder.

"I'm just glad he came to his senses."

"Me too. I really hope it's not like that when we tell my dad."

"I'll tell him the same thing as I told your brother."

Before I respond, a new customer comes up. I greet her and ask about what she's found so far at the market. She compliments my book earrings and buys a set for herself and her sister. The longer it goes on, the more I'm slammed with people. I even have a line at one point. Cole takes photos and videos of me in action since I'm too busy to handle it myself.

By the time the event is down to an hour left, I've nearly sold out of the stock I brought. Only some of my earrings and stickers remain out of what I overpacked.

"I'd say you killed it at your first event," Cole says.

I lace our fingers together, leaning into him. "It's because of you supporting me. Bumpy road and all."

"No," he says fondly. "This is all you and your talent. You did it. How's it feel?"

"Awesome."

There's something so magical about interacting with the shoppers in person today. Whether they bought something or not, it's wonderful to see what catches their interest, and feel the sense of community from the other vendors.

A content smile curves my mouth. I did it, despite the struggles. Because I'm not perfect, and that's okay.

As long as I have Cole to anchor me, I feel capable of anything I dream up.

THIRTY-SIX
EVE

AFTER EVERYONE finally goes to bed on Christmas Eve, I sneak upstairs to the guest room Cole's staying in. This year he's spending the night, along with our puppy in his crate downstairs. I text him to open his door and moments later he peers through the crack.

We both glance down the hall to my parents' room. The light's off. Dad was snoring when I tiptoed past.

He draws me inside and shuts the door.

"What's up?" he whispers.

"I can't sleep without you anymore."

He tugs me against him, burying his nose in my hair. "Me either."

"I'll get up early before everyone. They won't know."

He pulls back to tuck a strand of hair behind my ear. "I was sitting up here thinking about coming out to you."

Husky laughter bubbles out of me. I lean into his palm.

"Why are we like this?"

"Because being in love makes us act weird."

"I love being in weird with you."

His mouth quirks. "Back at you, sweetheart."

I hold up his present. It's better to give him this now since it's too big of a gift to pass off as his friend. I made him a different gift to open with my family tomorrow to match the hockey-themed scarf I knit him last year.

"Open your present," I whisper.

"I thought you were my present," he replies in an amused tone, leading me to the bed.

"I'm the gift that keeps on giving...you head."

He snorts. "Nice."

We settle on the bed facing each other. I hand it over, teeth raking my lip. He works his thumb beneath the wrapping to tear it, eyes flicking to me.

"Is it...an engraved whistle, or a World's Best Coach mug?"

"Nope, but that does give me an idea to have a custom Coach Bossy mug made for you."

"What about a nice big ribbon to tie you up with?"

"Just open it," I say in exasperation.

He's been complaining that his laptop from college is on its last leg. It always freezes when he tries to watch the livestream of a game. I'm proud I've made enough through my sales to buy him a new one. His eyes widen when he reveals it, then he releases a warm hum.

"Evie. This is amazing. Thank you."

"You like it?"

He clasps my nape to pull me in for a kiss. "Of course. I like everything you give me."

"But for real. It's not too much, is it? You're always annoyed with yours."

He stops me from twisting my fingers. "No. I love it. I needed this and I really appreciate you for getting me a new one."

"I'm glad. I also made you something to open tomorrow, but this is special. It felt too big to give you in front of everyone else when they're all getting handmade presents."

It would be nice not having to hide our real presents like this.

Impulse slams into me. I want to face Dad. I'm so tired of modifying how I act to hide that I'm in love with Cole.

Tomorrow. We need to tell him.

"I also have something for you. I left it at home to give you when it's just us."

I bite my lip around a smirk. "Is it something to tie me up with?"

His smoky chuckle makes me shiver. Once he moves the laptop out of the way, he's on me with a heart-stopping kiss that touches my soul.

I deepen it first, pressing against him. We tug at our clothes until we're down to skin against skin. He flips me, pulling my ass against him and reaching around to slip his fingers between my legs. I muffle a soft noise in the pillows, moving against his touch.

He nuzzles into my throat. "Can you be quiet?"

My nod is tinged with desperation, heat spilling through me already. He lifts my leg and I reach to line him up. We both shudder as he sinks into me. I arch at the full feeling of his cock stretching my pussy.

The only sounds are our hazy sighs and muted noises of pleasure as he rocks into me slowly so the bed doesn't creak. My toes curl as he kisses my throat, fingers dragging up my thigh to stroke my clit.

"Cole," I breathe.

"Just feel, baby." His lips brush my shoulder. "Feel us."

He pets my throbbing clit and curls the arm beneath me to hold me tighter against his firm chest. I feel his heartbeat syncing to mine as we move together, not rushing to finish this. The sensations of our connection are incredible.

A cry sticks in my throat. He hushes me, spreading his fingers to tease where our bodies are joined. My pussy clamps. He buries a pleased rumble against my flushed skin and finds my clit again, fingers slick with my wetness.

I tremble with pleasure as it crests within me. His steady thrusts light me up, hitting exactly where I need him to while he strokes my clit.

"I've got you, sweetheart. Let go for me."

His encouragement washes over me, tipping me over the edge into ecstasy. I writhe with the rippling waves of my orgasm.

"That's my good girl," he rasps against my ear. "Does that feel nice when I make you come?"

I nod, rolling my lips between my teeth to stop a moan from escaping. His thrusts grow sharper, then he stills, cock pulsing with his release.

When he recovers, he lays random kisses on any inch of skin within reach, murmuring praise that melts my insides into a puddle.

We stay like that for as long as possible, tangled together.

When he shifts to get up, I cling to him. He brushes hair from my face and kisses my forehead.

"Let me take care of my girl."

He doesn't let me lift a finger after he sneaks to the bathroom and returns to clean me up. I expect him to slip beneath the sheets. Instead, he lies between my legs, lapping at my sensitive pussy.

I gasp, thighs clamping around his head. "What are you doing?"

He taps my leg to make me let up. When I relax, he continues working me with his mouth until my back arches.

"Taking care of you," he mutters against my clit.

I shiver, giving myself over to him. He's not satisfied until I've come two more times on his tongue. I'm mush when he finally climbs back in bed with me. He drags my hips back to nestle against his.

My world aligns whenever I'm wrapped in his arms like this.

"Evie?" Cole murmurs when I've almost drifted off.

"Yes?"

He holds me tighter, kissing my shoulder. "Don't go giving my heart away to anyone else, got it? It's only yours."

I hum sleepily. "Never. Love you."

THIRTY-SEVEN
COLE

IT'S EARLY, I think. The first thing I'm aware of as I'm lured to consciousness is Eve's sweet scent tickling my nose and her ass wriggling against my dick. Cracking my eyes, I find the room brightening with the first light of sunrise.

With a playful growl, my arm sweeps from its position around her waist to band around her hips, holding her still while I grind against her.

"Good morning," I mumble into her hair.

"You're up?"

I press my erection against the soft curve of her ass. "When I open my eyes to you in my arms? Always."

"You're awake, I mean," she says.

"I am now. Someone was rubbing on me."

If we were in our bed at home, I'd already have her gasping out my name to wish her good morning.

"Oops."

She doesn't sound sorry at all. I give her hip a light tug and she turns to face me with a yawn. I tip her chin up and give her a kiss.

"Did you sleep good?"

"Mhm. I think I was having a pretty good dream before I woke up."

"Yeah?" Another kiss, this one more insistent. "Hey."

She winds her arms around me. "Yes?"

"You're mine."

Her smile curves against mine. My embrace cinches, pulling her on top of me.

"I think you mean you're *mine*," she sasses.

"Nope. Definitely mine."

"Oh yeah?"

I kiss her grin, tasting her stifled laughter. Her hands roam where she pleases, mapping my arms, shoulders, chest, down my abdomen.

"This? All mine."

"I could say the same," I say with a handful of her ass.

Her exploration moves lower. She peeks up at me through her lashes when she reaches my cock and gives it a tantalizing stroke. A low moan escapes me. She grips it firmer and jerks me until I'm rock hard.

I tease her with my teeth beneath her ear. She stifles a giggle when I roll her beneath me. It's early enough. We must be the only ones awake. There's time before she has to leave my bed.

"Need me again so soon, baby? If we sneak into the shower, I'll fuck you how you like. But you have to promise to be quiet. Your screams will wake this whole house."

"No," she says with a groggy laugh. "This is good."

"I'm about to make it a whole lot better," I promise, shifting to kiss my way down her perfect curves, intent on having my favorite meal.

We both freeze when there's a short knock at the door before it swings open.

"Cole, would you give me a hand? I don't want to spoil the surprise before Eve—"

Oh *fuck.*

Eve shrieks, yanking the covers up to cover herself. Somehow my bare ass ends up exposed. The color drains from my face. I gape at her, then whip my head around to face her father.

David is silent for a beat that feels like the longest second in history. Then he leaves without saying a word.

"Shit," Eve hisses as she winds the blanket tighter around herself. "Shit, shit, *shit.*"

I sit up, drawing my girlfriend-turned-blanket burrito into my arms.

"Shh, it's okay." I don't know who I'm trying to comfort more, her or myself.

"No it's not!" She squirms out of my embrace and darts around the room, grabbing the first random clothes within reach. "This is so far from okay. My dad just caught us in bed with you about to go down on me. Oh my *god*, I don't even want to think about it."

An uncomfortable band pinches my heart when she gets overwhelmed like this. All I want is to make her feel better. I'm panicking too, except my instinct to help her overrides any of my own worries.

I stop her from flitting around the room to pace nervously, and trap her hands between mine to keep her from raking her fingers through her hair. "Hey. Let's take a breath."

She holds my gaze, taking measured inhales with me. Once she's calmed down, I slip my arms around her and press my lips against her forehead.

"I'll talk to him. You stay up here, okay?"

She nods, freeing her trapped arms to lock them around my waist. Her heart beats as hard and fast as mine.

"I didn't want him to find out we're together like this," she says.

"I know. Neither did I." My embrace tightens. "It'll be okay."

Eve buries her face against my chest, tucking her head beneath my chin with a tiny distressed noise that breaks my fucking heart. I drop a kiss to her hair and throw on clothes before I leave the guest room to find David.

Christ, what do I even say to him? It was easier with Benson once he got his head out of his ass. After his reaction, I anticipate the worst. An echo of David's words from this summer haunt me. *Not worthy.*

I clench my jaw with a surge of determination. It doesn't matter. If I lose my job for this, I'll figure something out. I'm not leaving Heston Lake—or Eve. She matters more to me than anything else in my life. I'll prove to him I'm worthy of loving her.

I find David in the kitchen, hands braced on the counter, faraway stare directed out the window to the yard where Benson, Eve, and I used to play.

Before he opens his mouth, I speak first.

"First of all, I'm sorry for being disrespectful under your roof."

He grunts without turning around. I work my jaw, stepping further into the room.

"You've invited me into your home, your family, you've given me my dream job. It was wrong for me to deceive you by sneaking around."

At last, he turns with a raised brow. "Are you dating Eve?"

"Yes."

He nods once. "You were hiding it?"

It's a struggle to read him. He sounds as stern as he does when he critiques the team for every little mistake they made in practice or a game. Despite working alongside him for a year, I feel like I'm permanently fifteen in his eyes.

"Yes."

"How long?"

I'm expecting anger. For him to raise his voice for touching his daughter. Not his steady demeanor and mild interrogation. My stomach roils with unease, waiting for him to snap if he doesn't like my answers.

"About a year." I squeeze my nape.

He studies me somberly for an eternity before his next question. "What made you feel you needed to hide it?"

"I'm sorry. I know I messed up and that she's off-limits." My shoulders roll back. "That said, I'm prepared to face any consequence. I love being a coach for Heston, but I'd rather get fired than walk away from her. I'm sorry I broke your rule. You can't stop us, though. I won't give her up for anything."

His thick brows jump up. He hums into his coffee.

"There's only one thing that's important to me. Do you make her happy?"

I inhale sharply, stunned. "Yes. I care about her—love her," I correct fiercely. "And, respectfully, sir... Eve's the one who decides if I'm worthy of her."

A wrinkle appears between his pinched brows. "Of course you are."

My chest constricts. "But at practice anytime the guys got too friendly with her, and at the Fourth of July barbecue, you said—"

"I never meant you."

The world rearranges. I've relived the conversation in my head countless times since then. Christ, it did a number on me to hear my girlfriend's dad and brother remind me she was off-limits.

I scrub a hand over my face, the stubble shadowing my jawline scraping my palm. "So... You're not mad about me dating Eve behind your back?"

"No. My daughter will always be my little girl in my eyes, but she's an adult in charge of her own life. As long as you take care of her and treat her right, I have no business getting between you two." He squeezes my shoulder. "You've always been family. I'm proud of the man you've grown into, especially in the last year."

A lump lodges in my throat. I swallow thickly. His acknowledgement is everything I've been striving toward since I returned to Heston Lake to coach with him.

"Thank you, sir. That means a lot to me that I have your respect."

"You have it as long as you don't do anything to hurt my daughter. Then you and I will have a problem."

Blood drains from my face at his serious tone. He breaks a moment later, chuckling. I recognize Eve's mischievous side in his amused expression.

"I know I don't have to worry about her."

"No. Never," I assure him.

He peers through the doorway to the kitchen. "Is she going to come down?"

"Eventually. She's embarrassed. I'll check on her."

"Tell her I'm sorry for, er." He gestures aimlessly.

"I'll tell her."

"I'll see if Benson is up yet to move the camper."

"Thanks."

My heart beats double-time as I hurry back to Eve. The room is empty. Her slipper shoes are missing. My brows furrow.

I go downstairs and poke my head in every room, coming up empty. In the kitchen, Mrs. Lombard is yawning at the counter.

"Where's Eve?"

She blinks at me, stirring her coffee. "Hmm? Oh, she said she was taking Bauer for a walk when I went to go get him. Did you both sleep well? I know the guest bed is due to be replaced."

It's my turn to blink. "What?"

"She came from upstairs instead of the side door. I figured you both spent the night in the house instead of going out to the garage. I don't blame you, it was a cold one last night."

My mouth opens and closes. She says it so matter-of-factly I'm not sure how to process what I'm hearing.

"Wait. You know we're—?" I don't know how to form the question. "How long have you known?"

"Of course. I've known for months. You two aren't very subtle with all those longing stares. I worked it out at the end of summer when I saw you kissing from the kitchen window while everyone was here fixing her camper. I thought you were keeping it a secret, so I haven't said anything."

A short laugh puffs out of me. Maybe this whole time the only ones we've been fooling are ourselves.

It doesn't matter now. No more sneaking around.

I need to go track down my girl and bring her home.

THIRTY-EIGHT

EVE

FLEEING the house in the most epic of mismatched pajamas—part mine and part Cole's—to walk the dog isn't my finest moment.

But neither is getting caught in bed naked with my boyfriend by my dad. No one needs to experience that, especially on Christmas morning.

A fresh wave of mortification drowns me. I scrub a hand over my face, wishing it could erase the awkward memory from my mind.

I promised Cole I'd stay in the guest room, but it kept replaying in my head. I had to get out of there, powerless against the impulse to move. Panic almost got the best of me when I found Mom baby talking Bauer when I went down to get him for our escape, but she bought my excuse to take him for a walk without question.

When I'm two blocks from the house, I stop in my tracks. I've got enough steam to power walk across town if I don't pay attention. Bauer barks to get me to move.

"Okay, shh. Don't wake the whole neighborhood. Let's go this way."

We turn the corner to circle the block. I sigh, getting lost in my thoughts once more.

I was ready to end this last night. No more secrets. No more sneaking around. I wanted to tell Dad today, but I didn't expect it to be like this.

Dad's never been that enthused with the guys I've dated, least of all the ones like Shawn. It would break my heart for him to look at Cole with disappointment and disapproval, even though he's nothing like them.

Not only that, he holds Cole's job in the palm of his hand. He gave it and he can just as easily rip it away. A sting irritates my throat. Cole loves being a coach more than anything. My jaw clenches.

No. I won't let Dad do that.

What am I doing out here? Cole's the one that taught me I can't run from problems when things get hard. I need to face this with him together. Face Dad.

I have to go back and tell him myself. He doesn't get a say in who I fall in love with, and I won't let him punish Cole for being with me.

With a fire burning in my stomach, I spin around. Cole's there, jogging to reach me. His thick brown hair is windswept and his green eyes are bright.

"This is where you got off to."

"You tracked me down."

"Of course I did. Always will."

He seems in good spirits. I lick my lips, glancing past him as my stomach flips with nerves.

"Is it over?" I ask tightly.

Am I too late?

"Having to be together in secret? Yes." He cradles my face, giving me the tender smile that wraps my heart in warmth. "But us? No, sweetheart. We'll never be done. We're in this together, aren't we?"

My heart clenches. "Yes. I'm sorry I rushed out, but I'm going to give Dad hell if he thinks he can ruin what we have or mess with your job. It's an abuse of authority if he fires you for whatever you choose to do in your personal life, and I'll go over his head to argue with whoever I need to."

Cole chuckles. "I always want you fighting in my corner. HR wouldn't know what hit them."

Bauer runs around our feet, clumsily ramming his head into our legs. Cole kisses my forehead, holding me and breathing with me until my head stops rioting with information to plan out what I'll tell Dad.

Once my thoughts slow down, I process what he said belatedly. "Wait. What happened when you talked to him?"

He pulls back, lips quirking into a lopsided curve. "That's why I came out here to get you. Everything's fine."

"Fine?"

"Completely. He's not mad. As long as you're happy, he is. Oh, and your Mom's apparently known about us since summer. We weren't as sneaky as we thought, kissing behind the camper."

"Oh." I'm sapped of my fierce determination.

Without it to distract me, embarrassment flickers back to life, for what happened this morning and for running out of the house being dramatic over something that wasn't as big of a deal as I've been dreading. I worry my lip with my teeth.

"Are you ready to head back, or do you want to take another lap or two around the block until you feel better?"

A flutter fills my chest. He knows me better than I know myself. More than that, he understands what I need.

Blowing out a breath, I lean into him. His arm drapes across my shoulders.

"It's cold."

He rubs me. "That's because you left without a coat. I'll warm you up."

"Let's go back. It won't stop feeling awkward until we move past it."

He steers us around, laughing when Bauer keeps going the opposite way before reaching the end of the lead. With a click of his tongue, our puppy dashes to follow us.

"Your dad's sorry for what happened. I think he'll wait after knocking now."

I cover my eyes. "Don't remind me. I haven't recovered from the humiliation yet. Probably never will." I tap my temple. "It'll always live up here, ready to haunt me when I least expect it. Obviously, we're never doing anything in the same house as my parents again. I don't know how Jess and Benson handle this."

"You weren't complaining when I took you upstairs in the middle of the party. Or that time you answered the phone. And this morning was all you."

My nose wrinkles. "That was before we got caught. I think it's time for me to look for a new place. No more...unfortunate incidents for me to add to my anxiety-before-sleep memory rotation if I don't live at home. Or ten feet from my parents."

He squeezes me, kissing my cheek. "So move in with me. I already think of it as our home. When you're not there, it's just empty space for me and Bauer."

My steps falter, gaze snapping to him. His eyes bounce between mine as he clasps my chin between his fingers.

"What do you think?"

A delighted laugh leaves me. "Wait, you're really serious?"

His head dips, leaving barely a millimeter between us. "Are you surprised? You're my girl, Evie. My world doesn't spin without you in it. I want you with me when I wake up. When I go to sleep. In the middle of the week. Every—" Kiss. "—single—" Kiss. "—day."

"I'd like that," I murmur.

The walk back is short.

"I have another surprise for you," he says when we reach my street.

"You already asked me to move in with you and got Dad's approval. What else is there?"

His arm drops from my shoulders to take my hand. "Everything. I've told you before, anything you need? I'll be the one to give it to you."

"You're such a sap," I tease.

"For you, baby. Only for you. Now close your eyes."

"Okay, but make sure I don't trip."

His hand squeezes mine. "I've got you."

I let him guide me because there's no question he's the one I trust with my heart.

"You're about to reach the driveway. Morning, guys," he says as we start up the incline.

I keep my eyes shut. "Is everyone outside?"

"Freezing our asses off for you," Benson confirms. "Except Mom, she's inside with the baby watching through the window. Wave to them." He snickers at my attempt. "You're waving to the bushes."

"Your mom's only inside with Gracie because you won't let her out in the cold for more than two seconds. She'd be fine out here."

Jess' sarcastic retort drifts over from somewhere beside us as Cole murmurs directions. I smirk at them bickering about Benson being an overprotective dad.

"Not peeking?" Cole checks.

"Nope."

"Here, Benny, take Bauer's leash. Evie, come right over...this way." He moves behind me, holding my shoulders. "There, now you can open your eyes."

Cracking them open one at a time, I find myself before the camper. Dad, Benson and Jess are next to it with secret smiles.

I twist to look at him. "The camper?"

"I know how much it bothered you that it wasn't done in time for your first market. I recruited Benson and your dad to help me finish it."

"You have?"

"Go look inside."

He kisses the top of my head and nudges me forward. When I open the door, I gasp.

It's finished. The paint, the fluffy rug I bought but have been waiting to open, the cozy chair, the display shelves stocked with the small amount of earrings, stickers, and stationary I brought home from the market.

In the corner, there's the little library I wanted. I lay a hand over my thumping heart and drift to the book cart decorated with fairy lights and magnets I've designed.

"Cole." It comes out soft and emotional. "You did all this?"

"Don't give him all the credit," Benson says from outside. "Dad and I helped when he asked us to."

I poke my head out. "Thank you."

I bite my lip when Dad catches my gaze. Neither of us have to say anything. I step down to hug him and he crushes me the way he has since I was a kid. The awkwardness slips away. Benson pats my shoulder.

"I love you guys. Thanks for doing this."

"That's what family is for," Dad says gruffly. "No matter what."

I nod, understanding he's letting me know in his own way that he's happy for me. Benson pinches my cheek when I pull back. I swat at him and he laughs.

Cole follows me back inside. He leans in the doorway, forearm braced above his head while I wander the finished space, touching everything he put together to complete it.

"You like it?"

"I love it. This is perfect. It's exactly how I pictured it. How did you even—? It's like you pulled it right from my head."

He taps his temple. "I know what you like."

I rush to him, colliding against his chest. He catches me, keeping us steady like always.

"Thank you," I mumble into the neckline of the Heston U Hockey sweater he pulled on.

"I'm glad it made you happy."

I pull back to meet his eye. "You make me happy."

His eyes crinkle before he dips to kiss me. "Not as much as you make me."

"Are you going to fight me on this? I'll win."

"I will," he insists. "I'll out-stubborn your competitive streak every time, sweetheart, because no matter how much you love me, I'll love you back harder."

"Why are we like this?" I ask through laughing so hard my sides cramp.

"Because this is us," he murmurs before kissing me again.

When we first matched on Love Struck, I thought the universe was hating on me by showing me everything I wanted that I couldn't have in him. It turns out, it was showing me how much I needed him. How much we needed each other.

We're a match in every way.

EPILOGUE
EVE

May, Five Months Later

STOPPING outside the empty storefront window with a *coming soon* sign hanging in it, a smile breaks free for the millionth time in the last two months. It's all mine. I still can't believe I'm opening my own boutique after a year in business.

The lease opportunity was too good to pass up when this space in Main Street Square became available.

Plus, I have the best support system in the world. Cole, my family, and friends all have my back like they have from the beginning.

Upbeat music drifts from inside. I unlock the door and balance the coffees I stopped for on the way back. Another smile tugs at my lips once I walk inside.

Cole's dancing with Bauer's front paws in his hands. Pink paint splatters the white t-shirt stretched across his broad frame. There's some in his messy brown hair, I think.

The grand opening won't be for another month. Once we got the keys, we got to work right away on turning this space into my vision. Cole's even going to build me a fake camper display in the corner.

When I look back only a short while ago to how nervous and

freaked out I was leading up to my first market event, I shake my head at myself. There are still days I get jitters.

It's amazing to be in full control of my job and every decision that goes into it, though it all still falls on me. Sometimes I have a huge win and sometimes my choices are a flop. I have to own them either way.

Although when things are hard, I never have to face them alone.

These days I feel like I'm more settled. Days still pass me by quickly, but I no longer dread the end of the year because whatever I've accomplished, I'm proud of. I feel like I understand myself and what I want a lot better.

My business has continued growing steadily. In addition to opening my own boutique, I have interest for my first wholesale partnerships sitting in my inbox.

A year changes so much. I'd never be here without everyone's support.

I love my life now. And I love Cole with my entire heart.

"Hey," he says warmly. "How'd it go?"

I set the coffee tray down so I don't spill it before twirling and striking a pose. "You are officially looking at the full-time artist and owner behind Sweet Luxe."

Mr. Boucher was unsurprised when I finally gave notice today at the end of my shift. I've been putting it off despite my dwindling hours. Reagan's taken over most of my usual nights as a bartender.

It's so freeing to let go of the job I've kept since college because it was the only safety net I knew. Now I've built something for myself that I'm passionate about, a career that I wouldn't trade for the world. It feeds my creative soul and my need for new challenges.

Cole pats the puppy's flank when he lets him down from dancing and comes over to hug me. I fall into his embrace, comforted by his woodsy scent enveloping me.

"That's my girl. I'm proud of you."

"I'm proud of myself, too."

Bauer noses at my hip. I pull free to kneel at his level.

"And my sweet Bauer-boy is proud, huh?"

He gets worked up, responding with chatty barks. I ruffle his fur, then hug him. When I look up, Cole is taking photos of us on his phone.

"You got a lot done while I was out."

"Benson was here this morning to give me a hand."

The bond of their friendship hasn't been damaged by us hiding our relationship from him. They're closer than ever.

I hand him his coffee and sip mine. Bauer trots around the room before settling in his bed beneath the checkout counter in progress. I unlock my phone to check my email, but open my library app on autopilot. A delighted noise leaves me.

"The next book in the cowboy romance series I wanted to borrow is available." I waggle my brows at him. "This one's about the older brother's best friend."

He steps behind me, drawing my hair aside to kiss my shoulder. "Get it. We can start listening to it tonight."

I love listening to books with him. He's gone from being the guy I dream up for every hero to my real life book boyfriend.

The next song from the playlist he's listening to is slower. He plucks the phone from my hand and turns me around, drawing me into dancing with him. I giggle when he nuzzles my temple and plays with the scarf tying my hair back.

"You're beautiful."

My eyes crinkle with serene joy. "What's that for?"

"Just because."

I lift my chin for a kiss, smiling when his lips meet mine. He adjusts his grip on my hand and twirls me. I overcompensate, getting too into it. I wobble off balance with a bright laugh, steadying myself.

Cole holds out a hand. I slip mine into it without hesitation, glad we no longer have to love each other in secret.

"Ready to go home?"

My heartfelt smile could light up the whole room. I lean into him. He plants a kiss on my head.

"I'd happily go anywhere with you."

Because as long as I'm with him, there are no bad days.

EPILOGUE
COLE

November, Six Months Later

My palms won't stop sweating. I wipe them on my nice jeans for the third time in the last twenty minutes. The ring isn't even in my pocket anymore and I'm still going through it.

Bauer senses my distress, leaving my mom's side for the first time since my parents arrived back in Heston Lake for a visit. He leans heavily against me. I take a few breaths to steady my nerves while petting him.

Benson and David are the only ones that know the plan. This time I don't want to keep them out of the loop. I took them out for drinks and showed them the ring I bought for Eve and broke the news that I'm planning to propose before we sit down for Thanksgiving dinner as a family.

I didn't expect to be so nervous after I've spent months figuring out how I want to ask her to spend our lives together.

"Are you okay? You're looking flushed." Eve touches my forehead and cheeks in concern.

I clasp her wrist, sliding an arm around her waist. "I'm okay. It's just warm in here with everyone over."

"We're going to need a bigger table soon. It's nice we get to spend the holidays with your parents this year. I like having everyone together."

"Me too."

I wanted everyone important to us to be here when I ask her to marry me.

Eve's mom calls her from the kitchen. She presses on her toes to kiss my cheek, then goes to help.

Benson comes up behind me, massaging my shoulders. "You good, man?"

"Hanging in there," I mutter.

"Relax. You've got this."

I nod, turning to him. He slips me the ring box and pats my chest. "From the heart."

"Right."

He snickers with glee. "You look like you just took the biggest hit."

"Thanks, asshole."

"Do I need to get Dad to tell you to skate it off?"

I roll my eyes. "How did you survive this when you asked Jess?"

"Bro, I couldn't remember a damn thing. She ended up asking me."

I pinch the bridge of my nose, shoulders shaking with amusement. "That makes sense."

"Don't worry. She's going to say yes."

I rub at the burn tingling my chest. "I hope so."

"Say yes to what?" Eve leans around me from behind. "What are you two plotting? And before you say impromptu ski trip, no. I can't hit the slopes until I finish my new collection for my Valentine's Day launch."

Benson shoots me the same look he used to before our hockey games in high school. It's his way of silently wishing me luck.

This is it.

"I know. We're not planning a ski trip. Come here for a second?" I draw her to the center of the room.

A slow smile stretches across her face. "What?"

"Just—this."

I kiss her. She returns it. When I pull back, I'm overcome with how much I love her.

My gaze softens, eyes bouncing between hers. When I lower to one knee, her features slacken in surprise. She glances around, then refocuses on me with a shimmer in her gaze.

"Oh my god. Is this happening right now? Are you really—?"

A laugh huffs out of me. "I haven't said a word yet. Can I?"

"Right, okay." She mimes zipping her lips.

I offer a hand and she slips hers into it. My thumb sweeps her fingers and I bring them to my lips.

"Evie..."

Every word I practiced for this moment leaves my head. I'm always reminding her it's okay to be imperfect and embrace it. I draw in a shuddering breath, then let my heart do the talking.

"Sweetheart, you're everything to me. You make me want to be the best man I possibly can be, for myself and for you."

"Yes," she blurts.

My brows lift. "I'm not done yet."

"Oh. Okay. Keep going." She dances in place, grinning through the tears shining in her beautiful eyes.

"I love the life we're building. I want to spend every day by your side. Taking care of you. Making you laugh. Wiping your tears. The good. The bad. All of it. I'm in, sweetheart. I'm in with you forever."

"Cole," she whispers, moved.

I lick my lips. "So what do you think? Want to marry me?"

She's silent for a beat. My stomach ripples with unease. Then she jumps.

"Oh, you're waiting. I already said yes."

My head hangs with a relieved huff. "Yes. *Yes.*"

"Yes," she repeats affectionately.

With a delighted noise, she crashes into me, taking both of us to the floor. Our family laughs. My arms lock around her, mouth meeting hers. When we climb to our feet, we hug everyone as they congratulate us.

"Aren't you forgetting something?" Benson mouths *ring* at me.

Damn it. I pat my pocket, feeling the box I forgot to get out. A rueful smile crosses my face.

"Sorry, sweetheart."

Eve winds her arms around my waist. "It was a perfect proposal in my book. Perfectly imperfect, just the way I like it."

My lips twitch at the mantra I'm always giving her when she's being hard on herself. I drop a kiss on her forehead, then slide the engagement ring on her finger. With Jess and her friends' help, I found a custom jeweler to create something as unique as she is, setting her birthstone amongst a cluster of gold leaves to look like a bouquet.

"It's gorgeous." She admires it.

"You like it? The girls helped me pick it."

"I love it." She tips her chin up for another kiss, murmuring against my lips. "Love you."

"Love you too, Evie."

When we part, we pose for photos. Eve rests her hand against my chest to show off the sparkling engagement ring. I haven't stopped grinning since she said yes. Bauer jumps up on us, making both of us laugh. She bends to give him affection.

"Did you want to be in the photo too, my sweet boy?"

"I texted it to you," Jess says.

"Thanks."

Eve leans into me. I tug her closer while I pull up the photo on my phone.

"Send it to me, too," she says. "I want to text the girls."

I run my hand up and down her back, marveling that she'll be my wife.

Once I shoot the photo off to her, I pull up the group chat the guys on the team put me in. There are several messages of their backyards covered in fresh snow and their meals. I text our picture to them and moments later, responses from rookies to upperclassmen players flood the chat.

Easton
Holy shit, Kincaid. Congrats.

Noah
Yooooo! [confetti emoji]

Easton
Locking it down with Coach Lombard's daughter.

Elijah
Nice.

Madden
Congrats.

Cameron
The man, the myth, the legend.

Noah
Did you use my suggestion?

Cole
No. Only sent this so you'll stop sending me every viral proposal idea you see.

Easton
Don't lie. You love us.

Cole
And I question why often.

Cameron
Fuck off, bro. Go enjoy the good news with your family.

Chuckling, I show Eve. "Everyone's fired up for us."

She tilts her head. "The guys are so sweet. Tell them me and their favorite rink mascot wish them a Happy Thanksgiving."

"Who, you or Bauer? Because you're my favorite mascot," I tease.

She pushes my chest playfully, lowering her voice. "Meet me at the rink after hours and I'll show you my team spirit."

"What am I going to do with you, my naughty girl?" I mutter against her ear. "Feel like sneaking away?"

"Me? You're the one that bagged the coach's daughter, mister assistant coach," she sasses. "I'd say you're the naughty one."

My stomach drops. I text the group chat with the guys, a laugh of disbelief slipping out.

Cole
Oh shit.

> **Easton**
> What?

> **Cole**
> I'm marrying Eve. That makes David my father in law.

The little fucker sends back a long line of laughing emojis at my realization.

Eve catches my eye and gives me the bright smile that wraps tighter around my heart every time. My hand finds the small of her back and she leans into me. Our future is only getting started. We have everything ahead of us.

This is where I'm meant to be. Where I was always going to end up.

Coaching in Heston Lake and loving her with everything I've got.

* * *

Need more swoon-worthy Heston U Hotshots?
The **Heston U Hotshots** series features more swoony hockey romance with the irresistible players of the Heston U Knights and the feisty girls who bring them to their knees off the ice.

Read ICED OUT, Easton's college sports romance with his rival's sister.

BONUS DELETED SCENE

If you can't get enough of Cole and Eve, enjoy a free bonus scene! Additional bonus content is available on my website. Visit the address below or scan the QR code to collect all available bonus content.

BONUS CONTENT:
www.veronicaedenauthor.com/bonus-content

ABOUT THE AUTHOR
STAY UP ALL NIGHT FALLING IN LOVE

Veronica Eden is a USA Today, Amazon Top 30, and International bestselling author of addictive romances that keep you up all night falling in love with spitfire heroines and irresistible heroes.

She writes spicy contemporary romance and loves exploring the bond of characters that embrace *us against the world*. She's a fan of strong heroines and collecting as many book boyfriends as possible from swoony "*sin*namon rolls" with devastating smirks to gruff bad boys. When not writing, she can be found soaking up sunshine at the beach in Northeast Florida, snuggling in a pile with her untamed pack of animals (her husband, dog and cats), and surrounding herself with as many plants as she can get her hands on.

* * *

CONTACT + FOLLOW
Email: veronica@veronicaedenauthor.com
Website: http://veronicaedenauthor.com
FB Reader Group: bit.ly/veronicafbgroup
Amazon: amazon.com/author/veronicaeden

facebook.com/veronicaedenauthor

instagram.com/veronicaedenauthor

pinterest.com/veronicaedenauthor

bookbub.com/profile/veronica-eden

goodreads.com/veronicaedenauthor

ALSO BY VERONICA EDEN

Sign up for the mailing list to get first access and ARC opportunities!
Follow Veronica on BookBub for new release alerts!

New Adult& Contemporary Romance

Sinners and Saints Series

Wicked Saint

Tempting Devil

Ruthless Bishop

Savage Wilder

Sinners and Saints: The Complete Series

Crowned Crows Series

Crowned Crows of Thorne Point

Loyalty in the Shadows

A Fractured Reign

Heston U Hotshots Series

Trick Play (Prequel)

Iced Out

Standalone

The Devil You Know

The Player You Need

Unmasked Heart

Devil on the Lake

Jingle Wars

Haze

Fantasy & Paranormal Romance

Standalone

Hell Gate

Made in the USA
Las Vegas, NV
19 December 2023

83178069R00225